LADY ALONE

A LADY • A BOAT • ALONE

BASED ON ACTUAL EVENTS

Other Books By Steven Amory Twitty

- *TERROR BENEATH THE BAYOU*
- *SAVING MOSES*
- *BETWIXT AND BETWEEN*

LADY ALONE
A LADY • A BOAT • ALONE

STEVEN AMORY TWITTY

Waldenhouse Publishers, Inc.
Walden, Tennessee

LADY ALONE: A LADY • A BOAT • ALONE

Copyright ©2022 Steven Amory Twitty 1950. All rights reserved. No part of this book may be reproduced in any form or by any electronic or mechanical means including information storage and retrieval systems, without permission in writing from the publisher. The only exception is by a reviewer, who may quote short excerpts in a review.

This is a work of fiction. Names, characters, places, and incidents either are the products of the author's imagination or are used fictitiously. Any resemblances to actual persons, living or dead, businesses, companies, events, or locales is entirely coincidental.

ISBN: 978-1-947589-71-1

Edited by Tom Ehrhart

Type and design by Karen Paul Stone

Published by Waldenhouse Publishers, Inc.

100 Clegg Street, Signal Mountain, Tennessee 37377 USA

423-886-2721 www.waldenhouse.com

Printed in the United States of America

Library of Congress Control Number: 2023944002

One woman's struggle for survival at sea alone on a forty-foot sailboat. - Provided by publisher

FIC047000 FICTION / Sea Stories

FIC002000 FICTION / Action & Adventure

FIC000000 FICTION / General

TO

All those who see adventure beyond their front door.

CONTENTS

ACKNOWLEDGMENTS

With thanks to Kathryn "Springer" Healey
for her suggestions of all things sailing
and to the late Larry Rutledge of the sailboat, *Brisa Del Mar*,
for his friendship and guidance

TO THE READER

Dear Reader:

Lady Alone is based on a tale I heard from a sailor friend who claimed this story is fair dinkum, that in the 1980's there was a boat named *Atmosphere*, owned by a captain who haled from Hong Kong, and that while crossing the Pacific Ocean with an inexperienced woman as crew, he was lost overboard during a storm, leaving his hapless crew struggling for her life.

Though such a story is certainly plausible, I have yet to confirm its validity, though this in itself does not negate truth.

What calamities the unfortunate woman in my friend's story supposedly suffered, he did not elaborate, but those souls who sail or have sailed know how easily a safe and comfortable passage can be plunged from a satisfying sense of control into a harrowing struggle in a brief moment of time.

Whether due to sleep deprivation or simple oversight, the same issues the lady in my story faces, and worse, can and have put experienced captains and crew in life-threatening struggles. Throw inexperience into the mix and that struggle to stay alive in a deteriorating situation can become a monumental challenge.

For those readers who are or have been sailors and those who have dreamed of shaking out the canvas and letting the wind sweep you toward a destination beyond the horizon, it is my hope you enjoy this tale as much as you delight in fair seas and a steady wind over the stern quarter. And for all those readers who just like a good story, I truly hope you find this gripping tale of survival and determination as enjoyable to read as it was for me to write.

THE SAILBOAT ATMOSPHERE

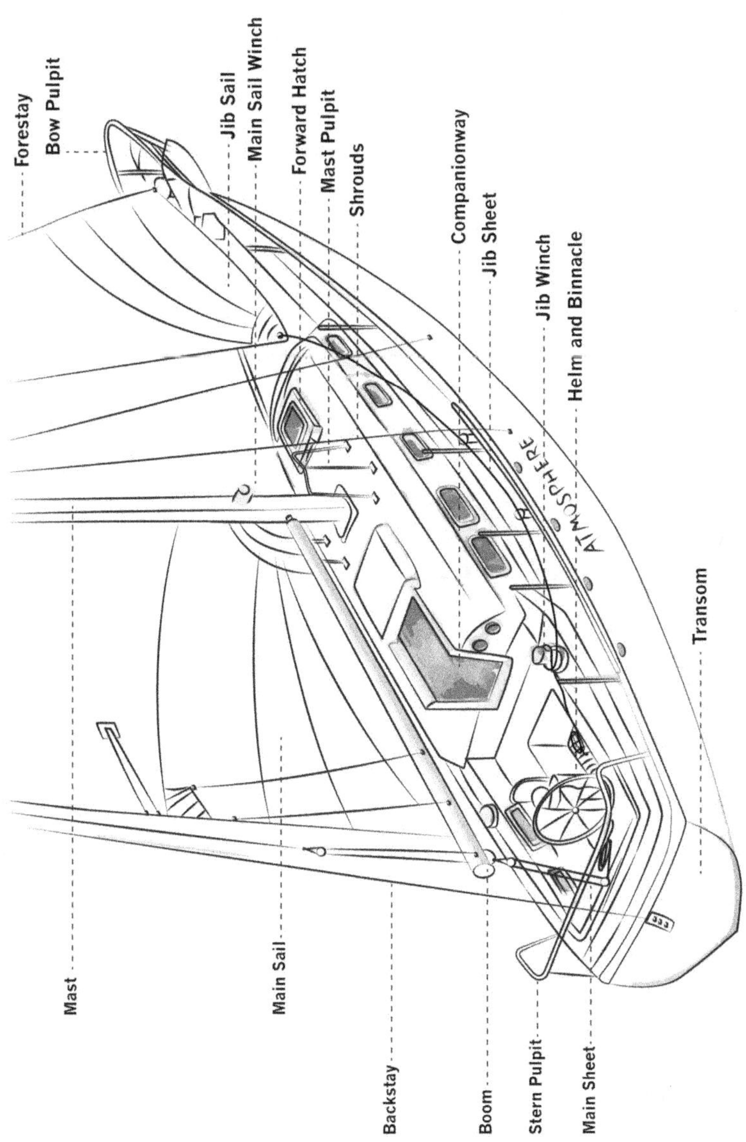

CHAPTER ONE

The outboard's tinny whir rose an octave as it accelerated the wooden fishing skiff away from an exposed sandbar connecting a low-lying, rocky islet to the lower end of a larger, densely forested island. The uninhabited island was a mile and a half long, a third as wide with an unbroken, white-sand beach lined with coconut palms crowned with their feather-like leaves, tight clumps of green fruit and trunks leaning as if the winds that sculpted them were still blowing.

Tangled jungle pushed hard up against the frontline defense of palms, spilling out onto the beach as if anxious to claim more of the island. Overhead, frigate birds circled in a clear mid-afternoon sky.

Clipped to the island like a necklace was an oblong atoll, extending four miles, north to south, and a third this in girth. A plethora of corals forming the impressive ring brimmed vibrant colors, beautiful and alluring but bristling with certain destruction for any sea craft venturing too close.

The fifteen-foot skiff skirting the atoll was a veteran of the sea, varnished by sun and brine to a dull gray covered in a patchwork of green paint more stubborn than time and abuse. The boat carried a seasoned, earthy smell of soured netting, stale, sulfury salt and every fish landed.

Bilge water sloshed in the boat's stern forming shallow eddies around a six gallon, red plastic carboy of gasoline into which the outboard's fuel line was plugged. Between the rear and middle seats were a gallon-size, aluminum cooking pot repurposed for bailing and a tattered athletic bag. Pushed to one side was a cobbled-together wooden box looking every bit as abused as the boat but still capable of holding an assortment of fishing hooks, lead weights and three monofilament hand lines wound onto red, plastic grips. A neatly folded casting net lay atop a sheet of canvas alongside a galvanized bucket half-filled with today's catch: three yellow and black rabbitfish, a blue unicorn fish and one green and yellow parrot fish. At the boat's bow was a four-hook Grapnel anchor on fifty feet of hemp anchor rope.

Atea Napil, a thin, ancient-looking fisherman with Polynesian features, sat on the vessel's rear seat, gripping the outboard's tiller with a knobbly, callused hand. His wrinkled face looked like a map of the ocean's currents, toughened, like his boat, by weather and brine. He was clad in a faded blue, long-sleeve shirt and knee-worn, brown slacks, no shoes. From under his fraying straw hat that looked like an unfinished basket, his mottled eyes, white with pterygium, looked back over the boat's stern to a forty-foot sailboat foundered on the island's white sand beach, a victim of the latest storm, one day past.

Atea's eyes followed two side-by-side sets of footprints in the sand, one left by his own steady gait, and the second, stumbling, struggling. Both tracks led from a wood and sheet-metal shed at the island's near end to keel marks on the sandbar where he had landed his skiff.

Skilfully guiding his vessel within calm water close to the outside edge of the atoll's gnarly coral, Atea twisted hard the outboard's throttle for all the power the old motor could offer. Glancing across to the atoll's opposing side, he perused a natural gap in the reef through which tidal water ebbed and flowed. This had been where the grounded sailboat had entered the ring of coral and strangely, its bow-mounted anchor had not been deployed. What the captain had been attempting was not clear to the fisherman but had the fiberglass sloop made good another twenty-five miles south, it could have escaped the storm's fierce winds by tucking into a safe anchorage.

Atea refocused on his unexpected passenger seated on the folded fishing net, facing him. The frail-looking woman's eyes were closed, each labored breath rocking her drooping head. She wore khaki hiking shorts and a soiled, gray T-shirt featuring the depiction of a straitjacket. She chewed on a sprig of beef jerky and clutched the fisherman's red plastic cup of water as if to lose it was to die. Her blonde hair was matted against her head, and her craggy face and body were drawn tight by dehydration. He guessed she was in her twenties but adversity had made her look older than him.

The woman's shaking hands raised the cup to her sun-cracked lips. She choked down a swig of water, grimacing as if swallowing broken glass and finding pleasure in doing so. Her eyes opened. She had a dead stare.

It was under the dull white ball of the midday sun in a hard blue sky that Atea had spied the beached sailboat and what he would find to be an incoherent woman sprawled on the sand at the island's lower end, near a storage shed he shared with two other fishermen.

In a rush to reach the unconscious woman, Atea had purposely run his boat's bow onto the adjoining sandbar near the motionless body and hurried to what he had figured was a victim of the shipwreck. Helping the gal to her feet, he had shouldered her weight down the beach to his boat, her struggling with every step in desperate need for water, food and medical attention.

"Is there anyone else with you?" he had asked as he seated her on the folded casting net, her back against the middle seat.

"No," had come the almost inaudible reply.

As he motored his skiff south, down the length of the atoll and toward his home port twenty-five miles distance, his eyes moved from the sailboat to his shed. He had not seen any indication there had been others on the boat and had not taken the time to check further. In this woman's dire need for medical care, that search would have to be arranged by the authorities.

"What port are you out of?" he asked, hopeful of adding to what little information he already had. This woman's condition bespoke of a struggle substantially longer than if the grounded sailboat haled from one of the local marinas on the main island.

Failing to get a response, he tried a different tack. "My name is, Atea."

He caught his passenger's vacant eyes. "What's your name?"

The question echoed in her muddled brain as if within a grand hall emptied and abandoned.

"Joan. Joan Mackland," she managed. Her body was responding to what little moisture she had consumed from the cup, thinning the fog shrouding her mind. Taking another sip of water, she rolled the moisture in her mouth with her swollen tongue and swallowed. Her eyes drifted out over the skiff's stern, past her savior at the tiller and to her sailboat beached and abandoned. A morose feeling of deserting a friend came over her.

Atea smiled affirmation to Joan that she would be all right, figuring she needed the encouragement. He transferred his hat onto her head.

"What happened, Joan?" he asked over the shrill of the outboard.

Atea's question crawled into Joan's brain and sparked a memory that dispersed the haze shrouding her thoughts like a wind-blown morning mist. Before her mind's eye appeared snapshots of the prior two weeks, from expectations for a distant landfall to awakening to a harrowing struggle for her life.

☧

Savoring the last sip of her Starbuck's latte, Joan dropped the spent paper cup into an empty, reinforced corrugated shipping box labeled; Mackland Gallery, 105 Kitchener Street, Auckland, New Zealand. She had arrived at her Uncle Phil's high-end art gallery earlier that morning to unbox and inventory his latest deliveries, something she had helped with since she had moved to Auckland four years earlier. Having recently completed a university degree in art history, she planned a career in museum administration.

Joan stepped back and took in the paintings she had already unpacked and placed on display racks, a variety of original paintings from as many artists, additions to those hanging on walls or seated proudly on their own display racks organized in two central rows.

Beyond the artwork a wide display window created its own work of art with a view of arboreal Albert Park, while on the shop's glass-paned front door, a Valentine heart hung above the business' stenciled name and address.

For the last few years Joan had celebrated Valentine's Day with friends by touring wineries in Northland and Gisborne, but this year was different. She had opted for an opportunity to put problems at home behind her for an out of character adventure on the high seas before settling into the more mundane affair of seeking employment.

From her jeans' back pocket, Joan withdrew a box cutter and thumbed out its razor blade. She cut the plastic straps on the last box of newly arrived stock and laid the knife aside. From the two by three foot shipper she lifted out a single, canvas painting framed in carved mahogany. The work's subject matter pulled her face tight with a smile; two Spanish galleons and their crews being swept over the edge of the world.

"Uncle Phil," she called, "don't say anything to mum about this one."

Phil Mackland, a pear-shaped man in his mid-forties, also clad in jeans but with balding head, stepped from a rear storage room, a steaming cup of tea in hand. He grinned satisfaction at the artwork his niece held.

"Wonderful," he said. "It arrived."

He took a sip from his cup and set it on a paper-cluttered desk at the back wall. Accepting the painting from Joan, he held it out like a doting father with his first newborn. He placed it on a vacant display stand.

"This is an original Ed Miracle," he declared proudly. He pointed to a caption engraved on a brass plate fixed to the frame below the painted scene, 'I TOLD YOU SO', before tracing with his finger the two ships' inevitable plunge over the edge of the world. His eyes shifted to his niece.

"Don't worry about your mum," he promised with a flick of his brow. "Not a word from me."

His late brother, Joan's father, had invested in the art gallery years before when it was only an idea on paper, and after his untimely death, his widow, Joan's mother, had inherited her late husband's part of ownership. A demanding woman of her husband, that albatross had fallen squarely on Phil, burdening him with her weekly phone calls for sales data and new additions to their inventory.

Uncle Phil's brow rose. "Since I haven't heard from your mum about your plans, you obviously haven't told her. Am I right?"

Joan made a pained face. "Well…" she stretched out the word. "I did mention it to her."

Uncle Phil's mouth drew into a thin line of disappointment. "You mentioned it, as in, 'This is what I'm going to do.'?"

When Joan's eyes fell to the floor, her uncle knew how that conversation had gone.

Phil understood Joan's deeply ingrained trait of avoiding confrontation, especially with her mother. His late brother's wife was a self-focused, hard-boiled woman near impossible when she disagreed. She had perfected the art of manipulation, a first-class narcissist, using pity to make her seem the victim in order to satisfy her own emotional needs. It was behavior she had used to box-in her late husband and still used to control her daughter.

Phil admitted he had been surprised when Joan had found the strength to talk her way past her mother's frustrating conduct when she moved from Christchurch to Auckland for university. At the time, her mother had been squarely against the move, even demanding that he, Phil, talk some sense into his niece. Fortunately, Joan had, for once, held strong and in the end, her mother, seeing her usual tactics had failed, had agreed to let her daughter leave the nest but not without a caveat that Joan owed her for this one. As for Joan's current plans, there was no way her mother would be willing to permit her only daughter to go so far afield on such an outrageous excursion.

"I know I should have been more firm," Joan lamented with a sigh. She pulled herself up straight as if suddenly becoming a new person. "When I talk to her later today, I'm telling her exactly what I'm going to do and nothing she says is going to change my mind." This was said more as a pledge to herself than a promise to her uncle.

"You remember your own words," Uncle Phil said. "Don't let yourself down."

Joan appreciated her uncle's support and concern. Ending up like the ships in Mr. Miracle's painting would be a blessing compared to living with the knowledge she had failed to take a major step in affirming her claim of independence with this grand statement.

Phil was not convinced his niece could hold strong against the coming onslaught, and as he set the empty shipping box by the desk and picked up his cup of tea, he gave her a fatalistic face. "This could finally end her hold on you."

He caught Joan's stare. "Do you have your plane ticket?"

"I have until five this afternoon to pick it up from the travel agent." She looked at her sports watch. "In fact, I better get going."

"The only person who can make this happen is you," Uncle Phil stated affirmation. "You are in control. Don't forget that."

"I know I am," Joan said with a glimmer of a smile. "This is something I have to do and I'm going through with it."

Phil hugged his niece. "You be careful. Don't worry about your mum. She'll get over it. And have a wonderful experience."

⊂ॐ⊃

Atea scooted his skiff past the atoll's lower end into open water where the ocean's floor dropped off, changing the water's aqua-blue color to an almost purple hue. The skiff rode on the backs of a short chop, the waves bobbing the boat as if tapping to a song's steady down-beat. The rhythmic motion swirled Joan's thoughts back to her present condition, far from her mother in Christchurch and far from her life in Auckland.

She raised the cup to her lips, took in one more sup of water and snagged another thread of events that had brought her to the edge of disaster.

The image before Joan was herself driving her blue VW Beetle across Auckland's Harbour Bridge on her return trip from downtown Auckland to her apartment in Birkenhead. The vista to her right took in a tight gathering of sailboats docked at Westhaven Marina, at the south end of the bridge, while a dozen sailboats scooted about Waitemata Harbour on a summer northeasterly, all set against a backdrop of Stanley Point, North Head Peninsula and farther out, the lone peak of Rangitoto Island.

Joan touched a plane ticket atop her black backpack on the seat next to her, a tangible token of her self-imposed hegira far beyond her own comfort zone. Having never been on a boat in the open sea was cause enough for apprehension but her long time friend and experienced sailor, Lois Tomblinson, was going which dulled the teeth of the unfamiliar. Even with the reassurance from her late father's brother, she had stepped into the travel agent's office with nervous anticipation only to have the table turned vertical.

"Hi Ms. Millwright," Joan had said to the travel agent, "I'm here to pick up my plane ticket."

Sally Millwright had given her customer a bewildered stare and leaned back in her chair. "Have you not spoken with Miss Tomblinson today?" the travel agent had asked. "She had a change in her plans and your trip has to be cancelled."

Joan stood as stark as stone processing the information. "Did she say, why?" and before Ms. Millwright could respond, Joan placed her hand on the travel agent's idle phone. "Can I use your phone? I need to talk to Lois."

"Of course," the travel agent had replied. She had nudged the telephone in invitation and busied herself with pending files stacked on her desk. The agent was a big-boned woman with short, curly brown hair and pale skin contrasting blood-red lipstick.

Punching out a phone number she knew better than her own, Joan's eyes had stared a hole in the phone's body, her anger gnawing within her as she had waited through ten anxious rings. When the phone's message mode clicked on, Joan coaxed the recording to run faster and then said with intent, "Lois, I'm at the travel agent's office. What's this about the trip being cancelled? I didn't go through all of this planning with you just to end up staying here. I'll call you again when I get home but as far as I'm concerned, I'm still going, whether you are or not."

Joan cradled the handset, taking a moment to consider what she had just told her friend. Her declaration had been made in the heat of anger and disappointment, but as preposterous as that proclamation had been, it seemed to tick all of the boxes for what she truly wanted.

Ms. Millwright, caught between astonishment and awe, had waited for instructions.

"I'll need my ticket," Joan had stated with no hint of apprehension.

Ms. Millwright had slipped a ticket from a file and handing it to Joan, she said, "One way to Guam." Pausing, she had added, impressed,

"I must say, you are a very brave woman going on a trip like this by yourself."

Joan saw an opening in traffic and worked her VW to the Harbour Bridge's far left lane. Pushing aside her reflections of how she had reached this point and her pending phone calls to Lois and then her mother, she turned up volume on her car's radio. The station's current event segment was in progress.

" ...pioneer in life raft design, Steve Callahan will be interviewed on One ZB's Monday morning show, sixteen February," the dee-jay announced.

"Mr. Callahan is the author of Adrift: Seventy-Six Days Lost At Sea, the true story of his survival in a life raft after his sailboat struck a whale and sank. Don't miss what will certainly be a riveting show. And now, a One ZB sports update."

Joan lowered volume as a jab of uneasiness tightened her stomach, not because she would be four thousand miles away on Monday and would miss the interview, but because Steve Callahan, an obviously experienced sailor, had lived through her own worst nightmare; the sinking of the boat he was on, and now, she had whales to worry about. Her jaw tightened at a danger she had not anticipated.

"I hope that was just bad luck," she commented to the radio's dee-jay of Mr. Callahan's ordeal. Surely, nothing like that could happen to the boat she would be on.

Joan exited the highway onto Stafford Road, at the north end of Harbour Bridge. The familiarity of her neighborhood niggled at her resolve. She was leaving everything she knew for the outlandish, a capricious leap into the unknown. Something that was definitely not her.

She caught her runaway musings and calmed her trepidation with the knowledge life in New Zealand may be the same upon her return from this adventure but for the people in her life, they would see her differently, a changed woman with the real possibility her mother would finally accept her as an adult.

Parking in a curbside slot fronting her second-floor flat on Battle Point Road, Joan slipped the plane ticket into her backpack, stepped from her car and slung the rucksack over her shoulder. She trudged up the two flights of stairs to her one-bedroom flat. Her apartment was furnished as it was with hand-me-down furniture and decorated with wall posters of New Zealand landmarks; sharp-peaked Mount Taranaki in Egmont National Park with its network of deep gullies disappearing into dense beech forests, Moke Lake and its clear water surrounded by pristine valley grassland and craggy mountains tufted with scraggly bushes and stunted trees and her favorite get-away, Punakaiki Beach with its roaring blow holes sounding like winded whales and unique 'pancake' rocks eroded into bizarre shapes, all backdropped by steep forested mountain slopes capped with sheer limestone cliffs.

She stepped inside her apartment and closed the door just as her telephone rang, a shrill sound that sent a biting pang of anxiety through her stomach. She wasn't ready if this was her mother.

Joan dropped her backpack onto the floor by a wooden dining table and took a tentative step to her phone set on a half-moon table next to her bedroom door. She waited for the unit's already blinking message program to engage. As edgy as she was about speaking to her mother and Lois, there was another call she refused to take. Her recorded voice switched on.

"Hi, I'm not home. Leave the usual and I'll call you back."

Her mother's voice was fringed with a displeased, sharp tone when she said, "Joanie, call me when …"

Joan snatched up the handset and breathed deep before speaking. From her mother's tone of voice, this conversation was starting with herself on the defensive. "Hi, mum." She leaned her back against the wall, not knowing what to say, only that it was time to get this call over with, once and for all, and focus on saving this trip.

"Good, you're finally home."

Joan slid her back down the wall to sit on the floor, girding herself for what would take all of her mettle to accomplish. "I was going to call you," she said. She bit her lower lip, building courage to be strong and tell her mother of her plans, no vacillation from rebuke.

"Is that why I had to call you?" Her mom's voice was tight with emotion, whiny, as if she were about to cry. "You and your father, always sneaking around behind my back. When were you planning to tell me?"

A sharp feeling of betrayal hit Joan head-on. There was only one person her mother spoke to on a frequent basis who knew about her plans. "Did you talk to Uncle Phil?"

"Your uncle? No," her mother stated flatly. "But I'm sure he has been egging you on. And that, after our little talk. Thank God, Lois saw reason."

Joan's brow shot up at her mother's knowing of the supposedly aborted trip. Lois rarely called her mother and had a standing agreement with Joan never to mention anything they were planning, no matter how mundane. "What about Lois?"

"I guess I should be happy you won't be adding to all of your disappointing behavior by traipsing halfway around the world to go sailing."

"Mum, when did you talk to Lois?" Joan was agitated. She had not planned to mention Lois' late decision, figuring if her mom was under the impression Lois was still in on this, it might tip things closer to reasonable limits.

Joan's mother's answer was edged with triumph. "Hasn't she told you? Your trip is cancelled."

"And when did you talk to her?" Joan pressed.

"Lois called this morning, looking for you. She said she left a message on your machine."

Joan was left flat footed, off balance. Lois's disclosure trumped Joan's mental gymnastics preparing for this conversation, leaving her on the downside of a pivotal event in which she was fully invested emotionally. The phone's blinking message light suddenly held immense but ill-boding significance for she had slipped down the ladder, back to square one.

"I don't have any messages," Joan lied, not wanting her mother to gloat anymore than she was. "I think you misunderstood her." No matter how small the step-up toward her goal, Joan was taking it.

"I know what she told me," Joan's mom said firmly. "Call her. See for yourself."

Overwhelmed by even a hint of such an opportunity snatched from her and under the pall of her mother's self-righteousness, Joan succumbed to an overbearing personality from which she had little resistance. "Mum, I'll talk to Lois but if in the end she does cancel, there still might be a chance for me to go. Please mum. This is important to me."

Joan clenched her fist, her face tight with self-reprimand. Bugger, there was no room in this for appeasement.

"Don't be ridiculous," her mother replied in a barbed tone. "It's not like you've ever been sailing."

"I went sailing in high school," Joan challenged. "With Betty McReynolds and her family."

"That wasn't real sailing. You know that. You were in Waitemata Harbour, not the open ocean. Besides, you know Betty. You don't know the man with the sailboat in Guam. How do you think I'll feel if something happens to you? What if he's a perv or you fall overboard or the boat sinks?"

Joan threw her head back, miffed at herself for allowing this conversation to drift onto her mother's side of the court, a distressing turn from her original plan. She strangled the phone's handset as if it were her mother's neck.

"Mum, please listen."

"Please listen? To what? Please listen to, I want to go alone to some far off place to meet some man, a complete stranger, and get on a sailboat with him and only him?" Her mother harrumphed. "Don't be wally."

"Mum, he's not a complete stranger."

Her mother's voice dropped an octave. "You know what I mean. If you love me you'll forget all of this nonsense. It's for your own good."

"Please mum, this means so much to me."

"And what about me?" her mother spat. "What do you think going off like this means to me or don't you care?"

Joan dropped her head, exasperated. Her fortitude was slipping backward into the darkness of submission. She felt tired. Old.

"Mum, why do you say things like that? Of course I care."

"Then show me. Come home and we'll have another talk."

"I'm twenty-three years old," Joan complained. "Old enough to live my own life."

Joan's mom reverted to a more appeasing tone. "I know you are, dear. I'm just thinking about your safety. If going sailing is so important to you, why don't you and Lois book a sailing trip around the harbour? That would be fun. I'm sure Darren would like to go."

"Darren and I broke up."

"Joanie, you're being unfair to me. All the years I have helped you make good decisions and now that you're older, you have no appreciation for all of my sacrifices."

Joan reset her resolve. This turn of events was indeed unfair, a single decision by a third person that could impact her own life in a profound way. Dragging a thread of courage from her pocket, Joan clutched it in her proverbial fist and taking a calming breath, clinging to her promise to herself, she said, "Mum, I love you and I do appreciate everything you've done for me but this is something I have to do. No matter what Lois has decided, I'm going."

In the after-moments of Joan's mutinous statement, her face was a study of contrasts, startled surprise at unexpected boldness that had leapt from her chest and relief at overcoming her usual avoidance to step beyond her comfort zone but for all she had accomplished, she had left herself in a quandary. The threshold she had crossed in her declaration was a demarcation between justifying a change of plan due to someone else's decision and full commitment to stay the course with no chance of return without inflating her mother's control.

A cold silence chilled the air. Joan's mother was planning what to say next, refusing to lose what she felt necessary to ensure her daughter made rational choices, and this latest decision was totally unacceptable.

Joan had tasted independence during her informative years and into her early teens. Her father had taken her on camping trips to New Zealand national parks with jaunts to points of interest on both the south and north islands but at age fourteen, two years after her father and mother had divorced, all of that had changed. Cancer had taken her father and she was suddenly marooned under her mother's narcissistic spell.

Thrown into a situation far beyond her choosing, Joan had quickly found isolation and appeasement the least stressful ways of dealing with her mother's emotional needs while memories of her father had carried her through the hard times.

At eighteen, Joan had taken it upon herself to enrol at Canterbury University in Christchurch and a year later, struggling through the minefield of her mother's ridicule and myopic view of her daughter's capabilities, she had transferred to Auckland University on the North Island to complete her degree.

Joan had not realized until confrontation with her mother over changing universities just how deeply her mother's emotional instability had impacted her own mental state. Even as an adult, she still strove for the acceptance she had sought as a fatherless teen.

Now, with university behind her and only days before her life's greatest adventure, Joan realized she had underestimated just how much she still craved confirmation that the one person she had so desperately attempted to please had a place in her heart for her daughter, that one day she would be accepted as an adult with applause for her accomplishments. Who she was and who she wanted to be seemed separated by an impasse too wide to cross yet she had a deep-seated feeling a grand statement like this would be a defining moment, a point in her relationship with her mother that would wipe the slate clean.

Joan held onto that thought and said, "I know you are going to worry."

Her mom's voice became heavy. "And that's the part that hurts the most. All I've done for you and to be treated like this."

Joan held herself together, not allowing her emotions to take her where she didn't need to go. For good measure she said, "Mum, I want you to remember what I told you before, that Lois' brother, Max, knows the captain and said he is very nice and has a lot of sailing experience. He even sailed around the world."

"What about seasickness?" her mother said condescendingly, working every angle. "You know how you get just riding in the backseat of a car."

"Only if Grandad Stuart is driving," Joan stated, "and I didn't feel sick on the McReynolds' boat."

Joan had never revealed to her mother that she remembered little about that daysail around the harbour due to severe drowsiness from motion sickness medication she had taken before stepping aboard. As for this trip from Guam to Hong Kong, Joan would carry seasick medication, though Lois had assured her that since they would be sailing downwind the boat would have a comfortable motion and after one or two days at sea, Joan would find her sea legs.

"Joanie, you're being selfish," Joan's mother stated.

"Mum. If I'm being selfish, it's just that … Please mum. This is something I want to do."

Joan's mother's voice became labored, frail. The only trip she was allowing her daughter to take involved guilt. "I wasn't going to tell you this. I fell yesterday. I think I fainted."

Joan clamped her eyes closed, shaking her head, appearing to have aged fifty years. "Mum, don't do this again," she pleaded.

No more than six months earlier Joan had cancelled a camping trip with friends to fly back to Christchurch after her mother had called, distraught over a diagnosis of breast cancer. It was only upon arriving at the family home that Joan had learned the truth. Her mother had already been informed by her doctor the suspicious tissue revealed in her mammogram and biopsied had been benign.

"Mum, why did you have me come back home for this?" Joan had complained about the blatant lie.

Pouting, Joan's mother had turned away. "Always thinking of yourself," she had mumbled loud enough to be heard. "If your father was still alive, he would have done anything to be here with me."

"Mum…"

And that conversation had ended along with any chance of Joan salvaging what had remained of her weekend.

As if to totally torpedo her daughter's current plans to go sailing into the unknown, Joan's mother's voice edged up with hope when she said, "Since you are out of uni, why don't you take this time to move back to Christchurch? You have friends here and you could start job hunting. Your Uncle Phil can handle our shop by himself." Her voice softened, consoling. "To tell you the truth, the last time I spoke with your uncle it seemed he didn't want you to come around anymore."

Joan stood her ground. "He said that?"

Joan's mother quickly backed off. "I didn't say he said it."

Joan could see her mother waving a dismissive hand at the phone.

Another lull. Joan's mother was unwilling to end this conversation unless it was her way.

"I don't know what else to say," Joan spoke up before her mother, "except, I'm going on this trip." She had learned early on in life, the longer she remained embroiled in a disagreement with her mother, the more pressure her mother would exert to get what she wanted.

There was no reply. Was her mother crying?

"Mum?"

Still no reply. This conversation needed to end. "Mum, I'll call you. Is that all right? I love y …"

Her mother hung up.

Joan lowered her own handset onto its cradle, disappointed in herself for failing to make the definitive statement of self she had so ardently attempted to orchestrate. Saying 'please' multiple times and ending the phone call by asking her mother's permission to call had only reinforced inappropriate behavior, and if Lois had torpedoed her chances of crewing, her mother would take that as a win.

"Uncle Phil, what have I done?"

For a long moment Joan stared at the phone's blinking message light, knowing at least one of the two calls would be from Lois. Even a message from Darren, her ex-boyfriend, would be more tolerable than Lois' apologies.

Accepting this next step, Joan pressed the 'Retrieve Messages' key. The phone's speaker clicked, a dull sound similar to her mother hanging up. "You have two messages," the machine's pre-recorded voice announced in a steady cadence, "First message, received one thirty-two PM on thirteen February."

A barely audible clack and the message from Lois. "Joan, call me." Lois rattled off the words as if the world were about to end. She hung up.

"End of message," the phone's voice stated. "Second message, received two seventeen PM on thirteen February."

Joan pressed the 'Stop' button, thought a moment and pressed 'Delete'. She had no desire to hear Lois' or her mother's voice yet again, and she was in no mood to deal with anything Darren Gentry, her ex-boyfriend, might say.

Joan touched the plane ticket atop her backpack next to her on the floor, a tangible token of her self-imposed hegira. Was she making the right decision? She dialed Lois' number again.

"Hello." Lois picked up after the first ring.

"Lois, I want to know what the hell's going on," Joan demanded.

"I was just about to call you," Lois said, her voice coated with guilt. "I'm sorry. I really am, but I'm cancelling the trip."

"Why? What's going on?" Joan stated in a voice filled with displeasure.

"Uhhhh, something has come up." Lois' voice carried a reluctance that signaled all Joan needed to know.

"It's Kevin, isn't it."

Joan was well-acquainted with Lois' own boyfriend. He had been her first choice to go on this trek but when he could not get the time off from his job, Joan was next in line. In retrospect, Joan admonished herself for not seeing the obvious. Lois was going nowhere without Kevin.

"He doesn't want me to be away for that long," Lois said in a mournful tone. "Ms. Millwright said we can get partial refunds for our plane tickets."

Joan's nostrils flared. She would have reached into the phone and grabbed Lois by her throat if she could but that display of her anger could be postponed. Regardless of what Lois had decided, Joan's own mind was made up. She would not be around to hear her friend beat an apology to death or to deal with Darren when he came knocking.

"I don't want a refund," Joan growled. "I want to go on this trip."

"Joan, I really am sorry but Kevin…"

"Do what you want," Joan sniped, her obstinance powering up her will with each word. "Does the captain know that you've cancelled?"

"Max is going to send a fax."

"And has he sent it?"

If Max, Lois' brother, had already followed through with contacting his friend, the sailboat's owner and captain, Joan could be traveling to Guam for no reason.

"I don't think so. Not yet." Lois said, quickly adding, "I'll make this up to you, Joanie, I promise."

"Yes you will," Joan declared, glad for small miracles, the cancellation was not yet official. "You're going to tell Max to let the captain know that I will be in Guam, at the marina in two days, as scheduled."

Lois was stunned. "You're serious, aren't you?"

"Dead serious," Joan said. "You just make good your promise." She added, piqued, "Can you do that?"

"Joanie," Lois said, clearly taken aback by her friend's abruptness. "I really am sorry. I didn't think you would mind, you know, having to deal with your mum. I certainly didn't figure you would go by yourself."

Joan caught her anger at Lois' mention of her mother. Venturing into water too deep to see bottom was only going to upset Lois and possibly thwart Joan's end game. "Lois," she said firmly, "if you really aren't going, make sure Max informs the captain that I am."

"Joanie, stop worrying. I'll see to it that Max tells the captain."

And Joan believed her.

CHAPTER TWO

A dusk-tinted view from her window seat of an astonishingly desolate ocean fed the hesitancy Joan had been unable to banish since slipping into the taxi that took her to Auckland's international airport. Now, as her plane descended to Tokyo's Narita Airport, her imagined idyllic cruise tanning herself on a sailboat's foredeck while munching tropical fruit and sipping a gin and tonic faltered at the sight of wind blown white horses on the unsettled sea. She would have a three hour layover in Japan before her connecting flight departed for Guam and though temptation urged her to use that time to cancel her next flight and return home to Auckland, she clung to what she had set into motion. The certainty of empowering her mother and emboldening an ex-boyfriend intent on rekindling their relationship was far more foreboding than the uncertainty awaiting her in the Western Pacific Ocean.

⊂Зℰᗡ

Joan pulled aside her hotel room's window curtain. Morning sunlight cast long shadows from palm trees across a grassy yard ending at a strip of white sand beach where an elderly couple strolled against a backdrop of a sand and reef that abruptly yielded to deeper water five hundred yards off Agat, Guam. A cargo ship inched across the western horizon on an invitingly calm ocean, drawing a confident smile from Joan that her own trip would be on the same docile sea.

Joan showered and dressed in loose-fitting shorts and T-shirt she had packed for the tropics. She clipped a bum-pack around her waist and slipped in her money and passport, protective of the document that would open doors to other countries and ultimately get her back home. Donning a safari hat that had been a loyal companion on hiking and camping trips on New Zealand's two main islands, she exited her room and took the stairway to the first floor for a complimentary buffet breakfast in a side room clipped to the hotel's lobby. Central to the cereals, eggs, breads and assorted fruit was a plate of boiled breadfruit, its off-white slices fanned into a ring pattern.

Thickening pressure in her stomach for her upcoming trip dampened Joan's appetite and instead of her usual granola, fruit and hard boiled egg breakfast, she downed a quick blueberry muffin and cup of hot tea, topped off with her first ever slice of breadfruit. The boiled fruit's soft meat had a taste and texture to a similarly cooked potato.

She exited the hotel onto its front, paver walkway shaded from morning sun by a massive breadfruit tree festooned with football-size, knobby-skin fruit among its oversized, undulated leaves. The air outside was soft and balmy with a floral back note from flowering hibiscus and plumeria. The heavy air muffled the sounds of morning traffic. She flagged an approaching taxi and slipped onto its backseat, butterflies turning her stomach. "I'm going to Gregorio Perez Marina," Joan told the taxi driver.

The taxi's driver, a middle-aged man with a mix of Filipino and Japanese features and a 1960's Afro-haircut, merged his vehicle into a break in traffic. He regarded his passenger's reflection in the rear-view mirror. "Are you with the tour group from Australia?"

"No, I'm crewing on a sailboat," Joan replied, feeling in an elite class for being able to make such a claim. "We're sailing to the Philippines and then to Hong Kong."

The driver sized up Joan in the mirror. "Guam to the Philippines and Hong Kong? That's off the beaten track."

Joan's mother's warning about storms and her own lingering concerns about how safe the boat would be on the high seas flooded over Joan. "Is that a problem?"

"No problem," the driver commented. "I used to work on a fishing boat, mostly west of Guam. Went to the Philippines once. That's where my father is from." He stopped at a traffic light. "Besides cargo ships and fishing boats," he continued, "there's not much out there. I don't recall ever seeing any sailboats."

Joan purposefully focused on the positives of her trip, paying scant attention to the surroundings outside the taxi. "The captain has already sailed around the world, so I'm sure he has been to the Philippines before, and he is originally from Hong Kong."

"Don't get me wrong," the driver said. "This is the perfect time of year to head west. The prevailing winds are blowing in that direction and so far this year there haven't been any typhoons."

"Are there typhoons this time of year?" Joan asked, not having expected weather as intense as tropical storms during the northern hemisphere's winter months.

"This part of the Pacific gets typhoons year round but not so many in February. This year, though, has been quiet."

With the driver's affirmation of what she wanted to believe would be smooth sailing conditions, Joan settled back in her seat and held onto her optimism that because her boat's captain knew what he was doing, and the winds were light, she would have a fantastic trip.

At a wide intersection, the taxi kept right onto Marine Corps Drive and continued along the west coast for three miles before the four lane curved to the right with a northern view through Joan's left window to breaking waves churning into white froth against a fringe reef and beyond, a deep, almost black sea capped with white horses under an intense blue sky.

Joan's unwelcome companion of anxiety rose in her throat. The waves on this side of the island were alarmingly larger than what she had seen from her hotel room. And then there was the reef.

"Have any boats ever hit that reef?" The concern in her voice was palpable.

The driver gave an uninterested glance at the ocean.

"A few have," he commented and seeing the uneasiness in her reflection, he added, "Since your captain has sailed this part of the world before, he'll have all of the navigation charts and skills for a safe trip. The only time you have to worry about reefs is closer to land and there's not much of that between here and the Philippines."

A sign tacked to a wooden post sprouting from a tuft of grass marked the entrance into Gregorio D. Perez Marina at the base of a twenty-five acre peninsula accommodating Paseo de Susana Recreation Park with its miniature Statue of Liberty and baseball diamond.

The taxi driver turned left at a traffic light and followed the park's curving entrance road to the marina's rectangular, gravel parking lot flanked by two opposing docks each accessed by two four-foot long steel ladders, one at each end of the parking lot. A dozen boats were slipped along the length of the dock to the right and half as many on the left where a gaggle of pale-skinned tourists in gaudy beachwear boarded a fifty-foot wooden hull excursion boat under the watchful eyes of squawking seagulls waiting for handouts.

Joan's driver halted at the parking lot's lower end in front of a single-story building clad in white weatherboard and decorated with a sun-faded sign over its front, screen door: Marina Office.

"Good luck is always welcome at sea," Joan's cabbie commented, "so, good luck and enjoy every minute of it. You're living the dream."

"Thanks," Joan replied as she slipped from his taxi.

Even if good luck was indeed traveling with her, she was aware how easy it would be to tell the driver to take her back to the hotel so she could gather up her gear and check out before hauling her to the airport. Stubbornly, she held onto her original decision. There was too much at stake to not stay committed and maybe she really was, living the dream.

Exiting the taxi, the sulfurous tinge of mudflats and stale seawater assaulted Joan's nostrils. She handed the driver his fare through the open window and shaded her eyes Indian-fashion when a raw-boned man with a bulbous nose patterned with a filigree of broken blood vessels pushed through the creaking office door. His gray shirt was embroidered with "Norm" over the heart, and his thin legs protruded from baggy, khaki shorts, making him look like a double stick ice block.

"If you're booked on the day cruise," he called to Joan in a voice as rough as his brown skin, "you'll need to hurry." He pointed toward the last few passengers boarding the excursion boat.

"Actually, I'm looking for Wayne Yao," Joan said. "His boat's name is, Atmosphere."

The butterflies in Joan's stomach kicked up their pace for yet another step toward the point of no return.

Norm descended the office's low steps in deliberate strides due to what was obviously a lower back problem and led Joan to a security gate and steel access ladder at the upper end of the parking lot, directly opposite the now loaded excursion boat. Norm keyed open the gate's lock, pulled up on its outer edge and swung it open. Motioning to the dock's lower end by his office, he said, "Atmosphere is in the last slip." He stepped aside to allow Joan passage. "Don't use the ladder by the office," he said. "It's closed for repairs."

Joan thanked Norm for his assistance and reversing her stance, descended the ladder facing the parking lot's sheer, concrete foundation to which the ladder was bolted. Stepping onto the wood-slated dock, she made her way toward the dock's far end which looked to extend to the rear of the marina office.

The main dock had perpendicular fingers jutting into the narrow bay, like a wide-toothed comb, with an assortment of motorboats and a handful of sailboats slipped bows or sterns to the main dock. Some of the boats were in pristine condition while other vessels had decks and coach roofs streaked with bird droppings and peeling rot. One particularly gruesome sailboat toward the dock's lower end had a delaminating teak deck and a dry-rotted dinghy atop its coach roof. Duct-tape sealed a twelve inch wide jagged hole just above the unfortunate boat's starboard side waterline.

The next boat past this derelict was a scuffed-up white forty-foot sloop, slipped bow-in with three inflated, cylindrical fenders cushioning its port side from the dock. ATMOSPHERE was stenciled in large letters mid-ships on the vessel's sides. The sailboat had dual perimeter lifelines, a sturdy mast with a single pair of spreaders, lazy-jacks cradling the furled mainsail, a roller furling jib and electric windlass on the bow for hauling up the plow-shaped anchor strapped to a bow roller. A reinforced inflatable dinghy with a fiberglass bottom was inverted on the boat's coach roof and a navy blue, canvas Bimini top on an aluminum frame shielded the stern cockpit from the harsh sun. Fitted to the boat's stern rail was an orange-colored life ring connected to an orange Nylon rope leading into a heavy-duty, canvas bag. Next to this was a four foot tall pole attached to a day-glow orange buoy and topped with a water-proof light and red and yellow signal ensign.

Midship, across the boat, on its starboard side, a fifty year old man of Chinese heritage, thin and fit, plugged a plastic funnel into an uncapped fuel ingress portal through the boat's deck. Just forward of the man's position were a half dozen, yellow, six gallon diesel fuel carboys shrouded with Nylon netting and secured to the boat's starboard rail.

Removing the cap from a seventh fuel carboy marked in black letters; Property of G.P. Marina, and conveniently staged atop the coach roof next to himself, the man tilted the container toward the funnel. Diesel fuel gurgled from the carboy into the boat's main fuel tank.

Joan refrained from interrupting the man's work but when the transfer was complete and he stood to stretch tight back muscles without acknowledging her, she spoke up. "Excuse me. Mr. Yao?"

Yao gave vague recognition to Joan's presence, too busy to be bothered with curiosity seekers.

"My name is Joan Mackland, Lois Tomblinson's friend."

Yao drew a hand towel from his back pocket and wiped sweat from his face. He fixed her with a flat look. "Max sent me a fax that said Lois had cancelled."

A hollow feeling replaced Joan's butterflies. After dealing with her mother and the anxieties she had overcome to travel to Guam, she hadn't come this far just to eat a slice of boiled breadfruit. "Max was supposed to have told you that I was still coming."

Yao's brow furrowed in an irritated look.

Joan set her mouth in a hard line. Lois' indifference was not going to nix her efforts. "Can I ask if you still need a crew member?"

Yao took an uncomfortably long moment to process Joan's question. "Lois indicated you have crewed before," he said. "Any passages or just local sailing in New Zealand?" He gave Joan the once-over.

Joan's hopes deflated in a rush. She could acknowledge having crewed and knowing her way around a boat but her lack of experience would shine through even the slightest embellishment. "No sir. I don't know why Lois told you that. I went on a daysail in high school but I wasn't crewing."

Yao's inexpressive face was hard to read. "Did you fly in from New Zealand?"

"Yes sir," she said lowly. "I arrived last night." She licked her dry lips, steeling herself for that return flight to Auckland and the explanations that would follow.

Yao swept his eyes over the string of boats on his side of the marina, teetering on a fine line of decision. Taking on crew was a serious matter, especially for someone with what he considered no sailing experience. He turned to Joan. "Are you willing to learn how to sail?"

"Yes sir, I am," Joan said, hope returning and bringing with it a sparkle to her eyes.

"Seasickness?"

Joan held her own with Yao's further questioning. She had figured seasickness would be brought up and she now had to provide an answer for what had been a concern of hers since Lois first mentioned the trip. It was true she became nauseous riding on any car's back seat but her malady was far worse in her grandfather's car with his oscillating pressure on the accelerator pedal. She managed much better up front with a clear view outside.

Joan considered the panorama from where she stood on the dock and rationalized that she would have a similarly open view from the boat's cockpit. Like a seat change in a motorcar, any discomfort from motion while below deck could be quelled by going topside. Whether this were true or not, she didn't know but returning home to face the out-of-tune melodies that had driven her to the precipice on which she now stood was still totally unacceptable, especially when a pill could cure the affliction. As for the medication's side effect, she would reduce the dosage to half a pill, problem solved.

"I get a little queasy sometimes riding in a car," she confessed, "mostly if my grandfather drives and I don't keep looking through the windscreen."

Yao had used this same question to cull other adventure-seeking hopefuls and was well aware severe motion sickness could be debilitating, even life threatening, and from what he had seen, sufferers had an acute aversion to willingly subjecting themselves to the causes of their infirmity. As for Joan, her revelation was notable but for Yao, not worrisome. He was acquainted with old salts who suffered likewise in automobiles.

"Most people feel a bit off the first day or two after leaving port," he offered. "They're fine after getting used to the boat's motion. Atmosphere will be sailing downwind which gives a smoother motion than working windward."

It seemed to Joan that Yao was attempting to convince himself to give her a chance and for that, she was suddenly filled with inadequacy of filling the shoes Yao would expect her to wear as his sole crew.

But Yao had not yet made his final decision, and that was clear to Joan when he said, "I've never taken on crew without spending a few days getting to know them with a bit of sailing thrown in to see how well they do." He stroked his chin with a glance over his boat.

Joan sighed acceptance of whatever decision Yao made. She knew deep within she truly wanted to go, needed to go, but also was fully aware of a string of reasons Yao could decide otherwise.

Yao turned back to Joan. "And you can spare two to three weeks?"

This roller coaster just started up again and she was not getting off unless ordered. "I'm between uni and finding a job," she said, "so I have whatever time it takes."

Yao posted his hands on his hips. Taking on a green crew member with no sailing experience was indeed a big responsibility, but the gal on the dock seemed determined to go and appeared fit enough to manage a trip he expected to be uneventful. He took the first step in his decision by motioning Joan to a gap through the lifelines at the boat's cockpit. "Take your shoes off and come aboard. I'll show you around."

Joan slipped off her sandals, stepped onto the boat's cap rail and ducked under the Bimini top, feeling as if she were isolating herself in another world. The spacious, open-air cockpit had cushioned seating all around and a central, binnacle-mounted helm with compass. There were two barrel-winches for the jib sheets, one winch each atop the port and starboard coaming, with the canvas Bimini top providing welcome shade from the bright ball of the mid-morning sun.

Yao joined her in the cockpit toting a coil of rope. He tilted up the port side cockpit cushion and raised the top of a storage locker underneath. The locker was filled with similar coils of rope, two white buckets holding scrub brushes and cleaners and forward of these, a round, wooden lid the size of an eighteen-inch frying pan and labeled, "Propane Gas." He dropped the length of rope into the locker and closed its lid.

"Come below," he said in the tone of someone used to giving orders.

He descended the companionway steps in the same reversed position Joan had used on the dock's ladder at the parking lot. She followed him down into the boat's wood-finished interior illuminated by sunlight streaming through port lights, five on each side of the cabin.

The galley was on the port side of the stairs. Yao pointed out a double sink and faucet, cabinets for plates, bowls and glasses and slatted shelves holding dehydrated beans and mushrooms, canned vegetables and salted nuts. He lifted the lid of an in-counter dry bin holding a five pound bag of white rice and a two pound bag of unrefined sugar. A miniature net hammock loaded with twenty oranges was strung between two port light latches.

Yao lifted the lid of a built-in, top-loading refrigerator. He sorted through the unit, stating its contents: a brick-size block of cheddar cheese, a round loaf of fresh-baked bread looking like a mummy wrapped in plastic film, a quarter pound square of real butter, nine stalks of Chinese cabbage, three dozen tomatoes, two bunches of celery and a dozen sweet peppers, plastic bags of leafy herbs and a plump finger of ginger root. "I'm a vegetarian, so you are on your own if you want anything else," he said and watched Joan's reaction.

"No worries about vegetarian food," she said. She was far from a fussy eater and cutting meat from her diet while at sea was fine with her.

"I was waiting for Lois and you to arrive before stocking for three people, but what I have is enough for two," he told Joan.

"It all looks great," Joan said, impressed, and added with hesitation, "Does that mean I'll be your crew?"

Yao crossed his arms like a teacher evaluating a student's performance. "And you're positive you want to sail?"

Joan took in the spacious cabin with its welcoming comfort, not forgetting why she was there, and her doubts slipped away.

"Yes, I am sure," she said, her answer bolstered even more by a feeling the boat was sturdy enough to take them safely across any ocean.

"Let's finish the tour," Yao said. "If after that you change you mind, no problem for me. I often single-hand anyway."

He eyed her sternly. "I just want you to be certain you want to go," adding, "Once we leave port, we're not turning back for any reason."

Joan understood and accepted that fact.

Yao slid open a cabinet door.

"Potatoes and carrots are in here. Onions in there. Over here, granola bars and dried apples."

He tapped a wide-mouth, gallon plastic jug filled with wadded paper towels.

"Raw eggs, individually wrapped."

Motioning to the opposite side of the companionway stairs, he pointed out the navigation table and an overhead radio fixed to a ceiling panel next to a cabin fan. An electrical control panel aft of the nav table featured two banks of labeled switches and above this, secured by a bungee cord, was a wooden box looking like a sixteen inch square hat box. Astern of the navigation table and extending under the cockpit's starboard side was a cushioned quarter berth, now stuffed with a storm jib, assorted gear and a four-man life raft packed in a valise looking like a black, oversized sports bag.

"I keep all my charts and navigation tools in here," Yao said of the nav table. He placed his hand on the wooden box like it was an old friend. "My sextant. When I bought the boat, it didn't have any electronics and that suited me fine. I prefer to navigate the old fashion way. In fact, the only electrical component I have on board is this VHF-UHF radio. The VHF antenna is mounted on the masthead. That's the top of the mast. Any boat you can see from up there, you can reach in VHF mode. Channel sixteen is pre-set. It's the VHF international emergency channel. From there, you just dial in the channel you want if it's not an emergency.

The back stay is the antenna for the UHF radio which is essentially a HAM radio, if you know anything about them."

Joan gave a knowing smile. "I have a cousin in Christchurch who is a HAM operator. He talks to people all around the world."

"In UHF mode, this radio can too, under the right atmospheric conditions. I use VHF when I'm close to a port or communicating with other boats. UHF is used mostly for talking to my brother in Vancouver."

He pointed out the electrical control panel. "That panel is connected to four house batteries stored under the pilot berth. The electrical panel is where the main switches are for the masthead light, running lights, cabin lights and fans. The radio and refrigerator are wired directly to the batteries. Any questions?"

"Is there a motor?"

"An engine," Yao clarified. "It's a forty horse diesel with its own starter battery. To get to the engine, you remove the companionway steps to an access door but that's nothing you will have to worry about."

The last part of his comment was a relief for Joan. She knew less about engines of any type than she did about sailing.

Yao moved into the roomy main cabin with its buffed white walls, cherry wood floor and teak bulkheads. On the boat's port side, a U-shaped settee wrapped around a central teak-wood table with ceiling-mounted cabin lights. To starboard, directly opposite the settee was the cushioned pilot berth. The bench-type seat ended at a forward bulkhead on which was mounted a barometer and digital clock. Joan noticed the timepiece needed adjusting, for it was set ten hours behind Guam time.

Inset cabinets along both sides of the cabin offered an impressive amount of storage with a port side bulkhead separating the main cabin from the head. Attached to this wood partition was a framed artist's rendition of *Atmosphere* in profile, a sleek boat with a fin keel and spade rudder.

Yao switched on a cabin fan, its artificial breeze pushing aside stagnant air. Taking a seat on the pilot berth, he invited Joan to sit across from him on the settee, the table as their prop.

"Tell me about yourself," Yao said.

"I'm twenty-three, originally from Christchurch but now I live in Auckland," Joan said. "I just finished uni with a degree in art history. I backpack and camp but I've always wanted to do something more adventurous. When Lois asked me to come with her on this trip, I knew I had to go."

Joan refrained from providing insights into the darker side of her decision to take a step into what for her was uncharted waters.

Yao's face darkened at the mention of Lois' name. "What happened to Lois? Why didn't she come?"

Joan gave a regretful frown. "She's crazy about a new boyfriend. In fact, she wanted him to come with her on this trip, but he couldn't get off work, so she asked me. He was the one who talked her out of coming."

Moving past a less than pleasant conversation about boyfriends, Joan regarded the artist's rendition of *Atmosphere*. "She's a beautiful boat," she commented.

Yao appreciated the compliment. "Yes, she is," he said, pride showing in his eyes. "I bought her last year, and after a few repairs, I'm taking her home to Hong Kong for a complete refit."

He scanned *Atmosphere*'s interior. "She's sturdy, constructed of aluminum, not a common building material for sailboats. As you can see from the drawing, she has a fin keel making her light-weight and fast. I like to say, her keel is a wing in the water, and her sails are a wing in the air."

Yao's comment about *Atmosphere* being sturdy and fast reinforced Joan's initial impression of the boat's soundness. "Atmosphere is an interesting name," she observed. "Why did you choose that?"

"The boat's previous name was, Baccus, which had no meaning to me," Yao explained. "Then I found an earlier certificate of ownership under some papers in the nav table. The certificate included the boat's first name, Atmosphere. That fit with what I was looking for, a name signifying that on which all life depends and which mankind must respect and preserve."

Yao's noble gesture in his choice of a name gave Joan a new perspective of *Atmosphere's* owner and captain.

Yao continued his tour. Leaning to one side, he flipped open a door to a standing locker, just forward from the navigation table.

"This is a wet locker for rain gear, life jackets, safety harnesses and diving gear. The drawer underneath is for hand tools." His voice was more authoritative when he added, "When you are in the cockpit, you are to wear a life jacket at all times. On night watches or in heavy weather, you'll also strap on a safety harness and clip onto either the binnacle or an attachment ring at the aft end of the cockpit."

Joan pulled a cautious look at the dangers she might have been purposely playing down. "By heavy weather, do you mean, typhoons?" she asked.

"Thunder storms, typhoons, any weather with waves and wind strong enough to jeopardize the safety of the boat and crew," Yao explained.

Yao's remark did nothing to alleviate Joan's concerns. "My taxi driver said there haven't been any typhoons this year. Is he right?"

Yao saw the issue of weather weighed heavy on Joan's mind, as he would expect. "Yes, he's right," he said. "Here in the West Pacific, tropical storms and typhoons pop up throughout the year but this year, most of the weather has been staying further south. The way it looks for the next week or so, we'll have rain and some wind but nothing close to a major blow."

Yao's "nothing close to a major blow" didn't sound too ominous to Joan.

Continuing his tour, Yao leaned down and hooked a finger through a hinged latch on a two-foot square floorboard between the settee table and pilot berth. Lifting the panel, he exposed the bolted-on inspection plate atop a stainless steel tank.

"This is the freshwater tank, eighty gallons." He held Joan with a pragmatic look. "Eighty gallons is not a lot of water. Use it sparingly. Showers and dish washing are with seawater. Rinse with fresh. There are two tethered buckets in the cockpit locker. The smaller bucket is for scooping up seawater and general cleaning. The larger one is for showers and dishes."

He slipped the floorboard into place and pointed aft to a second latched floorboard between the freshwater tank and the galley. This floorboard was half the dimensions of the first. "Under that panel there's an inspection plate on a fifty gallon tank of diesel fuel. The tank is full and there's another thirty-six gallons of reserve fuel in plastic jugs on deck. I expect a few days of light winds but considering the winds this time of year, that's plenty of fuel for the passage to Manila."

Just forward of the bulkhead on which was mounted the drawing of *Atmosphere*, Yao opened a door to the head. The camper-size bathroom had a grated floor, porcelain toilet and downsized stainless steel sink with a lower cabinet.

"To flush the toilet," Yao said, "use the hand pump. Seawater comes in to flush the contents and it automatically refills."

Forward of the head, a doorway opened into the V-berth, a cushioned cabin with additional storage on both sides as well as a reading light, a fan, and at the boat's bow, a crawl-through door into the anchor chain locker. An overhead hatch in the V-berth accessed the forward deck end of the cabin roof and could be opened for air circulation after removing the inverted dinghy strapped atop. Port light windows, two on each side, offered passive lighting and a view outside.

"This is your berth," Yao stated of the V-berth. "There's a hook and latch on the door for privacy. The only reason I would come forward is to get into the chain locker, but I won't need to do that until we arrive at the Philippines."

Captain and crew returned to the main cabin. Joan sat on the pilot berth as Yao lifted the top of the nav table and slipped out NGA nautical chart number fifty-two. The chart covered the top of the settee table and displayed the North Pacific Ocean from the Hawaiian Islands to the east, the Philippine Islands to the west, north to Japan and south to Papua New Guinea.

Placing his finger on the small dot that represented the island of Guam, at the southern end of the North Mariana Islands, Yao said, "We'll sail west from here, pass north of Yap and Palau and on to Manila, eight to ten days. We re-provision in Manila, pick up a wind generator from a friend of mine and then sail north to Hong Kong, another four to five days."

He paused, eyes on Joan. "I expect you to cook, stand your watches and keep the cabin clean. I'll teach you basic sailing but I handle everything on deck. Also, if you want to listen to music, bring your own. And absolutely no illegal drugs. That includes marijuana. Understood?"

Joan nodded with an accepting smile. "Yes sir, I understand."

"Are you familiar with port and starboard, mainsail, jib, stern and bow?"

"Yes sir, I learned all of that before the daysail," Joan smiled. "Port, left. Starboard, right. The big sail is the mainsail and the sail at the front, at the bow, is the jib."

"Where are your personal things?"

"At my hotel. We don't leave for a couple more days, right?"

"I brought forward the departure after getting the fax about Lois and you cancelling. I have a couple of friends in immigration and customs who are passing by here in about an hour, and they will clear Atmosphere for departure so we don't have to get tied up at their offices at Apra Harbor. He caught Joan with an uncompromising look. "Port officials are on a tight schedule. They handle both pleasure craft and cargo ships, and if you are late getting back before the clearing-out papers are ready to sign, you will not be on board Atmosphere. Is that clear?"

"It won't take me long to get my things at the hotel," Joan said.

"Where's your passport?"

Joan touched her bum-pack. "In here."

"Do you have photocopies of it, front information page and page with your Guam entry stamp?"

"No, but I can get copies made at my hotel when I check out."

"Get three copies each of the two pages. The third set is for the harbor master. My friends will take care of that too."

Joan nodded understanding of the very stringent schedule. "I'll be back here in time, I promise."

"Do you have seasick medication?"

"Not yet," Joan said. "I planned to pick it up here."

"You'll find it in any drug store, like Rexall," Yao said. "There's a patch called, scopolamine. I've never used it but I have heard it works well. Even if you buy scopolamine, get a pack of regular seasick pills, like Dramamine. It takes the patches about twelve hours to start working."

"I hope I don't disappoint you," Joan commented about her untested abilities as crew.

"I'll teach you how to sail," Yao said. "Follow my directions, stand your watches and you'll be fine." He slipped a key off a hook by the companionway and gave it to Joan. "You'll need this to open the gate when you return."

Joan reconfirmed to Yao that she understood the time constraint and hustled off the boat onto the dock. Even from the brief time she had been aboard *Atmosphere*, the effect of the boat's minor motion made the dock feel like it too was rocking. She took her slightly intoxicated gait to be the onset of her sea-legs, a comforting thought that immunity to seasickness came on that quickly.

As she ascended the ladder to the parking lot, Joan glanced back to *Atmosphere's* bow peering out from beyond the derelict slipped beside it. No matter what that unfortunate boat's captain and crew had experienced, she assured herself that hers would be a trip of self-enlightenment, adventure and fond memories.

CHAPTER THREE

Joan dropped her backpack on the floor at her hotel's Formica-covered front desk and slid her room key to a pudgy desk clerk with short, black hair. Pinned on the right side of the attendant's lime-green blouse was her name tag, Tess Palerma, and below this, a separate badge marked, Trainee.

"I'm in a hurry," Joan told Tess. After leaving Yao with her promise to return by noon, Joan had been lucky to catch a taxi dropping off a fare in the marina parking lot. Like this morning's taxi ride, the return trip to her hotel had taken only twenty minutes, but she still had a stop to make at a pharmacy for seasick medication, and she didn't know how much time finding a pharmacy would consume. Even so, she fully expected this jaunt to go smoothly, keeping her promise for a speedy return with time to spare.

Tess pulled Joan's registration form.

"Anything from the mini-bar?"

"No."

"Your bill is seventy US dollars."

"There is one other thing," Joan said in a flash recall. She pulled her passport from her bum-pack and opened the document to the data page displaying her photo and personal information. "I need three copies of this page..." She flipped past two pages. "...and three of this page." She handed Tess the passport.

Tess hesitated with an apologetic look. "I'm supposed to charge two cents per copy, if that's all right," she told Joan.

"That's fine," Joan said. She slid Tess her credit card and at the same time, checked her watch, more of a demonstration to the front desk clerk of her tightening schedule than for the current time.

Tess made a change to the digitized bill and printed a copy before attending to Joan's requested copies which she ran off quickly. She handed Joan the half dozen pages along with her passport and the credit card receipt.

Joan signed the credit card receipt, accepted the hotel's invoice from Tess, and as she returned her passport into her bum-pack she asked, "Do you know if there is a chemist close by?"

"A chemist?" Tess had never heard the term.

"A pharmacy, like Rexall."

"I'm not sure if there is a Rexall pharmacy close by," Tess apologized, "but there's a pharmacy in Agat Town, a couple miles up the road."

"Can you write down the address?" Joan asked. "For the taxi."

Tess slipped a phone book from under the counter, flipped through pages, found the listing she needed and wrote out the pharmacy's name and address on a page from a notepad. "It's called Sagan Amot Pharmacy," she told Joan as she handed her the jotted down information.

Joan stuffed her credit card receipt, hotel invoice and copies of her passport pages into an outer sleeve of her backpack and hefted the bag onto her shoulder.

"Thank you for staying with us and enjoy your day," Tess smiled.

Joan waved thanks as she hustled through the hotel's front door.

An anxious ten minutes passed before Joan was able to commandeer a taxi. The vehicle's driver was an ancient Japanese man with sagging skin, looking as if he would fall apart if touched. His driver ID card mounted on the dashboard's passenger side displayed his name and taxi registration number, "Kanji Suzuki - REG: 7639." He squinted at Joan's reflection in the rear-view mirror. "Yes?" he asked as if she were an uninvited guest.

Joan returned the stare at his dull, brown eyes. "I need to go to a pharmacy in Agat Town and then a marina, Gregorio Perez Marina." She slipped the transcribed business name and address through the pay window in the taxi's security screen. "First the pharmacy."

The driver looked at the written address as if trying to read hieroglyphics. "Saga?" he said in heavily accented Japanese.

"Yes, Sagan Amot in Agat Town and then marina." Joan was tempted to bail and hunt another taxi, but that decision was made for her when Mr. Suzuki swung his cab into honking horns of late morning traffic. A mile north on the two lane, he took a hard right onto a narrow street into Agat Town. The seaside community was a collection of single story concrete homes and a scattering of home-grown convenience stores. Mr. Suzuki's slow pace along back streets with frequent references to the written address made it painfully obvious to Joan that he was not familiar with Agat Town and possibly not even with this end of the island.

For a better view through the windscreen, Joan leaned closer to the Plexiglass partition separating the taxi's front and back seats. Mr. Suzuki drove like her Grandfather Stuart.

"This is not right," Joan protested. "Mr. Suzuki, turn around and go back to the main road." She jabbed her thumb over her shoulder. "There's a Shell petrol station further up." Just as Mr. Suzuki had turned into the small community of Agat Town, she had spied the station's iconic yellow scallop logo at the far end of the town.

Mr. Suzuki mumbled under his breath but complied to his passenger's demand and returned to the main road where he turned right, back on his original course. He sped on.

"Stop here," Joan nearly yelled, pointing to the Shell station. "Stop."

Mr. Suzuki whipped his taxi into the station's entrance, halting short of twin petrol pumps while mumbling under his breath.

A station attendant, looking every bit of fifteen years old and wearing dark slacks and a yellow, collared shirt, signaled the driver to pull up next to a pump.

When the taxi didn't move, Joan lowered her window and waved over the attendant. The name "Matthew" was embroidered on his shirt, opposite Shell's logo over his heart.

"I'm trying to get to Sagan Amot Pharmacy," Joan explained to the attendant, her voice heavy with annoyance. "The driver has the written address but can't find it."

"Yes ma'am, Sagan Pharmacy is about a mile and a half on this road, in the direction you were going," Matthew said in perfect American English. "It's in a strip mall called Agat Point. It will be on your right. You can't miss it."

"Can you explain what you told me to the driver?" Joan asked, grim-faced. She wasn't taking anymore chances.

Matthew stepped to the driver's window. The short conversation was in the local Chamorro dialect and ended with Mr. Suzuki reverting to Japanese by giving a drawn out, deep-throated, 'ahhhh' and a sharp, "HAI."

Stepping back from the car, Matthew said to Joan, "He knows where it is."

As the taxi pulled away, Joan called back a hasty "thank you" and closed her window. She checked the time on her watch again and shook her head. Her hour would be up in fifteen minutes. She mentally prepared herself for *Atmosphere's* slip to be vacant and her making an unplanned trip back to the airport.

To Joan's relief, Agat Point was indeed easy to find and Mr. Suzuki had no trouble picking out the pharmacy among the other tenants.

"Saga," he said like someone who had unwillingly driven miles out of his way.

"You wait," Joan told the driver. "I won't be long." She left her backpack in the taxi, figuring it would slow her down in the store while acting as a reminder to Mr. Suzuki that he still had a fare. She didn't worry about any of her possessions in the pack. There was only her Walkman, a few cassette tapes, personal hygiene items and her clothes. Her passport, credit cards and money were safely within her bum-pack.

Inside the shop, a twenty-five year old round-faced man in attendance directed Joan to the scopolamine patches Yao had mentioned. She selected a pack and added to this a bottle of Dramamine. Returning to the front counter, she queried the same helpful attendant. "Is it all right to use one of these patches and Dramamine at the same time?"

The attendant apologized for not knowing the answer. He lifted a telephone handset next to a box of Bic lighters and dialed three digits. "There's a customer wanting to know about mixing two different motion sickness medications." He replaced the handset. "The pharmacist will be right here."

Joan waited, appreciating the help but not the delay.

A short, Asian woman, looking to be in her fifties, with banged black hair streaked grey, light skin, eye-glasses and garbed in a white lab coat approached Joan, the only customer at checkout. "How can I help you?" she asked.

Joan held out her two selections. "I'm just wondering if I can take half of a Dramamine pill while using one of these patches."

"You can," the pharmacist cautioned, "but even with a partial dose of Dramamine, dizziness would be a concern. Both products by themselves can make you drowsy and the combined side-effect would be more pronounced." She looked at Joan from over her glasses. "Drowsiness can be severe in some people, so don't drive or operate machinery."

Joan could attest to Dramamine's side-effect. "I'll be on a sailboat."

"You'll apply the patch twelve hours or more before departure. If you are leaving within the next one or two hours, I recommend taking the Dramamine now."

The pharmacist's warning of drowsiness highlighted Joan's own worry that taking even a half dose of Dramamine could impair her ability to function and failing to impress the captain was no way to start the voyage. Both Lois and Yao had stated the boat would have a smooth motion sailing downwind and that was good enough for Joan. The medications she had selected would be a last resort. "I think I'll wait," Joan commented.

"As you like," the pharmacist replied.

Joan purchased both drugs, along with a new product from Pringles, baked potato crisps stacked in a canister. The attendant placed the medications in a white paper bag and crisps in a separate bag.

The transaction concluded, Joan exited through the store's automatic door on a high note. Slipping into her waiting taxi, she checked the time on her watch. The fact this was the same road her earlier taxi had taken meant that if there were no further delays, she should be back onboard Atmosphere at about the one hour mark.

"Marine?" the driver asked over his shoulder.

Joan leaned forward to make sure he heard her every word. "Yes, marina."

She glanced at his identification card again. "Mr. Suzuki, same as the motorcar."

Kanji's face brightened. "Hai. Suzuki."

"Mr. Suzuki, it's important I get to the marina as quickly as possible but please drive carefully." Her schedule was to return to the marina before the immigration and customs officers departed, not to be detained by police as a witness to a motor vehicle accident.

Suzuki flicked his eyes at Joan's reflection, either not having understood what she said, or not caring. He sped off.

As relaxed as she could be with time running out for securing her place on such a monumental voyage across an ocean, Joan's thoughts switched to the coming days and the anticipation of an adventure of a lifetime. For all of her uncertainties and concerns, she felt her worries and second-guessing had been exaggerated. The boat was more than she had expected, and she was as ready as she possibly could be for the high seas.

Mr. Suzuki slowed his taxi at a wide T-intersection and with a green light for his lane, turned left onto Marine Corps Drive, the same road the marina was on but alarmingly, he was traveling in the opposite direction. Ahead a dozen cars waited in line to reach a guard shack for security clearance onto; US Naval Base, Guam.

Joan's anxiety soared. She rapped on the Plexiglass divider. "Mr. Suzuki, where are you going? This is a naval base. You have to turn around."

Mr. Suzuki turned his head to his passenger's sharp frown, the loose skin on his forehead rising. "You go marine," he stated as if she couldn't recall her own request.

Joan's jaw muscles became as hard as rocks. The sinews in her neck stood out as concern turned to irritation. "Not marine," she yammered. "Marina. Gregorio Perez Marina. Boats. Not ships." If the security screen hadn't been there, she would have smacked his head.

Mr. Suzuki jabbered to himself in dialect and for all Joan knew, he was cursing her. With his understanding of English minimal and his pronunciation even worse, like his "Saga" for her "Sagan," her 'marina" must have been his "marine."

Joan struggled to control a scurry of anxiety and anger. Waiting in line to reach the guard shack just for an on-duty sailor to confirm to Mr. Suzuki that he indeed was going the wrong way was not something she would tolerate. Thinking fast and concerned Mr. Suzuki might reach his own limit and evict her, she spoke as calmly as she could. "Mr. Suzuki, please turn around and go back that way." Keeping her eyes on his, she pointed to the taxi's rear window. "Gregorio Perez Marina is that way. There's a park where they play baseball. Do you know where it is?" For all her determination to be as clear as possible, she couldn't recall the park's name.

As angered as his passenger was flustered, Mr. Suzuki made an accelerated U-turn and sped through the intersection, finally traveling north on Marine Corps Drive, in the right direction.

The four lane took a sweeping curve to the right, paralleling what for Joan was a familiar-looking, reef-fringed coastline. She scanned ahead through the windscreen for recognizable landmarks, having no confidence that Mr. Suzuki would not drive right past her destination. A few minutes later she tapped the security screen, motioning to a sign nailed to a stubby, roadside tree she had not seen on her earlier trip; "Gregorio D. Perez Marina - 1 mile."

"Marina," Joan stated to Mr. Suzuki in clear syllables, like a parent teaching a child a new word.

The driver fussed again in dialect as if he had caught the sarcasm. He turned his taxi left onto the entrance drive into Paseo de Susana Park and didn't slow until he reached the marina's parking lot. The car's tires grumbled gravel when he skidded to a stop to Joan's instructions. Ahead of the taxi, parked in front of the gated ladder, was a white sedan with a Port Authority of Guam decal on its front doors.

Joan reached *Atmosphere's* bow just as two port authority officials stepped from the boat's cockpit onto the dock. Both officers had the same slim frame with the taller officer clad in navy blue slacks and a light blue, short-sleeve shirt with matching epaulettes. On the garment's right sleeve was a Port Authority patch with embroidered lettering, "CUSTOMS," and the name, "P. SANTOS," etched white into a black name plate clipped to the shirt over his heart.

The second official wore a burgundy sports shirt with the same arm patch as P. Santos but with "IMMIGRATION" stitched on the front and opposite, over the heart, "W. LEUNG," was etched into the same type of name tag as his partner. Mr. Leung had sharp Chinese features and fisted a brown briefcase, making him look like a naval attaché.

Yao stood on the dock behind the two men. His stern face did not soften when he beheld Joan's late arrival.

"I hurried as fast as I could," Joan apologized, panting like an out-of-shape runner who had worked desperately to reach the finish line. It was painfully obvious to her that the check-out formalities had been concluded, and there would be no need for her to load her gear onto the boat. Still, she gave a quick explanation for the cause of her tardiness for whatever good that would do in changing her situation.

Mr. Santos smiled knowingly when Joan concluded the abridged version of her anxiety-filled sojourn. "One of the old guard, no doubt," the customs official commented of Joan's taxi driver. "There is a handful of them on the island. They were part of what was the Japanese garrison here during the war. From what I've heard, soldiers like your driver were either captured or surrendered to Allied forces, and after Japan's surrender, they returned to Guam to live, too ashamed of not fighting to the death to stay in Japan."

Mr. Leung gave Joan a quick look and nodded his mutual understanding, adding, "Those older drivers usually cater to Japanese tourists and the local Japanese community. They certainly don't speak much English, not like the younger drivers who speak English, Korean and Chamorro, the local dialect."

Mr. Leung turned to Yao. "Is this your crew?" he asked.

If the checkout formalities had been concluded a few minutes earlier, Yao would have accompanied the two officers to the parking lot and continued to the marina office to settle up his outstanding account before casting off, but with Joan's arrival, her anecdote and the two officers' unsolicited comments, he had come off his cold reaction to his crew member's delinquency. He took a quick look at the first hint of the outgoing tide and replied, "Yes, a bit late but she's here."

Mr. Leung slipped his briefcase under the bottom safety line and onto the cockpit seat. "Let's get this done so Yao has some companionship on this trip," he said to Joan. He gave Yao a wink and a smile and led the way on board. As the officer picked up his briefcase, Yao motioned to Joan. "Stow you things in the V-berth. We'll need you at the table."

Joan felt two-foot small as she lugged her gear down the companionway stairs, but all was not lost. She may have been late, but she was still crewing.

Holding to her captain's order, she hurried to the V-berth, dumped her gear and purchases onto the cushion, slipped out the copied pages of her passport and obediently joined Mr. Leung and Yao at the settee table where she took a seat on the pilot berth, intentionally closer to the immigration officer than her unsmiling captain. She laid her passport and the copies on the table.

Yao returned his previously completed documents to Officer Leung and caught Joan's forlorn look. "You like cutting things close, don't you," he said. His way of indicating things were back on track.

Joan gave a meek but appreciative smile.

From his attaché case, Mr. Lueng placed the original copy of his department's document over Yao's copy and filled in the appropriate information from Joan's passport before sliding the document to her for her signature. He also had her sign each of the copied passport pages. Producing a rubber immigration stamp, an adjustable date stamp and an ink pad, he compared Joan's face with that of the passport's photo and entered her exit stamp on one of her passport's many blank pages, overlaid with the day's date. He returned Yao's revised copy and filed Joan's passport copies into his briefcase.

The check-out completed, Joan followed the men into the cockpit. "Thank you so much," she told the officials as Mr. Lueng joined his partner on the dock.

"I'll phone you next month when I'm in Hong Kong," Mr. Lueng told Yao. "Good to have you here for the last year." The two men shook hands and the officials hurried off for their next appointment.

Joan turned to Yao, full of repentance. "Yao …," she started.

Yao held up a halting hand. "Let's finish up so we can cast off." He pressed a silver button mounted on the binnacle and the boat's diesel cranked with a muffled growl, settling into a steady coarse hum, barely audible from the cockpit. At the boat's stern, exhaust gases spewed and cooling water spit and gurgled from the engine's exhaust pipe.

Yao pulled from his pocket folded American currency and motioned to the borrowed marina fuel carboy set aside on the dock. "Take that fuel container on the dock back to the office and pay my bill," he told Joan. "Make sure you return the gate key. There's a rock by the gate to prop it open." He handed her the money. "Get a receipt. I'll finish up here and then we'll cast off."

Joan picked up the empty fuel carboy and walked with purpose down the dock toward the usable ladder at the dock's upper end. Even though Yao seemed to have a few more tasks to complete before casting off, she wasn't going to be the cause of any further delay.

Joan tip-toed for extra height and pushed the empty fuel carboy onto the boundary wall next to the ladder. She repositioned herself and as she stepped onto the ladder's lower rung, the edge of a partially submerged white paper bag protruding from under the dock caught her attention. She ascended to the parking lot wondering why someone would throw trash into the water when there were conveniently placed trash cans within easy reach.

An entrance bell jangled when Joan stepped into the dated marina office, a combination mini-store and tackle shop with a creaky wooden floor. An open terrace in the rear with a gathering of tables and chairs overlooked the barrier reef and rolling sea beyond. Norm stood behind a varnished plywood counter replenishing Guam lapel pins onto a paper display card.

"Mr. Yao is returning this fuel tank," Joan said. She displayed the carboy as she laid the gate key on the counter.

"Leave the fuel container at the end of the counter," Norm told her. He set the pin collection aside. "So you are crewing on Atmosphere?"

"Yes sir," Joan replied. She placed the empty tank as instructed and withdrew Yao's money from her pocket. "This is for Mr. Yao's account. He needs a receipt."

Norm thumbed through paperwork in a wire mesh tray atop a filing cabinet behind him and lifted out Yao's account documents. "You know, this will be that boat's second trip from here to the Philippines," Norm commented.

Joan was astounded. "Really," she said with a touch of unease as to a story different from what Yao had described. "Mr. Yao told me that he bought the boat a year ago and has done only local sailing."

"That would be right," Norm clarified. "A couple of years back, three boys from California stopped here on a circumnavigation. They were on the boat Yao bought, same name."

Another customer set off the entrance bell. Norm nodded greeting to a short, local man with curly hair.

"So Yao bought the boat from the three Californians?" Joan queried. That time-line of "a couple of years back" did not fit with Yao purchasing the boat a year ago or the fact he had said the boat he purchased was named, *Baccus*.

"Actually, Yao bought it from me."

"So the three previous owners never made it around the world?" Joan asked, curious about this more than convoluted history.

"No, they didn't," Norm said. "What happened was, about six weeks or so after the three left for the Philippines, two of them showed up here again. They said their friend, the third boy, had jumped ship in Palau and they had decided to give up their plans about making it around the world."

He gave a look of bafflement and said, "Why they would come back to Guam and not continue on to the Philippines, I don't know. Anyway, they registered the boat here in Guam, changed the boat's name to, Baccus, sold all of the electronics on board and disappeared. No for sale sign, incorrect contact information and at that point, a couple of months' unpaid slippage fee.

"After another month of no payment and no word from them, I reported the boat to the port authority and they designated it as abandoned. It was put up for auction, and I bought it with the intention of fixing it up and selling it, but before I started any work, Yao showed up looking for a sailboat. We worked out a price and that was that."

Joan's full confidence in Yao and her own decision to make this journey with him returned.

Norm rubber stamped "PAID" on the receipt, signed and dated the document and handed it to Joan. "Enjoy the trip," he said, looking past her to the waiting customer.

Joan returned to the ladder and once on the dock, hurried for *Atmosphere.* The white bag had either sunk or drifted out of sight under the dock. She gave it no further thought.

"Grab a life jacket from the wet locker," Yao instructed Joan as she stepped aboard. "I need you at the helm to take Atmosphere through the passage into open water while I shake out the mainsail."

While Joan had been dealing with Norm, Yao had completed preparations on board by stowing loose gear and tightening the straps holding down the inflatable dinghy over the forward hatch. *Atmosphere* and her supplies were secure.

Joan ducked below deck. Their imminent departure raised a sense of accomplishment in her, edged with unease at this threshold to adventure and self-discovery she had intentionally crossed. She was pleased with her decision to not subject herself to the drug-induced dullness of seasick medication and would prove to her captain he had made the right decision taking her on as crew.

Atmosphere rocked when Yao stepped onto the dock and released the dock lines. Pushing the boat away from its slip, he stepped back on board, a juncture Joan marked by committing the moment of casting off to memory, one forty-five on the afternoon of February sixteen, nineteen eighty seven, the official start of their expedition across the Western Pacific Ocean.

Severing ties with the marina dock meant more to Joan than the crack of a starter gun. It was a statement, an inescapable acceptance of what she had willingly set into motion. Her mixture of fear of the unknown and exhilaration of following through with this life-changing experience elevated her heart rate and reawakened stomach butterflies. Fear and excitement were one. She corralled her emotions in her clenched jaw, knowing the person she had been upon her departure from Auckland was on the brink of a transformation into a person even she may not recognize when this adventure was over.

Gears clunked and *Atmosphere* reversed into the marina's small bay. The engine idled momentarily as Yao turned the helm and his boat's bow swung around ninety degrees before he shifted gears again and the boat started forward, still at idle throttle.

In the main cabin, Joan opened the wet locker. Three orange life jackets were lined up along the bottom like slouching soldiers. She lifted out the newest looking jacket and carried it up into the cockpit. Yao stood behind the helm wearing his own life jacket over a safety harness, giving him the appearance of a power company pole climber preparing for a flood.

"You want me to steer?" Joan asked in a tone of uncertainty for something she had never done before.

"Yes," Yao said flatly. "Steer like a car. Stay in the middle of the channel to open water while I finish hauling the mainsail to the masthead. After that, I'll get the jib set and take the helm."

His brown eyes caught hers. "You've taken your seasick meds?"

"I picked up the patches and Dramamine, but I haven't taken anything yet."

Yao pulled a fleeting frown. "You should have taken the Dramamine."

"I was afraid it would make me drowsy."

"Take it now," Yao ordered, "and get back topside. I'd rather have you sleepy than seasick."

Joan returned below and hurried to the V-berth. She appreciated Yao putting seasickness above a medication's side-effects, and in retrospect, she should have taken the Dramamine when suggested by the pharmacist, but even now, she saw no issue with a delayed administration. Being topside with a grand view of everything around her would give her ample time for the medication to kick in before any ill effects from motion could set in.

Through the V-berth's starboard port light Joan caught sight of four teens running an impromptu foot race around the baseball diamond in Paseo Susana Park. A grounds keeper seated on a lawnmower cut grass fronting the scaled down replica of the Statue of Liberty. To the boat's port side was the wave-swept gnarly reef submerged now at high tide and looking less menacing than when she had first laid eyes on it. She smiled satisfaction that what she had set into motion had all worked out. Her adventure had indeed started.

Yao called down from the cockpit. "Joan, I need you up here, now."

Not seeing her purchases, Joan strong-armed her backpack aside, uncovering the bagged canister of baked crisps but no seasick medication. She dug through the pockets on her backpack, anxiety rising as she slung aside her Walkman cassette player, suntan lotion, a pack of Kotex and toiletries, knowing all the while she had not stowed the pills and patches inside.

In the cockpit, Yao could wait for his crew no longer. *Atmosphere* was approaching open water at the end of the cut channel, and he still had the sails to deal with. He steered past a breakwater of wooden pilings and boulders and took his boat into a rough northeasterly chop marching rhythmically toward the boat from a thousand miles of open sea. Waves struck the boat's starboard bow, lifting it over the crest of one wave and into the following trough, bringing an immediate uncomfortable motion below deck.

Still in the V-berth, scrambling to find her medication, Joan's desperation and concern ramped up at how quickly her stomach rebelled at the conflict between visual perception of static surroundings and abrupt motion. She shoved the backpack to one side and lifted the V-berth cushion. The medication was here in the V-berth, somewhere. It had to be. "Where the hell are you?" she moaned to the missing bag, refusing to believe she had left it in the taxi.

The image of what she had perceived to be someone's indiscriminately discarded trash floating near the ladder stabbed Joan's heart. That bag had not been litter. It had been her pharmacy purchase, lost from her grip when she had slipped and nearly fallen from the ladder. The thought of making a beeline to the cockpit and pleading with Yao to return to the marina and mount a search for her missing purchases was swept away by an all too familiar metallic taste blossoming in her mouth as if she was seated on the backseat of her grandfather's car. Her will was no match for this dreaded harbinger.

Despairing eyes glanced into the main cabin. The way to the companionway stairs was clear, but in that same instant, agonizing nausea overwhelmed her senses as if her Grandfather Stuart was at the helm. In defense of her rising dilemma, Joan fixed her gaze through the starboard port light, hoping against hope the visual reference of the foamy wave crests would abate her malady. It did not. Regret ripped at her soul for giving caution too much importance, for now the piper was demanding payment.

Joan retched, her desperation rising with her gorge. She knew her limits well enough to know she would never reach the cockpit before purging her stomach. She staggered from the V-berth into the head.

Ensconced behind the helm, Yao hunkered down for a view forward through the companionway. The fact his crew hadn't taken a Dramamine hinted she had been unconcerned about motion-sickness, but Yao knew, anyone coming off land needed to acclimate to a new reality that was constantly moving, and the fact Joan had not yet appeared topside frustrated and angered him. Either she had ignored his order to steer the boat, or her failure to medicate had taken her out of action. Either way, he was not impressed with his decision to bring her aboard.

Yao had no intention of returning to the marina to off-load Joan. They had both cleared customs and immigration and if *Atmosphere* returned to port, the check-out would have to be reversed before he could check-out once again, something that would require rescheduling with the port authority.

Yao stubbornly held to his original plan. If Joan was like other crew members he had had, she would get her sea-legs soon enough. All she needed to do now was get topside and keep a pill down.

A half mile out from the marina entrance, with Joan still a no-show and no other boat traffic nearby, Yao turned *Atmosphere's* helm, putting the boat's bow at a sharp angle to a steady twelve knot wind and four foot seas. Seaspray blasted over the foredeck and coach roof, soaking the strapped down dinghy.

Activating his boat's auto-pilot, Yao released the mainsheet, setting the boom to quavering, and clipped his harness' tether to the starboard side jack-line. This nylon strap, one of a pair, starboard and port, was stretched tight between the stern and bow cleats on both sides of the boat, providing a safeguard for staying attached to the boat as he moved forward or aft.

Stooping to lower his center of gravity, Yao made his way along the boat's side deck to the mast. He unclipped from the jack-line and secured his harness to an attachment ring welded onto the mast pulpit, a butt-high stainless steel frame that provided steady support from which to work the mainsail halyard and reefing lines.

Yao wedged himself securely between mast and pulpit and winched the flogging mainsail past the spreader, to the masthead. With the mainsail fully deployed, he cleated off the sail's halyard, unclipped his safety harness from the pulpit and worked his way back into the cockpit in a reverse procedure. Resetting the auto-pilot to a downwind course, he released the mainsheet from its clam cleat and fed out the rope as the boat's bow fell off the wind. The sail's boom swung over the boat's port side and the mainsail filled with air. *Atmosphere's* rigging stiffened, and the boat's pace quickened with a smooth, rocking motion.

Yao unfastened the foresail's furling line and hauled in the headsail's sheet, unrolling the jib from around the forestay. *Atmosphere* was under full sail and at its best.

Levering the transmission into neutral, Yao switched off the engine before shifting the transmission into reverse to prevent the propeller from free-wheeling. The diesel's constant drone was replaced by a soothing whoosh of water under the hull and a whisper of wind through the rigging, sounds that brought a contented smile to the captain. He set the auto-pilot to a course two hundred seventy degrees, due west, and readjusted the sails for a respectable six and half knots. Waves caught up to the boat's starboard stern quarter and passed under its hull, refining the vessel's motion to a dampened roll. He retrieved the five inflated fenders along the boat's port side and stowed these in the cockpit locker.

Boat, captain and missing crew glided past Adelup Point with its World War II gun emplacements perched atop a wooded limestone outcrop and a mile on sailed by Asan Point. Yao returned a friendly wave from tourists on Asan Invasion Beach. Clearing Cabras Island and the US Navy Reservation on Oroto Peninsula, *Atmosphere* and its two-person crew were free of land and on their thousand nautical mile passage across the Western Pacific Ocean. With seasonal storms sequestered farther south and no apparent threat of a tropical depression, good weather and fair winds were the order for the entire trip.

Yao ducked below, his face turning hard when he smelled vomit. The open V-berth door revealed Joan in the fetal position, motionless on the cushion. He started forward to rouse her, but the sight of vomit outside of the head brought him to a halt. He huffed. He had had seasick crew before but never someone who failed to pull their weight even when they felt like death warmed over. His decision to keep this crew member on-board seemed to have been a mistake.

CHAPTER FOUR

A desert-dry mouth and throbbing, low-grade headache dragged Joan from sleep plagued with black dreams of dying. The air within the darkened V-berth was stagnant and muggy. She reached up in gloomy twilight to open the hatch and her hand dropped in defeat when she remembered the dinghy lashed down on top. At that moment she would have gladly paid a king's ransom for a tree to hug.

Joan brushed aside a vomit-soiled towel, a souvenir of the worst bout of motion sickness she had ever endured, made worse knowing she couldn't banish the waves or get off the boat. Her happy beginning had not remained so, but at least the boat's more subtle motion offered hope the worst had passed.

She rose onto an elbow for a view through a port light. Night glow reflected from endless waves rolling past the boat in its direction of travel. She braced herself to face another unpleasant encounter with her captain.

Wadding up the soiled towel, she sat on the edge of the cushion to shake out the kinks in her body before standing. A red light in the main cabin illuminated Yao seated at the navigation table holding the radio's mike in conversation. The boat's engine softly grumbled in the background.

Joan stood on weak legs. Her splash of vomit in front of the head had been cleaned up, no doubt adding another grievance to Yao's list. She could clearly hear Yao's voice from where she stood.

"So far, I had to clean up her chunder and she missed her first watch."

"Take her back to Guam," came a man's radio-transmitted reply.

"I'll see how she fairs with the Dramamine. If she proves unable to follow orders, or her seasickness remains a problem, I'll put her off on Yap." Yao's firm tone signaled his intention of following through with this plan if need be.

Yao spied Joan. "Colin," he transmitted in a voice intended for Joan, "my seasick crew is finally awake."

Joan bowed her head sheepishly.

"I'll talk with you again in a few days," Colin radioed. "Good luck."

Joan walked awkwardly into the cabin, wadded towel in hand. "Yao, I'm so sorry," she said, full of regret. "Thank you for cleaning up my mess." She was referring to her vomit.

"It was either that or smell it for the rest of the night," Yao said, but his ire was much more deep-seated. "You told me that your seasickness wasn't severe."

Joan placed a hand on the table for balance, teetering on a precipice. Her eyes dropped to the floor. "I am sorry," she said in a meek voice. She raised her head to look him in the eyes. "I lost my seasickness medicine. I had no idea I could ever be so sick."

"When did you lose them?" Yao asked of her medication.

"I was in such a hurry to get back to the boat," Joan confessed, "that I nearly fell off the ladder. I must have dropped the bag with my pills and patches when that happened. I didn't realize it until I came below to take a Dramamine."

She didn't mention that she had a chance to recover them when she went to the marina office. At this point, it didn't matter.

Yao crossed his arms with clear meaning. Things with Joan were not as she had indicated earlier and even before speaking with his brother, he had decided on his only course of action.

"I have Atmosphere on a more southerly course that will take us closer to Yap Island," he said, holding her eyes with a gaze less threatening than adamant. "That gives us about three days to see how you fair with your seasickness."

Joan nodded acceptance.

"I have ginger in the refrigerator," Yao continued. "It helps relieve motion sickness."

"I really want to make this trip to Hong Kong," Joan commented. "I'll try anything," With her medication not on board, any potential remedy offered comforting hope.

"The ginger is in the refrigerator's side compartment. Suck on a slice as soon as you start feeling queasy. From what I understand, if you wait too long after the symptoms start, it doesn't work as well."

"I really am sorry for creating such a big problem."

Yao neither accepted nor spurned Joan's apology. Between the ginger and her inner ear acclimating to the motion of the sea, her condition should improve, and she had three days to prove it had.

Yao wasn't finished.

"I want you to understand," he stated, "that if your condition doesn't improve, with or without the ginger, you will have to leave the boat at Yap. There will most likely be weather between here and the Philippines and there's no sense in you suffering again as you did. I'll pay for your return flight from Yap to New Zealand."

"I understand," Joan said with a dispirited frown.

She hadn't known mal del mer could be as incapacitating as she had experienced, and though she indeed wanted to complete what she had started, it was foolish to allow seasickness to ruin the trip by torturing her and creating a source of aggravation for Yao.

What hinted to Joan of reprieve was the boat's improved motion that offered a respite from her suffering and with that, more time to gain her sea legs. Between that and the ginger, her calamity with seasickness might very well be behind her.

This optimism intensified when she captured a thread of the resoluteness that had put her on a collision course with this endeavor. Her desire to prove to her mother and to herself that she had the mettle to see this through was still just as strong as when she boarded the taxi to Auckland's airport. Crossing an ocean on a sailboat might not have been an advisable decision for her, but she was committed and would do all she could to stay the course. For her, there were no other acceptable options.

"No matter how badly I feel from now on," she told Yao, "I'm not letting you down again."

Yao accepted Joan's promised amends with justifiable skepticism. He uncrossed his arms and switched off the radio.

"Get some fresh air topside," he said, more a suggestion than an order. "The canteen is up there. Drink some water and stay in the cockpit as much as you can. The fresh air will do you good."

"Thanks," Joan sighed with a shadow of relief. "I think I'm already starting to feel better."

She stepped humbly past her captain and dragged her still fragile constitution up the companionway steps into the cockpit. Steadying herself with a hand on the binnacle, she closed her eyes, breathing in early morning's cool, therapeutic air. She sat on the starboard cockpit cushion feeling like the singer, Donna Summer. She would survive.

The cabin's red light spilled through the companionway, bathing the cockpit in its soft glow without impairing Joan's night vision. The canteen was US military issue wrapped in its olive-drab, cotton canvas cover. She unscrewed the quart-size, aluminum container's black cap and lifted the vessel to her lips. Each baby sip refreshed her like a healing elixir.

As she replaced lost fluids, she took in *Atmosphere* under full sail, caught between a dark sea and starry sky. Forward, the boat's red and green bow lights had a slow methodical motion caused by *Atmosphere's* response to the waves passing under its belly, stern to bow. Orion hung low in the western sky.

Yao brought Joan her life jacket and harness. "You forgot these," he said in his stern captain's voice. "Wear them when you are in the cockpit."

He switched off the engine and shifted the transmission into reverse.

Joan worked herself into the harness and overlaid this with the life jacket, feeling like an overstuffed puppet. She latched her gear onto the binnacle's connection point.

"I was thinking we would use the engine all the way to the Philippines," Joan commented. At the time she had succumbed to motion sickness, the engine had been running, as it had been when she awoke.

"The engine charges the batteries," Yao explained. "When we're sailing, I usually run it for an hour, every six to eight hours. That ensures the batteries are not drained too low."

The cabin's red illumination gave his skin a rough complexion and darkened his already dark eyes.

"Sunrise is in a couple hours," he said. "You can start your first watch then. Watches are four hours on, four hours off, twenty-four seven."

"Yes sir."

No matter how long watches were, Joan would not forsake her responsibility again after being out of commission within minutes of their departure.

"Exactly what do I do on watch?"

"Stay alert to what's going on around the boat, changes in weather or any shipping. There are no road signs out here and cargo ships don't always stay in the shipping lanes. They travel a lot faster than they appear, and they can easily run us down without them ever knowing."

"What if something happens?"

"Call me, even if you have to wake me. And you are not to go on deck for any reason without my permission. The safest places are here in the cockpit and down below. Also, before either of us goes off watch, we give the other a report, anything significant; changes in weather and wind, any problems with the sails or any shipping."

"It looks like everything now is all right," Joan observed, scanning the wind-filled sails and starlight flickering off of the rolling waves.

"This is what it's all about," Yao mused with more than a touch of reverence. "We've been making good close to seven knots. That's with a favorable current."

He lowered his head to view under the boom angled over the boat's port side.

"I've seen a few ships to the south but nothing to worry about." He regarded a sliver of moon hung low over the boat's bow. "The wind will probably freshen once the sun is up. I don't expect you to have any problems but you know the protocol."

"Wake you if any thing changes," Joan repeated with confidence.

"Are you hungry?" Yao asked.

"I think I am." She was feeling more herself again.

"If you are up to it, go below and get something to eat. I had one seasick crew member who swore by crackers and peanut butter."

"Crackers sound good," Joan said and cautious of aggravating her still delicate condition, she added, "I'll give the peanut butter a pass."

"After you get something in your stomach, try laying down on the pilot berth. There is less motion amidship. Be topside in an hour and a half."

Joan went below, snacked on a slice of cheese with crackers and taking Yao's comment about the pilot berth as a suggestion and not an order, she chose the privacy of the V-berth.

Joan silenced her wristwatch's shrill alarm after an hour's sleep and sat on the edge of the V-berth, calmed by the boat's subtle motion. She dressed and stepped into the darkened cabin, filled with a sense of security like in a warm, protective womb as inviting as her own flat. Sleep had erased the last traces of seasickness hinting that her affliction might have been conquered. She stretched out stiffness in her back and shoulders. Today, the captain would see her grit.

She visited the head. The view through the compact room's port light revealed a dark sky pressed low with clouds. Her personal needs satisfied, she passed through the cabin and switched on the galley's red ceiling light. On the cantered, gimbaled stove was a still hot kettle of water and a pan of rice porridge with boiled Chinese cabbage and onions. To her disappointment, the concoction included a slice of ginger. The herb might or might not relieve mal de mer but if her seasickness had not yet been defeated, having something that even hinted of benefit made losing the smallest slice a concern.

"Good morning, Yao," Joan called up through the companionway, proud of her early appearance.

The half dozen crackers and cheese she had consumed before retiring to the V-berth had replaced strength stolen by seasickness but hunger once again knocked.

"Can I get you anything from down here?"

"No thanks," Yao replied.

His ghostly image saluted her with an empty bowl and a half-peeled orange. "Help yourself to the rice and cabbage. I squeezed some oranges. The juice is in a Tupperware container in the refrigerator."

Joan spooned breakfast into a bowl and metered the orange juice into a glass.

"Before you come up," Yao called, "switch on the deck light. It's on the electrical panel, in the middle of the right-hand bank of switches."

Joan crossed the cabin to the nav table, found the switch on the panel and clicked it up. Reflected, white luminescence from a light mounted on the mast between the spreaders brought a sharper definition to the cockpit. She ascended the ladder with her meal.

Yao sat against the curved aft corner of the cockpit. The three-foot long tether of his safety harness fitted under his life jacket hung from his midriff like a strange umbilical cord. Next to him on the cushioned seat was a folded plastic tarp with a center drain spout.

Joan took the opposing position to her captain, the glass of juice secure in a cupholder on the binnacle and breakfast bowl on her lap. The switched-on deck light had turned the sails into brilliant white panels against a black sky. Her night vision was completely gone.

"The wind changed direction," Joan observed. The sails had been reset on the boat's starboard side.

"Just after you went below. Out of the south now."

Yao tightened his life jacket's strap. "There's a weak front passing through. I'm going to set up the rain catcher. Hopefully we'll get enough rain to top-up the water tank."

Joan was surprised. "We haven't used that much water, have we?"

"No, we've barely used any. I got a little behind in preparing to cast off and forgot to top up the tank. It's almost full, but I'll take on fresh water anytime I can get it."

He clipped onto the jack-line and went forward on the boat's port side, tarp in hand.

Joan ate her breakfast, watching Yao unfold the tarp and hang it with bungee cords from the mast and port shrouds, creating an oversized funnel. He knelt on the narrow strip of deck between the gunnel and coach roof and unscrewed a through-deck cap. Joan noted the cap was on the opposite side of the boat from where he had been filling the diesel tank upon her arrival at *Atmosphere.* As he inserted the tarp's drain hose into the open portal, a misting rain glistened like tiny snow flakes in the deck light's white beam.

With his rain catcher in place, Yao stood erect and reached for the mast pulpit for balance before unclipping his harness. At that moment, invisible to him without his night vision, an odd wave slapped *Atmosphere's* side. Sea spray doused the foredeck and the boat lurched, throwing Yao off balance. He slung out an arm but missed grabbing the pulpit. His harness tether snapped taut against his full weight, jarring the pulpit's attachment point but saving him from an unexpected swim.

Joan was on her feet the instant Yao lost his balance, as if she could have saved him from going overboard. Her bowl of soup tumbled from her lap, splashing its contents over the cockpit's grated sole.

Just as fast as disaster loomed, Yao reached out a hand, grabbed the mast pulpit and levered himself upright.

Joan wilted onto her seat.

Quickly recovering from his mishap and staying low, Yao unclipped the tether from the attachment ring and returned to the cockpit.

"I guess you saw what happened," Yao commented. He held up his harnesses snap-on buckle for emphasis.

"Yes, I did," Joan said with heavy relief. Yao's unexpected misstep had been a stark demonstration on just how vital it was to maintain physical connection with the boat.

Yao went below where he switched off the mast light returning the distinct, contrasting planes of a constantly moving sea and an all but static, star-filled sky.

Yao emerged through the companionway into the cockpit.

"You scared the piss out of me," Joan exclaimed as Yao took his seat.

"That is why safety gear is so important," Yao stated in a voice devoid of any unease. "We'll go over man-overboard procedures when it gets light," Yao stated. Had his crew been up to it, this training would have commenced soon after leaving port.

He studied Joan's face for lingering traces of mal de mer. "How are you feeling?"

"Better after that kip and a couple bites of food."

She sipped from her glass of orange juice and glanced at what was left of her meal scattered on the cockpit grating. "Lucky most of that went into my stomach," she commented of her lost breakfast.

Yao removed from the locker a well-used rag and the smaller of the two white buckets with its three-foot rope tether, and handed them to Joan to clean up the spill. The bucket held a bar of soap, a scrub brush and a toothbrush with frayed bristles.

"You can clean the cockpit during your watch," he said. He looked skyward beyond the edge of the Bimini top. "It doesn't look like we'll get much more rain." His hoped-for precipitation had not materialized beyond the brief sprinkle and patches of starry sky spoke of a front weaker than he had expected. "I'll replace the cap on the water tank. We don't need salt water in our drinking water."

Yao went forward on deck with due care, closed the in-feed portal for the drinking water tank and returned with the rain catcher. He stowed the modified tarp in the cockpit locker and descended halfway down the companionway ladder. Looking at Joan, he said, "If you need anything else to eat, come down and get it. Keep your eyes on the weather and get a piece of ginger whenever you think you'll need it."

He disappeared below.

Joan twisted at the waist and tugged on the upper, waist-high strand of the two lifelines ringing the boat. After Yao's near overboard scare, the plastic coated, one-eighth inch diameter steel cables seemed woefully inadequate to avert disaster. She gazed into the endless darkness beyond her world that was *Atmosphere,* and a chill ran through her at the thought of Yao having actually fallen overboard. She hoped what she would learn in the upcoming man-overboard session would never be called into action.

Alone with her thoughts, Joan delighted in the boat's tamed motion, a comforting improvement from hours earlier when *Atmosphere* was a bucking brumby. Across the boat's stern, orange-tinted lights of an impressively long ship passed south to north along the eastern horizon, probably calling into Guam. She recalled Yao's caution about the dangers of close encounters with shipping, and having seen the massive vessels at Christchurch's container port, she had a healthy respect for the behemoths.

In pale starlight, Joan tossed the spilled pieces of cooked vegetables overboard and set the bucketed accessories aside. Lowering the bucket over the boat's side, she hauled in enough water to rinse her spilled breakfast down the scuppers and into the long path of greenish phosphorescence from plankton stirred up in the boat's wake. With a second bucket of seawater, she washed her face and hands and rinsed away the salt with water from the canteen. It wasn't as refreshing as her apartment's shower but for now, she felt clean.

She reloaded the bucket with the cleaning supplies and stowed the gear in the locker. Across the boat's stern, clouds yielded to dawn's first light, bringing definition to waves seemingly coaxing *Atmosphere* west, toward the Philippine Islands. The early morning ocean was awesome, and for Joan, it seemed adversity trailed far behind in the boat's wake, and nothing else could go wrong on such an accommodating sea.

CHAPTER FIVE

Joan squirreled herself in the cockpit's aft corner, blinking her drowsy eyes in rapid succession to force herself awake. Morning's light in a sky devoid of clouds glinted off a rolling swell that had replaced white horses, calming *Atmosphere*'s motion. A faltering wind swayed the boom and jib to and fro as if the sails waited for further orders.

To the south, white clouds ran before a dark thunderhead crawling over the horizon, an electrified monster devouring the sky. Yao had another hour of sleep before his watch began, but he needed to know of the developing weather.

Joan crawled forward and leaned through the companionway. "Yao, I think you need to take a look at these clouds." There was more than a touch of uncertainty edging her voice.

Instinctively in tune with his boat when at sea, Yao was already shrugging on his life jacket. "I'll be up."

He emerged after a few moments and evaluated the southern sky.

"I didn't see that storm until the wind started dying," Joan confessed. "I hope I didn't wait too long." She was glad Yao hadn't found her dozing.

Yao took stock of the sea and sky around them. "You did fine. Just make sure you stay alert. Those storms can move quickly."

Any self-appointed accolades Joan felt she had earned by complying to onboard protocol were stolen by a lightning flash in the thunderhead. "Will that storm reach this far north?" Dealing with a pitching boat yet again was not in her plans for this day.

Yao was conscious of his crew's flushed features. After her bout of seasickness, the threat of a major storm had her spooked. "From the reports I've heard, I don't think it will get this far north," he replied with composed calm. "As I mentioned back in Guam, weather this year in this part of the ocean has been mild, and from what the fishing boat captains in Guam were saying, the storms south of here are tracking more to the west and blowing themselves out. We might get some stronger winds but more likely light and variable."

He adjusted the jib and hauled tight the main sheet, bridling the boom over the cockpit.

"Have you had anything to eat since earlier this morning?" He figured getting Joan's mind off of something neither of them could control would help her nerves.

"No," Joan replied.

"Get something to eat and then we'll go over man-overboard procedures." He paused. "And by the way, we're on a more westerly course now. Unless you want to disembark at Yap, I see no need to stop there."

Joan beamed her appreciation for his decision. Her body seemed to have acclimated to the boat's constant motion, for she could remain below with no ill affects, and this bolstered her confidence that heavier weather would no longer take her out of commission. She ducked below and shed her life jacket, secure that she was in this trip for the full monty. Removing the loaf of bread from the refrigerator, she peeled back its plastic wrap and cut two slices for a tomato and cheese sandwich, accompanied by one of five hard boiled eggs Yao had prepared during his last watch.

As Joan ate her meal seated at the settee table, she studied the general navigation chart. She located Yap Island, south west of Guam with Palau another two hundred miles further on. Due west were the Philippine islands, her next milestone.

Atmosphere heeled just enough to let Joan know the wind had returned. Her meal finished, she dropped her dish and silverware in the sink, donned her life jacket and returned topside anxious for Yao's man-overboard instructions. Having already witnessed how unpredictable the boat's motion could be, learning more about onboard safety could only make crossing an ocean a more enjoyable experience.

"That weather to the south is breaking up," Yao reported as Joan settled onto a cockpit cushion. "The wind is freshening from the east."

He released the mainsail's sheet, and the boom swung to port ninety degrees. The mainsail filled in the ten knot breeze and *Atmosphere* responded, a wonderful feeling for Joan, the boat in harmony with a steady wind and calming sea.

Joan was all ears as Yao began his lesson.

"The first thing you do if someone falls overboard," Yao instructed, "is toss this marker buoy as close to the victim as you can."

He shifted to the stern rail and gripping the flagged pole fitted to the buoy, shook it for effect.

"This marker gives you a reference point for the general area where the person went into the water. It's easier to see than this orange life ring or someone wearing a life jacket."

"If though, the person overboard is not wearing a life jacket, throw in this orange ring first and then the marker pole."

He motioned Joan to deploy the marker. "Just pull it up and out of its holder."

Joan disengaged the buoy. It was not as heavy as it appeared.

"Throw it off the stern."

"Now?"

Joan's knee-jerk fear of losing the marker gave way to understanding this was hands-on training, and to do first-hand was to remember. She heaved the buoy. It splashed onto the sea, its white signal light atop automatically switching on with a steady blinking as the marker itself settled into the rhythm of the waves.

"Next," Yao continued, "turn off the auto-pilot and start the engine if it's not already running."

He allowed Joan to complete this procedure, switching off the auto-pilot, taking the transmission out of gear, pressing the engine's start button and shifting the transmission into forward.

"Now, throttle up and come about into the wind. Head toward the marker."

Joan steered *Atmosphere* as instructed, feeling like she was driving a heavy vehicle crossways over low furrows in a field. The headwind set the sails flapping noisily. She was too engrossed in the lesson to think about the boat's more pronounced motion going windward.

"Now that you've come about," Yao said loud enough to be heard over the protesting sails, "haul in the sails as tight as you can. Maintain a course that will put Atmosphere upwind from me. If you don't have a visual on me, stay within sight of the marker pole. I will wave my arms, so watch for me."

Joan followed the instructions as if the bobbing marker were Yao.

He nudged another silver switch.

"Since you'll be alone, switch on the auto-pilot to keep the boat on course, and as quickly as you can, toss the life ring over the stern rail along with all of its tether. The bitter end is already secured to the rail."

Joan activated the auto-pilot and stepped to the stern. Lifting the life ring from the stern rail, she pulled from its bag a sixty foot long orange-colored, Nylon tether. She tossed the life ring and its coiled tether into the water.

On the stern's port side, Yao lifted a clump of knotted, one inch diameter hemp rope that Joan had seen their first day out but had not questioned.

"This is a rope ladder," Yao explained. "After you deploy the life ring, shake out the ladder and drop it over the stern. Then get back to the helm and switch off the auto-pilot."

Joan took over steering from the auto-pilot. *Atmosphere* continued windward at a moderate crawl, closing the gap between boat and marker with the life ring and its stretched out tether sliding up one wave and down to the next. The marker pole was twenty feet off the starboard bow.

"What about the sails?" Joan asked worriedly.

"Don't worry about the sails," Yao stated, wanting to eliminate as many distractions for her in what would be an already distressing situation.

Joan placed a hand on the throttle.

"Don't slow the engine," Yao cautioned. "Stay on course until I am about even with the stern, then throttle back and turn to starboard, to circle around me."

Joan steered as directed, making a wide turn, a maneuver that brought the tether closer to the marker pole, which in a real man-overboard situation would be Yao.

"As soon as I have hold of the tether or the life ring," Yao said, "put the transmission into neutral to let *Atmosphere* drift and pull in the tether. I'll use the ladder to get onboard."

Yao had Joan retrieve the life ring before coming about, and as the marker pole slipped along the craft's stern quarter, he lifted the pole from the water and secured it into its holder. The marker's signal light automatically switched off.

"Put the boat back on course," he told Joan as he hung the life ring on its bracket with its coiled tether.

Joan steered the boat in an about face, and Yao had her reset the sails before switching off the engine.

"To recap," Yao said, as if he were reading from a manual, and he highlighted each point of the procedure, "and what was the one thing you do after you deploy the marker?"

"Keep my eye on the marker and watch for you."

Joan had little doubt Yao was making this out to be simpler than it would be in a real man-overboard situation.

"What if I get to the marker and still can't see you?"

Yao welcomed the question. "Everything you do after deploying the marker will be dictated by the weather, and it is much more likely for me to go overboard in heavy weather which makes things a little more difficult."

He looked beyond the boat's stern to the on-coming sea.

"If I go overboard in conditions like this, you'll sail to the marker like you just learned and if you don't see me, you'll sail a grid."

"You mean, going back and forth?"

"Yes, but there's a pattern you follow," Yao said and he pointed to a theoretical point where he might be in the water. "Let's say you have deployed the marker, hauled the sails in, turned the boat around and motored back to the marker but still don't see me. In that case, you'll follow a specific grid pattern while watching for me."

Yao placed a finger to one side of a dark blemish on the starboard cockpit cushion. "Let's say this black spot is the marker." He moved his finger four inches toward Joan, passing the stain as he said, "Continue straight past the marker for five hundred feet, then steer ninety degrees to starboard. Go another five hundred feet and then turn to starboard again but this time, travel the five hundred feet back to the marker and another five hundred feet beyond that. That puts you five hundred feet on the other side of the marker. You can see how, as you extend each side of the pattern by five hundred feet, you form concentric, square rings. Make sure you don't go so far that you lose sight of the marker."

He refrained from alarming Joan that if he were farther out than that or the sea was whipped up in a storm, there would be little chance of her finding him. Instead, he said, "As for searching in heavy weather, your best option will be to heave to as long as you are not close to land. Heaving to is simply setting the jib so the wind stops the boat and pushes it sideways."

He sat back with a reassuring look that signaled to Joan heaving to was not difficult.

"To heave to, keep your course into the wind. Use the winch to haul in the jib as tight as you can and then release the main sheet."

Joan followed Yao's instructions.

"Now, turn the boat so the wind hits on the wrong side of the jib," Yao said. "That's called, putting the jib aback."

He motioned to the foresail.

"The jib right now is set to port and has the shape of an airplane wing," he said. "In fact, that is how a sail moves the boat forward, greater pressure on the windward side and lower pressure on the lee side."

"I see what you mean," Joan commented, understanding the basic physics of flight.

"To heave to, what you do is change the dynamics by hauling tight the jib and falling off the wind to set the jib aback, putting the jib amidship where it no longer functions as an airfoil."

Joan sheeted in the jib and released the mainsail sheet. She made the course adjustment and the wind caught the jib, slapping it aback, the mainsail flapping uselessly to starboard.

"Switch off the engine and the auto-pilot, if it's on. Tie off the helm hard to starboard. The rudder will be attempting to turn Atmosphere into the wind but set like it is, the jib doesn't have any forward force so the boat stalls and drifts sideways, downwind." He motioned to the mainsail. "At this point, you would get the mainsail down, but we won't do it for this session. Go ahead and heave to."

Joan killed the diesel and switched off the auto-pilot. She turned the helm hard to port and secured it to the port side winch. *Atmosphere* slowed to a stop. Joan was amazed at the boat's subdued motion on the sea as the boat slipped to starboard as turbulent water churned under the keel killing the energy within oncoming waves.

"You can sit like this in the worst weather," Yao noted. "Make sure you record the compass heading between the boat and the marker so when the weather has dropped, you can return in the direction of the marker." He paused. "And don't forget, never heave to close to land."

"I think the easiest thing is for you stay onboard," Joan said, more as an order than a comment.

"I will do that," Yao smiled.

He regarded the boat's hove-to position. "Do you feel up to a short course in sail handling?"

Yao's man-overboard instructions had eased Joan's fears about what to do if he went for an unexpected swim, while the search grid had given her confidence of locating him if he was not immediately spotted. As for heaving to in bad weather, Yao had reviewed this for Joan's own safety. Locating and rescuing a man overboard in heavy seas kicked up in a storm was not only a near impossibility, it also put everyone on board at greater risk.

"That would be good," Joan said about further instruction.

Yao placed his hand on the port side winch to which the jib's sheet was attached, the winch handle slotted on top.

"You already know this is the working winch and working jib sheet," he said. "The winch and jib sheet that are not being used are called the lazy winch and lazy sheet. And that line running from the roller furling spool on the forestay, along the deck, back to the cockpit is the jib's furling line, used to roll up the jib."

He picked up the bitter end of the furling line. "To haul in the jib, just point the bow higher up on the wind, release the working sheet and haul in the furling line. Each pull turns the spool which rolls up the jib."

Standing, he said, "Go with me to the mast."

He clipped his harness tether onto the starboard side jack-line and stooped down low. Gripping a lifeline with his right hand, he looked back at his crew.

"Follow what I do."

He shuttled forward, sliding his hand along the top lifeline while holding onto a handhold fixed to the coach roof with his other hand for added balance as if in heavy seas.

Joan clipped onto the jack-line behind Yao and mimicked his moves. She could sense that without being securely attached to the boat and not steadying herself with the lifeline and handhold, any sudden motion of the boat could easily catapult her overboard.

Still gripping the handhold, Yao released the lifeline, unclipped from the jack-line and grabbed the starboard side mast pulpit. He let go of the handhold and stepped to the mast, moving around to its opposite side before clipping onto the port side pulpit.

Again, Joan mimicked his moves and joined him at the mast.

"Stay on the starboard side," Yao instructed. "That's the side the mainsail halyard is cleated. Make sure you clip onto the pulpit's attachment point."

Joan was already familiar with the mainsail halyard cleat as it was visible through the spray dodger's windscreen. A second cleat on the mast's port side was for the jib's halyard.

She clipped in as Yao had instructed. Before her was the mainsail halyard running from its cleat to a pulley mounted on the masthead and then down to the head of the mainsail.

"To get the sail down," Yao said, "all you do is uncleat and release the halyard. Gravity will do all of the work and the sail will gather in the lazy-jacks. After that, cleat off the halyard so the bitter end doesn't flap around. For the jib, the halyard is on my side of the mast but with roller furling, you don't have to worry about getting it down. Just roll it up."

Yao glanced to the masthead.

"If there is much of a wind, the mainsail doesn't always drop. If that happens, you'll need to pull it down by hand."

He raised inquisitive eyebrows. "Does all that make sense?"

"Yes sir, it does," Joan stated with confidence.

They reversed the safety procedure to return to the cockpit.

"That's enough for today," Yao said. "We'll go over it all again to-morrow. You can run through man-overboard procedures by yourself."

He paused. "You're off watch now. Be topside again by noon."

Returning to the V-berth, Joan set her wrist watch's alarm for three hours, ensuring she would have time for a bite to eat before relieving Yao at the end of his watch, another show of her sense of responsibility and potential competence.

She closed the V-berth's door and undressed, satisfied with what she had learned in her man-overboard training. That and keeping to Yao's established watch schedule would go a long way in holding her captain's approval. She turned on the fan, slipped on the Walkman's headphones and stretched out on the cushion. This had turned into the trip she had hoped for.

CHAPTER SIX

With Yao's second man-overboard session having been completed the following day and Joan no longer under the dark cloud of motion sickness, the next two days passed without incident with life aboard settling into a routine of standing watches, Yao navigating by the North Star, meals eaten in the cockpit, sleeping and Joan learning the nuances of sail trim. Joan deemed herself a bona fide crew member now, full of new-found independence and self-confidence, her old self left standing on the dock in Guam. She looked forward to arriving in the Philippines in another seven or eight days and hoped her mother would be proud of her accomplishment or would at least recognize her daughter could manage her own life.

"How was your kip?" Yao asked Joan of her nap as she appeared through the companionway. *Atmosphere* heeled slightly in the steady ten knot wind. It was just before midnight on nineteen February, the fourth day of their passage, and Joan was fed and ready for her next watch. She sat opposite Yao.

"I'm sleeping a lot better," Joan commented to Yao's question.

A comfortable familiarity of *Atmosphere* had settled over Joan, a oneness she found in the boat's smells, the way it rode rolling swells and kicked up its heels on the backs of white horses with their hissing crests of cascading foam, all moving in the same direction as the boat. She embraced the lively sensation of a brisk wind filling the sails, the rigging humming like guitar strings and water rushing under the hull, a symphony played to a backbeat of creaks and thumps of the boat and its stores.

Joan especially loved night watches when the starry heavens and glittering sea made it appear as if *Atmosphere* were floating in space, suspended in the center of the endless universe with all directions open for exploration. It was a magical time wrapped in the clean smell of sea air, meditative isolation and a heightened sense of self. A time when she marveled at the wonder around her and pondered the course she was steering for her life, contented in what she had put into motion. She had cast off the shackles from her childhood, slipped past her regrets of never satisfying a demanding mother and too little time with her father before he had been taken from her. More recently, she had ended a floundering relationship with a boyfriend too selfish to look beyond his own needs.

The string of regrets that she had been convinced would one day strangle her had been broken. Her decision to crew for Yao was a clear statement, to herself and to the world, she would decide what would come next in her life, not her mother and not some mis-matched boyfriend. As for now, she welcomed this passage never ending.

"I'm going forward to get a position fix," Yao said, breaking Joan's reverie. He lifted up his sextant. "Stay alert. Remember what you have learned." Since her first session of man-overboard training, that had become Yao's new catch phrase any time he went on deck.

Clipping himself onto the starboard side jack-line, Yao worked his way forward in the starry gloom, gripping handholds in his free hand. He moved to the middle of the deck in front of the coachroof, clipped onto a connection point and took a firm stance, sextant held firmly, his form highlighted by the jib's triangle of ghostly white.

As he had done for previous sightings, he loosened the sextant's index arm and swung the instrument up to his face where he sighted the North Star through the eyepiece. After subtle adjustments to the angle of arc with the unit's index arm, he locked the arm, immediately checking the time on his watch.

Yao's competence in seamanship was another source of comfort for Joan, and with his strict, on-board protocol and clear explanation of safety matters, Joan had found reassurance early on that as his crew, she was in good company. *Atmosphere* may have been a sturdy craft, but the boat and its crew were a minuscule speck on an expansive ocean, and disaster was only one mistake away, a mistake she was upbeat neither she nor Yao would ever make.

Yao returned to the cockpit with the adjusted sextant. Shifting the engine's transmission from reverse into neutral, he started the engine and shifted gear into forward, still under sail. The batteries needed charging again. He adjusted throttle to a fast idle and *Atmosphere* moved ahead at a speed almost that of the waves, settling the boat's motion even more.

"I'll be below working on our position," he told Joan. "Not much to report from my watch. Shipping to the south and a couple of trawlers north of us. An hour ago there were flashes of lightning to the south, nothing much now."

He descended to the ladder's bottom rung.

"Can you make me a tea?" he called topside.

Joan gave a prudent three-sixty scan of the environs and seeing all was clear, slipped below to the galley.

"By the way," Yao said as he laid the sextant on the nautical chart covering the settee table, "I don't think I mentioned, the propane tank for the stove is low on gas. When it runs out, let me know and I'll switch over to the reserve tank."

From the nav table, he selected a pad of lined paper, a pencil, parallel rule, dividers, a compact digital calculator and a two-inch thick volume of Nautical Almanac. Setting these on the settee table next to the sextant, he busied himself with calculations.

Joan ran water from the faucet into a pot and placed it on a lit burner. She dropped a teabag into a mug for Yao and prepared coffee for herself. As she waited for the boil, she watched Yao, hunched over as he was, looking like a math student ciphering equations on a final exam.

"Would you like something to eat?" she asked.

"A chocolate cookie," Yao said without looking up.

When the water boiled, she filled the cups and gingerly carried Yao's order to him, placing the tea and cookie out of his way on the settee table. She returned to the galley for her cup of coffee and portion of cookies and rejoined Yao.

"Is it all right if I stay down here and watch what you're doing?" Joan was intrigued with the process of calculating their position with data from the heavens but had not taken the opportunity since their departure from Guam to learn the process.

"Sure, every crew member should understand basic navigation."

Yao referenced his sextant's arc and recorded the angle of his fix on a scrap piece of paper.

"Our latitude, our position between north and south, is the arc's angle between the North Star and horizon," Yao explained, "with adjustments for the sextant's height above the water and refraction, the offset of the star's image when it enters earth's atmosphere, along with a number of other factors. Those adjustments require using some mathematical equations with data from tables in this." He tapped the nautical almanac.

"It sounds complicated," Joan said.

"It takes practice," Yao commented. He shifted his eyes to Joan. "Longitude, our position between east and west, is more involved and we can go over it later today. The main thing to remember at this point is latitude is based on angle and longitude is based on time at Greenwich, England." He motioned to the digital clock on the starboard bulkhead.

Joan nodded, finally understanding the offset time on the clock. Impressed with Yao's navigational skills, she said, "I'd probably end up sailing in circles."

Yao slid his finger along the chart to his previous position mark, calculated twenty-four hours earlier. "If all else fails," he said, "dead reckon. That's simply plotting the course you have been on since your last known position, taking into account time traveled and estimated boat speed. It's a general fix on your position, not as accurate as knowing latitude and longitude, but it will get you in the general area of where you are going."

He handed Joan the dividers. "Give it a try. Dead reckon from where we are now ..." He circled that position's pencil mark on the chart. "... to where we will be in ten hours, assuming we stay on our present course."

Joan considered the calculation.

"How do I know boat speed?"

"Without a speed indicator, it's through experience, knowing how fast the boat sails at certain wind speeds or judging the speed of the boat through the water. For what you are doing, let's say your estimated boat speed over the last ten hours has averaged five knots with a favorable current of one knot. That puts our adjusted speed over the ground, over the ocean bottom, at six knots."

He slid his finger along the chart in a more northerly direction.

"If the boat is on a heading at an angle to the current, then you need to take into account sideward slippage, but for now, we'll keep it simple and use our westerly course."

Joan was not certain how to begin.

Yao placed his finger on the vertical Y axis of the chart. "Always pick up distance on the vertical, longitude scale. Longitude lines, called meridians, are the lines that run north to south but measure distance east or west. Distance between longitude lines never changes relative to any position on Earth and that's why longitude is used to measure distance. Latitude lines aren't used to measure because distance between them changes as you move north to south."

He tapped his finger on the chart's compass rose. "We know from the boat's compass that our heading is two hundred seventy degrees, due west."

He laid the parallel rule across the chart's compass rose, one edge aligned with the rose's center point and the same edge crossing the two hundred seventy degree mark, giving their direction of travel. Maintaining the rule at that pre-set angle, he scissor-walked the tool across the chart until its edge touched his previous marked position. From this point, he drew a faint line along the rule's edge from his marked point and in the direction of travel.

"If we hold our present course from this position, and boat speed over the ground and the direction and speed of the current don't change, we'll be somewhere on this line. All you have to do now is take the boat's estimated speed and walk off the dividers the distance traveled along this line in ten hours."

He sipped his tea and ate his cookie, eyes on Joan's work.

Joan considered the data and instructions. "Let's see, six knots per hour, ten hours, that's sixty miles which would put us ..."

Following the procedure she had seen Yao use on his earlier plots, she adjusted the terminal points of the scissor-like dividers to a ten mile plot distance, taken from the chart's longitude scale. In an intermittent rotating motion, she walked the instrument six steps along their line of travel from Yao's last marked position and placed a confident finger on their future position. "We should be here," she said.

"That's correct. Be sure to mark the position on the chart and record the day and time next to it, then enter the information into the log book."

The rigging jangled in a shifting wind.

Yao downed his tea. "I'll see about the sails," he said and went topside.

Joan cleared the table of cups, visited the head and retrieved her Walkman from the V-berth.

"Thanks for explaining a bit about navigation," she said to Yao after taking a seat in the cockpit.

Yao had adjusted the sails for an erratic, ten knot northerly. "Celestial navigation isn't for everyone," he commented, switching off the engine, the batteries fully charged, "but I believe it's essential for anyone who goes to sea to understand the basics."

Joan smiled and nodded understanding. She appreciated Yao's unsolicited instruction, and even though this voyage was fulfilling objectives she had set for herself, she doubted another sailing excursion would factor into her future.

Across the wide expanse of ocean, high altitude clouds littered the night-washed southern sky. A lightning flash domed over the horizon.

"I'm glad we're not heading south," Joan commented.

"I expect the weather will stay in the lower latitudes for another week or so," Yao said. "We'll be in the Philippines by then."

"There's some shipping," Joan observed, pointing northwest over the boat's starboard bow to a brilliant, white light above a short line of dimmer lights.

"That's a fishing boat," Yao said. "Probably one of the trawlers I saw earlier."

"How can you tell it's a fishing boat?"

"The boat's single elevated white light means its length is less than fifty meters. Cargo ships have two raised lights, one above the other, and they are well over fifty meters in length."

"Is the trawler coming our way?" Joan asked. It was difficult for her to tell the fishing boat's actual course.

Yao lifted the binoculars to his eyes. Sliding the field of vision along the interface between dark sea and lighter sky, he found his target. He adjusted focus.

"I can see its port bow light which means it is headed due east, maybe working a grid, maybe returning to Guam."

He handed Joan the field glasses. "Keep an eye on it. If you can see both the red and green bow lights, it means the boat is heading straight for us. No bow lights, its heading away from us. Call me if there are any changes to its course."

Yao went below to complete his latitude calculations before turning in.

Joan clipped her safety harness to the cockpit's aft attachment point and reposed against the curved starboard corner. She donned her Walkman's headphones and clicked on music, content with *Atmosphere's* gentle rocking on waves that nudged the boat's stern, coaxing it toward a preordained destiny.

Three hours into Joan's watch and the fishing boat was a single point of white light on the eastern horizon where fast moving cirrus gleaming night shine skidded north. Wispy fingers of more ominous clouds peered over the darker southern horizon. No doubt another storm destined to fizzle out, or was it?

The steady northeasterly fell away. *Atmosphere's* sails went limp. The line of dense, cold clouds crawling north devoured the sky. Joan pulled off her headphones to total silence, the air heavy with the pungent smell of ozone. The southern horizon had lost all delineation as if the sea and sky had coalesced.

Rain-shrouded lightning flashed, revealing the gray-black face of a shelf cloud and bringing definition to a storm front much closer to *Atmosphere* than it had first appeared to Joan.

Chilling fear stole Joan's breath when she realized how quickly the storm was moving. She threw aside the headphones in instant terror and lurched for the companionway, but her harness tether snapped taut mid-stride and jerked her to a halt. "Yao," she yelled.

The boat's red interior light came on.

The sharp report of thunder rolled over *Atmosphere*.

"Yao!"

Like throwing its own switch, a mule-kick of a southerly gale clobbered the boat in a cold blast of sea spray, slamming the boom across the cockpit as if claiming the sail and rigging for its own. *Atmosphere* laid hard over to starboard. Seawater poured over the starboard gunnel into the cockpit, sucking at Joan's legs as if to pull her onto the floor of the quickly filling cockpit.

"Yao!" Joan screamed, clinging to the binnacle and certain she was about to be drowned.

Yao rocketed through the skewed companionway, eyes wild with alarm and rage.

"What the hell are you doing?" he bellowed over the din, angered at his crew's late response to impending disaster. "Release the mainsail sheet," he shouted as he snapped tight his harness buckle. Spilling air from the mainsail would upright his boat, making it more manageable for reefing.

Before Joan could react to Yao's directive, the boat's weather helm out muscled its autopilot and *Atmosphere* swerved bow-on to the wind, spilling air from the sails. The boat shook violently to the flaying jib and slashing boom in the head-on wind that kicked up foamy, sharp-crested waves bringing an abrupt motion to *Atmosphere* on the confused sea.

Yao wrestled on his life jacket. He had to reef the main. A gray deluge of rain hissing on the breaking waves, swept over *Atmosphere*, taking visibility to naught.

Joan found her footing. She wrapped both arms around the binnacle, mumbling something, a prayer, an apology, but her words were lost to the bedlam of flogging sails, wind and rain.

Atmosphere's speed fell off, threatening to put the jib aback.

Yao extricated himself through the bucking companionway and hauled in the mainsheet enough for the sail's leach, its aft edge, to catch the wind, once again giving *Atmosphere* forward motion and more control. He rushed through an adjustment of the auto-pilot to a southwest heading. "Release the mainsail sheet when I signal you," he barked, his voice wrapped within the racket. He clipped onto the starboard side jack-line and crawled with urgent intent forward to the mast pulpit.

Overwhelmed with fear and guilt and following what she had understood Yao to have said, Joan lowered herself in the still flooded cockpit and reaching astern, yanked the mainsail sheet from its clam cleat.

The partially filled sail scissored the freed boom upward and heaved it hard to starboard, slashing the air with skull-crushing force. With the mainsail no longer providing balance to the endangered boat, the wind-strained jib veered *Atmosphere* to port, to its original heading. The abrupt, almost instant motion caught Yao off guard at the moment his harness' snap hook engaged the mast pulpit's starboard side connection point. The unexpected motion threw him sideways and back. Flailing, disoriented and unable to grab the pulpit, he fell backward on a course that would take him over the lifelines. His harness tether snapped taut against his full weight, jarring the pulpit at it foundation, but saving him from a worse case scenario. White-knuckling the mast pulpit, his head jerked around like he had been slapped.

"When I signal you," he screamed at Joan's horrified figure through the spray dodger's rain-soaked windscreen.

Joan could feel the force of his eyes.

Rain water on Yao's nose and chin blew sideways as he wedged himself between pulpit and mast. He mouthed his displeasure at being forced to the mast in such a blow due to what he considered pure negligence, and at this point he didn't care if it was caused by inexperience.

He freed up the mainsail halyard and heaved down on the sail's luff, dragging the sail down one pull after another to the second reefing point, reducing the sail's exposed surface by two-thirds. He pulled on a reefing line at the boom's gooseneck, where the boom was attached to the mast, and yanked, tightening the sail along the boom. Giving quick inspection to his work and satisfied with the trimmed sail, he unhooked his safety harness, latched onto the jack-line and crawled on the side deck to the cockpit. He pushed unceremoniously past his shamefaced crew and hauled in the main sheet. *Atmosphere* responded with what sounded like a sigh.

Yao worked the jib's furling line while letting out the working jib sheet to reduce and trim the headsail. *Atmosphere* was still wrapped in the storm's stinging rain and spray but at least was under control.

The immediacy of the moment quelled, Yao turned stern-faced to his crew, ready to tear her a new one, but Joan's pallid features were etched with lines of tormented misery. Her worst fears had collapsed onto her shoulders telling Yao he had once again lost his crew to seasickness.

For all he had in his craw, Joan's condition would mute any reprimand from him. He had indeed heard her call to alert him of the weather, but she had obviously not been aware of the storm's proximity until it was upon them, which to Yao showed a clear case of sleeping while on watch. His ire would be better served when she was back from the living dead.

Yao leaned close to be heard. "Are you using the ginger?" he asked gruffly.

Nausea twisted Joan's stomach filling her mouth with the dreaded metallic taste. She worked her tongue in an attempt to moisten her lips and shook her head at Yao's question, a feeble attempt at both an apology for upsetting him yet again and an answer to his question. Panting desperation, she pressed her eyes closed and vomited onto the cockpit sole.

"Chunder over the side," Yao blustered, but Joan was unresponsive, consumed by her malady.

Yao surrendered to the situation. Joan was a greater liability remaining in the cockpit than any support she might offer, and he didn't need to be stepping over her in his struggle to bring his boat safely through this ferment.

He shuttled below and moments later strong-armed himself back into the cockpit with a thick slice of ginger root. Holding his forearm in front of his face to shield from the stinging rain, he said over the storm's roar, "I need you out of the way." He pressed the ginger slice into her hand. "Suck on this. Get below. Lay down and keep your eyes closed."

Joan was past caring about her promise to never again shirk her responsibilities as crew. She pushed the ginger slice into her mouth not knowing if Yao's remedy was fair dinkum or only a mariner's myth, but the root's pungent flavor at least overpowered the metallic taste and eased her urge to retch. A welcome improvement, though the horrible queasiness still consumed her.

Yao had enough pity to unclip Joan's harness and assist her to the companionway. "Chunder in the sink or the head," he ordered. "I'm not cleaning up after you again."

Every bone in Joan's body seemed to have dissolved, and she felt as if she were flowing down the companionway steps like thick syrup. Her breathing came in short gasps and her heart raced.

Straight-arming a stance at the galley sink, desperate to defeat the nausea, she bit down on the ginger slice and chewed the woody mass. Stress lines creasing her face deepened at the fibrous root's spike of sharp flavor and spicy heat. Struggling to not spit out the masticated herb and determined to get every bit of medicinal benefit from the coarse ball, she breathed deep, shoulders rising, and swallowed. Hope replaced misery when her suffering mercifully eased a notch.

Joan unbuckled her life jacket and harness and shed them onto the galley floor. She moved through the cabin like a gibbon in an earthquake, her rubbery legs threatening to give out like a drunk. Ignoring the pilot berth once again, she muddled into the V-berth for the privacy it offered. Closing the door of her sanctuary, she braced herself and peeled off her wet clothes. She dragged dry clothing from a storage compartment and lay down on the cushion, eyes closed to lessen the affect of seasickness. She wrestled on panties and a T-shirt for what warmth they offered. Exhausted and praying the boat would run aground like Noah's ark, she cursed the gods for her feeling like this again after thinking she had found her sea-legs.

Heavy wind and building seas intensified the boat's motion, revving up Joan's distress no matter how tight she clinched her eyes or in what position she lay. Nausea swept through her body. Her throat tightened. Her skin felt as cold as the grave. She swallowed, attempting to keep her gorge down but to no avail. Slinging open the V-berth door, she beelined into the head.

Sweat soaked Joan's forehead as she stood over the toilet waiting for whatever was left in her stomach to come up. The air in the confined room was hot and stagnant, further raising her level of misery. Fumbling open the head's port light, she leaned in close, ignoring the splattering rain, but even a deep breath of fresh air failed to hold back what the ginger supposedly prevented. A flood of nausea overwhelmed her, and she purged her stomach into the toilet.

Joan's ordeal pulled long her face. She pleaded to the same gods she had cursed to either drive away her affliction or let her die. With no change in her condition, she took what relief there was in vomiting again and staggered from the head to the galley. The cabin's red light cast faint illumination into the cockpit, revealing Yao's ghost-like figure shouldering the wind and rain and resetting the jib sheet.

Holding her silence as if this would not remind the captain she was on board, she kicked aside her discarded life jacket and harness and yanked up the refrigerator lid. She reached a desperate hand into the side compartment where Yao said he stored the ginger, but the root was not there. She ripped through the layered produce. Her last hope was not to be found.

Feeling as if failure to find the ginger would surely kill her, she shoved her hand deeper into the side compartment and her fingers wrapped around the smooth, lumpy root. She whipped out the already carved on ginger and slapped it onto the cutting board. With a paring knife from a drawer, she chopped the rhizome into a dozen pieces, pushed two slices into her mouth and chomped down.

A supercharged rush of flavor and heat exploded in Joan's mouth and nostrils like a spoonful of Japanese wasabi. Her eyes welled-up and the lining in her mouth tingled. She cringed at the powerful sensation, uncertain if the double shot was an ounce of cure or pound of torture. Tilting her head back, she let her hopped-up saliva drain down her throat, again easing queasiness in her stomach.

Relieved her tactic soothed the curse within her and praying the remedy would suppress her symptoms until sleep arrived, she scooped up the ten remaining slices and worked her way forward in the jostling boat to the V-berth. With a short kip and a stockpile of ginger, she had every intention of gleaning whatever redemption she could by taking her next watch no matter what the weather.

Atmosphere bucked and swayed. Sharp-crested waves battered the boat's port side, the unyielding wind clattering the rigging and stressing the vessel's every fiber. The sleep Joan craved refused to take her and with every passing regretful minute her trepidation and disappointment rose. Like old chewing gum, the pungent flavor of the two ginger slices taken in the galley had been exhausted, leaving only a residual taste as subdued as a whisper.

Unwilling to lose the "ginger" edge, Joan swallowed the woody mass and repeated the relief with two more pieces, one at a time. Death might not be as close as it seemed. She hovered at the edge of sleep, feeling weak and frail, until the last two slices had been sapped of flavor. She was too exhausted to swallow and spit it out in her hand. Where it ended up she knew not nor cared. She slipped into a restless slumber.

Sharp intestinal cramps pulled Joan from a foggy slumber. Rumbles in her lower tract and a horrible rancid taste in her mouth were side-effects of consuming too much ginger. She elbowed herself to sit up, grimacing to throbbing temples, sensitive to a methodical clank of sails and rigging. She didn't know how long she had been out of commission, but the boat's subdued motion announced the bad weather had passed. Clenching her teeth against a shooting pain in her belly of a self-inflicted infirmity, she hauled herself from the berth and double-timed into the head.

Leaning forward and lifting the rain-spattered toilet seat lid, Joan caught a glimpse through the still open port light to the dull light of morning in a sky of broken clouds. She plopped onto the toilet seat to address her urgency, relieved at the passage of the heavy weather, but the respite she felt from physical discomfort was tainted by regret. Yao's fiery behavior clearly belied his belief she had been negligent in not warning him sooner of the approaching storm and to that, he was right. She had indeed been remiss for not having been more attentive to weather she thought was still far off. There would be the inevitable retribution she knew she deserved, a breach of her promise that might end her voyage early. Her only option was to ensure Yao understood darkness had concealed the squall's true nature.

A wisp of cool, soothing air cascaded through the port light caressing the back of Joan's neck, cooling her negative thoughts and willing herself to believe this, the sixth day of their journey, marked a turning point, a promise from the gods of fair winds and clear skies with her continuing to crew on *Atmosphere* to the Philippines and beyond. She prayed her hopeful intuition was right, for like the weather, this trip had been a series of highs and lows, moments of awe at the sea's beauty and stretches of misery from its fury.

Joan tilted her head back, fixing her eyes on the ceiling as if expecting to see what was happening topside. Yao had yet to trim the clanking sails which, for him, was a first. He clearly took pride in maintaining maximum efficiency of …

Joan's face went slack. She became as still as a statue, her ears peeled for the sound of movement, footsteps on deck, the ratcheting of a winch or rustling in the main cabin. And then, reality stole her breath. "God no," she gasped.

She rushed through the formalities on the toilet and barged from the head. Through the boat she ran and up the companionway steps into the empty cockpit where *Atmosphere's* auto-pilot steered a straight course in a steady ten knot wind that tugged at the reefed mainsail and joggled the poorly trimmed jib.

Joan ignored another cramp that tightened like a fist in her belly and cast her eyes on the boat's feeble wake trailing out to a red dawn. She pivoted and looked forward through the spray dodger's window. Yao wasn't at the mast.

She leaned out beyond the edge of the Bimini top for a better view forward. Running her eyes from the mast to the wavering headsail and beyond to the bow pulpit, her face drew wide in instant alarm. Yao was not on deck.

Joan rushed down the companionway. The quarter berth was unoccupied as were the settee and pilot berth. She hammered her fist on the door to the head perchance she had not seen Yao sleeping when she had hurried through the cabin to the cockpit, and he was now inside relieving himself. She opened the door and her soul was sucked from her. The compact room was empty.

"Yao," she screamed with the intensity of finding someone in an angry crowd. She bolted through the cabin and up the companionway. Mounting the stern, she scoured *Atmosphere's* wake with her eyes, frantic to find Yao but seeing nothing, nothing but the ashen sea in morning's first light. She checked both sides of the boat, imagining Yao had fallen overboard and was hanging by a jack-line but her agony flared into horrified desperation when she confirmed both jack-lines lay flat on the deck. Yao was no longer on his boat.

Panicked, Joan rushed forward with no thought of her safety gear, refusing to believe what she knew was true. She wrestled up an edge of the dinghy and peered underneath the very last place on the boat he could be. The cold hand of reality gripped her. She was alone mid-ocean with a basic knowledge of sailing, no idea how long it had been since Yao had been lost overboard and no help within sight.

She scrambled to the stern again. Clinging to the backstay and rail, she leaned precariously over the transom.

"Yao," she screamed. "Yao. YAO."

She listened for his voice, hoping against hope for a whisper of proof that he was within hearing distance but only the waves and wind answered.

"Oh God."

Joan jumped to the helm. She yanked the wheel to come about but the auto-pilot was in control and the helm held firm. She mentally zipped through Yao's man-overboard procedures. The first step was to deploy the marker flag but that was immediately after he had gone overboard. Tossing the marker flag into the sea now was pointless without some knowledge of his general location.

Joan toggled off the auto-pilot, freeing up the helm. She spun the wheel. *Atmosphere's* languid speed rounded up the boat into the wind excruciatingly slow, setting the jib aback. The mainsail flogged, shaking the boom over her head. *Atmosphere* slowed to a stop, in irons.

Tears of anguished frustration flooded Joan's eyes. She jabbed the engine's starter button with her thumb. The diesel rumbled to life. At least one thing was going right. She shoved the throttle full open and jammed the transmission into forward. Gears ground and thumped. Black smoke rolled from the stern exhaust vent. *Atmosphere* shivered under strain and lurched forward. Its bow crashed into on-coming waves in showers of spray that soaked the foredeck and spray dodger, blurring Joan's view through the dodger's windscreen. She aimed the boat as best she could along its own barely perceptible wake and switched on the auto-pilot.

Praying that her effort was enough to save Yao, Joan rushed below and grabbed her harness and life jacket from the galley floor. She clambered topside again and threw on the safety gear. Whether she was ready or not, she was now *Atmosphere's* captain.

CHAPTER SEVEN

The fear that blew through Joan had ramped up into full blown panic when she forced herself to stare into the eyes of grim reality. It had been an hour since she had discovered Yao missing, an hour in which she had backtracked, scanning the sea on both sides of the boat and seeing only sea and sky. She was alone in the middle of an ocean, on a boat she had only minimal knowledge of handling, and unless luck was with her, sighting anyone among the choppy waves and glinting sunlight seemed all but impossible.

Joan brought her focus back to the challenge at hand. The jib was still set aback in a tug-of-war with the autopilot. She grabbed the headsail's furling line and pulled but the rig's spool refused to yield. Realizing her oversight, she released the jib's working sheet from its winch, setting the head sail snapping sharply. Putting all of her angry frustration into her arms and legs, she pulled again and the roller furling spool turned, each hand over hand pull claiming two more feet of line from around the rig's bale and wrapping the sail tightly around itself on the forestay.

With the headsail out of the equation, *Atmosphere* picked up speed. Crouching low, Joan clipped onto the starboard side jack-line, and gripping handholds as she had been trained, she left the autopilot in charge of the helm and made her way forward to the mast. She took up position between mast and pulpit for a more unencumbered view of the rolling sea that seemed to have grown in immensity since she had first awakened. She slid her hand down the safety harness' tether to clip its carabiner onto the pulpit's attachment ring and was further shocked to find the attachment point had been snapped off by force, leaving only a bare weld.

What seemed evident to Joan was that Yao had clipped onto the starboard side mast pulpit during the storm and lost his balance as he had when she released the main sheet too early. The excessive force of his body weight in the first incident likely had weakened an already compromised weld. When stressed yet again, the weld had failed, sending him overboard.

Remorse and guilt seized Joan. Missing her watch and not being in the cockpit where she could have put into practice what she had been taught could have cost Yao his life.

Joan realized emotions would do nothing to improve the situation. She released the mainsail halyard and the reefed sail slid unencumbered down the mast, gathering in the lazy-jacks. For all of her regrets for being thrown into this life and death situation caused by her own mistake, she felt thankful Yao's decision in Guam had put her on the boat. At least she had a chance of saving his life. She secured the loose halyard and retreated to the cockpit where she hauled tight the main sheet, securing the loose boom overhead. Under power only, with no resistance from the sails, *Atmosphere* responded and gained speed.

"Please let this be the right course," she prayed. The boat's original wake stretching out in front of her appeared as a quickly dissipating slick.

Desperate for a full range of vision, Joan clipped onto the jackline once again and crawled forward along the teetering deck awash in drenching sea spray and broaching waves. She reached the pitching bow and wrapped an arm around the furled jib to avoid being pitched overboard. Forward of the blinding spray, she now had a clear view ahead and on both sides.

On-coming waves hurled the boat's bow to their frothy crests in rhythmic cadence, each apex offering Joan a grand view of an endless onslaught of white-topped waves advancing from the sunlit horizon and then, like some breath-taking carnival ride, crashing down into a flurry of salty spray to meet the next wave. If Yao was out there, her best chance of seeing him would be on wave peaks.

"Yao," Joan scream over wind, waves and the diesel engine's whine at full tilt.

"Yao!"

As if Poseidon himself had been conjured from the depths by Joan's emotional cries, a dark, foreboding wave, sharp and straight, appeared seemingly from no where, creating its own horizon. The steep-sided rogue glistened in morning's light, its peaked crest curling into a surfer's dream. The face of the huge wave undulated like a living organism with a score to settle. The sea had given birth to a monster and that monster was heading straight for *Atmosphere's* starboard bow.

Joan's terrified eyes scaled the thirty foot wall of destruction rushing toward her. With no time for retreat to the safety of the cockpit, she threw both arms around the furled jib in a tight hug. Her life and that of Yao depended on her staying on board.

Atmosphere plummeted into the huge wave's leading trough. The boat's bowsprit ripped into the demon's side in futile defense. The boat pitched hard to starboard. The wave's white claw of boiling foam rained onto the deck like a cloudburst, the wave's base churning with an unstable, whirling motion. *Atmosphere's* bow was catapulted upward and the freak wave heaved and collapsed, roaring over the boat in a tsunami of green water that threatened to flip the boat upside down.

The avalanche of water savaged Joan, breaking her hold on the furled jib and sucking her overboard like a rag doll into a drain. Her jack-line reverse-looped around a lifeline stanchion leaving her dangling in her harness as the roiling water did all it could to pull her under.

Diesel exhaust, as thick as a swarm of black flies, whipped about in turbulent air over *Atmosphere's* stern to the clank and thump of the vessel's engine fighting against the backsliding boat.

Atmosphere heaved over the massive wave's fallen crest and charged bow first into the following wave. The up-swelling water lifted Joan under the lifelines and slammed her onto the deck like some strange sea creature dredged from the depths.

Exhausted, sputtering for breath and desperate to abandon the foredeck before another deck-clearing dousing, Joan righted herself on hands and knees and scurried for the cockpit. Mid-crawl, her harness tether snapped tight and she face-dived onto the deck, splitting her lower lip and bloodying her nose.

Recovering and ignoring her injuries, Joan unclipped her harness from the jack-line with a spooked glance forward to the unrelenting onslaught and belly-crawled astern, cursing each rush of water over the deck. She tumbled into the cockpit trembling from her ordeal as the labored engine drove *Atmosphere* headlong into assaulting waves.

Joan yanked back the struggling diesel's throttle, mercifully bringing a quieter, more kindly motion to the boat on the rough sea. She clipped onto the cockpit's attachment point, horrified she had been plunged into a man-overboard scenario eclipsing what felt like insufficient training.

"Yao, I'm sorry," she murmured, overwhelmed by her dilemma. For all of her good intentions, her failure to stand her watch had turned a life-threatening, man-overboard situation into an untenable disaster. The marker pole still secure in its holder on the boat's stern spoke of just how serious this unholy mess had become.

With little chance of spotting Yao in the turbulent water, Joan rushed below, switched on the radio, and grabbed up the radio's mike. She increased volume. Faint hissing emerged from the ether, fading in and out amid background noise from the engine driving *Atmosphere* onward into a churning sea.

Joan thumbed the radio's mike. "Hello, hello, can anyone hear me?" she yelled into the mike, her voice cold with dread.

She released the switch to the hissing static, and after a long moment with no response, she radioed again. "This is an emergency," she screamed into the microphone as if no one was responding because they didn't sense the urgency. "The captain fell overboard. I'm alone and I don't know what to do. Can you hear me?" The VHF radio's silence was an agonizing reminder of her isolation.

She twisted the radio's tuner again and again, searching for some other channel on which there were voices, but found only silence. She turned up volume and a moment later, the radio automatically switched back to channel sixteen, the international emergency channel, still as silent as it had been. She left the unit turned on. Someone, somewhere had to have heard her.

Spooning the last of Yao's cooked rice into a bowl, she slung the binoculars over her shoulder and hustled topside to continue her vigil for Yao, for a ship, for any form of help.

Joan replayed in her mind Yao's man-overboard instructions for anything she might have missed. What he had not included in his training sessions was what she needed most, details for search and rescue of a victim whose general position was unknown. With the sea like it was, the reason for his omission was obvious. Spotting someone among the infinity of waves with no point of reference was less than improbable and if that search dragged on into the dark of night, that challenge would be stretched to the impossible.

Joan had not forgotten Yao's concentric search pattern, a procedure to bring order from chaos, but with no knowledge of when Yao had gone overboard, her search would be as random as it was now. The only way to tilt the table in her favor was a reversing grid, retracing *Atmosphere's* original path as she had been doing and staggering an about-face course, using an estimated three hours of travel based on the time frame between when she retreated to her cabin and when Yao could have gone missing. With an adjustment for speed going against the wind and waves, she reasoned dead reckoning would take her back to the point where she had taken to her bunk. That reasoning may have been flawed but it was all she had.

Under a pale gray sky that merged with an equally gray ocean, making it appear as if there was no horizon, Joan ticked off the hours, staggering her return leg at her calculated three hour mark with nothing on the sea but disappointment.

Evening crawled over the eastern horizon, stealing the day's light and bringing with it a low ceiling of clouds. Joan's biggest fear since setting out on this quest had been passing Yao unseen and unheard, and the approaching darkness pulled from deep within her an empty feeling of total futility. Sound of a voice somewhere among the surrounding waves would soon become her only way of locating him and though her resoluteness to accomplish this still filled her every fiber, she reluctantly resigned herself to an effort that seemed more symbolic than practical.

In preparation for her all-night vigil, Joan had moved the plastic-wrapped bread, peanut butter and half of the dozen remaining oranges into the cockpit to limit her time below deck. The cockpit's floor grating served as a makeshift urinal with seawater for flushing. In this way she passed the uneventful night.

A brilliantly clear sunrise in a cloudless sky with light winds gave a fresh feel to the air, raising Joan's spirits for an improved chance at redemption. During the night she had tried to radio two distant ships but failed to receive a response from either and with seemingly no one on a VHF channel, she had switched the radio to UHF, figuring the greater transmission distance would increase her prospects for a hit. So far, it hadn't.

Daylight and a calming sea brought opportunity for more substantial meals and after scanning the sea with nothing but waves and sky in view, she slipped below to prepare instant noodles and a fried egg with frequent glances through the port lights.

Topside again with her meal, she scarfed down the sustenance with no thought beyond filling her stomach and after chasing it with water from the canteen, she donned her life jacket and harness. Slinging the binoculars around her neck, she made her way forward to the mast, clipped onto the port side pulpit and planted her feet firmly on the coach roof. Stubbornly holding onto renewed hope that today she would find Yao, she searched the sea on both sides of the boat in the direction of travel. The wind had dropped steadily over the morning hours from eight knots to four and the clear southern sky signaled benign conditions, one less worry for Joan.

By late afternoon on this second day of Yao's disappearance, Joan returned to the cockpit feeling wasted. The sun had sapped her energy and left her with a raging thirst no amount of water seemed to slake. Poseidon had mercifully quelled the sea to a low, rolling swell which boosted Joan's faltering confidence, but night lurked below the eastern horizon and would once again shrink her world into a minuscule speck on a featureless ocean.

Joan stretched tight back muscles and lifted the field glasses to her face. Her tired eyes scanned the sea from port to starboard and back again as she clung to more hope than expectation that Yao was out there and her effort to find him was not in vain.

She lowered the binoculars and studied the eastern sky where the edge of night drew her hope into a thin, frail line. Even the engine's thrum sounded godforsaken as if sensing the pointlessness of her quest. Though the clear sky promised star glow, that paled to the radiance of a clear day.

As evening came down, Joan switched off the auto-pilot and veered *Atmosphere* south, ninety degrees to starboard. When the boat's previous wake had nearly slipped from view, she turned the helm hard to starboard again, returning *Atmosphere* to its original course, due west, and parallel to her previous track, holding to her established grid pattern.

Reactivating the auto-pilot, she set the binoculars aside and hurried below with the empty canteen. She refilled the vessel from the faucet, coaxing the water to flow faster until the container was full. She grabbed a flashlight from a cabinet by the nav table and returned topside where she hung the topped-up canteen from the binnacle and set the flashlight at the back corner of the cockpit. Picking up the field glasses, she sat on the starboard cockpit seat and continued her methodical, visual sweep, extending the range of field astern in case Yao had slipped by while she had been below deck.

A flash of movement off the starboard stern flicked through the binoculars' field of vision, an animated image that spiked Joan's heart rate and fired her senses. She did a double-take, pressing the field glasses hard against her wide eyes as if added pressure would increase magnification. As she worked the binoculars focusing thumbwheel, anxious hope leapt into a flood of unbelieving relief. A raised arm waved, desperate.

Joan vaulted from the cockpit for a better view astern. In her rush, she tripped on the cockpit coaming and crashed hard against the stern rail, scraping her forearms and loosing the binoculars from her grip. The field glasses tumbled overboard and disappeared into the mile deep water.

Her injury of no importance and lost binoculars ignored, Joan scrambled to the helm. Whether dumb luck or divine intervention, she had found Yao. She switched off the auto-pilot and spun the wheel hard to starboard. Even without the aid of magnification, she could make out what was indeed Yao.

"Oh God, thank you, thank you," she called to the heavens. She increased throttle. The diesel hummed and *Atmosphere* cut across the wide, rolling sea, closing the gap between the boat and its rightful captain. She took a deep breath and exhaled tension held too long. Her attentiveness to a structured search had paid off.

The gap narrowed. Joan became as still as a corpse and with a gasp, her ecstasy faltered. Something was not right. Yao's arm was unusually straight, ending in what would have been a blue and red hand. Maybe he had been wearing two-tone, sailing gloves when he had been cast into the sea, but anxious uncertainty gave way to recognition and Joan's body slumped as if life had been sucked from her. Tears flooded her eyes. She throttled back the engine. What only moments before had been Yao haling rescue was nothing more than a drifting, Styrofoam fishing buoy with a wind-tattered marker flag on a three-foot pole. Visible just under the water's surface was a fifty foot length of the buoy's severed, monofilament anchor cord stretched out in the ocean current.

Joan yanked the boat's transmission into neutral, incensed at a god who had forsaken her with such deception. She ran anger-stiffened fingers through her hair in righteous indignation as the boat coasted past the barnacle-covered buoy that continued swaying to and fro as if mocking her. So much hope, shattered in an instant.

"Damn you," she screamed at the buoy, enraged enough to have snatched the marker from the sea and thrown it at God.

Tossing her head back in frustration for being thrown back into an empty arena, Joan caught herself and stifled her emotions. Her face hardened. For all of her fears, lost hope and resentment, she would not forsake Yao with any thought of defeat. If she could spot a fishing buoy, she could damn-well find her captain. She jammed the transmission into forward and turned the helm hard to put *Atmosphere* onto its course west, leaving the bobbing buoy in the propeller's turbulence.

Joan straightened the boat's course as a rhythmic thumping below the waterline vibrated *Atmosphere*'s throttle. The boat's engine growled under load and black, oily smoke whirled from the vessel's exhaust. The buoy jiggled like a fishing bobber and skipped across thirty feet of water toward the boat's stern as if pulled by some giant fish hooked on the end of the line.

Confused as to what was happening, Joan hesitated if only for a brief moment but a moment too long. The buoy smacked *Atmosphere's* stern and was dragged under the hull. The struggling engine shuddered, coughed and died bringing an uneasy quiet to the edge of night.

"Great," Joan spat scorn at herself for not taking quicker action before the full length of the buoy's tether had wrapped around the prop. She yanked back on the transmission lever like she wanted to rip it from the binnacle, but the propeller was jammed, seizing the drive shaft and gears. No amount of manhandling by Joan could shift the transmission into neutral.

She thumbed the engine's start button, cursing again when the motor groaned protest against a defiant drive train. Slamming her palm against the wheel, she burst into tears at a succession of mishaps that had brought her to this end. If luck existed anywhere in the world, it was far from this stretch of ocean. She desperately looked around as if against all hope help was close by, but only evening's twilight greeted her.

A deep sense of helpless ineptitude overwhelmed Joan. She plunked down on the cockpit seat and buried her face in her hands. No matter how hard she tried, no matter how methodical were her attempts to save Yao, her inexperience and foolish mistakes continued to move her further back toward the end of the queue.

"Joanie, I told you this was too much for you."

Her mother's voice was as clear in Joan's befuddled brain as if she were sitting in the cockpit with her daughter.

In Joan's mind's eye, her mother raked her from head to foot with judgmental scorn. Her signature smile pulled at the edges of her mouth, a sarcastic grin that preluded a self-righteous declaration. "Serves you right for not listening to me."

The words echoed in Joan's head, reminding her how much she resented her mother's malice while playing the loving matron. It was a relationship that had plagued her since childhood and caused her father to file for divorce. It seemed to Joan that no matter how far she distanced herself from New Zealand, her mother was always within earshot.

Once again gaining control of her emotions, Joan found the inner strength to push back her rancor. She could not allow this mishap to become even more of a disaster by obsessing over her gloating mother. Joan still had some control over her very limited world and by whatever means, she would make things right. After all, the boat was still afloat, there was food and drinking water and the wind and sea were calm.

"Okay Joanie," she coaxed herself, "you wrapped fishing line around the propeller. Now get it off."

Below deck, Joan switched on a ceiling light, bringing high noon to the cabin. She stepped to the forward bulkhead and studied *Atmosphere's* framed drawing. The boat's propeller was midway between its central keel and spade rudder, easy to access, at least on paper. She looked through the open companionway where twilight beckoned the stars. There was only one remedy for this situation and with stoic determination she accepted what must be done.

Gathering skin-diving gear from the wet locker, Joan selected the sharpest knife in the galley, a fillet knife in a leather, strap-on sheath. She switched the cabin light to red and carried the gear topside.

Joan's determination to get underway and rob her mother of the final word wavered when she shined the flashlight into water as dark as death. Twilight of late evening had claimed the sea along with any chance of a quick fix.

Joan dumped the diving gear at the boat's stern and plopped onto the cockpit seat, disgusted with herself. One moment she had been searching for her lost captain and the next, her boat was dead in the water from a careless mistake. "Jesus, what have I done?" she lamented of her folly.

Abandoning the task of freeing the propeller until morning's light, Joan retreated into the lit cabin and flicked the toggle to illuminate the running lights. Tired and unwilling to exert the effort to boil rice, she ate a handful of oil-roasted peanuts and a hard-boiled egg, followed by a cheese, tomato and cabbage sandwich with a tall glass of water. She returned topside for its more open view and where she felt closer to Yao.

Viewing the ocean from a sandy beach at night had always been a peaceful, alluring occasion for Joan, wonderment of what exotic lands waited for her beyond the horizon with dreams of traveling there but the veil of darkness over the sea that stretched out to what appeared to be eternity had become fearful and cold, holding uncertainty that burrowed deep into her soul.

She set her wristwatch's alarm for two hours and stretched out on the cockpit cushion to the rhythmic motion of low-peaked swells that rocked the boat like a gentle hand on a cradle. Sleep was almost instant.

Atmosphere drifted.

CHAPTER EIGHT

Joan's wristwatch alarm dredged her from exhausted slumber. She silenced the shrill ring and sat up, pulling a face at her painful chest and shoulders from the previous day's collision with the stern rail. The sea had calmed to ghost-like wavelets flickering starlight. A quiet night had slipped into early morning, but before accepting sleep's promise to soften her plight, she scanned around *Atmosphere* and sat bolt upright when she spied orange-tinted lights of a cargo ship moving snail-like across the edge of the southern horizon.

She scampered below into the still red-lit cabin and picking up the radio's mike, she switched the unit from UHF to VHF mode.

"Hello to the ship south of me," she said with renewed vigor. "I am on a sailboat and I have an emergency. Do you hear me?"

She waited. When there was no response, she turned the tuning dial to another channel. "Hello ship, this is an emergency. I am on a sailboat just north of you. I need help. Do you hear me?"

She waited again for a reply, and it came to her that compared to those ocean-going behemoths, *Atmosphere's* running lights were feeble specks of illumination on a seemingly limitless ocean. Since no one seemed to be receiving her radio transmissions, something visual was needed, something of the same or greater luminosity as those of the freighters.

Joan shuffled through one drawer and then another, knowing she had previously seen what she was searching for. She pulled open a cabinet at the nav table and dug out a day-glow orange, snub-nose pistol with a three-inch barrel the diameter of a sixteen-gauge shotgun. Attached to the hard plastic, single-shot handgun was a plastic bandoleer loaded with four out of the original six flare cartridges, like so many beers on a plastic ring holder. She pressed a button on the weapon's side marked, "Open," and tilted the barrel forward. Slipping in a cartridge, she swung the barrel into position. This was the edge she needed.

Flare-gun in hand, Joan hurried up the steps topside and positioned herself on the stern, away from the sails and with a clear view south to the ship's lights. The ship was still visible and *Atmosphere* was about to be also.

Holding the pistol at arm's length, aimed at the water, she thumbed back the gun's hammer. As she raised the firearm to shoot over her head, her finger prematurely engaged the pistol's hair-trigger with a deafening roar. The sharp recoil nearly kicked the gun from her grip. Like a poorly batted cricket ball, a red-orange orb of fire and smoke skipped across the wavelets where it sputtered and went out.

"Dammit," Joan cursed. She rushed the reload and pulled back the hammer again. Holding the gun overhead, she focused on her grip and purposely squeezed the trigger. The hammer snapped against the firing pin with a loud click but there was no following report or fireball rocketing skyward.

Joan's anxiety spiked. The ship's lights were drifting lower on the dark line of the southern horizon and would soon be out of sight. She extracted the dud cartridge, dropped it at her feet and ripped the third cartridge from its holder for the reload. Taking deliberate aim, she discharged the aerial signal. The fiery shot arced two hundred feet into the air, casting a circular red aura over *Atmosphere* and the sea. But all too quickly, the flare dimmed into a flickering ember that dropped from the heavens onto the water a hundred feet from the boat.

The cargo ship's three fairy lights merged. The vessel was turning. The ship's captain was responding to the distress signal. Joan jammed the last flare into the gun and shot it into the sky, willing it to go higher and burn brighter.

As the aerial signal rocketed overhead, she extracted the spent cartridge and grabbed up the dud. With the gun reloaded and trigger set, she held her stance and fired but with no better results than before.

Joan hustled below. There had to be more than four flare cartridges. She rifled through the drawers and cabinets again, frustrated when she came up empty-handed. Turning her attention to the quarter berth, the only area she had yet to check, she hefted aside the tightly packed life raft to rummage around a folded sail marked, 'Storm Jib', a case of fuel filters and a roll of blue canvas, no doubt extra material for the Bimini top. She scooted back to the life raft. Printed on its valise were launch instructions for deployment and a drawing of the inflated craft with a list of what was apparently its complete onboard inventory; a knife, a sea anchor and a quoit or ring of rope, nothing that Joan needed. What was not listed on the valise and what Joan could not have known was that during the raft's last annual inspection, Yao had added to its inventory three hand-held smoke signals for daytime use and three hand-held flares that she so desperately needed at that moment.

Empty-handed but certain rescue was nigh, Joan clambered up the companionway stairs only to have the wind pummeled from her like a sucker punch. The ship had indeed turned but not toward *Atmosphere*. Minutes later, its lights disappeared over the horizon.

Joan wilted. Her failure to catch the ship's attention meant she was still alone, and at first light, no matter what the sea's condition, she had no other choice but to go for a swim. For now, she would catch more sleep in preparation for her dive.

🌐

A red dawn topped the gray sea when Joan emerged from below on this eighth day out of Guam. The previous night's failure with the visual alarm had been disappointing, as had this morning's lack of response on another radio call. It seemed to Joan no matter what she did, failure tracked her every move.

The brilliant ball of sun broke above the eastern horizon and caught *Atmosphere's* stern-mounted marker pole in its sharp light, intensifying the marker's day-glow orange buoy and red and yellow ensign. If Joan had been in the cockpit when Yao had fallen overboard, that signal flag would have been deployed, and the fact it was still onboard highlighted her predicament. She knew nothing about when Yao was lost at the start of her search, and at this point, she had even less knowledge of her own position. To continue looking for Yao was to rely on the dint of luck that so far had eluded her. The decision did not sit well, but she saw no other option. She had to abandon this floundering, one-person hunt and rally more resources. For that, she had to set a course south for the shipping lane or the nearest landfall, Yap Island. But with only whispers of wind, her trek south would be only after she had dealt with the fouled propeller.

With her nerves fluttering in her stomach and knowing she would need energy for her undertaking, she forced down a fried egg and buttered bread. No matter how she looked at what she was about to do, she couldn't deny, this was the scariest thing she had ever attempted.

Joan went topside and draped the rope ladder over the stern. She undressed. The cool morning air refreshed her skin, propping up her wavering confidence that her commitment to clear the boat's prop and decision to seek help could only improve her situation and with that, Yao's. She strapped the dive mask and its attached snorkel onto her forehead and worked her feet into the closed-heel dive flippers. Yao's feet were two sizes smaller than hers, making the flippers excessively tight, but they would have to do. She strapped the knife to her bare, right thigh and stepped over the stern rail to stand on the transom's cap rail. With a steadying hand on the back stay, she took a calming breath at what she was about to do. Planning was one thing but execution, alone, in the middle of the Western Pacific Ocean, was an entirely different kettle of fear.

Joan eased her grip on the back stay and squatted down, as if bringing her body closer to the water would make this less traumatic. She set the dive mask in place and half jumped, half fell from the safety of the boat into the tropical ocean's dark water.

Joan grabbed the rope ladder, battling her nerves as she oriented herself to the boat. Fear raced her heart and clamped her throat with a feeling of helplessness that howled her folly. Being on the ocean, in the bosom of a sailboat was sobering enough when the wind and sea conspired to create havoc, but being eye-level to the sea, even when its surface was calm, and exposed in its seemingly endless vastness to unseen threats lurking in its black, fathomless depths, was infinitely more frightening.

Struggling to conquer her fear, Joan released the ladder and swam to the boat's port side. She plugged the snorkel's mouthpiece into her mouth, listening to her own fear-filled breath hissing rapid cadence through the breathing tube. No matter how hard she inhaled, the snorkel's restricting air intake was a discomfort she was not willing to endure. She yanked out the mouthpiece and took in a deeper, unimpeded breath.

She ran her hand along *Atmosphere's* hull, physical contact with her sanctuary easing her tension. From her vantage point the boat appeared as big as a battleship. She took in a series of still shaky breaths, drew in one final deep breath and dived.

A feeling of separation and vulnerability remained alongside Joan as she skimmed along the smooth curvature of *Atmosphere's* black painted hull. The boat's keel and spade rudder were reassuring landmarks. She didn't dare look down.

Joan felt a sliver of relief seeing with what she was dealing. The buoy's twisted line had wrapped around the prop shaft and shrouded the propeller. One of the prop's flukes had become embedded deep into the hard Styrofoam float, compressing the bobber against *Atmosphere's* hull, locking the boat's transmission. The trammeled float may have been the only impediment to the shaft turning, but Joan was going to cut away all of the tangled line to ensure no encore performance would be needed. The float and every strand of the rig's line would go.

Joan had seen enough on this first dive to feel comfortable with what lay before her. She retreated to the surface for air and unsheathed the knife. Its sharp, narrow blade was perfect for the job at hand. She reminded herself that being careful and not dropping the tool into the depths was more important than resolving this problem in record time. She sucked in another lungful of air and returned under the boat.

Positioning herself to face forward, between prop and rudder, Joan gripped the propeller's shaft tube with her free hand for stability and purposely ignoring the eerie immensity below her, severed the line from the float. Resheathing the knife, she clamped her hand around the buoy and pulled. The float refused to budge. She yielded the struggle to the urge to breathe and headed up for more air.

Lifting the mask onto her forehead again, Joan worked the flippers to keep her head above water while reconsidering her plan. As fast as the buoy was jammed against the boat's hull, it would not come free until its hold on the prop was weakened. That would take blade work she hoped her knife could dole out without breaking. After extrication, she would tackle the buoy's line and be done with it. Readying the mask, she took another breath and dived.

Chunks of squeaky Styrofoam popped out like loose bricks as Joan jabbed and sliced the buoy. The knife blade flexed once or twice but did not break. Prying out a length of screeching mid-section, the parent float sighed as it expanded to fill the gap. Out of air again, she resurfaced.

Joan raised the diving mask onto her forehead. Physical exertion while holding her breath underwater was not part of her usual day and her strength was ebbing. Added to this was annoying tightness of the flippers that made her feet ache. It was time to finish this task and return aboard the boat. Gathering her mettle, she adjusted the mask onto her face, took a breath and disappeared underwater.

Joan positioned herself on the buoy's uncut side. Gripping the sphere with both hands, like a basketball, she set the heel of a flipper against the prop shaft. Tensing her arm and leg muscles, she yanked and the tortured buoy shrieked protest as it parted from the fluke. She pushed the bobber away and it scuttled along the hull to the surface. Out of air yet again, Joan retreated.

The heavy burden of rectifying the jammed propeller eased tension in Joan's chest. With the buoy having been eliminated from her predicament she was all but ready to give up on her commitment to tackle the buoy's anchor line. She couldn't get out of the water soon enough, but as it was, she saw no difficulty removing the monofilament, an insurance policy for not having to leave the boat again. One more dive should turn this scrum into a winning try.

A distinct sound, like a hand slapping water, spun Joan's head around. Her face paled and gooseflesh crawled up her neck. Fifty feet from *Atmosphere* a miniature whirlpool was an unmistakeable sign that she had attracted unwanted attention.

The full weight of Joan's fear returned as the blackness she had tried so hard to ignore seemed to rise up to swallow her, intensifying her urge to scramble to safety but this job had to be finished. She dived.

Joan fixed her eyes on the snarl of high test monofilament and stabbed the tangle as if it were some menacing sea creature. With each jab, the tightly wound anchor line blossomed into a nest of split ends. This would indeed be her last dive.

A shadow, more a feeling than optics, swept over Joan like a cold hand. She jerked away from the prop and looked out across the boat's curved bottom to clear, sunlit, bluish-green water caught between the sea's slick, glassy surface and its dark depths. She pivoted her body to check astern, past the boat's rudder, and her terrified eyes filled her mask. A ten-foot shark, more than just curious, made a tight loop back toward the boat, its cold predator eyes fixed on Joan. The grayish brown creature had a stocky body, whitish belly with white markings on the tips of its rounded dorsal fin and long pectoral fins. At the top of the food chain in its three dimensional world, the creature knew it had the undeniable advantage.

Joan panicked. She shoved herself back from the prop and whacked her head against the rudder's forward edge. Stars scattered before her eyes. Fear numbed the pain. She tore through the water along the hull and broke the surface at *Atmosphere's* stern. Snagging the dangling rope ladder with one hand, she turned to face her adversary, the knife in her other hand cocked over her shoulder as if her feeble weapon would scare away the shark.

Joan flicked her eyes over the water and did not see the shark, but she had read enough newspaper articles about shark attacks along New Zealand's coast lines to be certain enough the beast had not lost interest in her.

Releasing the ladder, she pulled at her right flipper, instantly welded by anxiety when its over-tight slipper refused to yield. She dug her fingers in between her foot and the stretched tight rubber, working the other flipper to keep her balance. She ripped the one flipper off, set it free and grabbed the ladder, her worked-up breathing hissing from her mouth. To remain in the water was to die.

With the knife held at the ready, Joan's attempt to remove the second flipper became a struggle against gravity and her own buoyancy. Unable to dislodge the flipper without her head sinking below water, she latched onto the ladder with her free hand just as movement caught her eye. In that single, terrifying moment, her throat clamped tight as the shark passed within feet of her. Overwhelmed by total horror, she stabbed wildly into the water and found her mark. Scarlet billowed.

Joan slung the knife away. The beast was now aware she too could bite, but that did not mean it had lost its appetite.

Joan's effort to pry her foot from the stubborn flipper yielded to the expediency of getting out of harm's way. She cocked her right leg and caught the ladder's lowest rung with her bare foot, grimacing at a jolt of sharp pain in her right thigh. In her wild defense to drive away the shark, she had stabbed herself with the razor-sharp knife, making herself a more enticing target.

The uninjured and hunger-frenzied shark's white-tipped dorsal fin broke the water's surface thirty feet from Joan. The beast powered up for the kill, its dark, bulky body looking like a torpedo at full speed.

No self-inflicted injury trumped getting back on the boat. Super-charged with adrenaline and feeling as if the entire world was pinwheel-ing out of control, Joan jammed down her right foot on the ladder's rung and catapulted herself shoulder high to the stern's cap rail, the pain of severed tissue in her wound lost in her terror. She wrapped the fingers of her right hand in a death grip around the backstay and fore-armed the top of the cap rail with her left arm. Kicking both feet with all she had, she heaved herself up and then …

A flash of wild terror gripped Joan's face. Her body stiffened and she was jerked violently downward. She managed to hold onto the boat, saving her from being dragged from her precarious perch, but her twisted, desperate face was flushed with the unbelieving shock of someone who had just suffered a catastrophic injury.

Besieged by horror more visceral than any fear she had ever felt, Joan found a stern cleat with her left hand and muscled herself on-board, her eyes black saucers of dread. She tumbled onto the cockpit seat where she lay on her back like a dead fish. Her body quivered as an icy chill ran through her. With no medical support, her injury would be fatal.

A trembling hand peeled off the diving mask and let it fall to the cockpit sole. She fixed her dark eyes on the blue canvas of the Bimini top and braced herself for the rush of pain that came with such a devas-tating wound, her mind racing around a single thought. Had the shark taken only her foot or her entire lower leg?

The reality of bleeding to death brought Joan's focused attention to the here and now. As difficult as this was going to be, she could not allow fear to conquer courage. She had to at least attempt saving her own life. Digging deep, reaching past the gnawing revulsion of beholding a blood-gushing stump, she raised her head and blinked to clear blurry eyes.

Joan swooned at the full score and collapsed onto her back. Her eyes welled up, pouring forth emotions she could not control. The beast had not taken a pound of flesh. It had ripped off the tight-fitting flipper and the spurting blood she had dreaded was from the oozing wound she herself had inflicted on her right thigh. Compared to the injury from a shark's bite, the laceration seemed no more serious than a mere scratch.

Stretched to her limit, physically and emotionally, Joan lulled on the edge of exhaustion. The boat's propeller was freed up, she was injured but would live, and once her strength returned, she would set out for Yap.

Sharp sunlight through the spray dodger's windscreen roused Joan to the day's rising temperature. The elusive wind had not returned and the ripening morning promised yet another day of heat and humidity, but at least she had the boat's engine to get her moving again.

Joan relaxed her injured leg, using her upper body to sit up. Her leg wound had formed a medallion of blood on the cockpit cushion but had stopped bleeding, indicating no major blood vessel had been severed. She stood, favoring her wounded leg. Her close encounter with the ocean's most terrifying creature was not something she would ever forget, and looking down at her legs, she marveled at still having both feet on which to stand. Astern, the two halves of her sacrificed flipper floated on the sea's oily-looking surface. The shark, it appeared, had moved on to more productive hunting grounds.

Rinsing away dried blood from around her wound with water from the canteen, Joan hobbled below and retrieved the boat's first aid kit from a cabinet behind the nav table. She seated herself on the pilot berth and placed the first aid kit in front of her on the settee table. The half inch wide puncture wound was deeper than she had thought and probably warranted stitches, but with only basic medical supplies at hand, improvisation was her only immediate recourse. She doused the injury with alcohol, showing teeth at the sharp sting, and dabbed the wound dry with gauze. She applied iodine solution, let it dry and closed the wound with one of two butterfly bandages from the kit. She finished off her handiwork with a wrap-around, gauze covering.

Immobilizing her injured leg was the fastest way to full recovery, but Joan could not afford the wasted time. She was anxious to get underway, and she had yet to start the engine to confirm her underwater handiwork had resolved the problem.

Back in the cockpit at the helm, Joan held her breath in nervous anticipation. She tugged back on the transmission lever and heaved a sigh when the gear popped into neutral. The relief she felt was well-worth the price paid.

She patted the binnacle, coaxing *Atmosphere's* guardian angel to grant her one more wish. "Please," she whispered, coddling to whatever extra mercy there might have been and holding her breath, she pressed the silver ignition button. The engine's starter clicked and the diesel rumbled to life, a grumbling sound that lifted the burden of doubt and worry from Joan. There was a merciful god.

Joan scanned the dead calm sea, still as alone as she had been since Yao's disappearance. She shifted the transmission into forward. Swirling water kicked out behind *Atmosphere's* stern, a long awaited signal that the boat and crew were once again underway. Turning the helm, she watched the compass rose rotate until due south lined up with the compass' lubber line. She increased throttle.

Fifteen hours had passed since the boat had been set adrift by a fouled propeller and at least forty-eight hours since Yao had gone missing. The calm sea and clear weather had improved her chances of spotting Yao, something with which she struggled, second-guessing her decision to seek help. Taking in the infinity surrounding *Atmosphere* and the reality of the dangers lurking below, she knew she was right. If there was any chance of finding Yao alive, a much greater effort was needed than a single, meandering boat. She switched on the auto-pilot and slipping on her panties and T-shirt, went below to the galley.

After filling a cooking pot with water and adding a portion of rice, Joan ignited the burner and left the raw grain to cook. She carried the remaining crackers topside, still compelled to keep her vigil for her missing captain. Across *Atmosphere's* bow and unchanging sea, a dark thunderhead peered over the horizon. Joan could only hope the shipping lane was well north of the weather.

Finishing her cracker snack, Joan leaned through the companionway to check on her cooking rice and frowned when she found the burner's flame extinguished. She hobbled below and closed and reopened the burner's control knob but the burner refused to reignite. She placed an ear close to the open burner and her suspicion was confirmed. The partially filled propane tank Yao had warned her about was finally empty.

Joan knelt on the floor in front of the oven-stove and reached a hand behind the unit. With her fingers, she traced a gas hose from the oven-stove, aft to a hole through the cockpit bulkhead behind which was the storage compartment marked Propane. Thoughts of switching the hose to the unused tank abruptly ended when the diesel engine coughed, choked and stopped with a clank.

"Shit. What now?" Joan hissed, frustrated. No sooner did she resolve one problem than another swung down from the yardarm.

She levered herself up with the countertop and gimped topside, aware of the strain on her bandaged wound with each step. She pressed the engine's ignition button. The diesel turned over with a wavering growl but refused to start. She released the button. Annoyance tightened her jaw, her face showing blood when she jabbed the ignition button with her thumb and held it as if settling a score. The engine's mechanical groan dropped from a snappy soprano to a tired baritone before the engine dragged to a stop, leaving only the clicking of its starter. The battery no longer had enough juice to turn over the diesel.

"Dammit," Joan snarled. She grabbed the helm with both hands and shook it as if to teach *Atmosphere* a lesson. Disgusted with this entire situation, she tromped below to check the fuel gauge located next to the companionway steps. The gauge's indication needle said it all; EMPTY.

"Bloody hell." Joan moaned.

She forged topside and snatched the funnel from the cockpit locker, rightfully cursing herself for not considering the fuel she had used while running the engine for two solid days. Slamming the locker lid closed like she was blaming it for all of her problems, she went forward on the starboard side and unstrapped the six reserve carboys of fuel. The filled containers were heavier than they looked, close to fifty pounds each, but even with her injured leg, she was able to hoist each one onto the coach roof above the fuel port as she had seen Yao do. The fuel tank's receptacle included a screw-off cap with thumb tabs within a black collar inset into the deck.

With thumb and forefinger, Joan unscrewed the fuel tank's cap and shoved the funnel into the open portal. Yao had stated the fuel tank held fifty gallons and with a total of thirty-six reserve gallons, she would pour them all in, eliminating the need to repeat this exercise.

She tilted the first carboy forward and directed its pour spout over the funnel. A steady, gurgling flow of fuel whirlpooled down the funnel, edging Joan off her anger high. She set the empty container aside and poured in the next four carboys in the same fashion, one after the other, stretching her back after each vessel was emptied.

Dragging over the sixth and final carboy, Joan blew out the remainder of her pent-up stress. She didn't know how far thirty-six gallons of fuel would take her but as soon as the wind kicked up again, *Atmosphere* would be under sail power with hopefully fuel in reserve for charging the batteries.

Joan started the transfer from the final carboy into the tank. Once underway, she would find the spare propane tank and finish preparing her now well-deserved breakfast. Her musings abruptly halted when the last gallon of fuel in the carboy backed up in the funnel and topped the tank's in-feed portal like an artesian well. The oily liquid ran along the deck and dribbled onto the sea, spreading out like some strange amoeba in an explosion of iridescent rainbow colors set off by bright sunlight. The fuel tank was full to its brim with a pint or two of fuel remaining in the carboy.

Pleased with herself at having a more than full tank of fuel, Joan extracted the funnel and dogged down the tank's cap, glad that smelly task was behind her and her situation was back on track. She returned to the cockpit. The shipping lane awaited.

Positioned behind the helm, her confidence high at thwarting fate's dirty tricks, Joan depressed the engine's starter button again. The engine struggled through a half dozen anemic groans before it choked to a stall. The battery, already low from her previous attempt to get the engine running, had gained back a portion of its original charge but still not enough to start the engine.

Joan fisted her hands tight, every fiber of her being focused on a mile deep resentment of the god who refused to take pity on her. Yao's fate and that of her own were seemingly being influenced by forces far beyond her control, and the building tropical heat from the harsh sun in a washed out sky bespoke of weather that, like her struggle to take another step, was far from cooperating.

A long moment passed before Joan broke from her reverie and redirected her dark thoughts from the problem of a dead starter battery to its solution. Conflating an inconvenience with a disaster offered no resolution, only a deeper feeling of helplessness. She was dealing with a depleted battery, not a sinking ship.

Moving to the companionway, Joan scanned *Atmosphere's* dusky interior for a thread of an idea. There must be an easy solution to a nearly dead engine battery, and that solution flooded over her in an 'aha' moment. Of course, one of the four house bank batteries could be swapped with the drained engine starter battery, end of story. With a full tank of fuel she would be ready to …

Joan's face drew tight with a jab of unease at where that thought had taken her. She distinctly recalled that during his tour of *Atmosphere*, Yao had indeed stated the fuel tank held fifty gallons, and if that were true, which she had no reason to doubt it wasn't, how could she overfill the tank with only thirty-six gallons? The simple fact was, she couldn't, which meant even though the fuel gauge had registered empty, there had been fuel remaining in the tank when the engine stopped. Taking that to its logical conclusion, she realized the engine was not suffering from a lack of fuel. There was a mechanical problem.

Joan felt a sense of accomplishment at not allowing emotions to cloud her reasoning. She acknowledged her total lack of knowing how a diesel engine worked, much less repairing one, but there was no reason to worry about something she could not control. Her next step would be to swap the batteries and crank the engine again. Either the engine would start or it wouldn't. For now though, it was time to swap out the empty propane tank with its spare and finish cooking her breakfast.

Joan opened the locker and lifted off the removable plywood panel atop the locker's side compartment, exposing the propane tank with an attached black hose, the same hose she had traced from the oven-stove. She twisted the tanks' valve and confirmed it was already fully open. "So, where the hell is the spare?" she wondered. Yao had clearly stated a second propane tank was on board.

Joan dug deeper into the locker's main compartment, under the buckets, dock lines and dock fenders and not finding the partner tank, she limped below deck.

Stagnant air in the cabin pulled perspiration from Joan's forehead. She switched on a fan to a wispy air stream and set about rifling through closets, storage bins and compartments. If the spare propane tank wasn't in the topside locker, it had to be somewhere down below.

Coming up empty-handed from her search in the main cabin, Joan slumped onto the settee feeling the weight of this still young day. Her eyes narrowed in angered frustration for yet another glitch. In his rush for an early departure, Yao had overlooked a deficient inventory, creating yet another problem for her. With no propane gas, she could no longer cook rice, boil potatoes or even boil water for instant noodles. It did not take a lot of imagination for her to understand she was slipping toward an untenable plight.

Sweat beaded Joan's face and ran down her back. She slipped a drinking glass from a cabinet and held it under the faucet for a long overdue drink of water. The tropical heat was sapping her body of moisture and she had a lot of catching up to do. Cranking open the tap, the water pump whirred and water gurgled forth, quickly filling the glass.

Joan guzzled the portion of water and set her empty glass aside. Energized by slaking her immediate thirst, it struck her how much better she would feel by cleansing the salt from her body. She opened the tap again and cautious of not overusing what water remained in the tank, she cupped her hands and splashed cool water onto her face, wishing she could dump the entire tank over herself.

The tang of diesel fuel nipped Joan's nose, a sullied odor between that of lubricating oil and kerosene but with a sharper, more pungent bouquet. She palmed closed the faucet's handle and stood back, putting on a look of astonishment at beads of water on an oily glaze covering the bottom of the sink. Its persistent smell turned her stomach.

Uncertain how fuel ended up in the sink or why she hadn't smelled it until now, Joan opened the tap again. Immediately the foul smell overwhelmed her as rivulets of water, looking like so many veins of plasma, coursed through a thickening layer of diesel fuel coating the sink's bottom and splashing onto its sides.

Fighting against believing what she was seeing, Joan turned off the faucet again and checked the fuel gauge. To her consternation, the gauge's indicator needle had not moved from her previous check, bringing brute reality down on her. The engine had indeed stopped due to lack of fuel, and the fact diesel had shown up in the drinking water made it painfully clear the nearly thirty-six gallons of fuel she had poured into the tank had somehow been diverted into the freshwater tank.

Alarm dropped Joan's bottom jaw. How was that altered flow possible? When she had first arrived at *Atmosphere*, Yao had been on the boat's starboard side pouring diesel fuel from the marina's borrowed carboy into the fuel tank's portal, the same portal she had used. She had also witnessed him setting up his rain catcher on the boat's port side, opposite the fuel portal which made sense. This layout would eliminate cross-filling the tanks. What didn't make sense was that this seemingly practical solution had not stopped the disaster it had been designed to prevent.

Up the companionway steps she hobbled, pushing past the aggravating pain in her thigh and ignoring the bandage's red tattoo of blood. She stomped forward to the capped fuel tank portal, confirming in her mind this was where Yao, and then she, had added fuel into the diesel tank. She ran a hand over her hair, baffled as to why none of this added up. And then a cold tightness gripped her stomach in horrid reality when she beheld the missing denominator, an unforgiving oversight that had set her on a spiraling downward slope into a worse case scenario.

Three feet astern from what she took to be the diesel portal was a second tank portal she had failed to notice until now. This in-feed port had a stainless steel screw cap fitted in a low-set stainless steel collar embossed with a single word; DIESEL.

"No," Joan yelled, not believing providence could be this cruel. She scurried across the boat to its port side and what she saw brought agonizing clarity. There were two sets of in-feed portals on both sides of the boat, clones, a dual system that allowed both water and diesel to be filled from either side, a not so minor detail that if she had known, would have made her future infinitely more certain.

"Bugger all," Joan spat, crushed by such a monumental misstep. She staggered to the cockpit and collapsed in defeat onto the starboard cushion. All that she had endured, all of her noble intentions, and now this. Her string of oversights were no longer just annoyances or delays that could affect Yao's rescue. They were blunders that had put in doubt her own tenuous survival.

Joan was drained, used up, on the verge of her frustration becoming depression. She needed water and food. Only then would she have the energy to mentally and emotionally deal with her flagging situation.

Returning below, Joan scarfed down the last hard boiled egg followed by a mindful drink from the canteen. Because of her bungle with the fuel, the half-filled water vessel had become her only source of drinkable water which meant strict rationing was in order, at least until the weather brought rain. In that event, she would break out the rain catcher and fill every pot, pan and vessel on the boat. What else she didn't know about the life raft was that along with the smoke signals and flares, Yao had also packed a solar still, a balloon-like contraption that evaporated and filtered seawater, capable of providing up to twenty ounces of drinkable water a day.

Joan considered the boat's galley stores. Without propane, her diet was constrained to those foods not requiring boiling water or heating and that offered moisture without a high salt content. This narrow regimen of food limited her selection to fruit and vegetables, raw eggs and raw potatoes, each in limited supply. Disheartened by her food restrictions, she retuned topside for one of the half dozen oranges she kept in the cockpit.

Seated in the shade of the Bimini top, she dug her thumbnail into the orange's rind, breathing in its refreshing acidy scent that made her mouth water and dulled the sharp edge of her fouled emotions.

Feeling the slightest of reprieves from the morning's stress, Joan methodically peeled the fruit in a concentric strip, a habit she had picked up from her father. As she worked the peel free, the fruit's cheerful aroma swept her back fifteen years to a camping trip she had taken with her father at Tokomaru Bay, outside Gisborne on New Zealand's North Island.

Joan had been eight at the time of the outdoor excursion, and in between hikes through native bush, coastal forests and green valleys, they visited Tairāwhiti Museum with its native and local artwork, watched surfers at Wainui Beach and picked a kilogram of navel oranges at a visitor-friendly plantation.

On a nature-sculpted landscaping boulder along a narrow country road flanked by fields of fragrant orange trees, her father had taught her how to peel the fruit in what he considered the proper way. Young Joan had caught on quickly and every orange she had enjoyed since that trip had been peeled with her father in mind.

It occurred to Joan as she sat on a sailboat going nowhere, that due in part to her own mistakes, as trapped as she was, mid-ocean, with limited fresh water and food options, peeling oranges was about all she could get right.

She completed the full spiral of rind and tossed the fruit's skin overboard where it floated alongside *Atmosphere* on the glass-smooth sea, making it appear as if the boat were welded in place. She made quick work of the orange's slices and sipped just enough water from the canteen to purge her mouth of sticky saliva and a sugar-thirst. She slipped off her T-shirt in the day's rising temperature, hopeful the heat would bring the wind and the wind would send her rain.

The day matured and time for Joan was measured by sunlight chasing shade across the cockpit, rousing in her a more somber memory, a week-long motorhome excursion with her father to Akaroa Beach, on the south island, shortly after his cancer diagnosis. He and Joan's mother had divorced two years earlier, when Joan was eleven, and having learned his disease was terminal, he had rented the motorhome for one-on-one time with his daughter.

Closing her eyes to what appeared as a blank theater screen, Joan's mind brought forth those past images of her younger self with her father in their temporary home on wheels. His tall stature had always been comforting to her and his firm jaw, hazel eyes and short brown hair had made him look like a military man. He had rarely smiled before separating from her mother, but this trip, even under the circumstances, had been one continuous grin for them both.

Just past noon, as young Joan had watched her father in the vehicle's kitchenette, making egg salad for sandwiches and expounding on their planned afternoon trek, her attention had been drawn to a dagger of sunlight streaming through the back window onto the floor. The streak of light had grown ever longer, creeping across the floor toward him and conjuring in her young mind a musing that the shade between the narrow wedge of illumination and her father represented the remainder of time until he would be gone from her forever.

All of these years later, Joan recalled the sadness that had overtaken her with that thought and how she had pleaded to God to make her father well again. Through all of his torturous medical treatments, their final outing together, and all he had endured before his death, her prayers had gone unanswered.

Young Joan had watched that insidious strip of sunlight sulk across their chariot's floor, devouring the shadow, and she had reacted in the only way she could. She hurried to the window and drew closed the curtain. It had been an insignificant gesture on her part, but it was more than God had done.

Joan opened her eyes where she sat alone on a sailboat named *Atmosphere*, seemingly the only person in existence. It was just past noon and the harsh glare of sunlight on the flat sea dragged her from the past and threw her acrimoniously back into the limited world she herself had created. She thought of the past and how no matter what she had done, no matter how many times she had prayed or curtains she had closed, she had been unable to halt the inevitable, and now life seemed to be attempting to turn the table on her again.

As Joan pondered her own predicament, stranded on a boat and at the mercy of a temperamental sea and petulant wind, she realized her helplessness in saving her father did not translate into the same finality for herself. There was hope based on her will to save herself and do everything possible to save Yao, but that would take wind.

A crimson evenfall crowned the western horizon, turning the sea to amber glass. The wind had not returned and Joan was facing yet another night alone and in want. She stared out over the featureless expanse picturing in her mind's eye Yao returning on foot across the water's solid-looking surface to reclaim his boat. That scene quickly faded leaving nothing but a barren wasteland under a dreary twilight, a scene that fills mariners' souls with melancholy until dawn releases them from bondage.

Joan broke from her reverie and slipped below deck to air as still as night. She flipped on the red-tinted cabin light and to her consternation, the cabin remained dark. She turned on the flashlight. The fan was as motionless as a held breath. She checked the electrical panel. Nothing had changed.

Tracking the flashlight's beam around the cabin, she bit her bottom lip as it all came clear. Because of the many distractions over the last twenty-four hours, she had failed to consider that between freeing the boat's fouled propeller and running out of fuel, the engine had not run long enough for its alternator to fully recharge the house batteries which, with the direct-wired refrigerator and radio constantly running and the cabin fan she had failed to switch off, the boat's house batteries had been completely drained.

She switched off the refrigerator, radio and fan for whatever good that would do before scooping up a handful of uncooked rice from the cold pot. She shoveled the starchy grain into her mouth. Even after soaking for hours, the centers of the kernels were starchy hard and inedible. She spat the grainy mash into the sink and lifting the pot to her lips, drank the whitish, opaque water that remained to supplement her meager ration in the canteen.

From the refrigerator, she lifted out the block of cheese. The aged cheddar was soft, holding the slightest coolness. Unwrapping the brick-size block, she nipped off a corner, relishing its burst of sharp, pungent flavor, a salty taste as tantalizingly addictive as any narcotic but which carried with it a warning of dehydration if she consumed too much.

Setting aside the cheddar, she cleared a side shelf of wilted, thin-leaf vegetables, piling the compromised greens into the sink. From another shelf, she inspected twenty-eight plump tomatoes. They wouldn't last long in the tropical heat.

She lined up the canned vegetables on the galley counter. These offered another source of water, though the salt content would limit the amount she could drink without exacerbating her thirst. These would be held as a last resort.

Lamenting that for every step she took forward her own mistakes and oversights snowballed her imperiled condition, she carried topside the flashlight and another orange, her only food choice with some amount of water and no salt.

After peeling the citrus fruit, Joan discarded the long strip of peel over the side where it floated with the remnants of her previous meal, twin spiral reminders that wherever the current was carrying the rinds, *Atmosphere* would arrive at the same time. She ate the orange's plump slices and cleansed her mouth of sugar-thick saliva with a sip from the canteen. Switching off the flashlight and with no shipping in view, she stretched out on the cockpit seat. Sleep was mercifully swift.

CHAPTER NINE

Orion, the hunter, stared down from a cloudless sky to the insignificant speck that was *Atmosphere*. Becalmed on the sea, the boat's lone crew member was in restless sleep, haunted by sharks and parched desert sands.

The flash of dream images coalesced into a scene from the movie, "Ben Hur"; a muscled *pausarius* on a Roman war-galley beat out a rowing cadence, his body glistening with sweat. Battle speed. Panic-stricken oarsmen shackled to their seats pulled for their lives on long-shafted oars, and a camera shot through an oar-portal showed the source of their terror. An enemy vessel had set a course to broadside the Roman ship. The rowing cadence quickened, growing louder. Death was about to make a catastrophic entrance amidship.

Joan's dream morphed from the ancient sea battle in the Mediterranean to RMS Titanic steaming across the North Atlantic on an eerie, moonless night. Within the mighty ship's belly huge steam engines roared and hissed, turning massive propeller shafts the girths of trees that drove the ship toward disaster.

The din within the huge ship's bowels thundered. The boilers hissed louder, the crescendo meshing in real time with motion so violent it thrust *Atmosphere's* bow up at a severe angle, thrashing the boat's port side and hurling Joan onto the cockpit sole. Fully awake, she slung both arms around the binnacle to stay on board as water rushed into the cockpit. It seemed another monster wave was about to send her and the boat to the bottom of the Western Pacific.

Screeching steel against aluminum assailed Joan's senses. Her head whirled as if overwhelmed by the pass-by noise of a thundering freight train. Her eyes turned upward in the night-gloom, not to a towering breaker frothing destruction, but to a wall of black iron sideswiping *Atmosphere* at twenty knots.

The listing sailboat's port shrouds connected with the passing ship, flexing the mast like a drawn bow. *Atmosphere* recoiled, releasing the rigging's excessive strain in an explosion of kinetic energy that shuddered the boat like a stomach punch. The severe motion snapped the tri-color light, VHF antenna and wind direction indicator from the mast-head and flung them into the sea.

Atmosphere belly-flopped in an eruption of water and mist and spun full circle as it was sucked into the freighter's churning wake like the insignificant piece of jetsam it had become.

Joan scrambled to her feet in the dizzying aftermath of the mael-strom. She found the flashlight floating in the draining cockpit and half walked, half crawled to the stern rail garbed only in her panties. The crew of the freighter had to have heard the deafening collision and some curious crew member was surely peering astern from the deck or an upper level window to see what had happened. Joan's only thought was raising the alarm and if her nakedness was enough to stop the ship, then bring it on.

Joan flashed the light at the big ship's superstructure sixty meters above her. "Help. Down here," she screamed over the grumble from the vessel's engines that shook the very air. She turned the light onto her-self to beguile. "Look down here."

The cargo ship thundered on into the darkness. Salvation steamed away.

Joan jerked her head around, fully expecting another ship to be bringing up the rear but found only the night-darkened sea under a starlit sky.

For Joan, knowing there were people aboard that ship who could have rescued her felt like a cold hand gripping her heart, leaving her with an empty feeling of abandonment. Was there no end to her suf-fering? She collapsed onto the cockpit seat, all but ready to give up and accept what seemed her predetermined fate.

Cursing herself for not being awake to signal the ship as it ap-proached, a sobering thought touched Joan's soul. The freighter that nearly sank *Atmosphere* could have been a rogue ship on a course less traveled or maybe luck was indeed with her and *Atmosphere* had drift-ed into a shipping lane. No matter how fortuitous her situation, her near-fatal encounter was a wake-up call. Without signal flares, even in the light of day, a similar ship on any course might not see a floundering forty-foot sailboat and its buggered, one-woman crew.

Joan pleaded with providence to turn the cargo ship around until the vessel's lights melded into a tight cluster. If someone on board had reported to the captain about seeing the incident, even if the captain would not alter his course, surely he would at least call in the coordinates of the accident to some coast guard or official agency.

Turning from the unwavering ship to *Atmosphere's* condition, Joan limped down the companionway steps to inspect the boat's interior and any water the boat was taking on. The galley and main cabin looked like the aftermath of a drunken brawl. The passing cargo ship had spider-webbed two port-side port lights and scattered settee cushions, books and charts across the floor like the dead after battle, but there was no apparent flooding.

She tossed a cushion aside and lifted the removable floor board over the freshwater tank, giving her visual access to the bilge. *Atmosphere's* hull had not been breached. She felt a profound relief the collision had not doomed her and her boat.

Topside again, she inspected the standing rigging. The shrouds appeared to be intact but were loose due to a bent spreader. She shined the flashlight on the mast itself which looked sound enough not to fail when the wind picked up, but to her disappointment, the masthead components were missing which meant even if somehow she restored the charge in the house batteries, the VHF radio would still be useless. She had a desperate feeling *Atmosphere* was like a block of ice slowly being chipped away by an unseen hand wielding an icepick.

The cargo ship was a single speck of light when Joan returned to the cockpit. She sipped from the canteen, a luxury she knew could not be abused. She checked her wristwatch. Another two hours until dawn. She hoped the light of day would lift her forlorn feeling that to even try was futile.

Joan looked out to the horizon encircling *Atmosphere*, wary of other ships on a collision course. Anxious to be as visible as possible, she deployed the jib and cautiously raised the mainsail in short spurts, seeing no indication the port side shrouds or their spreader might actually fail. With the sails set, she returned to the cockpit, set her watch's alarm for one hour and lay down to let sleep quell her loneliness and fear. She had no way of knowing what fate had prepared for her was far more heartless than even her mother at her most domineering.

Dawn brought white cirrus, appearing as fingers of a bony hand, that revealed another change of weather somewhere south that maybe, Joan perused, would bring wind and rain her way.

Joan flexed at the waist to loosen tight joints. Constant thirst had set in and every bone and muscle in her bruised body ached from the beating the night before. For all of her increasing need, she had to carefully ration what water remained in the canteen and to be ready if the weather god found an ounce of compassion to at least bring precipitation.

Joan assessed the calm sea where wisps of air curried gray patches of wavelets on the water's surface. As alone as she had been three days ago when her world became a boat taking her no where, she reflected on the reasons for her decision to leave her life in Auckland for such a bizarre adventure. At the time, it had all made sense. She would raise her sword of independence to broadcast a clear statement to her mother that her daughter was going walk-about, on her own path, while signaling her ex-boyfriend he was only someone she used to know.

Her thoughts drifted back a week, to what now seemed like a year, to her apartment and the maps she had accumulated of the Western Pacific Ocean; Guam, where the real adventure would start, Yap and Palau Islands and further west, the Philippine archipelago. She recalled questioning her sanity for agreeing to accompany Lois on such a hastily thrown together sailing trip, but an incident involving someone Joan had thought was finally out of her life had pushed her over the edge.

On that fateful evening, Joan had been skimming over maps of the Philippine islands in a World Atlas when an unexpected knock on her apartment door had interrupted her musings. Figuring the visitor to be Lois, Joan had not known all of her doubts about signing on for the trip were about to hit a breakwater.

Joan had opened her apartment door with lingering questions about their trip for her soon-to-be travel companion but instead of Lois, she had been face to face with Darren Gentry, her twenty-four year old ex-boyfriend and the very last person she had wanted to see. Darren was a lanky man with a crewcut, an oval face with almost boyish features and a tattoo of a killer whale on his right forearm.

"Why are you here?" Joan had asked, miffed at his gall to show up at her door. She had broken up with him a fortnight before with a clear mandate that their relationship was over and he would no longer phone or come to her apartment. Her decree had fallen on deaf ears.

Darren had given her a hard look from where he stood outside her door, revealing his contempt. "Why didn't you tell me that you and Lois are going on a sailing trip?" he had demanded.

Joan had stood her ground. She would not allow Darren to exploit any openings in their hopefully short conversation. "I broke up with you, remember?"

Darren's voice had been as tight as a fist when he said, "Even if you meant it, I'm not letting you throw away a beautiful relationship."

Joan had scoffed. "Darren, your beautiful relationship had me somewhere after footie and beer with your mates."

Darren's brow had furrowed. "You're dating someone else, aren't you?"

"Darren, don't do this." Her demanding eyes caught his. "You need to go."

She had stepped back to close the door and Darren had blocked the threshold with his foot. "Whose sailboat are you and Lois going to be on?"

Joan had been well aware from Darren's tone of voice that he would not leave until he had had an answer that suited him. "A friend of Max, Lois' brother," she had said. The less revealed, the better.

Darren had given one of his cynical laughs. "You, on a sailboat?"

Joan had stood tall, refusing to give in as she had done too often in the past. "Yes, me on a sailboat."

Darren had moved to step inside but Joan had barred passage.

"We need to talk," he had said in his hurt little boy voice.

"How many times have we already talked?" Joan had pointed out. "It never goes anywhere." She had given him a look that could kill. "Now, leave and please, don't come back." Joan had had no intention of pursuing this subject any further, whether now or later.

Joan's continued belligerence had surprised Darren. She had never been this stubborn in the face of his demands, and he had finally begun to get the idea she actually meant what she said about things being over. This concern had cranked up a few notches in his belly that for him to press too hard could cause her to actually follow through with her threat, as much as he had found that simply impossible to believe. "It's just local sailing with Lois, her brother and his friend, right?"

Joan had considered lying but realized that would not have garnered the independence she was seeking. "No, actually, Lois and I are sailing from Guam to Hong Kong."

Darren's face had dropped in shock and then a contemptuous smile had touched his lips in righteous disbelief. "Okay, I get it," he had smirked at what he saw as intentional exaggeration. "Whatever you say." His brow came down. "I expect you to call me as soon as you get back from your, daysail."

She had dodged his intended kiss.

"I love you, Joan Mackland, and I'm not going to let you give up on us."

As far as Joan had been concerned, Darren had had his final say. "Darren, good-bye."

She had swung the door against his foot and when he relinquished with a dumbfounded look, she had closed the door and locked it, proud she had found the strength to stand her ground and relieved their conversation had not deteriorated into another argument.

The rustling mainsail dragged Joan from her memories of that fateful evening to the cockpit of what had turned into the biggest mistake of her life. She gripped the starboard winch and pulled herself to sit up. The easterly had returned, caressing her face with zephyrs that sent the makings of waves skating across the sea. The soft patter of water passing under the hull mended her spirits. *Atmosphere* was finally on the move again.

Joan turned the helm, and the compass inched to a southerly heading, the course she should have been on for the last day had she not been delayed. Whether she had somehow drifted into the southern shipping lane or not, sailing south would lead to her closest port, Yap Island.

The wind livened to a steady ten knots, pushing aside Joan's fatigue. With the autopilot non-functional due to no battery power, she tied a line from the helm to a cleat as Yao had done, allowing her freedom to move about. She adjusted the sails with confidence her luck had changed.

Returning below deck, she piled the jumbled seat cushions onto the settee and collected Yao's charts scattered on the floor. She laid the chart of the Western Pacific on the table top and plopped down on the settee. She passed a weary hand over her face, dredging from her memory Yao's navigational instructions.

"Okay Joanie, you're going to have to dead reckon," she said as if it were Yao speaking. She located his last penciled in position that included time, date and estimated boat speed, recorded just before midnight on the fourth night out of Guam, only hours before the storm had driven her to her bunk and cast him into the sea.

"Okay, about three and half hours from Yao's fix to when the storm hit and another three hours before I found he was ..." Emotions stopped her from finishing her statement.

She leaned back and closed her eyes forcing herself to focus. "I worked the grid from that position for three hours and found the buoy on day two of my search, maybe two hours west of where he went missing. Fifteen hours drifting west in a one knot current and motoring an hour south at five knots. Then out of fuel and maybe another twelve hours drifting west at one knot."

She wrote her calculations at the chart's bottom margin. "A total of maybe twenty-five miles west," she assumed with the information at hand.

Picking up a five mile reference on the chart's longitude scale, she walked off the total distance on the chart with the dividers and circled her assumed position. With the dividers reset to ten miles, she measured the distance from this estimated position to Yap. "One hundred seventy miles north of Yap Island."

Laying aside the dividers, she considered the distance. "If the wind stays like this, maybe two days to Yap," she said and regarded the artist drawing of *Atmosphere*, once again taking in the detail of what had been Yao's home. As much as she wished he was back on board, she had to accept her unwitting position as proxy captain. *Atmosphere* was her boat now, at least until she reached land.

"Yao, I'm sorry for the way things have worked out," she stated as if Yao were standing in front of her. "I am doing the best that I can. If you were here you would not be happy with the mistakes I've made or the condition of *Atmosphere,* but I'm still alive and as long as I am, I'll do everything in my power to find you. But I need help and I need first to keep myself alive."

Joan returned topside to a faltering breeze and *Atmosphere* crawling along at a discouraging two knots, putting into question her previous estimation. She steered the boat due south, toward knobby heads of dark cumulus that teasingly brought the prospect of a welcome change in weather, but as precious as rain was for her, the storm appeared far more substantial than those before and could bring devastating wind. For now though, rain-filled clouds offered nothing more than tempting enticement.

Joan dragged the rain catcher from the locker and tied its spout closed to trap and hold whatever precipitation she could catch, more hope than belief. She set it aside until needed.

Slipping into shade under the Bimini top, she settled her back against the aft end of the coach roof and gazed astern. *Atmosphere's* feeble wake pulled from within her a loneliness as deep as the sea under her boat's keel. She had played in her mind the scenario of Yao's loss a hundred times, always ending with the same regrets. It was true Yao had fallen overboard due to a physical defect on the mast pulpit, but if she hadn't lost her seasick pills or had seen that early morning storm soon enough to administer the ginger, she would have remained in the cockpit and possibly been able to save her captain. She pressed her palms together, fingers to her lips, and offered a prayer that wherever Yao was, he was no longer suffering.

Cramps in Joan's lower back from her sitting position refocused her thoughts. She leaned forward and tilted her head back, twisting her hips to loosen tendons and ligaments. As she swung down her legs and stood, the flighty breeze shifted again, this time from the northeast, quickly strengthening to a twelve knot blow that sculpted wavelets into waves.

Joan made a sail adjustment that bellied out *Atmosphere's* sails, taking the boat up to Joan's calculated five knots. The boat was not making up for lost time but at least was no longer losing. She readjusted the rope-tied helm to correct her course. The sensation of the boat's power was invigorating and gave Joan a reprieve from lingering worries and uncertainties.

Taking a final look of a portion of the vast sea she was beginning to know too well, she went below again into the musty cabin. With a cup of fresh water remaining in the canteen, she would inventory again all of the foods she had on board with the hope she had missed something of lifesaving value.

She set out the two pound bag of unrefined sugar, followed by the jar of eleven wrapped raw eggs, two boxes of chocolate chip cookies, four pounds remaining of a five pound bag of rice, two packs of salted peanuts and a jar of salted cashews, seven granola bars, a nearly full jar of instant coffee, a can of powdered milk, a bottle of soya sauce, a netted bag of garlic, two cans of peaches in syrup, five purple onions, a partial bag of dried apple slices, ten carrots, a box of chicken bouillon and a multi-pack of instant noodles, none of which fit her requirements of high moisture and low to no sodium.

Lifting the refrigerator top, she removed the twenty-eight remaining tomatoes and set aside four that were tattooed with darkening bruises and black dimples ringed with white fuzz. Selecting the ripest of the unblemished fruit, she leaned over the sink and bit into it like an apple. Musty tasting juice spurted into her mouth and flowed in rivulets down her chin. She gagged on the tomato's acidy taste but swallowed what was in her mouth. With her desperate need for water, this was no time to be a picky eater. She lowered her head over the sink and choked down the remainder of the love apple.

Drying her mouth with a paper towel, Joan placed the quartet of moldy tomatoes into the sink. This was followed with the wilted cabbage, a slimy red bell pepper and the entire stack of exhausted celery, all to be jettisoned overboard.

Of all her choices for sustenance, she was acutely aware there was nothing, not even the canned vegetables, tomatoes or oranges that had enough moisture to keep her sufficiently hydrated. Without another source of pure fresh water, none of the available food on board could save her. She loaded the six remaining oranges below deck into a bowl and ascending half way up the ladder, set the bowl of fruit on the starboard cockpit seat.

The unsalvageable veggies and fruit were hauled topside and dumped overboard, a ritual Joan knew would be repeated in the days to come. The green and red produce rode over waves like specks of condiments in the world's largest bowl of salted broth.

All too soon, approaching night stole the day's light. Joan brought the first aid kit topside and reposed in the cockpit, uplifted by *Atmosphere's* steady speed but humbled by her lack of water and food. She removed the gauze from her neglected leg wound and peeled off the butterfly bandage. Even with the physical activity she had endured over the last day and a half, pinkish signs of healing offered solace that she had properly tended to the laceration, though she needed to stop moving about for it to fully heal. She dappled the wound with an alcohol-soaked cotton ball and applied fresh iodine solution before tossing overboard the spent butterfly bandage and replacing it with its lone mate. Her handiwork was once again overlaid with gauze.

Laying aside the first aid kit, Joan wet her mouth from her meager ration of water and set her watch's alarm for what had become her standard one hour of rest. No matter how drained she felt, no matter how much her body ached, she was determined not to miss another chance at rescue. With no lights anywhere in view on the darkening sea, she stretched out on a cockpit seat. Clinging to the thought of a better tomorrow, she closed her eyes and gave herself to the rhythm of the sea. She dreamed.

Joan's dream-self was seated at *Atmosphere's* settee table dead-reckoning her position on the navigation chart while speaking with her mother on the radio that now hung from a ceiling panel above the table.

"Well Joanie, maybe next time you'll listen to me," her mother gloated with no attempt to hide her satisfaction of once again being right over any worries for her daughter's safety.

"Oh, hi Mum." Joan laid aside the pencil and dividers. "How did you get this number?"

"Never mind that. In case you haven't noticed, you are out of fuel."

"Yes, I did notice."

"And are you aware that the batteries are knackered?"

Joan's dream-self didn't miss a beat. "I'm picking up a wind generator in Manila."

"What you are going to do is pull into the next petrol station and fill up."

"Mum, the nearest station is miles out of my way."

"Joanie, you turn around right now. You're too close to the edge of the world."

Joan's watch alarm dragged her back into her reality of want. She pushed aside her aches and pains and sat up, working her dry tongue in her mouth, searching for moisture. Full darkness covered the sea. She snitched a quaff of water from the canteen, struggling with herself not to consume more and resigned to whatever the new day brought. Every drop of fresh water was as priceless as life itself.

The sails quavered impatiently to be trimmed. Joan mustered the strength to step to the binnacle. Either the wind direction had changed yet again or *Atmosphere* was off-course. The compass provided the answer. *Atmosphere* was aimed twenty degrees too far west. She fumbled through untying the cord holding the helm and adjusted the wheel to her original course, not knowing how long the boat had been off-track and at this point, not caring. She secured the helm and all but collapsed onto the cockpit cushion, already exhausted from what little energy she had expended.

Beyond the boundary of her confined world, the dark sea and cloud covered sky offered no hint of anything existing beyond the edge of her world that was *Atmosphere*. She thought of Yao again. As terrifying as her own plight had become, being lost at sea had to be far more horrifying than she could ever imagine.

"I'll reach Yap, tomorrow," she whispered as if such a statement begot fact.

CHAPTER TEN

Dryness crept down Joan's throat, a feeling as if her internal organs were turning to sand. She doled herself another sip from the canteen, again scuffling with her inner self not to turn up the vessel and guzzle to the last swallow.

Shunning further temptation, Joan dropped the hollow-sounding canteen onto the cockpit floor and trammeled below. It was time to test the resources at hand.

Within the flashlight's luminescence, she opened a can of green beans and posted her back against the counter for support, knowing this would be a bitter-sweet meal. She took a deep breath, tilted back her head as she brought the open can to her mouth and sucked down its thick, slimy liquid.

Joan's facial expression soured. Even with a dire need for water, the starchy brine was a disgusting substitute for clear, unadulterated water. She devoured half of the can's solid contents and dropped the half-spent can into the sink. Having something more than wishes in her stomach heartened her spirits, especially when she considered the three remaining, unopened cans, but just as quickly that recompense slipped away when she spat a wad of viscus saliva into the sink and her companion thirst tapped her on the shoulder.

The cold hand of reality once again pulled at her soul, attempting to drown her in despair. Everything on this boat was conspiring to kill her. Driven by an acute sense of desperation, she picked up the radio's mike, as if the unit had electrical power. "My name is Joan Mackland," she breathed in a hoarse, labored voice. She drew back, harrumphed another gunky feeling in the back of her throat and spat on the floor without a second thought. "I am from New Zealand. I am alone. On a sailboat. The captain is gone. Please answer."

She dropped the dead radio's mike onto the nav table with thoughts as black as the sea. Crossing to the galley, she tapped the faucet's spout with a finger and pressed her glistening fingertip to her tongue. The acrid taste of diesel highlighted the cornerstone of her plight.

"Tomorrow, it must be tomorrow," she coaxed herself on her arrival to Yap. She would make it. The alternative was too horrible to consider.

She crawled up the companionway steps and collapsed onto the cockpit cushion, lying there, motionless, feeling her breath going in and out as her beating heart radiated a blunt throbbing pain deep within her brain. She closed her eyes. Sleep was her only relief from physical and mental torture.

Joan's dream-self stood tall at *Atmosphere's* helm, fit and strong, a seasoned sailor on a course toward a mid-ocean service station off the starboard bow. The floating petrol station had a pontooned fuel pump, mooring buoy and an office constructed of driftwood and set on a rusty barge. *Atmosphere* passed a sign on a bobbing fishing buoy announcing a last chance to fuel up before the edge of the world.

Joan brought *Atmosphere* alongside the diesel pump, skilfully doused the sails and picked up the mooring line. Yao appeared from the office. He shaded his eyes to take in his only customer of the day and boarded a skiff tied alongside the barge. He motored the skiff toward the fuel pump. He was garbed in Hawaiian beach attire, his shoulders draped in seaweed like some odd scarf. Switching off his boat's chugging outboard motor, he glided up to the pump and tied off on a cleat.

"Nice to see a sailboat for once," the ex-captain turned grease-monkey smiled. "Don't see much more than an occasional fishing boat from Guam."

He lifted the nozzle from the pump and punched it through *Atmosphere's* side as if the sailboat's hull were made of paper. The pump's meter whirled and clicked.

"I need drinking water too, if you have any," Joan said.

Yao licked his own cracked and dry lips. "Won't have any of that until we get some rain." He wiped his sweaty forehead with a rag from his back pocket. "If you want, I can fill your water tank with diesel fuel."

Joan's dream-self made a pained face. "Thanks, but I already did that." She flashed hopeful eyes. "My nav chart shows an island south of here. It's called Yap. How much farther is it?"

Yao looked surprised. "I don't know what chart you have," he said with a shrug, "but as far as I know, there's no island south of here, just the edge of the world." He gave Joan a sage look. "Best you go back the way you came."

He plucked off a particularly annoying strand of seaweed irritating his cheek and tossed it away, adding, "That sign is out there for a reason."

"Well, the chart I have shows an island south of here and that's where I'm going."

The pump's nozzle snapped closed. *Atmosphere* was refueled. Yao removed the nozzle and the hole in *Atmosphere's* side vanished. He fit the nozzle to the pump. "Suit yourself," he said with a shake of his head. Women, they just don't listen. He uncleated and pushed his skiff clear of the pontoon, cranked his boat's outboard and motored away.

Sleep ebbed like the tide, leaving Joan's dream as vivid in her mind as if Yao were still alongside her boat. What would have been his service station was the low arch of a pastel sun on the eastern horizon and his cautioning sign any one of the infinite waves marching toward her.

Except for her dream, Joan's fifth night alone on the vacant ocean had passed, uneventful, and only the wind-filled sails and water passing under the hull let her know *Atmosphere* was taking her somewhere, and at this point, she found it hard to care if that somewhere was the edge of the world.

Atmosphere's course had drifted west again. Joan made the correction and retied the helm with no more thought than breathing. She absently pressed the engine's ignition switch, astounded when the engine hacked a growl. She perked up. Enough time had passed for the engine's starter battery to have recharged itself, possibly enough to get the engine running again. Temptation to press the button again yielded to the fact the battery may crank the engine but with a fuel tank as dry as her mouth, it would be for naught.

Adding another bobble of disappointment to the emotions strung around her neck, Joan mentally prepared herself to the very real possibility she was out of options and all but out of time. If she did not reach Yap or find rescue by a passing ship in the next day, she would surely die and her body would go undiscovered until *Atmosphere* washed up on some distant shore.

Joan moistened her cracked lips with a dab of water from the canteen and went below. Seated at the settee table, she focused her muddled brain and hazy eyes on the nautical chart. Dehydration and hunger were affecting her concentration, but even with that affliction, it was clear to her that after drifting off course two times, she could no longer trust what had, from the very beginning, been questionable dead-reckoning. Reality stabbed her like a spear when she realized she could have unknowingly passed through the southern shipping lane and worse, completely missed Yap. She dragged a finger past her elusive destination and across seven hundred nautical miles of open ocean to Papua, New Guinea.

Joan wilted. Not only was seven hundred miles an impossibly long distance in her condition, any storms that found *Atmosphere* would send her and the boat to the bottom of the sea. The dream warnings from her mother and Yao about the edge of the world took on new meaning.

Alternatives for Joan were no better. She estimated from her only dead-reckoned position that Yao's original destination, the Philippines, was equally as far as New Guinea and if indeed she had sailed past Yap, the only other accessible land she could possibly reach was Palau, an island two hundred miles southwest of Yap and just as fanciful.

"Yap is out there and I'm going to find it," Joan said, a statement wrapped in shaky confidence and tied with a thin thread of hope. Given her life threatening predicament, she would hold to a southerly route another day and failing to find Yap, she would steer toward her last chance at survival, the Republic of Palau.

Pulling up her suffering body, Joan steadied herself with a hand on the table. Every joint was stiff and sore and her cracked lips burned, peeling like old paint. The survival she sought was more painful than surrender.

Like an undernourished prisoner returned to solitary confinement, Joan took in the boat's compact interior, overrun by her gloomy funk. She was crossing a barren wasteland where drinkable water lay within angry thunderheads she both feared and welcomed. She wondered if *Atmosphere* was her chariot or her coffin.

Driven by need, she lifted and slid aside the floorboard in front of the settee table and stared longingly at the contaminated freshwater tank. She imagined herself reaching down through the interface between the two immiscible liquids to scoop up clean water as cool as a mountain spring and ...

Joan's drawn face softened. Furrowed stress lines vanished as revelation returned focus and determination. Of course, water and diesel fuel do not mix, a game-changer. All she had to do was transfer the fuel from the water tank into the fuel tank. That would allow her not only to restart the engine, if any of the boat's batteries indeed had sufficiently self-recharged, but would also activate the alternator, and that would once again give her access to water from the faucet. Even if the pumped water was contaminated, she could fill a glass and skim off what fuel rose to the top. Any lingering taste of diesel would be a minor inconvenience compared to having enough water to save her life.

Joan took her gaunt body on another trip topside. The closeness of having both power and drinkable water had given her a refreshing reprieve that brought strength to her suffering body. Gathering the two white buckets from the cockpit locker, she returned below and set the buckets next to the exposed water tank before removing the aft floorboard over the fuel tank, anxious to get this operation underway.

Armed with an adjustable spanner from the tool drawer, Joan lowered herself onto the floor at the fuel tank, sitting side saddle, and lumbered through removing the twelve securing bolts in the tank's ten inch diameter inspection plate. She slid the cover aside to a repelling waft of diesel fumes.

She scooted along the floor to the water tank and in labored movements set about with the spanner loosening the first of ten securing bolts on this tank's inspection plate. As she extracted the first bolt, diesel fuel from the overfilled tank spewed forth through the open bolt hole like a mini-artesian well, pulsing from *Atmosphere's* rolling motion on the sea.

Leaning back as far as she could from the foul vapors, Joan worked the fuel-slippery spanner in a slow and steady rhythm, removing each of the remaining nine bolts, creating a ring of golden wellsprings. The inspection plate had adhered to its gasket and she had to pry it off with a screwdriver, streaming the last of the overfill into the bilge.

Joan sucked the diesel-laced air between her teeth, as if this would filter out the noxious fumes, and slid aside the inspection plate. The malicious stench was suffocating. Her head reeled as nausea seized her stomach.

Woozy-headed from the effluvium, Joan wobbled to her feet, fighting for each breath and holding back her gorge. She swiped her fuel-glistened hands on a dish towel and dragged herself up the companionway steps like a spent mountain climber scaling a high altitude precipice. Free of the tainted environment below deck, she collapsed onto a cockpit cushion. The fuel's pernicious odor clung to her nostrils and her lungs felt as if they were filled with glue. She willed herself not to vomit while squeezing the bridge of her nose between thumb and forefinger to allay a sharp pain sprouting between her eyes.

Joan's flagging condition highlighted her quandary. As much as she needed water to rehydrate, her intoxicated body could not endure another close encounter with the toxic fuel, even after she had sobered up. Her plans to access water in the tank and restart the engine had hit what seemed a fatal snag.

Joan scooted to the aft end of the cockpit to distance herself from the stench below and caught a sound, seemingly distant but clear, a chirruping cadence as if her cousin in Christchurch had received one of her distress calls and was tapping out a message in Morse Code. She glanced forward, along the port side deck, toward the source of the sound and drew herself up in astonished surprise. Amidships, perched on the top port side lifeline was a white tern sporting a red beak and a red streamer-like tail the length of its pigeon-size body. Land!

Joan's eyes slipped past the stowaway and over the bow but instead of elation at beholding a tranquil anchorage fronting an idyllic beach on an inhabited island, her heart sank. Reflected sunlight off of the choppy sea was backdropped by a solid bank of dark, angry storm clouds. The sixty mile wide front had a wedge-shaped shelf cloud with a twisting, ragged base that formed the leading edge of its green-tinted cumulonimbus parent. Lightning flashed within veils of gray rain obscuring all behind it. Muffled thunder announced pending disaster.

Atmosphere was aimed at the center of a tempest it could not survive. Joan's only chance out of the razor's edge appeared to be a course change, due northwest in the hope the squall would blow itself out before it reached her. It was a long shot but it was the only shot she felt she had, or was it?

Five miles distance, directly south, between *Atmosphere* and the storm, a patch of sunlight highlighted a white line of beach under the wild face of the black demon. The strip of sand was no more than a comma on a blank page but for Joan, the beach and the deep green jungle behind it were not only shelter but possible life itself.

As if coaxing her to shed the affects of her inhaled diesel cocktail and take action, the steady northeasterly kicked up to a fifteen knot northerly being drawn into the cold wall of heavy weather. The bird took flight as if sensing a train wreck was in the making and it needed to be elsewhere.

Pushing through her residual inebriation, Joan took in the island with the interest of a prisoner planning escape. She made an instant decision, a defiant gamble, betting her life and *Atmosphere's* existence on a desperate race against the dark weather. She let out the sails to snag as much wind as she could. The boat gained speed, six and half knots.

"That island is mine," she swore to the advancing front, not willing to yield.

Joan swallowed a larger than allowed portion of water from the canteen, a cleansing shot of stamina. Having the boat as her world since leaving Guam ten days ago had given her a boost in courage that bolstered her daring she could sail *Atmosphere* well enough to save herself, but she had to have the strength to do so. She also knew that if she didn't win this race to the island, the single gulp of water remaining in the canteen would be lost with the boat.

Steadfast in getting herself through this challenge in one piece, she tied the helm and slipped on the safety harness and the life jacket. Clipping onto the binnacle, she freed the helm once again, taking control of her boat.

To starboard, across two miles of building seas, waves crashed against a reef protecting a low-set sandbank capped with a tumble of gray, barnacle-covered rocks looking like a sleeping whale.

The nearness of the islet and its rocky companion was an enticing invitation for shelter, but with the driving wind from the north and the storm's contrary winds that would come from the south, *Atmosphere* would be totally exposed no matter on which side of the islet Joan anchored. She held her course.

The larger island took on more definition. It was maybe a mile in length and half as wide, cantered to the southeast, away from *Atmosphere*.

Joan craned her head around the spray dodger for a more clear view of what lay before her. Her spirit rose. Fronting the island's north end was a feature that welded her resolve, a turquoise lagoon and the deepest water she could see along the island's sand and rock beach. No matter what the storm brought, the lagoon would make a perfect anchorage with the island's thick foliage of dark, leafy trees and scattered coconut palms offering protection against the storm's counter punch.

Atmosphere drove forward toward the rolling waves that appeared as an assaulting army on a fortress. Every ounce of the boat's speed was a must. Joan pushed aside her thoughts of dining on coconuts and trimmed the jib. It would take all of her focus and limited sailing skills to safely enter the small but accommodating harbor, drop anchor and furl the sails before the storm showed her its fury. She slipped on her shorts and T-shirt in anticipation of finding help.

A white sand bottom swept up from the depths changing the sea's deep blue to a softer hue dappled with dark shapes of brown sponges the size of bushel baskets, sea fans and knobby coral heads, looking like a submerged floral garden. The shallowing water sharpened the wave crests and jabbed Joan with jitters. If the water's depth became much shallower, her pursuit to safety would come to an abrupt end when the boat's keel met the sea's bottom.

But any concern Joan had for water depth was scattered like sea spray when she spied, a quarter mile ahead, a frothy line of crashing waves battering an impenetrable guardian reef blockading the lagoon. The solid-looking coral curved around the near end of the island like a snarl.

The water to port appeared too shallow to track down the length of the island in search of another possible anchorage. Joan had no other choice but to concede to an alternative approach to the lagoon. She steered to starboard, a course that would skirt the fifty-foot wide cor-al barrier and hopefully to the reef's terminus. Her desperate endeavor would either deliver her to safety or cast her asunder in the storm.

Atmosphere charged past the island's northern end where breaking waves battered the coral rim as determined to rip apart the immoveable obstacle as Joan was to reach safety. The boat's bow pointed like a spear at the dark, apocalyptic front that was clearly growing in intensity.

The folly of her decision not to try to sail down the length of the is-land washed over Joan in a tsunami of horrid surprise when *Atmosphere* rounded the island's tip and the reef revealed its true form. This was not a single bastion of coral protecting a placid lagoon but the top end of an impressively long atoll extending four miles south of the island to where the leading edge of the advancing wind and rain churned up the sea like a buzzsaw.

Across the atoll's half-mile-wide, aqua-green lagoon, a sandbar sprouting from the lower end of the main island's unobstructed sand beach connected a trio of in-line islets like dots and dashes to complete the odd corral.

The dense wall of the massive storm devoured the atoll's lower end and charged north to claim the island and anything in its path. Rising clouds born of the shelf cloud's ragged base scudded across its gust front to be torn apart by the storm's shear winds rushing under warmer air being inhaled by the deadly front.

The leading edge of the shelf cloud passed over the boat, a cold, humbling moment that turned day into the dusky half-light of what the edge of the world must look like. The parent cloud rolled up the atoll in an avalanche of blinding rain and hurricane-like winds that whirled and dug up the sea in a roiling mist of ruination.

A blast of swirling, tropical wind drawn by the storm ripped at the sea behind *Atmosphere* like an angry fist. The boat's sails and rigging clattered and moaned. Seaspray blasted the boat's stern, drenching the cockpit and pummeling the Bimini top, fair warning to the boat's sole crew member that the runaway juggernaut barreling down on her from a mile away was about to mete out a reverse punch.

Doubt and indecision twisted Joan's stomach and raced her heart. She might possibly save *Atmosphere* and herself from the storm's onslaught by turning the boat into what was likely the last of the following wind. Reefing the mainsail would make *Atmosphere* a smaller target, but the violent storm's speed and closeness gave her precious little time to complete that task. To be caught at the mast with a broken attachment point on its starboard pulpit was a terrifying thought.

Flurried reflections ran through her mind like a tornado, flashing images of all she had experienced and learned since leaving Guam. Desperation to snag something, anything, that might offer hope brought to the forefront one particular incident, the insidious storm that had caught her unawares and ultimately led to Yao's loss overboard.

In that tragic event, Yao had not yet made his way through the companionway into the cockpit when the raving wind had overpowered the sails, heeling *Atmosphere* hard onto its starboard gunnel. Joan had been certain the boat was doomed to the sea, but to her amazed relief, the boat's weather helm had wrested directional control from the autopilot and swerved the bow into the wind, spilling air from the sails. *Atmosphere* had been uncontrollable during the direction change, but the boat's tendency to turn windward when severely heeled had saved the boat and its crew from imminent disaster.

As she faced off with the black monster about to engulf her and her boat, Joan understood that for any chance of surviving this encounter and not being shipwrecked on the reef, she had to extend her fifty yard distance from the atoll's coral ring. The yardage she gained would not be much, but if she turned *Atmosphere* onto a port tack and lay on the cockpit sole, the weather helm would once again take over. This was mere assumption on Joan's part, based on the brief encounter with a blow far less intense than the raging bluster barreling down on her. What the approaching wall of destruction would actually do with her boat, rip the sails to shreds, drive it onto the reef or spawn another mountainous wave, Joan didn't know. All she did know was, she had no better option.

Joan took the jib sheet in hand, ready to reset the headsail once she veered the boat onto a port tack, away from the atoll, and in that same instant of preparation, fate tossed a wild card into this unpleasant game, offering her the slightest of cheats.

Breaking waves to port revealed a sand and coral appendix jutting out from the reef's near side, a natural breakwater created by a twenty-foot wide breach through which tidal flow entered and discharged from the atoll.

Joan didn't think twice. She accepted the challenge, winner take all. *Atmosphere* was going to catch the storm's full force no matter what she did, but if she could take the boat into the atoll before the winds nailed her, she could steer for the island and those same winds would drive the boat onto the beach. Such a maneuver would end any chance she had for reaching Yap's main island, but at least she would be back on land with access to lifesaving food and water held within coconuts and maybe even rescue, if perchance this island accommodated residents.

Adjusting the jib and turning the boat to port, nose-on toward the beckoning passage, Joan prayed this dramatic attempt to scoot into the atoll was more heroic than foolhardy.

The northerly dropped to a panting twelve knot gust that dampened *Atmosphere's* speed. Temptation to scuttle this audacious gamble tugged at Joan's will. She was riding the cusp of catastrophe, and if the wind across *Atmosphere's* port side failed completely, the boat would become fodder for the reef.

An uneasy stillness fell upon the island's trees foretelling of an imminent change in wind direction and speed. Cooler, reverse air chilled Joan with a fear-provoking premonition as the boat's momentum dropped in the defeated northerly. The hand she had been dealt, even with a wild card, had not been as solid as she had thought.

In one final, defiant breath, the northerly stiffened the sails, a short but steady gust that glided the boat into the tidal gap where an incoming tide eddied patterns of clear seawater into the lagoon's turquoise-tinted water two hundred feet away. Undulant crags of coral formed the gap's two sides bristling with knobby, coral protrusions colored with blues, greens and reds, and similarly hued patches of sea fans and sponges extending into the distance along the reef's partially exposed top.

The advancing storm's wind and rain turned the water's surface into a dense, gray mist, vibrating the air and sounding like a steam locomotive on worn out rails. Bucket size rain drops walloped the water around *Atmosphere* like mortar shells, a warning of the barrage to come.

The last wisp of the northerly rustled the sails, too weak to propel *Atmosphere* faster than the feeble current. Joan and her boat were caught between hammer and anvil with no cavalry charging over the proverbial hill.

The coconut palms along the island's beach fell still again as if suddenly turned to concrete, the northerly no longer able to move their leaves or the boat's sagging sails. The storm's might was set to take everything Joan had, including her life.

A punishing wind borne of the parent cloud bitch-slapped aside its dying contender and slammed into *Atmosphere's* starboard side like an enemy war-galley. The hard, gale force wind bellied the sails and snapped their sheets taut like bullwhips, setting the jib aback and the rigging to humming like overtightened guitar strings.

Atmosphere groaned as lateral force rolled the boat onto its port side, laying its sails onto the reef like discarded rags. Green water poured over the port gunnel into the cockpit like marauding pirates. The torrent grabbed Joan in its swirling fist seemingly in an attempt to severe her harness attachment point and sweep her from the boat.

Terror-stricken, Joan clawed the air, struggling to keep her head above water. She found the helm and pulled herself above the incoming flood as the invading sea discovered the open companionway and sluiced into the darkened cabin. The unrelenting wind held *Atmosphere* down for the count.

As if announcing the storm's full fury, a flash of impossibly bright lightning exploded in instant, head-spinning thunder. A waterfall of wind-slanted rain hissed and churned the lagoon's surface like boiling water.

Joan failed to catch her breath in the suffocating downpour. She grabbed the mainsail sheet and pulled, hand over fist to haul her shoulders above the flood, unwittingly wrenching the mainsail sheet from its clam-cleat. The freed mainsail slammed hard to port, dumping the wind's full force and yanking the sheet from her hand. The boat righted.

Still set aback, the jib clenched the gale, vibrating like an overcharged electrical transformer and driving the boat's already damaged port side against the jagged reef in a nauseating screech of aluminum against coral.

Joan spit up water, and on an adrenaline high, struggled to her knees in the flooded cockpit. The thrashing boom banged and slashed like a wild beast, seemingly intent on toppling the mast or shaking the boat apart.

The reef's coral teeth gnawed at the aluminum hull threatening to disembowel *Atmosphere*. Joan attacked the cleated jib sheet with the ferocity of the storm and let the headsail fly. The raging gale whipped the loose foresail in a frenzy, sounding like a machine gun.

The anguished cry of *Atmosphere* suffering against the coral was wrapped in the deafening roar of the wind and clanging rigging, but mercifully, the torturous passage was over. The boat broke free from the reef and was swept into the lagoon, freewheeling through stinging rain so heavy Joan was unable to distinguish sea from sky.

The boat veered to port. The howling blow sulked across the stern and caught the mainsail full-on, forcing it hard against the already damaged port side spreader. Joan braced herself against the helm as *Atmosphere's* stern rose and the boat powered up, rounding to port and doubling back on itself. The out-of-control boat was on a collision course with the reef.

Atmosphere continued to turn, putting the oncoming weather slightly forward of midship. The maelstrom snared the mainsail's leach, curling the sail's outer edge and threatening to slam the mainsail back across the boat in a jibe powerful enough to shatter the already compromised spreader and topple the mast.

Dead ahead, the water darkened, looking like a submerged fortress wall. Joan slung the helm to starboard less than one boat length from the reef. The boat wheeled hard over, throwing Joan onto the port cockpit seat, the boom's aft end furrowing the water only feet from her head. The turnbuckle of a starboard shroud exploded, threatening to dismast the boat as the jibe would have.

The helm shuddered when the boat's keel and rudder plowed through a sandy bottom where deep water transitioned from fathoms to feet. The churned up swill of water and fuel in the boat's flooded belly surged forward and sloshed back against the companionway steps in a breaking, glistening wave.

Atmosphere's grounded keel and rudder swerved the boat violently to starboard. The sudden motion threw Joan onto the cockpit sole. The boat's bow was now dead-on to the relentless wind that shook the mainsail with such violence the boom's gooseneck shattered, turning the unattached beam into a death-dealing bludgeon. Below deck, the still stirred up diesel-water mixture sloshed over the already soaked settee and the galley's stove and counters.

The rudder spun the helm and driven by the wind, *Atmosphere* lurched to port, flogging the tattered jib and forcing the mainsail and its broken boom against the now buckled port spreader.

Joan pulled herself up onto the port cockpit seat, not daring to reclaim the whirligigging helm for fear of losing an arm. From over the bow, through the gray rain and mist, emerged a line of breaking waves on a beach. She scrambled back onto the cockpit sole and braced herself for impact.

The keel thwacked a coral head, a sharp, unforgiving thud that tensioned Joan's every muscle in horrid anticipation. The helm snapped full around with bone-breaking force and the boat zagged bow-on to the wind again. *Atmosphere* stalled, quivering as if in its death throes, and collapsed like a toppled tree onto its starboard side.

Joan dangled from her safety harness tether like a marionette in amateur hands, inches over the convergence of the Bimini top and wave-swept shallows.

Her teeth clinched to pain from knocks and bruises, she unfastened her life jacket and let it fall. Too weak to pull herself up to unclip her harness from the binnacle, she unsnapped the safety gear's buckle and shrugging a strap off of her shoulder, lowered herself against the Bimini top where it met the water. Unable to slip under the canvas cover, she crawled astern and slithered from the boat into foot deep water. Wind and waves pummeled her weak and damaged body. She found her footing and schlepped ashore.

Physically and emotionally drained on the downside of an adrenaline rush, Joan had nothing in her to go further. She dropped to her knees at a high tide line, delirious, and collapsed onto her side. Too weak to move, her breathing came in ragged breaths.

⬡⬡⬡

Sand wrens skittered and hermit crabs snapped into their shells as Joan roused from where she lay between a retreating tide and deep green jungle. The sun's disk was low in a western sky of broken clouds. Frustrated by not getting its pound of flesh, the cold storm had slinked north in pursuit of other prey, dragging rain and wind with it.

Joan strained to her feet as reality sunk in. For all she had suffered and all the elements thrown at *Atmosphere*, the sea had not devoured her. She took in *Atmosphere* where the boat lay at the receding waterline. The vessel cast a long shadow onto the beach, appearing as a grounded leviathan forsaken to the coming night after its gallant struggle. The boat's name on its upturned port side was no longer legible, dented, scrapped and scarred as it was from the collision at sea and further marred, like its black-painted hull, from the boat's encounter with the reef.

A monumental relief of standing on terra firma overcame Joan. From the moment she had stepped onboard *Atmosphere* in Guam and especially after her first days at sea, the boat had been an alluring mode of transportation taking her from a North Pacific island to somewhere else she had never been. All of that had changed when fate had thrust her into a desperate strait with Yao's disappearance. In an instant her vehicle to adventure had become a prison, seemingly as permanent as if she had been on death row. Only now, looking at *Atmosphere's* corpse did she feel released from the topsy-turvy world she had grown to hate yet had so much depended on.

Joan's body sagged with weariness. She teetered on the edge of unconsciousness, fearful if she lay down again, even for a moment, she would never get back up.

Thirst still owned Joan's throat but strangely, she felt the urge to urinate. She gathered what wits she could and plodded to a nearby coconut tree at the jungle's edge, a conditioned reflex for privacy brought with her from the world to which she was so anxious to return. She assumed the position and when her stream finally came, it was weak, dark and carried a heavy, rank odor. For the last two days, her body had been restricting blood flow to her kidneys in an attempt to maintain sufficient circulation to her other organs. Between the soppy air and simplest exertion, even with the nutrition from the oranges, canned beans and what water she had consumed from the canteen, she faced renal failure and a death as frightful as shark attack.

Finishing up, Joan examined her injured right thigh. The damp dressing drooped and the underlying wound was sore to the touch. She peeled off the soggy gauze. The butterfly bandage had failed completely but the wound had closed up, and though its border was tender to the touch, it didn't appear to be infected. Still, she would need to get back onto the boat for the bottle of medicinal alcohol and medical kit. All she could do now was keep the cut clean and exposed to the air while she set out in search of help. Failing that, she would harvest downed coconuts for food and water.

Joan tossed away the soiled gauze and took in the beach from one end of the island to the other. *Atmosphere* had ended its doomed voyage midway along the mile long island, and no where did she see any skiffs pulled up onto the sand, no footprints or other telling signs that anyone else had ventured onto the beach after the storm.

The length of the beach was strewn with dozens of green coconuts. Joan picked up a nearby drupe and shook it. The sloshing within was too tantalizing to ignore and her plan shifted from seeking help to sustenance.

Joan had seen in New Zealand grocery stores carved green coconuts with their flat-cut bottoms, shaved sides and steepled tops. She had sampled the water and chewy white meat. What she had never done was breach the fruit's dense, fibrous husk, a feat that would require a broad-bladed knife or a hammer and chisel, all of which were onboard *Atmosphere*.

A deep, guttural drone of a labored diesel engine caught the edge of Joan's hearing, pulling her eyes to the lower end of the island. The dark shape of a fishing trawler, with its furled net looking like a bird's broken wing, was on a southerly course past her island, down the length of the atoll.

Joan's hopes were seismic. She dropped the coconut and lacking the strength and stamina to run the distance to the island's terminus, she raised weak arms and waved.

"Here," she wheezed, her raspy voice no more than a strangled cough. "I'm here."

The trawler's crew appeared as moving pips, their brighter clothes standing out against the dark wood of the fishing boat. At her distance from the island's end, if anyone aboard the trawler looked in her direction, they might see *Atmosphere's* black painted hull but would not know if the boat was animal, vegetable or mineral. Distance soon stole rescue from her.

From the island's lower point where Joan was looking, her eyes tracked along the exposed sandbar linking the main island with the three successive islets that made up the atoll's eastern side. Open water beyond the atoll's barely perceivable southern end separated the oblong reef from a more substantial island twenty-five miles distant. The larger body of land appeared as a dark cloud floating on the sea, possibly the trawler's home port.

With boat traffic and a likely port, Joan held onto hope that if she found no one living on this island, the day's end would likely bring other fishing boats, possibly close enough to her island for a crew to see her or *Atmosphere*.

In the opposing direction, at the island's upper end, a rocky outcrop marked the head of the western side of the atoll, the side she had passed through. Miles out at sea, visible along the interface between sea and sky, a scattering of trawlers were, like the first trawler, making their way south.

The nearness of potential rescue cut through Joan's despair, mustering from within an urgency to reach a vantage point that offered a better chance of rescue, but first, she had to address her immediate need, water and food.

The heavy chop kicked up by the storm had diminished to wavelets lapping the stranded boat's starboard cap rail. Joan waded to *Atmosphere* in knee-deep water and slipped under the severed boom. She stepped around the aft edge of the Bimini top and settled onto the crook of the slanted cockpit sole and base of the starboard cockpit seat. Diesel fumes from below deck mingled in the light breeze, a warning to Joan her beached home had a forbidden zone.

Joan's plan was simple. With all the oranges she had in the cockpit no longer on board, she would make her way below deck to collect the hammer, a chisel or screwdriver and return to the beach for a life-refreshing meal. After her coconut feast, she would take advantage of the day's last light to make her way to the island's lower end while searching for signs of habitation. She might even turn up other varieties of fruit, like breadfruit or mangoes. That was her plan, but plans, especially when everything else has gone awry, don't always work out.

Golden sunlight of a storm-cleared sky shown through the companionway at an oblique angle deepening the amber tone of two inches of diesel fuel layered atop thigh-deep seawater. The swill filled the tilted main cabin to the starboard port lights, submerging the pilot berth and its underlying house batteries and topping the main cabin's lockers and tool drawer. The lid to the navigation table was cocked open, its buoyant contents mingled with floating settee cushions, Yao's bed sheet and pillow, the two white buckets she had taken below, navigation charts, books and assorted packaged and fresh foods. Populating the bottom of the wallow were undissolved sugar still in its plastic bag and four pounds of spilled rice scattered about like so many drowned maggots. The radio and Yao's sextant had a diesel sheen and the jug of individually-wrapped eggs floated in front of the door to the head. From what Joan could see the V-berth appeared to have been spared the carnage.

The tool drawer was underwater and no longer accessible and the galley drawer with the knives could only be reached if Joan lowered herself into the slop, a tempting thought, but one that signaled due caution. The canted, fuel-coated companionway stairs were treacherously slippery and once her legs and feet were covered in diesel, she would play hell getting out again, especially with her flagging strength. As for the forward hatch, it had been latched tight from the inside before they had departed Guam. Even if she could have gained access into the V-berth, she would still have had to wade aft to the galley and then return forward again without losing her footing or being overcome by noxious diesel fumes.

Unable to reach what she needed inside the boat, Joan planted her feet against the cockpit's lower side and extended her legs. Shoulder-high to the port side locker, she lifted the storage compartment's lid and peered inside like a child just tall enough to see into an almost open drawer. The locker's top layer of dock fenders and coiled ropes would have to be lifted up and out to see what was underneath, but working against gravity and the boat's severe angle was beyond her physical capability.

Panting her exertion and feeling as drained physically as she did emotionally, Joan dropped the lid closed and slid down against the skewed starboard cockpit seat. Her only option now was to rely on what resources the island provided. Failing to find immediate help or an appropriate tool to open coconuts would sentence her to another long and painful night of deprivation.

A deep animosity engulfed Joan for the anonymous hand that had delivered her from yet another disaster only to cast her onto an island with food, water and possible rescue, yet she still wallowed in desperate straits.

Abandoning the boat, Joan remained on the wet, hard-packed, lower beach where walking was easier, and hobbled toward the island's lower end. The beach was strewn with clam shells and wave-worn shards of coral, all too brittle to withstand impact against a coconut's outer husk.

Fifty yards along the beach, at the edge of the jungle's deepening shadows, Joan spied a trailhead. Even with the day's end nigh, realization that someone cut this trail pulled Joan up the beach and onto the narrow path where sallow sunlight offered enough illumination to keep her footing.

Gnarled branches scratched her bare arms and legs as she made her way deeper into the jungle. Squadrons of mosquitoes and biting midges seemed to appear out of thin air, searing her exposed skin like hot cinders. She fanned away the pesky bugs from her face and neck and plodded on, lured by the promise this trail led to more than another letdown.

Minutes later the path ended at an acre clearing swept by late afternoon's long shadows and littered with beer cans and whiskey bottles.

She made her way past a tattered fishing net strung between two stunted trees to a wood and thatch lean-to at the rear of the compound. Laid alongside a stone-ringed fire pit fronting the eight foot square structure was a scorched sea turtle carapace, looking like an ancient warrior's shield. Under the hut's sagging roof a rotting canvas tarp partially covered a rusted outboard motor. The fact the camp was here spoke volumes and raised Joan's belief that if someone didn't live on this island, at least there were occasional visits, and among their trash could be treasure.

Scouring the ground for some forgotten tool or piece of rusty iron with an edge, her foot kicked up a fist-size chunk of coral with a protruding clam shell. The primitive tool was solid and looked stout enough to take on a coconut and win.

A wave of light-headedness blurred Joan's vision. Her legs suddenly felt too weak to support her. She was giving up precious moisture to the stagnant, soggy air and blood she could not afford to lose to the attacking insects. Swiping away a trace of sweat from her face, she slapped at a particularly painful mosquito bite on the back of her neck and prudently yielded to the warning signs.

Joan lurched from the gloom-filled trail onto the open beach with its caressing breeze and cooler temperatures. The western sky was afire with a reddish tint of the day's last light that sharpened the outline of the distant island. The air around her hummed with what seemed the island's entire host of ravenous blood-suckers.

Under a nearby palm that leaned as if it too was about to topple over, Joan hiked a coconut under her arm and made for the water's edge where the steady breeze thinned the ranks of the relentless attackers. Along the darkening horizon, both east and west, lights of squid boats congregated in clusters, offering bitter-sweet awareness that rescue was close yet too far away to matter.

Expending what little energy she had remaining to breach the coconut's two inches of hard, fibrous husk battled with her desire to lie down on the wet sand and let the next outgoing tide carry her away. Those tangled thoughts hung around her neck like a garland until she found herself standing next to *Atmosphere's* foundered corpse. The ebbing tide had surrendered a foot of beach and retreated from the boat's gunnel.

She dropped her coconut into the aft end of the pitched cockpit, followed by the coral chisel, and crawled in herself, huffing to the strain on her body as she settled into the crook between the cockpit sole and the seat. Moistening her swollen lips with what saliva she could coax from under her scaly tongue, she didn't have to dredge for strength to get to her meal. Her urgent need to drink and eat were enticement enough.

Joan laid the coconut on its side in the angle between the cockpit seat's base and sole. Her makeshift tool was too abrasive to grip bare-handed, so she slipped off her T-shirt and folded it together to create a buffer between skin and coral.

Armed and anxious, Joan's first hack at the coconut snapped off the clam shell where it sprouted from the coral nodule, leaving her with-out a chopping edge. Undeterred, she grated the coral's coarse surface against the drupe's rounded top edge, heartened by the moist, fibrous shavings that snowed onto her supporting hand.

Joan halted her work to extinguish burning shoulder and wrist muscles. Setting the coral rock aside, she lifted the coconut in both hands and pressed its abraded surface to her lips, touching it with her tongue. The sensation of even a trace of moisture swept through her, a desperate need that drove her on. She set the coconut in place and picking up her makeshift tool, set to work as if possessed.

A high pitched, grinding sound of raspy coral against a hard sur-face announced she had reached pay dirt. She expanded her effort, ex-posing more of the internal seed until her coral tool, chafed to half its original size, fractured into three pieces.

Joan tilted her head back in agony, her arm muscles screaming for mercy and her breathing coming in short pants. A drop of sweat crept down her right temple. She recovered and discarded the broken coral. Her fortuitous find had served its purpose. Blunt force would do the rest.

Joan disengaged the winch handle from the starboard winch and cocking the tool like a hammer, she brought it down on the exposed coconut shell with all the force she had. The repurposed tool's drive head struck the shell's rigid surface in a sharp, hollow clack, opening twin cracks oozing moisture.

Anticipation was an anxious knot in Joan's stomach. She bashed the drupe again. The second assault opened a one inch hole in the compromised shell revealing the coconut's watery prize within. Dropping the winch handle as if experiencing a religious conversion, she peered through the breach for a moment, hypnotized by the liquid contents inside and filled with a sense of triumph. Like some Robinson Crusoe, she had proven to herself the island's resources were hers for the taking.

Drawing herself up in great expectation, she pressed the coconut's opening to her lips, tilted her head back and gulped a shot of the cloudy water. Her body's response was immediate and dramatic. Her mouth and tongue tingled like sponges soaking up every molecule of the moisture. The supercharged water coursed down her throat, a succulent revival that spread through her body and rocked her soul.

Consumed by the titillating uplift of spirit, she upended the coconut a second time and gulped the remaining nourishment, holding the fruit steady until the last drop before digging out and sucking down what slimy meat she could corral with her finger.

The liquid meal was the turning point Joan had been anxiously awaiting, but with darkness descending over the island and surrounding sea, and too exhausted to mount another search for a tool, she realized her next meal would have to be in morning's light.

Joan tucked what she could of the limp mainsail into the crook between cockpit sole and starboard seat and lay on her crude bed with her life jacket as a makeshift pillow. Above her was a patch of visible sky at the upper edge of the Bimini top. Sighting on a single star, maybe the first star that night, she offered a prayer that sleep would hold her captive until morning's light, and when she awoke, for her to be in her own bed, safe from this terrifying nightmare. This might have been a more than improbable prayer, but with all she had suffered, she figured it was the least owed her. Spent from the challenges of a very long physical and emotional day, she closed her eyes and slept.

A single white cloud high overhead lingered above a filled swimming pool set atop a rippled sand dune somewhere in the Sahara Desert. Joan sat poolside on a beach chair within a triangle of shade cast by *Atmosphere's* repurposed mainsail set on three sturdy poles. She wore a bleached white Bikini and sipped ice-cold coconut water from a crystal glass. Gathered within a rear portico clipped to one end of the pool area were a half dozen white-suited waiters, looking every bit like Chippendale dancers, each holding a tray of oranges and glass pitchers overflowing with fresh coconut water.

Joan tapped her finger on the rim of her empty glass, nodding to the staff for a refill, and like soldiers on parade, the waiters filed from the restaurant. Overhead, the lone cloud darkened and released a stream of diesel fuel that quickly covered the water's surface to the pool's brim.

A wind stirred, swirling together the water and golden fuel and turning the blended liquids into desert sand as if by alchemy. The eatery's entire staff vanished, replaced by a leafy tree adorned with breadfruit dripping nectar. A bird sang within the massive tree's branches, a siren's song beckoning Joan from her shaded chair.

CHAPTER ELEVEN

Musty dampness tainted with the stench of diesel fuel wafted through *Atmosphere's* companionway, pulling Joan from her dream, back to reality and a new day. The poignant smell of the fumes of the vile mixture from below deck had kept biting insects at bay during the night, but the precious little coconut water she had consumed the evening before had not been enough to slake a thirst she had lived with for too long. Aching joints and a persistent headache etched her features.

Joan recalled waking during the night when high tide had inundated her makeshift bed and soaked her left shoulder and side. Too tired and weak to rearrange her bedding, she had shifted as far forward on the crumbled sail as she could and let sleep return her to a refuge of intermittent dreams that had since faded from memory.

Joan extracted herself from her still damp bed and slipped from the boat's stern quarter into ankle deep water. She waded ashore under scattered cumulus clouds tinted dawn red and drifting west as if on a slow migration across a blue savannah. The pastel sunlight caught the island's rustling tree tops with its roseate hue, bringing definition to individual trees, a reminder that she had yet to discover all of the island's resources.

Squinting to see the island's upper end and the sea's light chop beyond, Joan perceived no sign of boating activity, no sign of possible rescue, only sea and clouds.

In the opposing direction, between the boat and the island's lower end, Joan spied one of *Atmosphere's* cockpit cushions lost overboard during the boat's knockdown. The flotsam had been deposited along the high tide mark two hundred feet from where she stood. Along with the cushion was what appeared to be one of her lost oranges.

Joan lurched down the beach to the cushion and snatched up her unexpected meal. The outer layer of the orange's rind was mushy from extended contact with seawater but still held a citrusy, sweet smell that galvanized her hunger.

Hurriedly rinsing sand from the fruit at the water's edge, Joan dug her fingernails into the squishy peel and tore at the flesh inside with no attempt at her father's more meticulous technique. In excited anticipation, she brought the partially denuded orange to her mouth like an apple and bit the fruit's exposed flesh.

Every food Joan had ever eaten, every flavored drink she had ever consumed failed miserably in comparison to the orange's mouth tingling, almost orgasmic acidic sweetness. She swallowed the liquidy wad, seeds and all and reveled as the mouthful of nourishment traced down her esophagus, for this source of moisture and nutrition included bulk that let her know she was consuming something substantial. She devoured the orange and tossed away the tattered remains.

The spike of the orange's succulent flavor and boost from its sugary juice swelled Joan's morale and overwhelmed her with an urgency that above all else, she had to find her other precious oranges before the tide stole them from her or the sun and saltwater turned them to sludge. Tracking down another chunk of scabrous coral while scouting the remainder of an island she felt certain was uninhabited could wait. Her oranges couldn't.

Joan tromped down the beach just above an incoming tide. Her hungry eyes swept the beach with desire driven anticipation, as if an entire bushel basket of juice-dripping fruit was somewhere on the beach. But the cockpit cushion was the only other offering the tide had brought her.

Joan didn't have the strength and stamina to search the entire beach, even for oranges. The bright ball of sun had topped the trees, and cooler morning temperatures retreated from muggy air, threatening to steal what moisture she had consumed. Refusing to accept her oranges were lost to the sea, she swept her gaze over the near side of the lagoon in the same pattern she had searched for Yao. In her mind's eye, she could see her oranges rafted together on rippled water kicked up by a freshening northerly sweeping down from over the trees.

Beyond where the shallows dropped off into darker water, Joan's eyes latched onto olive-drab debris floating fifty yards out from the beach. To her amazed relief it was the canteen, and at that moment, suffering as she was from cognitive impairment due to insufficient water and nutrition, she was struck with an overpowering conviction that, like her oranges, she had to forsake what else may be on the island for what was a certainty, water in the canteen.

For any chance at retrieving the canteen, Joan had to act quickly The eight knot breeze was contrary to the incoming tide, nudging the water bottle even farther out into the lagoon.

Joan returned to her foundered boat and donned the life jacket. She waded to waist-deep water where the white sand bottom was dotted with shadowy shapes of coral heads, yellow and blue sea fans and brown sea cucumbers. A few more steps from where she stood, the bottom's gradual slope abruptly fell away into another world, giving the lagoon the ominous air of hiding more than just its depth.

Niggling intuition whispered Joan's folly of ignoring the island's resources to swim in unknown waters with a barely healed wound, all for a single quaff of drinkable water. But she stubbornly clung to her steadfast belief that her only salvation was in that canteen.

Joan further rationalized that because the atoll appeared to have limited access through a single entrance, ocean predators would find the bounty of the open sea more enticing. Whether any of this was true, Joan didn't know, but in her state of mind, it did not take much to convince herself the benefit of retrieving the canteen far outweighed the risk.

Time was putting distance between Joan and the reason for this mission. Fear would be her companion on this swim, but surely her boldness would garner pity from providence and safely deliver her back to the beach with her all important swallow of water.

Armed with nothing more than blind determination, Joan lowered her torso into the water, pushed off the bottom and set into a steady breaststroke. Her vantage point at water level made the lagoon appear as if she had either shrunk in size or the atoll had doubled its dimensions. To her right, the line of the scraggly reef's exposed coral was a thin brown, watery swatch broken five hundred feet beyond the canteen by the entrance gap. On the atoll's opposing side, the sandbar and wooded islets appeared as a trio of sea serpents connected by thin white lines of sand.

Fear tightened Joan's chest when she crossed the confluence where the sandy bottom fell away into the murky depths. The image of the shark that had nearly taken her leg flashed in her mind, making her internal organs feel as if they had turned to clay. Her pace slowed as fear rose. She teetered on aborting this mission and returning ashore, but her very real need for fluid had played its trump card, and this deal was sealed. She sighted on the bobbing canteen and picked up her tempo.

Every breaststroke farther from the shore, every ragged breath carried a skin-crawling reality. What she wanted to be true about the atoll's lagoon may not be so, and one of the sea's apex predators could very likely own this hood.

The thought of being devoured was, in a bizarre way, acceptable to Joan, an end to her unrelenting suffering, but she had stepped aboard *Atmosphere* for a specific reason, and she was intent on seeing this through.

The northerly had kicked up, turning ripples into confusing chop that stymied Joan's low-set view. She halted to re-sight on the canteen. The water bottle was farther from her now than when she had set out. She shot a nervous glance over her shoulder to the drop off three hundred feet behind her. The tenuous grip she had had on her resolve slipped a notch as reality whispered she was losing this race. The wind and waves had staked their claim and she was going no further.

And then, the page turned.

An indistinct flash of movement underwater caught in Joan's peripheral vision snapped her head around. Her heart raced. All of her rationalizing was swept away in a whirlwind of fear. She became as still as death, wishing herself invisible to the eyes she knew were upon her.

The dark, nebulous shape passed ten feet below Joan, creating a pressure wave and plunging her into absolute terror that thickened into panic. With a surge of strength that surprised her, she turned and tore at the water toward the shore. If she could have walked on water, she would have run.

WHOOSH!

Joan's head spun in dizzying fright and she recoiled as the black behemoth, looking every bit the size of a house, rocketed from the water mere yards in front of her. Flapping its ten foot wing span in mock flight, the black and white manta ray belly-flopped the water in a monumental splash and dived. A second manta, equally as large, zoomed past Joan in playful pursuit of its mate. The dark shapes of the twin rays veered across the lagoon and angled into the dark depths.

Any solace Joan should have found knowing these benign creatures were of no threat wilted with the reality that if the rays would enter the atoll, some other creature of size and far more deadly might also have joined them.

Joan locked her horror-struck eyes onto the green wall of jungle at the top of the beach and swam. Her skin crawled with the rising feeling that as she drew closer to the shallows, whatever monster was tracking her from below would become more compelled to strike before its intended meal escaped.

Joan crossed the sheer drop-off where fathoms changed to feet, still not out of danger but relieved she could at least see bottom. Exhausted from raging fear and exertion, she was too used up to sprint the final distance to shore. A jittery glance over her shoulder confirmed no dorsal fin was rushing toward her, but that was little comfort for she was still in water deep enough for attack.

Swinging her head toward the beach in her last struggle for shore, Joan's eyes welded onto a single point at the island's lower end. Where the jungle greenery fell away to beach were symmetrical lines of a man-made structure. The rectangular, brown and gray building looked no larger than a shed but with a pinch of luck, could be a shack in which island inhabitants lived. Whatever the case, the building proved there was more human activity on this island than a rotting lean-to. For the first time in what felt like years, her forever ordeal seemed finally at an end.

Joan found her footing and stumbled from the water onto the beach with a release of angst that fell away like a ship's anchor. Not stopping to acknowledge her weariness, she put one foot in front of the other, focused on any sign of movement at the island's beckoning structure.

CHAPTER TWELVE

The eight foot by twelve foot windowless shanty was not a residence but a crudely built wood-planked shed with a single-pitched roof of rust-streaked sheetmetal and a low-set door fitted with a hasp and padlock too rusted to close. The structure faced an overturned, ten-foot fiberglass skiff chained to a scarred coconut tree. Between shed and the rolling sea, fishing nets shrouded wind-stunted bushes.

Joan slung aside the padlock and folded back the tarnished hasp, driven by the thought that within these walls could be any number of tools suitable for cracking into coconuts. There could also be water and food. She swung open the door and lurched into the shadows, the embodiment of living death.

A grimy barrel of diesel fuel fitted with a dirt-caked hand-pump was front and center on the hard-packed, sand floor. To her right, casting nets draped two wooden sawhorses along a wall of rough-cut wooden shelves stacked with an assortment of hand-tools, sundry engine parts, jars of screws, nuts and bolts, and coils of ropes and wire.

On the floor along the opposing wall were seven wooden fruit crates heaped with a random collection of scrap metal; corroded turnbuckles, the lower half of an outboard motor, a three-bladed bronze propeller missing a fluke and sundry steel plates and aluminum piping.

Fishing buoys hung from ceiling rafters over an identical skiff to the vessel chained to the tree outside, but this second boat looked new and appeared to have never been pressed into service.

Behind the newer boat was a well-worn, aluminum-framed patio chair and a cobbled-together wooden table with three bottles of Perrier water lined up on top.

Joan tripped on her own feet and nearly went down in her rush for the table. She snatched up the closest bottle and twisting off its already loose cap, she chugged.

A shock jolted Joan's system. Her eyes clinched and her face twisted in horrid surprise. She coughed out what liquid remained in her mouth and doubled-over. She retched. The bottle slipped from her hand and she vomited kerosene and bile.

Clinging to the chair with one hand like a drunk trying to stay erect, Joan wiped her mouth with the back of her shaky hand. Her entire body trembled. She drew in short, ragged breaths, as if she had been cast into *Atmosphere's* fume-filled belly. She staggered through the shed and broke out into the bright sunlight.

Fighting a dizzying whirl in her head, she careened down the beach toward the lagoon. She had to cleanse the acrid liquid from her mouth, but the effort was too much for her. She collapsed onto the sand no more than ten steps from where the sandbar sprouted from the island.

Joan's mind swirled in some alternate state of being, conjuring up an image of her gazing down on her prone body laid out on the sand like a corpse on a morgue table.

In her out-of-body experience, a dry wind swept across the island, withering jungle foliage as if scorched by fire and shrinking her pallid gray skin tight over her body. Her nose shriveled into a mound of dried flesh and her closed mouth constricted into a mummified frown. The toes of her bare feet curled like fists and her fingers twisted, bony hard. Time stopped.

A shadow crept over Joan's remains as if a single cloud in the clear sky had blotted out the sun. Her extended self tumbled downward like a fallen angel. Her body gasped air. Opening her eyes to slits, she took in a tattered, wide-brimmed hat atop a deeply tanned, narrow face hovering over her.

"Miss, you can hear me, yes?" the phantom image was saying. "Can you walk?"

"Water," Joan's dry, cracked lips mimed.

Strong, supporting arms lifted Joan to her feet letting her know this was no apparition. Rescue had arrived. She was half-walked, half-carried to a wooden skiff beached on the ocean side of the island's point where the sandbar originated. She managed to get a foot over the small boat's gunnel and was suddenly sitting on a dried fishing net, her back against the boat's middle seat, facing astern. The voice spoke again.

"Miss, drink this."

Her savior was a lean man with weathered features that made him look older than his sixty-five years. He uncapped a half gallon "Hello Kitty" water jug and tilted it to her lips.

Joan's reaction was swift. She grabbed the jug with both hands. She could not drink fast enough.

The man firmly pulled the jug from Joan's grip, spilling her next intended swallow onto her lap. She wretched and spewed up what just went down.

Slipping out a blood-red, plastic coffee cup from a frazzled athletic bag at Joan's feet, the man poured water from the jug into the smaller container. He pressed the filled cup into Joan's hands. "Miss, you must sip or it will come up again," he instructed.

Joan nested the cup in both hands as if it contained a precious secret and took in a teaspoon-size sip. Overwhelmed by what marked the turning point of her ordeal, her head drooped and she sobbed heartfelt relief, a deep-throated sound, like a languid cough. "Thank you," she managed.

"My name is Atea," the man said. He slipped a thin strip of beef jerky from a cloth pouch in the athletic bag. "Here, eat this," he said. "Eat slowly." He inserted the dried meat between her lips.

Joan let the piece of jerky linger in her mouth, overwhelmed by its rush of salty, almost sweet flavor. She chewed in a slow, steady rhythm, turning her face up to the blue sky and breathing in refreshing reality. Her ordeal was over. Though she was too spent to cheer, she was able to force her cracked lips into the hint of a smile, the first in days. Against the worst the gods had thrown at her, perseverance had ultimately brought her through. She had indeed survived.

Atea asked Joan her name and when she replied, he queried if anyone else had been with her.

Joan sipped from the cup again, allowing the swig of water to carry the dollop of chewed meat down her throat. "No," she said, barely audible.

Lolling back against the boat's seat, Joan's eyes closed, and she let her mind drift back to a time that now seemed distant, to the path that had brought her to this crossroad and in such a sad condition.

଼ଵ

The outboard motor slowed, a drop in pitch mimicking Joan's own sense of remission of the downward spiral from her fateful decision in New Zealand to all of her suffering from the sea and the weather, made more acute by her own blunders. She pulled her eyes open, vaguely aware of voices from somewhere above her.

Atea cut off the outboard and brought his boat alongside a concrete seawall fringed with barnacles exposed by a low tide. The air was thick with the soured, sulfury smell of dead sea life, old concrete and the musty, chemical odor of diesel exhaust. Joan didn't know where she was or how long it had been since her rescue but she was more than ready to get on solid ground and stay there.

"Is that Constable Udui's car?" Atea called to a short, broad figure on the seawall. "I need him over here." Atea handed up his boat's stern line to another helping hand as more activity appeared above. Voices spoke in dialect.

Joan refused to relinquish the red cup, and Atea didn't force the issue. He assisted her onto still wobbly legs and guided her to outstretched hands of two men as weather-worn as himself. She was lifted onto a wide, broad concrete and dirt pier, suddenly free of the sea.

For Joan, the change in her condition seemed surreal. What seemed like only moments before, she had been alone, stranded on an island, on the brink of death and risking her life for what had been barely enough freshwater to wet her throat. Now, as if reborn, she was back in a more structured and forgiving world.

Atea was given a hand up onto the **pier. He** took Joan's arm to steady her, and with assistance, lifted her from the boat. "Joan," he said, waiting until she looked at him. "This is Police Constable Udui." He motioned with his chin to a blocky, athletic Polynesian uniformed in navy blue slacks and short-sleeved, white shirt with a police patch on the right shoulder. The sea blue emblem was gold trimmed with a central embroidered rendition of a gold badge flanked by depictions of sprigs from a breadfruit tree. A silver badge pinned over the officer's heart was opposite his name tag, J. Udui.

Constable Joshua Udui gently took Joan's other arm. He was accompanied by Andre Santiago, a Polynesian man with a round face. Andre was the marina's manager, a man with light brown skin and an overhanging gut. His shoulder-length black hair made him look taller than his six foot frame. He wore blue coveralls over a gray shirt.

The marina he managed was comprised of the two hundred fifty foot squared pier built with a concrete retainer wall and filled in with hard-packed gravel and dirt. Perimeter service buildings lined three sides of the structure, while fishing skiffs and scarred trawlers docked along the platform's outer periphery added their own fragrances to the tangy perfume of the sea. At the platform's far end with a grand view of the comings and goings was Andre's office, a white, board and baton, single story building with a shiny-new metal roof. A one lane causeway constructed of compacted dirt and crushed coral laid atop rip-rap connected the pier to the only road through the small fishing village of Ollei.

The police constable looked Joan over. Her face was smeared with hardship and topped with matted, blonde hair, her skin wind-reddened and sun-darkened and her body drawn tight by dehydration. She looked ancient.

"Joan, have a seat in my Jeep," the police constable said. "Can you do that?"

Joan gave a faint nod and took an uncertain step. Standing had intensified her throbbing head.

Atea and Constable Udui baby-stepped Joan the short distance to the officer's white Toyota Land Cruiser. Andre followed.

"Is your leg injured?" Udui asked Joan of her limping gait.

"Yes," Joan replied, too spent to offer details.

The men placed Joan on the Toyota's front passenger seat. Atea gently slipped his hat from her head. She seemed to find comfort in holding onto his now-empty water cup and he silently bequeathed it to her.

"What happened to her?" the constable asked Atea.

The fisherman explained how he had been going to his fishing shed on Kayangel Island to pick up a fishing net when he had spied a sailboat grounded on the island's beach and Joan unconscious near his shed. He informed the constable that Joan had indicated she had been the only person on the sailboat but that he had not taken the time to check her statement due to her own desperate condition.

Udui turned to Joan. She looked pathetically fragile. "Joan, I'm taking you to a clinic but I need you to think. Was anyone else with you on the boat, on the sailboat?"

"The captain, we have to find him," Joan mumbled.

"Did the captain leave you on the island?" Udui was confused. If the boat's captain could get off the island, then why would he not have taken his crew, unless, of course, there were more than two people and he had to leave someone behind. But why her, in her condition?

"He fell overboard," Joan added in an almost whisper.

The three men were shocked.

"Joan, where did he fall overboard?" Udui pressed to get the full story.

"I couldn't find him." Her voice trailed away like a lost cause.

"Try to remember," Udui said in a slow and deliberate voice. "The captain's life is at stake."

Regret twisted Joan's face. Even though she had placed herself in a perilous situation that had jeopardized her own survival, it seemed to her in retrospect that if she had resumed her search grid for that single hour before her fuel ran out, Yao would be with her now. It might have been a long shot but a shot it had been.

"Did he go missing near here, near Palau?" Udui asked.

"This is Yap Island," Joan muttered correction.

The men were even more baffled.

"I need to get her to the clinic," the constable told Atea and Andre. "She's not making any sense in her condition."

He hurried around the jeep and clambered in next to Joan. Medical care would help to bring clarity to Joan's memory. In the meantime, with a reported man-overboard and lack of details thereof, he would make the grounded boat a crime scene. He lowered his window to speak to Andre. "I need you to arrange transportation for Domingo, to Kayangel."

"Makoa can take him," the marina manager said.

Udui pulled away. As he drove across the pier toward the causeway, he thumbed his radio's mike. "Domingo, I need you to come to the marina."

"What's up, boss?" Deputy Domingo Vegas transmitted in his deep voice.

"There's a sailboat grounded on Kayangel," Udui told his deputy. "I'm taking the lady who was onboard to the clinic. Andre is arranging Makoa to transport you to the island."

"What do you want me to do when I'm out there?"

"It's possible there was at least one other person on board the sailboat. Contact Waipuna. He is to follow you to Kayangel. Get on the sailboat and see if there's anyone still on board. If not, you and Waipuna are to search the island for anyone from the boat. Waipuna is to stay overnight to secure the site. Treat it as a crime scene. No one except you is to go near that sailboat."

Waipuna Sikyang operated the village's only mechanic shop located at the top of the community's dirt road's gradual grade where it took a dog-leg to the right and continued its winding path past Badrulchau stone monoliths, Ngarchelong Community Clinic near the village of Mengellang and on to Koror, Palau's capital city, forty miles south. Waipuna was deputized and on permanent call.

"Are you coming to Kayangel?" Domingo asked.

"Yes, after I get more information from the woman," Udui told Domingo. "I don't know how long that will take. She needs medical attention. In the meantime, get what information you can, including anyone else associated with the sailboat, and get back here."

Ollei police department's five watt, handheld radios were not powerful enough to reach the twenty-five miles from Kayangel Island to the police station's four hundred megahertz transmitting and receiving system, and Udui wanted important details about the sailboat as quickly as possible.

"Anything else you want me to do?"

"That's all for now."

"Ten-four."

Udui ended the transmission as he navigated potholes on the causeway, crossing onto the sloping, graded road through the fishing village. The compact dirt track was as rutted with potholes and subsidence as the causeway and lined on both sides with a scattering of cinder block and wooden houses with corrugated metal roofs, guttering to concrete cisterns and Louvre windows. Chickens scratched and pecked among banana, breadfruit and coconut trees. The front of one home had been converted into a mom and pop store selling general groceries and beer. Motorcycles buzzed past the Land Cruiser and pedestrians walked roadside, carrying supplies purchased at a local fresh market.

"Joan," Udui said with urgency, "it's important that you tell me everything you can remember about what happened to the captain."

Joan took a deep breath as if to speak but remained silent.

"The captain disappeared near Yap?" Udui asked, figuring yes and no questions would net him more timely information.

"Yes."

"That's over two hundred miles northeast of here. How long ago did he go missing?"

Udui passed Ollei's only petrol station, an open-sided shed stacked with red drums of diesel fuel and a manual fuel pump hung from the structure's rafters. Slowing, he swung his vehicle off the road, stopping behind a white Dodge Dart parked on a roadside strip of sand dotted with crabgrass. Joan blinked her eyes and raised her brow as if awakening from a long sleep. Through her side window she took in a gray, double-wide trailer with a sign posted above its front door: "Clinic."

Udui stalled getting out of his vehicle. He had not finished this part of his questioning.

"I need to know when the captain was lost," he pressed. He waited and when an answer was still not forthcoming, whether she was no longer being cooperative or, more likely, just couldn't remember, he slipped from his vehicle. He trundled to the passenger door where he helped Joan onto uncertain legs. She clung to his arm with one hand and held the empty cup to her chest with the other as if the drinking vessel contained her soul.

Keeping in step with her invalid's gait, the constable walked Joan across the clinic's sand and grass front yard to steps to the double-wide's narrow porch. Passers-by on the roadside stared at Joan and her desperate appearance.

The clinic's front door opened and a hefty sixty-six year old man with subtle Asian features descended the front steps to help the constable with his charge. The man had graying hair and was missing his left eye, something he did not feel compelled to cover-up.

"What do you have here?" he asked the lawman, taking Joan's left arm under her shoulder.

"Joan, this is Doctor Reklai," Udui said and to the doctor, "Her sailboat ran aground on Kayangel."

Joan was half carried up the porch steps and into Ollei's only clinic, established to tend to minor injuries and stabilization of more serious trauma before transportation to Ngarchelong Community Clinic, three miles south. The front half of the double-wide was divided between an examination room with a unisex bathroom on the right and an office area to the left. The doctor's residence was in the back half of the building.

The clinic's receptionist, Iolani Tellei, was already on her feet when Joan was brought in. Iolani had seen the constable's arrival through a front window of the clinic and had alerted Dr. Reklai of their obvious next patient. Iolani was a big-boned woman with a pleasant face and smooth, honey skin. Her black hair was tied back into a ponytail, and she was garbed in a white blouse and flower-pattern sarong. She wore no shoes and had a hibiscus flower over her right ear, looking every bit like she had been cast for a part in a South Pacific movie with a high dollar budget.

From the doctor's residence stepped a tall, thin woman with brown hair and European features. She wore a white lab smock over a sky blue blouse and blue-printed sarong.

"Oh my, let's get her seated," the woman blurted in a Dutch-accented voice upon beholding Joan. She deftly unfolded a wheelchair set along the clinic's back wall and rolled it to Joan.

"Her name is, Joan," Udui said for the woman's benefit.

Joan was seated.

"Joan, this is Christina, Doctor Reklai's wife and nurse," Udui said.

Joan didn't care who she was meeting and certainly wasn't remembering names. All she wanted was a tall glass of cold water and to lie down and sleep.

"How long was she on Kayangel?" the doctor asked the constable of Joan.

"At this point," Udui replied, "all I know is that she was found on Kayangel in this condition. I still haven't gotten much information from her."

"She has had some water?" the doctor asked Udui, motioning to the red cup Joan held.

"I believe so," Udui replied, "but I don't know how much. Atea was the one who found her and brought her in." He turned to Joan. "Joan, I need you to answer a few more questions."

Dr. Reklai took hold of the wheelchair's hand grips, his own statement to the lawman that questions would have to wait. "I need to check her vitals," he explained to Udui. He rolled Joan into the examination room accompanied by Christina.

Udui followed, undeterred. "Joan, do you have any ID with you?" he asked.

"Everything is on the boat," came the reply.

"When was the captain lost overboard," Udui asked with a side glance at the doctor that her statement was critical.

Joan rested her eyes on Udui's with a far away look. The answer was too slow in coming.

"I need you to remember," Udui stressed. "How long ago was the captain lost at sea?"

Joan rolled through flashes of memory that seemed more like a trailer to some upcoming disaster movie than anything she herself had lived through, five days out of Guam, two days spent searching for Yao, a day, or was it two, with a fouled propeller and then no wind, two days to reach an island she now knew was named, Kayangel, and another day before rescue.

"I think five, maybe six days," came Joan's feeble answer.

Udui was astounded. "A life raft?" he asked. "Is the captain in a life raft?"

"The life raft is on the boat," Joan said. "He always wore a life jacket."

Udui shook his head with a defeated frown and yielded to the doctor. If what Joan had said was true, the only way the captain could have survived was if he had been picked up by a passing boat or ship or had fallen overboard close enough to land to where he was able to reach shore. Udui needed more clarification but with what he knew now, the urgency to find the captain was no longer there.

Like the constable, Dr. Reklai was fully aware unless the captain they were speaking of had somehow been rescued shortly after falling overboard, there was no chance he was still alive after a week adrift in the sea in only a life jacket.

The doctor brought his thoughts back to his patient. He noted her discolored, sunken eyes and weak, rapid pulse. He lifted the neckline of her T-shirt to access under the garment's soiled exterior. A check with the stethoscope did not improve his opinion of her condition. "How do you feel? Any pain?"

"A headache."

"Are you on any medication?"

"No."

"Open your mouth, please."

Dr. Reklai inspected her dry mucous membranes, noting a white, bacterial coating on her tongue giving her breath a sharp, musty odor. The skin on her arms was dry and 'tented' when lightly pinched. He checked her blood pressure. "When was the last time you urinated?" he asked.

Joan paused, searching her fuzzy memory again. "Yesterday, I think." Just walking to the clinic had taken a lot from her.

"Do you have to urinate now?"

"No."

Dr. Reklai gently tugged on the mug and Joan let it slip from her grip.

"How much water have you had in the last twenty-four hours?" he asked.

Joan had lost track of time. "Yesterday, a coconut." She was clearly not certain. "And today an orange." Her eyes drifted to Atea's mug. "Maybe one. Today."

The kerosene she drank from the Perrier water bottle had slipped her mind, but it had not stayed down anyway.

"You are severely dehydrated," the doctor stated the obvious. Stepping to a cabinet, he pulled a sachet from a box in a side cupboard, filled a clean glass with water from a top-loading water dispenser and mixed in the packet's powdered contents. He stirred the mixture, turning the liquid the color of a morning sun.

"This is an electrolyte," Reklai told Joan as he brought her the beverage. "Drink it slowly. We don't want it coming up."

Joan's first sip was an explosion of mixed fruit flavor, as vivid tasting as her orange, and with the salty sweetness of the beef jerky, reawakening a body craving sustenance. She slurped down the remaining mixture in manageable sips.

The doctor took the empty glass from Joan. "I would like to start an IV, an electrolyte with glucose," he said. He looked into her dull eyes. "Is that all right with you?"

Joan nodded, caring not what the doctor did as along as it improved her condition.

Christina rolled a stainless steel service tray alongside Joan's wheelchair. On the portable table was a stainless steel bowl of warm water, a bottle of Dettol disinfectant soap and a white towel. Protruding from the front pocket of the nurse's smock was a packaged butterfly needle with its transparent tubing and connector.

Christina washed Joan's right arm from armpit to finger tips. What looked like Joan's Polynesian complexion darkened the water in the bowl, leaving her arm with a lighter, natural tan.

As Christina dried Joan's arm, Udui spoke to Dr. Reklai in a subdued voice. "There are still unanswered questions about the missing captain," the constable said. "For now, I need you to keep her here or at the police station."

"She needs to be transported to Mengellang after this IV for blood work and further tests." Dr. Reklai was referring to Ngarchelong Community Clinic.

"You can't treat her here?"

Dr. Reklai's brow rose. Udui obviously had reason to keep her on the shortest of leashes.

"I'll need to see how she responds to the IV," the doctor said. "We can draw blood and send it off for analysis."

Dr. Reklai said to Joan, "I would like to get blood work done on you. Is that all right?"

"Yes," Joan said, more relaxed from the recharging effects of the electrolyte drink.

"What is your full name," Christina asked.

"Joan Mackland."

"Age?"

"Twenty-three."

Christina jotted the information onto a label before peeling off the backing and pressing the adhesive paper onto a blood collection tube.

Returning to Joan's cleaned arm, Christina was unable to find a suitably pronounced vein due to her patient's dehydration. She applied a tourniquet to Joan's upper arm, just above the elbow, and had her patient make a tight fist. Still unable to find an acceptable vein, she located a barely distended blood vessel below Joan's wrist, on top of her hand. Swabbing the area with alcohol, the butterfly needle was prepared and with an experienced touch, Christina inserted it into the vein and secured the hypodermic with tape. Confirming blood flow, she drew blood into the pre-labeled specimen tube and placed the filled tube into a blood transportation bag.

Iolani was quick to take the non-absorbent packet to her desk where she lifted her phone's handset and called a local man named Kedeb. He would transport the sample to the community clinic.

Kedeb was one of only six residents of Ollei's population of one hundred who owned an automobile which he used as a local taxi as well as providing Ollei Clinic with services for collection and delivery of supplies, equipment and bio samples. Transportation of trauma patients was by Ngarchelong Community Clinic's ambulance.

Christina wheeled Joan to the back wall of the examination room where Dr. Reklai had staged an IV pole and bag behind a portable curtain for privacy.

"Once your vital signs improve," Christina told Joan, "I'll help you wash up."

"How long will the IV take?" Udui asked the nurse.

"About an hour," Christina replied. She attached the bag's flow control tube to the butterfly needle and started the drip.

Udui brought in a chair from the reception area and took a seat next to Joan. "Joan, do you know the boat's coordinates when the captain was lost?" the constable asked.

Joan inhaled and released a ragged breath, wanting a respite from all of this questioning, if only for a moment. She shook her head. "There was a storm," she said, finally understanding what information she had was of little value in finding Yao after so much time. "I was in the V-berth, seasick."

"You said the captain was wearing a life jacket. How do you know that if you were below in your cabin when he went overboard?"

"He always wore a life jacket and harness when he went on deck." She drew a tight frown. "Is there any chance of finding him alive?" Her voice was edged with a trace of hope that by the slimmest of margins Yao could still be alive.

Udui's blank face showed no hope. "There's a lot of ocean out there, five, six days in the water, the current …"

"I did everything I could." Joan's voice caught in her throat. They all had to understand the effort she had made to find him.

Deputy Vegas' voice broke over Udui's belt-hung radio. The deputy's voice was wrapped in the steady vibrating whir of an outboard motor at full throttle.

"Hold on," the constable radioed his deputy. He stood and stepped outside onto the clinic's front porch where he wouldn't disturb Christina's work but more importantly, ensuring whatever information Domingo had recovered on the island would not prejudice Joan's interrogation. "Go ahead," he transmitted.

"That sailboat is a big one, forty feet," the deputy reported.

"Is it a local boat?" Udui asked.

"Registered in Guam."

"Ruth, do you copy?" Udui radioed.

"Go ahead, Domingo," Ruth replied, "what is the registration number?" Ruth Vegas was the police dispatcher and Deputy Domingo Vegas' wife.

"Golf, Uniform, seven, five, four, seven, Lima, Echo."

Ruth repeated the number.

"Ten-four."

"I'll check with the port authority in Koror," Ruth radioed, "and see if the boat already passed Palau clearance."

"Domingo, where are you?" Udui asked.

"Just passing Konlei Point," the deputy replied. He was on his return trip to Ollei.

"Did you find anyone else?"

"No sir," Domingo replied, "no one on the sailboat. Tekuu was just arriving when I got there." Domingo was referring to the trawler, *Tekuu*, that haled from Ollei. "Esebei loaned me his Filipino crew to help speed up the search. Waipuna is there too. He brought Sifa. They are still searching. I headed back as soon as I could. If there is anyone else on the island, they will find them."

"Did you get on board the sailboat?"

"Yes sir, but only in the cockpit. The boat's interior is flooded with diesel and water. There was no way of going inside, but from what I could see through the companionway, two tanks under the floor are open. No indication of why but that's likely where the diesel came from."

Udui ran a hand over his chin. "Is anyone watching the boat now?"

"Sifa is. Everyone there has been instructed it's a crime scene."

"Good work," Udui said. "Any damage to the boat's hull? Can we re-float it?"

"I didn't see any holes in the hull, but the side facing up, the port side, is damaged above the waterline, some type of collision that took the boat's name clean off. But it should float."

"How high up on the beach is it?"

"It's laying in shallow water," Domingo reported. "I guess at high tide it can be pulled into deep water. There's an easterly, so not much wave action."

The outboard slowed, signaling Makoa and Domingo had arrived at the marina.

"Wait for me at Andre's office," Udui ordered. "I need more information from our lady, and then you and I are going to Kayangel."

"What about the DMLE?" Domingo asked of Palau's Division of Marine Law Enforcement.

"I'll contact them after I have a look at the boat, and the search for other crew is completed," Udui told his deputy.

Three days ago Udui had heard from a colleague in Koror that the DMLE had posted a vacancy for a detective position due to a retirement from the department, and the constable had his application completed and ready to deliver. He figured with this latest development on Kayangel

Island, recording evidence that could be lost before DMLE investigators could arrive would catch a decision-maker's attention and give him a leg-up in filling the open position.

Udui's transmission with Domingo ended.

A 1978, light green Daihatsu Hijet flatbed with a canvas cover parked behind Udui's Land Cruiser. Kedeb stepped out. He was short and skinny, early fifties, with a distinct limp from one leg two inches shorter than the other. He wore black-rim glasses and a white bucket hat with a frayed brim atop a bald head.

Udui hung his police radio on his belt and nodded greeting to Kedeb as the courier ascended the steps to the clinic's front porch. The two men stepped inside.

With quick salutation, Iolani handed Kedeb the bagged blood sample. "The doctor already phoned the lab," she told him, "so they know this is to be rushed but you remind them."

Kedeb was a man of few words. He flashed a wave to Dr. Reklai through the open examination room door and hustled on his way.

Udui returned to his seat facing Joan. She was dozing, the harsh conditions she had lived through still lingered on her features.

"Joan," Udui said softly. When she failed to respond, he touched her hand.

Joan's eyes drifted open. The redness of their sclera had faded to a light pink.

"Joan, I'm going out to your sailboat for an inspection. I need a little more information from you."

"Okay," Joan said, still drained.

Udui leaned closer so she would hear every word and said with slow clarity, "I need you to confirm that you and the captain were the only two people on the boat."

Joan gave a slight nod to this important point in the officer's fact finding mission. "Yes. Only Yao and me."

"And he fell overboard while you were sleeping."

"I was seasick," Joan replied. She looked up, wishing the ceiling above her was that in her own apartment.

"Look at me," Udui stated, getting to the crux of his questioning and feeling pressed for time.

Joan brought her eyes down and focused on the constable's stern face.

Udui spoke clear and deliberate. "Joan, I need to know if there is anything on board the sailboat that I should know about. Any contraband."

"Contraband?" Joan said, not fully understanding what his meaning of contraband was.

"Is there anything that could be considered illegal. Drugs maybe? Firearms?" As a law officer, he was aware of the recent rise on western pacific islands of internationally trafficked marijuana, cocaine and heroine, and with the tale Ms. Mackland was telling, he was approaching his investigation with due suspicion.

"No," she said almost in a whisper, still not catching the seriousness of this line of questioning.

She clinched her eyes. "I need something to eat." The glucose in the saline drip had quelled the sharper pain of her hunger but her stomach still felt like a tight knot in her belly that only solid food could alleviate.

Dr. Reklai appeared next to Joan, an indication the constable would have to yield once again.

"She needs rest," the doctor confirmed to Udui.

Feeling pressure lifted from her shoulders at a pause in further inquiry, Joan drifted back into an exhausted rest.

Udui stood. "I'm going out to Kayangel," he told the doctor. "If you decide to transfer her to Mengellang, let Ruth know."

Even in Joan's current condition, Udui was not taking any chances that what he had been told was less than the truth, and he was not letting this bird in the hand slip through his fingers. His concern wasn't that she might flee the country if given the chance. Her pockets appeared empty, and she had stated all of her personal items were on the boat which would no doubt include her passport. His apprehension was that if left unattended, she might attempt to slip away after regaining her strength and end up as a guest at the central police station in Koror, which would no doubt snatch from him any chance for a promotion.

"We'll let Ruth know," Reklai said to Udui, "but Christina would be the one to take her, and if you want, Kedeb can stay with her at the clinic." The doctor appreciated the lawman's concerns, but his patient's health came first.

"I prefer Ruth to take her," Udui said of Joan. If Joan had anything further to add to her story, Ruth was deputized and her participation would make anything Joan said an official statement.

"We'll work it out for Ruth to go also," the doctor agreed.

Udui exited Ollei's clinic and walked to his vehicle. "Ruth," he radioed after hoisting himself behind the steering wheel, "you may have to escort our boat lady to the community clinic with Christina. Doctor Reklai will let you know. If you do go, stay with Joan until I get there. Take down anything she tells you."

"I'll alert Sueleb," Ruth replied.

Sueleb was Waipuna's wife and filled in for Ruth when the dispatcher was indisposed.

"I checked with the port authority," Ruth continued, "they have no record of any sailboats from Guam clearing in."

CHAPTER THIRTEEN

Makoa throttled up his boat's two hundred fifty horsepower outboard in oncoming waves as *Tilai*, the marina's twenty-six foot center console, V-hull, passed Konlei Point, the northernmost extremity on Palau's largest island, Babelthuap. To starboard, a fringe reef and mangrove swamp made the point impossible to reach by water. Behind *Tilai* was Ollei village.

Makoa was a sun-darkened, fifty year old man with a round face, portly body and a belly overlapping his Harley Davis belt buckle. His left hand was missing, having been amputated after a trawler accident three years earlier. He now worked as Andre's assistant.

Constable Udui and his deputy sat on the boat's rear bench seat holding their caps from blowing off their heads. Udui glanced at the top of Konlei Point's one hundred twenty foot high, forested hill to the pinnacle of a crumbling, World War Two, Japanese lighthouse visible above the wooded summit. As a young boy, he had visited there while his father had been a conscripted laborer for the Japanese army, assigned to help in the lighthouse's construction, and Udui always liked seeing the site as it reminded him of his father.

They passed Ngerkeklau and Ngerechur islets on calmer water, just north of Konlei Point, and scooted north fifteen miles to the end of Kossol Reef with its riverine tidal cuts and vivid colors of corals, sponges and sea fans.

At the reef's northern end, Makoa held his boat's speed, planing over the choppy seven miles of open water to the dark green swatch that was Kayangel Island and its three companion islets. The trawler *Tekuu* had returned to fishing, signaling the search of the island had been concluded.

Makoa navigated through the atoll's tidal opening under the stark scene of *Atmosphere's* helpless corpse pointing its angled mast toward a distant horizon. Waipuna's lone twenty-foot fiberglass skiff was bow-on the beach with its stern touching the low tide mark. A rope extended from the skiff's bow to a Grapnel anchor imbedded in sand higher up on the beach.

The approach of Makoa's boat prompted Waipuna and Sifa, his eighteen year old son, to slip from their hammocks strung end to end between coconut palms. Sifa picked up breadfruit rind from the sand and tossed it into the bordering foliage as if expecting to be scolded by the lawmen for littering.

Waipuna, the shorter of the two, greeted the arriving trio at the water line. He had light brown skin, bony legs and was missing the pinky finger on his left hand from a childhood run-in with a spinning outboard motor prop. He pulled Makoa's boat's bow onto the beach.

"Sulang," Makoa thanked Waipuna.

The three men stepped from the launch onto the hard, wet sand. Udui retrieved his utility backpack, and the team convened above the high water mark.

"Alii, Sifa," Udui greeted the boy as he joined them. Sifa was a skinny lad, like his father, and had shoulder-length black hair with a complexion a shade darker than the other men.

The team took in the reason for coming to the island.

"Has anyone else been here?" Udui asked Waipuna. Word of the grounding would have spread quickly and there were those, who, if given the chance, would happily rifle the wreckage.

"After Tekuu left," Waipuna said, "Neihana showed up."

Udui shook his head knowingly. Neihana was a local man who had been a fishing guide until his sour personality and laziness ruined his business. He now spent his time selling second hand appliances out of his house, always looking for anything that would bring him fast money. It was no surprise to the constable that Neihana saw the opportunities with an abandoned boat.

"He didn't get on board, did he?" the constable asked.

Waipuna motioned his son to answer.

"No sir," Sifa explained to Udui, "I told him he has to talk to you. He wasn't very happy. He said all he wanted to do was check out what electronics the boat has." Sifa smiled. "When he saw my dad, he left but I'm sure he'll be back."

"I need you and Sifa to stay the night," Udui noted to Waipuna.

"Domingo already told me," Waipuna commented.

Udui extracted a Canon F-1 camera from his backpack. The men stepped closer to *Atmosphere* where the chemical smell of diesel was pronounced. He worked his way around the slanted boat, taking photos of the vessel's exterior from every possible angle. He saw no leaking diesel or tale-tail glistening colors of fuel contamination on the sand or water which indicated the diesel smell came only from inside the boat.

With his exterior photos completed, Udui and then Domingo carefully stepped onto the tilted boat at the aft end of the Bimini top. Udui photographed the canted cockpit from the boat's stern and worked his way forward to *Atmosphere's* open companionway where the diesel smell was nearly overpowering.

Switching on his Maglite, Udui held his breath and leaned in through the companionway to inspect the boat's interior. Due to the vessel's incline, the quantity of liquid was deceptive but he judged two inches of amber-colored diesel topped at least two hundred gallons of water.

The constable swept his light's beam across the swill to one and then the other of the two open hatches in the floor, each exposing the open inspection portals of stainless steel tanks, one, logically being for fuel and the other, probably for fresh water. Why Joan or anyone would have removed and not replaced the tanks' access plates was beyond Udui, but he would flush out that information through his continued interrogation of Joan. He photographed the soggy clutter and moved his light's shaft of illumination forward, spotlighting a backpack in the V-berth, another source of forensic data.

Udui settled his hat higher on his head with a determined look.

"Don't even think about going down there," Domingo stated concerning his boss' clear intentions. "You don't need to be breathing those fumes."

Udui understood the dangers of going below but within that backpack could be revealing evidence, and it was too enticing to not at least make an attempt to get at it. "Can we get through the forward hatch?" he asked.

"That dinghy will have to come off," Domingo pointed out.

Udui stepped back from the foul brew for a breath of unsullied air and spied a dash of blood under the spray dodger, on the companionway's starboard side. The relatively fresh evidence could add credence to Joan's story if it matched her own blood type but would raise further suspicions if it didn't. He photographed the blood smear.

"Let's secure this blood evidence and then see about that front hatch," Udui said.

From Udui's backpack, Domingo retrieved a roll of painter's tape and a Zip-lock baggie containing squares of bakery paper. Following standard procedure, he taped a square of the non-absorbent paper over the blood evidence for preservation until a DMLE detective could take a sample for analysis.

After shielding the blood sample from further exposure, Domingo raised the cockpit locker lid and held it open while Udui photo-recorded its jumbled contents. He removed the cover over the propane tank storage bin, and as the constable snapped a photo of the exposed tank, reflected afternoon sunlight revealed a second object under the pressurized gas tank. Udui handed his camera to Domingo and hefted up and out the empty tank, exposing its twin underneath.

"A spare tank," Udui commented on the elusive tank Joan had searched for but had failed to find. He had his deputy hold the empty tank while he lifted out the spare. Seeing nothing of interest underneath, he returned the two tanks as he had found them and Domingo closed the locker's lid.

Both men retreated to the boat's stern and took in cleansing breaths.

"Have Sifa check the forward hatch to see if it opens," Udui said to his deputy. "If it's dogged down, leave it for the DMLE."

"Sifa," Domingo called to their young helper, "we need you to see if the forward hatch will open."

Sifa clambered onto the boat's sloped foredeck with simian agility. He untied the dinghy's straps and lifted the tender's lower side. Reaching a hand under the dinghy's inflated tube, his body contorted as he wrestled the hatch. "It's latched tight," he told the constables. "Do you want me to see if I can pry it open?"

"Leave it for now," Udui replied. "I need to get back to Ollei." He had been on the island for an hour and was anxious to continue his interrogation. As for the backpack, he would deal with it once the sailboat had been towed to the marina the following afternoon and its flooded interior pumped dry.

Sifa slid down to the starboard gunnel and scampered onto the beach with an athlete's finesse, leaving Domingo figuring he still had a trace of the younger man's dexterity. Moving to the angled cockpit's gunnel, he stepped out over the lifelines, aiming his extended foot for the edge of a rising tide. He let go of the Bimini top, and stepping up and out, his trailing foot snagged the top lifeline and he took a hard fall into shallow water. Pain was immediate.

"Are you all right?" a worried Udui asked.

"It's my ankle," Domingo said through clenched teeth, disgusted with himself for not waiting for assistance. "I think it's sprained."

Much more in tune with his physical limitations than his deputy, Udui waited for Sifa's steadying hand to lower him into ankle deep water as Makoa and Waipuna helped an embarrassed Domingo stand. The deputy grimaced when he put weight onto his injured foot.

Supported by Waipuna and Makoa, Domingo hobbled to Makoa's boat where Sifa, already on board, assisted the injured lawman over the gunnel and onto the back seat.

The three other ambulant men assembled alongside Makoa's skiff.

"Do you and Sifa have everything you need?" Udui asked Waipuna of their supplies for their night vigil.

"For tonight, yes," Waipuna said. "What about tomorrow?"

"Andre is arranging one or two trawlers to be out here, mid-morning," Udui said. "High tide will be about one o'clock."

"We will be fine until then." Waipuna said, giving a wry smile. "At least I will be. The boy misses his girlfriend."

Sifa shied from looking at the constable who chuckled. If Sifa blushed, it wasn't obvious on his dark brown skin.

Udui and Makoa climbed abord *Tilai*. The constable joined his deputy on the back seat. "You get the doctor to look at that ankle," he told his injured deputy.

"I'll put ice on it. It'll be fine," came the stoic reply.

Udui looked down at Domingo's injured ankle and shook his head with a dissenting frown. "It's already swelling," he noted, and in an uncompromising tone added, "Get it X-rayed."

Waipuna and Sifa pushed *Tilai* into deeper water. The launch's owner pulled himself over the side and took his position behind the boat's console. He pressed and held a toggle button. The boat's outboard swiveled, lowering its propeller end into the water to the whir of an electric motor. A silver button next to the toggle cranked the engine. He reversed his boat into deeper water, swinging around the craft's bow as he did so and aimed for the entrance gap. "It may be bumpy on the way back," he told Domingo, "so let me know if I need to slow down."

CHAPTER FOURTEEN

Christina wheeled Joan into the clinic's bathroom with its western-style toilet, wall-mounted mirror over a porcelain sink and walk-in shower with a stainless steel grab bar and shower stool.

"Poor dear," the nurse said as she brushed a spot of dried dirt from Joan's cheek. "I'll help you with your clothes."

"Thank you," Joan replied, feeling on the mend after completing her IV infusion and appreciative of the help. To have caring people assisting her after being alone and in so much want made all she had endured up to that moment seem like a dream, and though she was slowly coming to grips with dark reality, she had no way of knowing the nightmare had not yet reached a conclusion.

Joan placed both hands on the sink and stood with Christina's help, shock widening her eyes at the image staring back at her, a thin, drawn face from a horror show. She touched her peeling lips and ran her fingers through her matted hair. Her throat tightened and her head dropped with remorse as she was overwhelmed by guilt. "It's my fault," she confessed in a whisper, more to herself but loud enough for Christina to hear.

"You don't fret about that now," Christina said, unable to hold back a sympathetic squeeze of Joan's hand. "Let's get those clothes off. You'll feel better after a shower."

Joan drew up as if struck by a thought. "I have to urinate," she said, a relieved air coming over her that her organs were still functioning.

Christina asked Joan to wait and left the bathroom, returning moments later with a specimen cup.

"Start your stream before you collect your sample," the nurse instructed. She set the uncapped cup on the sink and stepped outside to give Joan privacy.

Joan unfastened and slipped off her shorts and panties, leaving on her T-shirt. She sat on the toilet seat, legs spread. Her urine sample was dark yellow, a lighter, less troubling color than her previous discharge on the island, a good sign. She emptied the remainder of her bladder into the toilet, capped the half-filled jar and stood. She would clean herself in the shower.

Christina knocked on the door and peered inside. As she reached in for the capped urine sample, she noticed Joan's injured thigh. "What happened there, on your leg?" she asked and moved in for a closer look. The half-inch wide cut was deeper than a scratch but showed signs of healing.

"I stabbed my leg with a knife." Joan said this as if it were a minor injury.

"The doctor needs to look at this after you clean up," Christina stated.

The double-boost from the IV and urination gave Joan a feeling of nearing the summit in a long mountain race, and taking care of her stab wound and what had become a nuisance pain was low on her list of importance. Even so, getting proper treatment for the cut would be another step closer to the finish line.

Christina helped Joan remove her dirt-streaked T-shirt, exposing the outline of Joan's bra and her natural skin-tone tinted with grime and salt.

"I'll get you some of my daughter's old clothes," Christina told Joan as the nurse started the flow of water from the shower head. She adjusted the water's temperature. "She wears a couple of sizes larger than you but it's only until we can get your things washed."

Joan limped under the stream. She tilted her head forward so the steady spray doused her hair and ran down her back and off her nose and chin. The contrast between deprivation and abundance was striking. She straightened up and let the deluge flow down her front taking with it what seemed half of the salt in the sea.

"Would you like me to wash your back?"

"Yes, thank you," Joan said.

Christina had Joan sit on the shower stool and lathered a wash cloth. She gently scrubbed Joan's back and shoulders before giving her patient the wash cloth and bar of soap. "I'll be outside," she said, moving to the door. "If you need anything, just call. When you are standing, hold onto the grab bar. We don't want you to fall."

Joan washed her face before cleansing the rest of her body. The caked on grime seemed layered like the rings of an ancient oak tree, bespeaking of each calamity that had befallen her over the last week. What she could not wash away was the deep-seated guilt for her being safely quartered and Yao still missing.

"How are you doing?" Christina asked through the door when Joan turned off the shower's water flow.

"All right."

Joan toweled off and stared in the mirror at her clean but still dour features. Her cheek bones were pronounced and eyes puffy from too much sun and seawater. Her contrasting sun-darkened patchwork on her ashen skin tingled all over with a first time newness, as if she had been a mummy unwrapped and revived after two thousand years.

The door swung partially open. Christina slipped inside. "Here are those clothes," she said and displayed a well-worn, white 'Tears For Fears' T-shirt and morning-blue sarong.

The sarong fit Joan. The T-shirt was larger than what she usually wore and draped her emaciated body like a tent.

Christina wheeled Joan from the bathroom. Dr. Reklai and Constable Udui were seated in the waiting area. The law officer had just returned from his trip to Kayangel Island. The two men ended their conversation and stood. Joan's appearance was both inspiring and sad.

Dr. Reklai gave Joan a general look-over and queried about the wound his wife had mentioned.

"I jabbed myself with a knife," Joan explained. She stood and pulled up the right side of her sarong to expose the wound. Dr. Reklai leaned down for close inspection.

"How did you manage this?" he asked of the still livid lesion.

"I stabbed at a shark that attacked me and cut myself instead."

Dr. Reklai gave a confounded expression to Christina and Udui. What Joan had obviously been through was the stuff of a blockbuster, Hollywood movie.

Dr. Reklai learned from Joan the knife that caused the injury was shiny clean and penetrated, she guessed, no deeper than its width. She also revealed her last tetanus vaccination had been four years earlier when she had stepped on a nail at an old home site where she and friends had been camping. The doctor confirmed another tetanus shot would not be needed for this most recent injury. "The wound looks to be healing well," Dr. Reklai commented. He gently probed around the cut. "No swelling that I can see. Any pain?"

"Only when you push on it or I put weight on that leg."

"I would like to start you on a regimen of antibiotics," the doctor said. "Other than that, there is not much I can do. You'll likely have a scar."

"I'd rather not take antibiotics if it's not absolutely necessary," Joan said with hesitation. "I'm not much of a pill taker."

Dr. Reklai understood. "The wound is healing so that should be fine. Take things easy for the next week and if you note a change in redness or the pain doesn't subside, have a doctor look at it."

Doctor Reklai had Joan sit in the wheelchair again and rechecked her blood pressure and pulse. It had been nearly two hours since she had been brought in, and after the glass of electrolyte and IV, she was more responsive.

"Your blood pressure is still high but it is coming down. Your heart rate is acceptable." He stepped back, a signal to his wife.

Christina moved in and applied antiseptic cream to the healing wound before reapplying a dressing. She uncapped a six ounce, straight-sided, white plastic jar filled with a creamy, white ointment. "I make this myself," she explained to Joan. "It's a skin moisturizer with aloe vera and herbs, for sunburn and skin rejuvenation. Use it on your face and your lips."

Joan spread a healthy dollop onto her bottom lip. The ointment's soothing effect on her sore, cracked skin was almost instant. She brought her lips together to transfer a portion of the balm onto her upper lip. Tears of relief glistened her eyes. "Thank you," she said to the nurse and doctor, two words that she knew failed to fully express her appreciation.

Christina applied her cream to Joan's deeply reddened cheeks, ears and forehead. "When you have access to a pharmacy," the nurse said, "pick up any skin moisturizer with aloe vera for your arms and legs."

Joan nodded understanding. "When can I get something to eat?" she asked. The glass of electrolyte-glucose solution she had consumed along with the IV had kick-started her energy level, but the power boost had stirred within her a hunger as acute as her first days with limited food on *Atmosphere*.

Dr. Reklai shot a telling look at the constable that was not lost on Joan. Something was in the works to which she was not privy.

"Joan, I'm releasing you to Constable Udui," the doctor said. "He'll arrange something for you to eat." He regarded the constable. "I suggest soup but nothing too heavy."

To Joan, the doctor said, "After you eat, I want you to lie down. As soon as your blood work is faxed here, I'll come over to check on you. If at any time you feel dizzy or faint or do not urinate again within the next hour, tell Ms. Vegas; she's the police dispatcher, and she'll let me know."

Joan sat back, trepidation touching her face for it was clear she was bound for a police station. "When will I be able to go home?" she asked.

"The police station is very close to here," the constable said without offering Joan an answer. "There is a bed and bathroom facilities."

"But when can I go home?" Joan queried again. She wanted an answer.

Udui's smile was the kind that is hard to read. "Your boat will be floated tomorrow afternoon and brought back to the marina, and I still have additional questions for you."

He purposely held off revealing that having taken this investigation as far as he felt comfortable, he had contacted the Department of Marine Law Enforcement in Koror. As a result, the department was sending detectives who would take charge of this case, ultimately deciding if and when Joan was free to leave Palau.

Joan refrained from reading too much into the constable's brief comment. Further questioning was not beyond anything she already expected. The lawman needed confidence that she was not involved in drug smuggling. That would take more explanation from her and a thorough inspection of *Atmosphere*. For now, relocating to where there was food and a bed, even in a police station, was fine. All she wanted at that moment was something to eat and a place to lay her head. It was for this reason she once again ignored the niggling voice deep in her sub-conscience that there was more to all of this than was apparent.

Fifty yards up the village's graded road from the clinic, Udui parked his Land Cruiser on the gravel parking lot fronting Ollei Police Station. Late afternoon sunlight with its pink-hue struck the sheet-metal roof of the brick and mortar structure, intensifying the greens of manicured hibiscus hedges lining the building's facade.

The constable again helped Joan from his car, though she was more capable now managing under her own steam. Even so, he lightly held her right arm, lest her legs not fully support her.

Ollei police station's interior was as spartan as the building's exterior with a VHF radio on an executive-size desk center stage, facing the door. A main-line telephone on the desk sprouted two extension lines, one each on two smaller desks, set to one side, one behind the other. A pint-size refrigerator was set against a side wall next to a unisex bathroom. Taking up half the width of the back wall was a single jail cell featuring a wall-mounted table with a red, plastic chair, a ceiling-mounted hospital curtain isolating a stainless steel commode, and a single cot, far from the constable's insinuation of 'comfortable' but as tired as Joan was, she was not complaining.

Thirty-seven year old Ruth Vegas was a bulky woman with permed curls and Japanese features. She sat at the central desk pecking the keys of a typewriter. Her brown eyes flashed wide when Udui escorted Joan inside.

Ruth got to her feet. "This must be the lady," she said with surprise at Joan's stark features. She had heard all of the radioed conversations and knew the basics of what had happened to their newest guest, but to see her in person, that was sobering.

Udui guided Joan to a chair at the first unoccupied desk. "This is Joan," he told the dispatcher as he helped Joan onto a swiveled chair. "Doctor Reklai just checked her over and she had a shower."

"Dear," Ruth asked Joan, "do you need anything?"

"Pick her up some soup," Udui told Ruth. "Something not too heavy."

Ruth took money from a green petty cash box stowed in her desk drawer and hurried off for Joan's meal.

Udui filled a glass with water from the chiller and returned to the desk.

"I know you're hungry and tired," he said as he set the filled glass in front of Joan, "but I need you to tell me as best you can exactly what happened." He picked up a pen and notepad and took a seat on the opposing side of the desk, facing Joan. Giving her a cautious look, he said, "You need to be aware everything you tell me will be compared with what I find on the boat and can be held against you."

Concern about remembering everything that had befallen her darkened Joan's face. She ran a pensive hand over her mouth and down her neck as details of the past days coalesced from the ether into snapshots; sounds and images she would have just as soon forget.

"There was a storm," she began, almost with reluctance, "and I missed my watch. When I woke up, Yao was gone." She took a swallow from the glass and ran her tongue nervously over her lower lip. Christina's cream had softened dead skin and subdued the raw pain.

Udui fixed his eyes on Joan's, patient but expectant. "The captain's name is, Yao. Is that correct?" he asked.

"Yes sir, Wayne Yao. It's his boat." Joan downed another portion of water. She hoped the soup would arrive soon. Hunger was stealing her concentration and she needed a refresher of sustenance to keep her thoughts coherent.

Udui leaned back in his chair with a look of assessment. "Where is your passport?"

"On the boat with the boat papers. They are in a cabinet at the navigation table. All of my things are on the boat."

"Was your port of departure Guam?" Udui asked.

"Yes," Joan said.

"How many days ago did you leave Guam?"

Like answering his earlier question about how many days ago Yao had disappeared, Joan struggled to remember details. She recalled the storm that had driven her into the atoll and onto the beach, the shed and the gulp of some horrible-tasting liquid that she had thought was water, but events and a timeline before all that had become jumbled together. "I don't know exactly how many days," she said, her eyes wandering across the desktop as if the timeline she sought was within its varnished wood grain. She looked at the constable. "We left Guam on February sixteen."

Udui was well aware today was the twenty-seventh. "That was eleven days ago," he commented. "And when did you run aground on the island?"

"Yesterday, I think." She didn't sound convinced. "There was a storm."

"Where were you and the captain going?"

"To Manila and then Hong Kong."

"And you and Yao have sailed this route before?" Udui couldn't conceal his suspicion.

Joan's face sagged with ebbing strength. Her concentration had slipped another notch. "Yao has," she said. "This is the first time I've ever been on a sailboat out on the ocean."

Udui jotted down this unexpected and to him, strange answer. If what she had told him were true, there had to have been a strong incentive for a total novice like Joan was claiming to be to knowingly step aboard a boat bound for the open sea. To him, that incentive likely involved a large amount of money. "You told me before that there was no one else on the boat, just you and the captain."

"Yes sir, just me and Yao."

"And your final destination was Hong Kong."

"Yes sir, Yao is from Hong Kong. That's all I know."

As the constable added this information to his notes, Ruth returned. She placed in front of Joan a styrofoam bowl of yam soup, grilled fillet of snapper and plastic silverware. "Be careful, the soup is hot," the dispatcher cautioned.

Joan took a bite of the grilled fish, savoring its rich, almost sweet flavor. She spooned up a steaming portion of broth and swallowed her hunger while the first bite of soup cooled.

"What is the boat's name?" the constable asked Joan.

"Atmosphere."

Udui gave a tight grin. People had personal reasons for their boats' names but *Atmosphere* was the strangest name he had ever encountered. "Was the boat's side damaged when you left Guam?"

Joan closed her eyes for a brief moment of contrite recollection. "A freighter hit Atmosphere," she replied. "It was at night and I was asleep." She tipped the first spoonful of broth over her still delicate lips, followed by another bite of fish. Relief etched her face when she swallowed.

Udui took in all that he knew, mentally comparing it with what Joan had revealed so far. "Did Atmosphere stop at any port between Guam and here?" he asked.

"No sir," Joan said. "Yao was sailing the boat west, toward the Philippines. After he was gone, I looked for him for two or three days and when I realized I needed help in the search, I sailed south, trying to find Yap. I thought the island I ran aground on was part of Yap." She scooped up another spoonful of soup.

Udui turned to his dispatcher. "Send a fax to Yap, to the police department in Colonia. Tell them we have information about a sailboater named Wayne Yao, lost at sea about a week ago, somewhere in their vicinity. Ask if they have any information on anyone, living or deceased, being recovered."

Ruth got to work on the fax.

"Actually, Yao didn't fall overboard close to Yap," Joan clarified. "We were about two hundred miles north."

Udui gave Joan a long, dull stare, his shoulders slumping with the futility of the situation. He did not rescind his order to Ruth but had no doubt what the reply from Yap's authorities would be.

Udui regrouped his thoughts. "So, what happened between the time Yao disappeared and you ended up on Kayangel Island?" he asked. Joan must have dealt with issues far worse than her boat's collision with a freighter to end up in the condition she was found.

Joan ate another piece of fish and slurped down a dollop of soup, hovering the spoon over the bowl as she gathered her thoughts. As clearly as she could, she explained to the constable how severe weather had overwhelmed her with seasickness and a faulty harness attachment point had set up Yao's loss overboard. Finishing the last portion of fish, Joan sipped down a spoonful of the cooling soup and described how she had searched the grid pattern Yao had taught her, had run out of propane gas, fouled the boat's propeller with an anchor line from a rogue fishing buoy, of the shark attack, running out of fuel and the *coup de grâce,* her mistakenly pouring the reserve diesel fuel into the freshwater tank. She finished her doleful tale with her attempted transfer of fuel from the water tank to the fuel tank which was interrupted by the storm that drove *Atmosphere* onto Kayangel Island.

Udui scribbled the enlightening details, glad the mystery behind *Atmosphere's* opened floor tanks had been solved.

Joan ate the tepid soup at a more rapid pace, satisfied her description of events seemed to have dispelled any suspicions with what she felt had been an accurate recount of events.

Constable Udui was suitably impressed by Joan's survival after such a string of disasters, but no matter how remarkable her feat, he still had to compare her statements with further evidence from the boat. "And there is nothing else you have to add to this?" he asked.

The meal Joan had consumed had brought her body and mind further from the abyss. "No sir, that's everything, I swear," she said.

Udui sat full upright in his chair and crossed his arms like a leery parent. "I want you to confirm again there is nothing illegal on the boat," he said, eyes on Joan's. "Maybe Yao stowed something that could be considered contraband."

A chill ran through Joan. This line of questioning suddenly felt like a noose tightening around her own neck. How was she to prove what Yao may have hidden on the boat was not hers? "I don't know everything Yao had onboard," Joan confessed, aware being defensive was not going to help her situation but feeling compelled to state what, as far as she knew, was the truth. "I don't use illegal drugs or have anything to do with them, and I didn't bring anything illegal on Atmosphere."

She halted, ensuring her words were leading her down the right path. "But there are a lot of places on the boat that I had no reason to go," she added for insurance, "and where Yao could have stowed something before I got onboard."

Dr. Reklai arrived, toting a black medical bag. He signaled quick greeting to Ruth and walked to Joan. "Am I interrupting?" he asked the constable.

"We're just finishing," Udui said, sitting back as a signal the doctor was free to check his patient.

Reklai looked Joan over, saying, "It's a good sign that you're able to hold that down." He motioned to her empty soup bowl and remnants of fish. He set his medical bag on a nearby chair and extracted his sphygmomanometer and stethoscope. "If you don't mind, I'll check your vitals."

Joan pushed the bowl aside, feeling sated, at least for the time being. She swiveled her chair to face the doctor. Her light meal should hold her for the time being, but Constable Udui's line of questioning had tightened her stomach with second-guesses on the reasons for Yao's rushed departure from Guam. Considering all of the nooks and crannies on *Atmosphere*, there were indeed ample places where contraband could be stored, out of sight and beyond easy detection.

Dr. Reklai gazed into Joan's eyes. The pinkish tint had faded to white, and they were more clear, but the stress on her face was easy enough to diagnose. "Do you have any pain or concerns about your condition?" he asked, aware the psychology of her demeanor could have been from her interaction with the constable.

"No, I'm just tired," Joan said.

"Any diarrhea or nausea?"

"No. Only my headache but it is better."

"Have you urinated since leaving the clinic?"

"Not since before I took a shower."

Dr. Reklai checked Joan's blood pressure and heart rate. "Your blood pressure has come down but is still higher than I like. Your heart rate is down to eighty-two."

Joan gave a pensive smile. Her blood pressure and heart rate would shoot back up again if indeed Yao was into something dubious.

The doctor slipped a faxed document from his bag. "I have your blood work from the clinic," he said and gave the page to Joan to review as he explained the results.

"As I would expect," the doctor said, "all of your markers are high but they should have improved since the IV and now your meal. I'd like to follow up with another blood sample tomorrow morning, if you're still here."

Joan's eyes flicked to Udui, appreciative of Dr. Reklai's concern but hopeful she would be traveling back to New Zealand by then, something Udui picked up on.

"The boat will have to be towed to the marina and pumped out," the constable explained for both Joan's and Reklai's benefit. "And that won't happen until tomorrow. Some DMLE detectives will be here in the morning. They will be the ones to set the schedule for the inspection."

Joan's thin face drew long, her eyes welling up at the thought of a lengthy stay. "What if I give you a signed statement about me not knowing of any contraband?" she pleaded to the constable. "You can make copies of my passport, and I'll leave you my home address and contact information." As tired as she felt, one night in Palau, even in a small fishing village, was infinitely better than what she had experienced during the last days on the boat, but she was more than ready to trade the tropics for her subtropical home.

A heavy silence held the office. Joan's teary eyes locked onto the constable's, her waiting for an answer and him, considering how to handle the delicate issue of a possible criminal case that could hold her in Palau for an extended period.

"At this point there is nothing more I can tell you," the constable stated. "You have to wait for the detectives to complete their inspection."

Joan sighed with a despondent nod.

Dr. Reklai stood and quietly packed his medical instruments into his bag, leaving Joan the medical report. "Keep yourself hydrated and if there are any of the symptoms I've mentioned, especially if you don't urinate again in the next hour, let me know."

Udui disengaged himself from Joan and walked Dr. Reklai to the front door.

"So, she won't need to be transferred to Mengellang?" Udui asked the doctor, referring to the better equipped community clinic.

"I see no reason for that right now with her improvements. Whether here or in Koror, it would be best if she recuperates a few days before making the trip back to her home."

"She won't be going anywhere until her boat has had a serious going through," Udui stated. "What happens to her after that will be up to the DMLE."

The doctor departed and Udui returned to his conversation with Joan. He called over Ruth.

Addressing Joan, the constable asked, "What's your full name and what country issued your passport?"

"Joan Eliess Mackland. I'm from New Zealand."

Ruth jotted down the information.

"Is there anyone you would like to call? Family?" Udui asked Joan.

The thought of speaking to someone familiar to her reconnected Joan emotionally to a life that had seemed so distant and released her from a feeling that she was dealing with this aftermath alone and unsupported.

"Yes, Phil Mackland, my uncle. He lives in Auckland." Just saying his name was a relief to her.

Ruth slid the pen and paper to Joan. "If you don't mind, write down his name and phone number and I'll see what I can do. Don't forget the country code."

Joan jotted down both her uncle's work and home phone numbers.

"Do you know what the time difference is between here and New Zealand?" Ruth queried their guest.

"I don't know about here," Joan confessed, "but Guam is three hours behind Auckland."

"Palau is an hour behind Guam," Udui noted to Joan and added, "Our back-up dispatcher, Miss Sueleb, will be in later this evening. She will stay the night and tend to your needs."

Deepening worry touched Joan's face at the very real prospect her ordeal was far from over. "Am I being arrested?"

"It's just until we get things sorted out," Udui said.

"But I've told you everything that happened," Joan stated firmly. "I don't know anything about drugs or anything else that might be hidden onboard."

Udui stared at Joan to let her know this was more complicated than just drugs. "There is also the issue of the missing captain."

Joan's face suddenly looked old. This was far beyond anything she could have imagined, from suspicion of smuggling to murder. "You think I killed him," she gasped. She slumped in her chair. Proving her innocence concerning drugs on *Atmosphere*, drugs that might not even exist, was one thing, but murder?

"I'm only stating a direction this case could go," Udui said matter-a-factly. "There's a boat grounded on Kayangel Island, a missing captain and the potential for contraband."

Joan's face paled as a tornado of worried thoughts spun through her head. Her explanation of what happened, as factual as it was, could easily lead to any number of conclusions, and what if Yao did have illegal drugs on-board? That would be motive for murder. Greed, confrontation and when the opportunity presented itself, Joan hadn't hesitated. Catch Yao when he least expected it, push him overboard and steal his boat and drugs. Clean and simple, unless of course, the fact you didn't know how to sail had not been factored into the plan.

"If you're finished with your meal …" Udui said. He stood, ending their conversation. Whatever happened now would be based on what the detectives decided.

Joan's hands tighten into fists. Was this never going to end? "I can't believe any of this."

"Miss Mackland," the constable said, "this is only until what you have told me can be matched with what evidence there is on the boat." He took Joan by her arm and helped her stand. He walked her to the jail cell and slid the cell door open.

Joan stepped into the enclosure to a wave of desperation. No sooner had she escaped one form of incarceration than she was consigned to another. She slouched onto the cot, feeling as trapped as she had on *Atmosphere*. All she wanted was to be back in her Buckhead apartment, back to a life that may have had its ups and downs but was absent of the uncertainty of a situation that had no middle ground.

Udui closed the cell door but refrained from locking it, an intended statement to Joan that things were not as terminal as she appeared to believe. "If you prefer," he told her in a further attempt to calm her fears, "feel free to use the office bathroom." He had little reason to believe her story would not prove true, but until the DMLE had reviewed the evidence and made their own evaluations, he had protocol to follow.

Stepping to Ruth's desk, he said in a subdued voice, "Contact the authorities in Guam. Let's see what they can tell us about Atmosphere and who was included on the clearance papers."

Ruth glanced at Joan, lying on the cot, staring at the ceiling, as still as stone.

"That poor girl," she sighed of Joan. "I already phoned her uncle in Auckland but there was no answer. I'll try again later."

Udui pulled his car keys from his pocket. "I'll be at the marina."

Ruth got on the telephone and Udui departed.

CHAPTER FIFTEEN

The white, forty-three foot sport fishing boat named, *Chedeng*, charged past Konlai Point heading north. Its nine hundred horse diesel engine was at full throttle, pushing the vessel at sixty miles per hour, as if the boat itself were on a mission. Owner and captain, Chris Addison, sat at the boat's controls on the flybridge with a grand view of Kossol Reef stretching north on the boat's starboard side like an irregular white road submerged under a foot of water. He partially opened his boat's upper windshield for a breeze to cool the rising morning temperatures as he steered his boat past Ngerkeklau and Ngerechur islets.

Chris was a thirty-two year old, sandy-blonde Californian who had lived in Palau for two years with his Palauan wife, Melai. Chris was of medium build with shoulder-length hair hanging from under a brimmed hat pulled hard onto his square head. His puffy eyes were those of someone recovering from a hangover.

Below the flybridge, in the boat's open cockpit, Melai stowed in a side compartment newly purchased eighty pound test monofilament fishing line and a sealed plastic box containing an electric fishing reel. She was a petite woman, two years younger than her husband, with black hair tied in a ponytail and a weathered but gentle face. She was also Chris' business partner, a woman with enough perseverance to deal with the most obnoxious foreign tourists and seasick newbies. Her friendly and supportive personality added a spark of appreciation that brought return clients to her and her husband's fishing guide business.

With the gear stashed, Melai entered the boat's enclosed cabin and ascended well-worn wooden steps to the flybridge. She sat in the observation seat next to her husband with its panorama view to an extended horizon. *Chedeng* scooting across smooth water at speed, and with no customers to entertain, gave Melai a feeling of freedom, and today that freedom was taking her and her husband to Kayangel Island.

Earlier that morning, in the gray light of a nondescript dawn, Chris and Melai had been seated in *Chedeng's* cockpit finishing their day's first cups of coffee while they reviewed preparations for a charter group from Canada. As they completed their check list, Neihana, a hot-head and one-time competitor of theirs, had stopped by to quip about the time and fuel he had wasted on a trip to Kayangel Island the previous afternoon.

In his gruff way, Neihana had informed the couple that his visit to the island had been to check out a grounded and abandoned sailboat and see what gear was onboard. He said he had figured on making an early offer to buy the vessel if perchance the unfortunate owner wanted to sell, but Waipuna and his son were already there, supposedly guarding the boat for the police. Unable to get on board, Neihana had returned to home base with little more than he had known before.

Chris and Melai usually tolerated Neihana's rants if his grievances were short, and when they weren't, the couple would set about with on-board chores until the man realized he had lost his audience and moved on to unload on someone else. This day had been no different and to them, the man's complaints had been of little interest. It wasn't rare for an occasional ship or local pleasure craft to end up on one of Palau's many reefs, and Chris figured this grounding was just the latest.

"What size boat is it?" Chris had asked with general curiosity after Neihana had gotten the gripe off his chest.

"Looks to be about forty feet," Neihana had said. "Guam registration."

That statement in itself had little significance to Chris until Neihana had added the vessel was constructed of aluminum, a revelation that had caught Chris' full attention.

"What's the boat's name?" Chris had asked. Aluminum was not a common construction material for sailboats, he knew of only a handful, but only one forty footer.

"Can't tell what the name is," Neihana had replied. "The boat is on the island's beach and the side facing up was damaged and the name scrapped off."

"So the name is on the boat's side and not the transom," Chris had said.

"Yes, that's right," Neihana had commented. "Why? Does that mean something to you?"

"Nah, just curious," Chris had stated.

"How many people were on board?" Melai asked. She had given her husband a fleeting, inquisitive glance at Neihana's mention the boat's name was on the vessel's side and not its transom as was far more common.

"Supposed to have been a lady rescued," Neihana had said, "in really bad condition. Nothing about anyone else. Just her." He had stroked his chin, eyes on Chris. "I'm figuring the lady who was on board is the owner and will want to sell." A friendly smile had crept across his face. "Do you want to go in as partners and buy it, me and you?" His eyes had flashed as if offering the deal of the century. "You're guaranteed to make money."

Chris had answered by setting his coffee mug aside and slipping on his black, Daiwa ball cap, a signal he had more important things waiting his attention. "Thanks but no thanks," he had said. "We have our hands full with Chedeng."

Neihana's face had darkened. Chris had been the one person he had thought would jump at this opportunity, and without the American, his grand scheme was just that, another grand scheme.

Neihana had grumbled to himself, giving Chris a hard look, and as he walked away, Melai had collected Chris' coffee mug, aware of his far away look and knowing exactly what was rolling around in his head. "You heard Neihana say it's a crime scene," she said to cool her husband's introspection, "so nothing is going to happen to that boat anytime soon."

"I have to see for myself," Chris had stated, certain his suspicion was correct, that he not only knew the boat but also knew at least one, possibly two, other people who would have been on board.

"No drama when we get to Kayangel," Melai told her husband as *Chedeng* approached the north end of Kossol Reef from where Kayangel Island was a dark green sliver on the northern horizon. "It's been two years and whatever is out there, you let it be."

Melai had been working at a travel agency in Koror those two years ago when three men, looking to be in their late twenties, had halted outside of her office's windowed front ensconced in a mulish conversation. Each of the men had shoulder-length hair, and one had a scruffy beard and a gray, overstuffed backpack. The two other men faced off with their bearded colleague, their bantering voices revealing an ongoing tiff that didn't appear anywhere near resolution. The mainly one-sided conversation had quickly ended with raised voices before the two dissenters stormed off.

A long moment had passed as the bearded man stood stark still, seeming to consider what the other two lads had said. Breaking from his reverie and realizing he had been standing in front of a travel agency under surveillance, he had pushed through the business' front door as if he now had a grievance with the lone staffer inside.

Melai had dropped her head with a guilty look of being a voyeur caught red-handed, but instead of admonishing her for being nosey, the young man had dropped his passport on her desk.

"I need a flight to America," Chris had said. "To California."

Melai had relaxed and opened the passport to the identification page. "Yes sir, Mr. Addison." She had said this with a touch of confusion. "Do you not already have a return ticket?"

She had gone on to explain what he already should have known, that tourists were required to have a round-trip ticket before leaving their country of departure for Palau.

Chris had motioned to his passport. "I arrived here on a sailboat with the two guys I was talking to. We got our visas when we checked in at the port authority."

"What day would you like to leave?"

"I don't know," Chris said with a touch of disgust and a shake of his head. "I have to get some personal things off of the boat first. I guess for now, all I need is a flight schedule and a hotel."

"There are daily flights from Palau, with connections in either Manila or Tokyo with service to the US west coast. Whenever you are ready to leave Palau, just let me know."

"What about a cheap hotel?" Chris had asked, his face adamant. "I mean, a real cheap hotel."

Melai had felt sorry for Mr. Chris Addison. He had seemed a nice person, holding his temper in check when the taller of his two sailing partners had taken things to the next level by poking a finger against Chris' chest to make a point. That restraint by Chris had impressed her, for her own older brother would have broken the man's jaw.

"If you don't mind waiting a few minutes while I close the office," Melai had told Chris, "I'd like to invite you to dinner at a restaurant, not far from here. After that, I'll show you a couple of cheap hotels." Smiling, she had added, "I mean, real cheap hotels."

Melai's selected eatery was an out of the way shop serving local cuisine: taro salads and soups, rice dishes, broiled fish with ginger and garlic and their specialties, deep-fried shrimp with squash fritters and fruit bat in coconut broth.

In a casual conversation while sipping wine before ordering dinner, Chris had learned that Melai had been born on Peleliu Island, where her parents, brother and relatives still lived. She had moved to Palau three years earlier, when she was twenty-one years old, to start-up a travel agency targeting sport fishing.

"What does your husband do?" Chris had asked, attempting a nonchalant tone but failing. Melai hadn't been wearing a wedding ring, but maybe in Palauan society some other jewelry, like her pink coral necklace, signified her betrothal.

Melai had given a timid smile, her wheatish complexion showing a soft, blushing glow when she had said, "I'm not married."

Their waiter had been hovering.

"Are you ready to order?" Melai had asked Chris.

"Let's finish our wine first."

Melai had spoken in dialect and the waiter busied himself with clearing a just vacated table.

Chris and Melai had both stared at their wine glasses for a long, thoughtful moment before Melai had spoken. "What about you?" she asked, immediately embarrassed at the insinuation. "I mean, where are you from," she clarified, "and why did you sail to Palau?"

Chris had explained how he was one third owner of a sailboat on which he and the two other owners, Bruce and Damion, were on a circumnavigation that had started from San Diego, California, from where they all haled. He had gone on to explain that besides a few personality quirks that on occasion raised tensions, their passage to Hawaii and further west had been pleasant enough, remaining so until shortly after they had sailed from Guam for the Philippines. This last leg of their passage across the Pacific Ocean quickly deteriorated into irreconcilable arguments that tanked all comradery between himself and his two shipmates. Chris had not offered specific details of this falling out, something Melai had respected, but he had commented that the trio had agreed to an unscheduled stop in Palau where Chris would take a few days away from the boat to let them all reconsider their future together. If indeed he would be ending his around-the-world adventure in Palau, they would meet Chris at a local bank to get the money to pay Chris his one third ownership before Bruce and Damion set sail again for Manila.

Disclosure to Melai about his aborted trip had boosted Chris' confidence that leaving the boat had not only been his best option but his only option, especially since he had met Melai. Even before he and Melai had ordered their meals, his attraction to her had grown into a need to spend more time together, and he had sensed for Melai, that feeling was mutual.

That evening had ended with Melai breaking her promise to take Chris to a low-cost hotel. Instead, she had escorted him to her apartment two blocks from the restaurant where he had bedded down on a futon in the apartment's small but adequate living room. Breakfast in the morning had included a continuation of their conversation the previous evening with his impromptu confession to Melai about his growing feelings for her. That unsolicited revelation had led to consequences he had not expected. Between breakfast and washing dishes, she had relocated Chris' pillow to her own bed.

Three days later with Chris having decided not to leave Melai, he had proposed marriage, and she had accepted with a stipulation. The wedding would be an early morning ceremony at Ngchus Beach in two weeks, giving sufficient time for her parents and brother to arrange travel to Palau and before Chris' visa expired.

The day following his proposal, after a breakfast of fresh coffee, boiled breadfruit and fried sea bass, Chris had escorted Melai to *Atmo-*

sphere to collect personal belongings and inform his two soon-to-be ex-shipmates of his plan not to continue the voyage.

Chris' appearance on the dock had turned into an icy reception when he informed Bruce and Damion of his plans, and that he would meet them at the Bank of Hawaii, as agreed. He had refrained from mentioning his pending marriage, instead telling the two that he would be returning home to California at thirty thousand feet. Chris had no desire to ever see the two men again, and the less they knew about his own life's change and whereabouts, the better.

"I figured you would come to your senses," Bruce had stated, but had accepted Chris' decision. Giving a waggle of his head, he had said, "I guess you want to pick up your stuff." He was referring to Chris' remaining belongings. Without stepping aside to allow passage, he had turned to Damion and said, "Bring his stuff topside, and get my wallet."

"I need on board and I want to show Melai around."

Bruce had stood his ground, holding firm his control.

"That's all right, Chris," Melai had said, clearly seeing the deep riff between the men.

"Yeah, Chris, listen to the lady," Bruce had commented.

Damion had lugged through the companionway a half-filled, black, plastic garbage bag, Chris' remaining clothes and toiletries not packed into his backpack. Bruce grabbed the makeshift travel bag and pushed it into Chris' arms.

"You don't forget," Bruce had said with intended malice, "you were onboard all the way from San Diego so you're as much a part of this as we are." He had held up a halting hand when Damion started to speak.

"All I want is to get back home," Chris had said.

Bruce had taken his wallet from Damion and unfolding it, extracted a stack of greenbacks. He had stripped off ten bills and crammed them into Chris' free hand.

"That's goodwill, a thousand dollars," Bruce had declared. "Meet us tomorrow afternoon, two o'clock, at the bank. I'll transfer the rest of the twelve thousand, and we can sign whatever sales agreement you have."

Chris' trust in Bruce had lagged long before they had sailed into Guam and now, with their relationship as tenuous friends at an end, all he wanted was to get what was rightfully his and be done with Bruce, Damion and the boat that had held so much promise, yet had turned into what had felt to him like prison.

"I'll be there," Chris had agreed and promptly turned and walked away with Melai. There had still been two items on board he had wanted to retrieve, but under the circumstances, with Bruce refusing to allow him onboard, his possessions were certain to have disappeared had he revealed to Damion or Bruce his property's whereabouts. At least he had had the next day to see if he could get back on board.

Early afternoon the following day, armed with a map Melai had sketched during their lunch, Chris had navigated a twenty minute hike along Koror streets to the Bank of Hawaii, a two-story structure looking similar to a Super 8 motel. Chris had arrived just before the agreed meeting time with Bruce and Damion, a meeting that was not to be. After waiting an hour for the two no-shows, he had made his way back to the marina only to find he had been duped. After he had pocketed Bruce's one thousand dollars of goodwill, and he and Melai had departed the boat with what belongings he was allowed, the conniving duo had cleared customs and immigration, hustled back to the boat and disappeared over the horizon. Chris didn't know if he would ever see *Atmosphere* again, but he vowed to Melai that if the opportunity ever presented itself, he would somehow board the boat to take back what was his.

"It may not even be them," Melai stated as her husband steered *Chedeng* north toward Kayangel Island.

Chris reduced throttle in choppy waves as his boat passed through the three mile gap between Kossol and Ngeraul reefs.

"Don't worry," Chris replied. "All I want is to see if it's them. After that, I'll take things as they come."

Fifteen minutes after passing Kossol reef, Chris reduced speed again on his approach to the tidal opening into Kayangel's atoll. The Ollei marina's launch and Waipuna's personal skiff were pulled up side by side on the island's beach.

The fishing boat *Iwalani* was there too, inside the atoll, holding a position in deep water, the boat's stern to the island's shallows. The thirty-seven foot wooden, shrimp trawler had a forward pilot house and windowed cabin with a stout central mast from which twin nets were draped from two opposing outriggers, now raised and locked into mast-mounted stabilizers. The boat's try net was secured to a modified boom angling up toward the vessel's stern.

Iwalani was the old lady of Ollei's small fleet, built in nineteen forty-nine, its seasoned hull and marred deck attested to the craft's long and arduous life harvesting from the sea. She was smaller than the fleet's more modern vessels and one of the few local trawlers with a narrow enough beam to safely navigate the atoll's craggy entrance. The old trawler may not have been pretty, but it could do its job and then some.

"Looks like things are about ready to rock and roll," Chris commented to his wife of the sailboat's imminent removal from the beach. He slipped *Chedeng* through the atoll's twenty-foot-wide tidal gap while he and Melai monitored the two feet of clearance between the jagged coral and each side of the boat's hull. The incoming tide was slackening which made for an uneventful passage.

Motoring halfway across the lagoon, Chris turned *Chedeng* bow-on to the foundered sailboat, out of *Iwalani's* working area, and shifted his boat into neutral. He picked up binoculars stowed in a side pocket by his seat and focused on the beached sailboat. After a long moment, he said to his wife of the boat, "That has to be her."

His visual inspection followed the shoreline, taking in the goings-on ashore. Waipuna and his son were providing the grunt work while Makoa directed the show, something Chris would have expected.

From what Chris knew of the onsite locals, Makoa had the most experience with ropes, having worked on trawlers since fresh out of high school. His long career had ended three years ago when a junior deckhand had misinterpreted a hand signal from another crew member and switched on the trawler's power winch to deploy the net. At that moment, Makoa had been untangling a water hose from the net and his left hand had been crushed between net and winch barrel. By the time he was delivered to a Koror hospital nearly two hours later, his hand could not be saved, leaving him unfit to continue in his chosen career. After convalescing, he had taken a job at Ollei's marina.

Also on the beach were Constable Udui and two uniformed police officers Chris had seen arriving at the marina with the constable earlier that morning. The tallest visiting officer had a medium build and his light blue shirt and dark slacks where finished off with a tan-colored bucket hat set firmly on his head. His partner, a pudgy-faced man with a pear-shaped body and a skin tone more olive than brown, wore a navy-blue baseball cap displaying a patch Chris could not read. Chris figured correctly the two men were from Koror.

Through the binoculars, Chris scanned the entire beach, his curiosity piqued when he saw no one who might be associated with the sailboat. Still, he was convinced the woman rescued from the island had not been alone.

Udui pointed toward *Chedeng*, no doubt explaining to the two uniformed officials who their newly arrived audience was.

Chris and Melai were well-acquainted with Constable Udui due to their frequent trips to Ollei from their home in Mengellang. They rented space for *Chendeng* along Ollei marina's pier wall and overnighted onboard when preparing for a paid fishing excursion, the next of which for them would be in two days.

Through Makoa's hand-signal instructions, a length of triple-strand manila rope attached to the base of *Iwalani's* mast was passed over the trawler's transom and ferried to shore by a skinny crew member in an inflatable dinghy. The onshore crew dragged the rope to the sailboat's bow where it was tied to a shackle joining two harness straps. One strap passed behind a bow cleat, across the foredeck and behind the opposing cleat with the strap's bitter ends brought forward under the boat's bowsprit like a hangman's noose.

The second, longer noose passed behind the boat's keel and led forward with its two ends shackled to those of the shorter strap, a good rig for distributing the pulling force without stressing any one part of the sailboat.

Wanting a closer view of the sailboat, Chris crept *Chedeng* to within a hundred yards from the beach and refocused the field glasses.

"Neihana was right," Chris commented to Melai about the sailboat. "It's side is too damaged to read the name, but I can make out the first letter, A, and it looks like there's a, P, in the middle."

He lowered the field glasses and turned to his wife with a hungry smile. "That's Atmosphere, for sure."

"Okay, so, it's your boat," Melai commented, still concerned her husband would push this to confrontation. "That doesn't mean either of them were on board. Maybe they sold the boat to the lady Neihana mentioned."

Chris shook his head at the suggestion. His voice held no doubt when he said, "I've never known anyone who bought a second-hand boat and didn't personalize it by changing the name."

"You've never told me why it was named, Atmosphere," Melai pointed out.

"I guess I haven't," Chris agreed and said, "The guy we were buying the boat from let us stay onboard one night so we could make sure we liked it. Once we got settled in, the main cabin became filled with so much reefer smoke you got high just going below deck."

Melai thought that was funny.

Chris smiled with the bitter-sweet memory. "Dame was the one who came up with the name," he said.

Their attention was drawn back to Kayangel Island. Makoa was inspecting the harnesses and appearing satisfied, stepped back a safe distance. He raised his right arm, signaling *Iwalani*.

The trawler's diesel engine growled louder and the trawler inched forward. As the rope snapped taut, shedding water like a drenched dog, *Iwalani's* captain worked his boat's gear lever to hold the tension steady while his five-man crew waited on deck for further instructions.

Makoa rechecked the tow rope's connection point and raised his right hand again, giving a forward motion.

Iwalani responded with a rev of its engine and crept forward again. The straps creaked tight. *Atmosphere* pivoted, half in and half out of the water, its keel and rudder furrowing the sand with a dampened grinding sound audible on *Chedeng*.

Makoa waved *Iwalani's* captain to continue. *Atmosphere* slid forward from knee-deep into waist-deep water, thumping against melon-size coral heads and plowing up sponges and sea fans. As the water deepened, the boat's keel dipped and the port side cap rail rose above the water's surface. *Atmosphere*'s mast angled higher. The pull continued.

Atmosphere's keel crossed the drop-off into the depths and the boat righted, its mast rocking like a spent metronome. The boat's rudder, still in shallow enough water to touch bottom, dug into the sand and spun the helm erratically as if by a maniacal helmsman. The rudder crossed the transition point into deep water and *Atmosphere* settled onto its waterline, afloat and in full display of its battle scars. The crew on shore clapped with Sifa adding a cheer for what looked to be a speedier than expected return to his girlfriend.

With the successful operation concluded, Waipuna delivered his son and the pudgy police officer to *Atmosphere*. Sifa took a position behind the sailboat's helm to steer the vessel straight during the tow to Ollei, while the lawman seated himself as an observer at the aft end of the cockpit, as if shunning something in the main cabin.

On *Chedeng*, Chris and Melai waited as the two smaller boats, Waipuna in his skiff, and Makoa, Udui and the pudgy officer's partner in the marina's launch, followed *Atmosphere* through the atoll's gap like a pair of cygnets behind their mother.

Chris cranked *Chedeng's* engine and brought the boat slowly about. He gingerly took *Chedeng* through the gap behind the other boats and dialed up the throttle on a heading toward Ollei.

CHAPTER SIXTEEN

Udui pulled his Land Cruiser alongside the DMLE's white SUV parked in front of Ollei's police station. The visiting vehicle's front doors were decorated with circular, navy-blue decals sporting silver fringes and lettering; PALAU, Department of Marine Law Enforcement.

Detective Nakamua slipped from the passenger side of Udui's vehicle under a bright afternoon sky. The men entered the station. Ruth was at her desk and Joan was dozing on the cot.

Before leaving for Kayangel that morning, the constable had stopped by his office to await two DMLE officers who were driving the forty miles from Koror to Ollei. At the time of his early arrival, Udui had found Joan seated at her "interrogation" desk, breakfasting on boiled breadfruit, broiled fish and fried taro chips with a cup of hot tea.

Ruth had been there too. She had come to the office an hour earlier than usual to relieve Sueleb, informing Udui the assistant on-call had reported Joan had not slept well the night before, with frequent trips to the bathroom, but had recovered enough before Sueleb had gone off duty to order breakfast.

"You're looking better," Udui had commented to Joan of her condition.

"I feel better," Joan had replied. "My headache is gone, and I'm not as achey as I was. I'm just constantly tired."

The office door had opened, and in had stepped a tall police officer, Detective Atonio Nakamua. The detective was fifty-five years old with a soft brown complexion and graying hair. His oval face had marionette mouth lines and his almond eyes, like his family name, revealed his Japanese heritage. He had slipped off his cotton bucket hat and shook Udui's hand.

"Good to see you again," the detective had said to Udui.

They had met the previous year when the detective had visited Ollei to update local commercial fishermen on his department's efforts to thwart illegal fishing by intruding Chinese trawlers.

Nakamua had been introduced to Joan. "I look forward to speaking with you a little later," the detective had told Joan. It had not been difficult for him to see by her appearance, even with what was no doubt her improved condition, that she had been through more than a little strife.

Accompanying Detective Nakamua, the thin police officer Chris had seen on Kayangel with Constable Udui, had been his pudgy partner. "This is Detective Kaiea Sanna," Nakamua had made introductions. "Kaiea is our latest DMLE team member, brought on board yesterday."

The new DMLE recruit appeared to be ten years Nakamua's junior and had short, curly black hair protruding from under his billed cap embossed on the front with "DMLE" in silver stitching. His uniform was identical to Nakamua's but without epaulettes.

As Udui had shaken Sanna's hand in the introductions, the constable's smile had concealed his disappointment that the department had already filled the position for which he had intended to apply. Still, he would submit his application in preparation of the next hire, whenever that might be. For now, he would take whatever points he would get for securing what he had designated as a crime scene, like taping the protective covering over the blood smear and setting into place the equipment and personnel needed to re-float the stranded sailboat.

"The detectives and I are leaving for Kayangel to oversee Atmosphere's extraction," Udui had told Joan. "After that, your boat will be towed back to the marina, pumped out and inspected. If what you have told me is verified by the detectives, I'm sure you will be free to return home." Udui had added this last part figuring worry was not helping Joan's recovery.

The three officers had departed for the marina.

Ruth got to her feet when her boss and Detective Nakamua returned from their jaunt to Kayangel. Both men looked thirsty. She filled two glasses with water from the dispenser and placed them on the constable's desk and gave a quick glance at Joan's prone body. "Doctor Reklai was in earlier to draw Joan's blood," she informed her boss.

"What about her uncle?" Udui asked his dispatcher.

"I called both his home and office again but no answer," Ruth reported. "I left him another message and our phone number."

She returned to her desk. "Also, Chief Ramarui phoned about an hour ago," she said to Detective Nakamua. "He wants you to return his call."

Holding up a fax and not knowing which of the two men should get it, she said, "This came in a short while ago. From Yap."

Udui took the fax and read the message to the detective in a low volume voice intent on keeping incoming information on an as needed basis perchance Joan was only resting. "Confirming, no reports of any boaters living or deceased arriving in Yap. Require time of loss and boat's position."

Udui handed the fax back to Ruth. "Fax them that we will send details if and when available."

Ruth slipped her boss a second fax. "This is from Guam."

Udui read to the detective the short message that confirmed sailing vessel *Atmosphere*, registration number GU 7547 LE, with Wayne Yao as captain and Joan E. Mackland as crew, had cleared Guam's immigration and customs on the sixteenth of February, nineteen eighty-seven bound for Manila, Philippines.

Knowing Mr. Wayne Yao had indeed been aboard *Atmosphere* when the boat departed Guam was one thing. Learning the true story behind the man's disappearance was another.

The two officers walked to the jail cell.

"Miss Mackland," Udui said through the bars.

Joan stirred. Groggy.

"Miss Mackland, I'm sorry to wake you," Udui said. "Detective Nakamua would like to speak with you." The constable slid open the cell door.

Joan rubbed sleep from her eyes. She fumbled her legs over the edge of the cot and for a long moment stared at Udui, getting her bearings.

"Please step out," the constable instructed Joan. His voice carried a formal tone Joan picked up on.

Joan got to her feet and Udui directed her to her usual seat at his desk. The two officers took seats facing her.

Detective Nakamua gave Joan a reassuring smile, figuring someone needed to. "Miss Mackland," the detective said, "we've had confirmation from Guam authorities that both Mr. Yao and yourself were on Atmosphere when the boat cleared Guam. What I need to understand is, what happened after your departure from Guam and before you arrived here, in Palau."

The office phone rang. Ruth answered in a voice that wouldn't disturb the ongoing conversation.

"You mean, about Yao?" Joan asked the detective, her eyes on Ruth perchance the call was from her uncle.

"About everything," Nakamua replied.

"Joan," Udui spoke up, "you need to pay attention. Detective Nakamua needs more details of what you've already told me."

Ruth hung up the phone and held up a hand to get Udui's attention. She touched the phone, referencing the call she had just taken. "The sailboat is at the marina," she half whispered, half mimed.

The constable nodded thanks.

Joan pulled a sigh of disappointment her uncle had not yet called. As instructed, she refocused on the two officers, piqued by a rising suspicion this was a good cop, bad cop interrogation but unclear who the bad cop was. Her stomach felt cold and tight as she asked, "Do I need to contact a New Zealand embassy?"

What the constable had said earlier this morning, before he and the detectives had departed for Kayangel, about her possibly being on the verge of going home, seemed to be dangling precariously from a question mark.

"Miss Mackland, you have not been charged with a crime," Nakamua stated in a tone of fatherly appeasement. He did not feel it necessary to tell her the nearest New Zealand consulate was in Manila, Philippines.

The detective's statement of not having been charged with a crime did not settle Joan's nerves. "But you think I killed Yao," she said as a fact.

"Miss Mackland, I ..." Nakamua started.

Joan cut in, her voice assertive, defensive, when she said, "I almost died trying to find Yao after he fell overboard. If I hadn't had so many problems with the boat, I would still be out there searching." She balled up her fists, fighting frustration. She felt caught between a hungry shark and a jagged coral reef. No matter what she said, without physical proof of how Yao was lost, she would still be tainted with guilt.

"Joan, from the condition of the boat and yourself," Nakamua said with understanding, "it is clear you suffered through a very difficult ordeal, but there is blood on board and still the matter of the missing captain."

"I didn't kill him," Joan croaked as if making a last moment's plea before the Guillotine blade dropped.

"Joan, I'm not saying we don't believe you," Nakamua pressed assurance, "but with a missing person, we have to investigate and that means searching the boat for evidence and getting all of the information from you that we can. Everything you told Constable Udui, and what you tell us now, will help to piece together what happened."

Joan's shoulders sagged. She let out a long breath, bobbing her head.

"Let's start with this," Nakamua suggested to Joan. "Walk me through the events, from the time you became seasick and took to your cabin, to the boat's grounding on the island."

Joan's eyes clouded over as she gathered her thoughts, struggling with a feeling that the same gods who had tried to destroy her at sea had not yet concluded their game.

Sucking in a deep breath in an attempt at absolution, Joan described to the officers the progression of events that now seemed surreal, like another lifetime, her words less of an explanation than a confession of her failures. Ending her tale with *Atmosphere* grounded on what she thought was an outlying island near Yap, she sat back in her chair, feeling she had to say more but not knowing what that would be.

Joan' face tightened with a double-shot of anxiety when she added into the mix the other part to this equation, the part related to what Constable Udui had referred to as contraband.

"I know this has not been easy for you," Nakamua continued. He truly sympathized with Joan for what she had suffered at sea, and though he had a gut feeling she was indeed innocent of any misdoings, he, like Udui, also believed that for a woman of Joan's purported novelty to sailing, setting out across an ocean on a sailboat with a captain she supposedly had never previously met hinted of a strong incentive to make such an excursion, and it was his duty to uncover the truth behind what that incentive had been.

"Constable Udui has already asked you," the detective continued, "but I need to ask you again. Are you aware of anything on your boat that we should know about?"

"It's not my boat," Joan stated, cold apprehension crawling inside her at not knowing what Yao may have secretly stowed onboard. "It belongs to Wayne Yao. I was just a last minute crew member."

"What items on the boat are yours?" Nakamua asked.

"My backpack. A Walkman, my clothes and personal things. That's all."

"Once the boat has been pumped out," the detective said, "Detective Sanna, who you met earlier, and I will do a search inside and outside. From what you have told me, Yao fell overboard while you were seasick, you injured your leg fending off a shark while clearing the boat's propeller of a fishing buoy, and your only possessions are what you brought in your backpack."

"Yes sir."

"Thank you," Nakamua said in conclusion to this part of his investigation.

Udui stood and walked Joan back to the cell. "Ruth is still trying to get through to your uncle," he told Joan. "Is there anything you need?"

Joan pressed her eyes closed, attempting to squeeze her predicament out of existence.

"I need to go home."

CS80

Constable Udui and Detective Nakamua arrived at Ollei's marina after concluding the detective's initial interview with Joan to find pumping out of *Atmosphere's* flooded interior, as arranged by Detective Sanna and Andre, was well underway.

A gaggle of onlookers had gathered on the pier close to where *Atmosphere* was tied off. With Andre were two gangly marina workers handling the pump's discharge hose. The young lads, both in their early twenties, had already transferred the boat's top layer of diesel fuel through a sieve screen set atop a spare fuel drum, and when the officers arrived, they were in the process of diverting the diesel-tainted seawater through the same sieve into empty drums used for collecting used engine oil. A third worker, mid to late twenties, was in the boat's cockpit with Detective Sanna. The worker onboard was in charge of the pump's suction hose from where it passed through the companionway into the boat's main cabin while Sanna photographed the boat's interior at different stages of the pump-out.

After having delivered *Atmosphere* to the marina, the captain of *Iwalani* had returned his boat to the upper end of Kossol Reef to anchor in calm water where the crew could catch up on sleep. When the day's heat lifted toward sundown, they would once again set out for a night of dragging nets culling by-catch and dumping the shrimp into the boat's live well, repeating the process until the live-well was full.

Chris and Melai had returned to the marina behind the delivery of *Atmosphere*. *Chedeng* was once again tied off at the boat's rented slot, adjacent to Andre's office. Chris and his wife had joined the gathering of sightseers but stood back from the activity after having given the sailboat closer scrutiny from the pier. Boat fenders buffered the vessel's undamaged starboard side against the concrete wall with the top half of boat's name visible above the pier: *ATMOSPHERE*.

When Detective Nakamua moved closer to the sailboat to speak with the other detective, Chris made his way to Udui who also stood apart from the activity, observing the work at hand. "Constable, good afternoon," Chris greeted the lawman.

Udui gave a nod of casual recognition.

"Why is the DMLE pumping out the boat?" Chris asked. "Seems that would be the owner's responsibility."

Chris was aware the Department of Marine Law Enforcement was involved in patrolling Palau waters, arrest and seizure of vessels for illegal activities as well as search and rescue, and he was certain the department did not help with repairs to salvaged vessels unless …

"There's an on-going investigation," Udui confirmed in his blunt reply.

This confirmation piqued Chris' further interest. "I heard there was only a woman on board. Is that true?"

Udui didn't respond.

"The reason I ask," Chris lied, "is because my wife and I are interested in buying this boat to expand our charter business. That is, if the owner will sell. Do you know if that woman is the owner?"

"Chris, you'll have to talk to the DMLE," Udui said, and he walked away to join Nakamua, having nothing more to offer on the case.

The marina's sump pump cavitated, sucking air from *Atmosphere's* now drained interior. One of the workers on the pier switched off the pump. The sieve screen with its contents of two stainless steel bolts, three keys on a ring and soggy paper was set aside.

"Do you want everything inside brought out?" Andre asked the detectives about the waterlogged cushions, charts and other gear still inside the boat.

"Yes, bring it all out," Nakamua told Andre, "and stage it on the ground out here." The soaked materials were unlikely to provide any clear evidence after marinating in diesel fuel and water, and even the doused interior may not reveal much, but at least he and his partner wouldn't be stumbling over debris in what would be an already slippery environment.

"Bung," Andre called to the stoutest of the two boys manning the discharge end of the hose, "get up on the boat and help Tuu. Hand everything to Ngau. Ngau, you stay down here with me."

Andre and his three workers were further briefed by Detective Nakamua that his priority was the backpack in the V-berth and whatever documents they could find elsewhere.

Tuu and Bung were to haul out of the boat whatever else was not nailed down while keeping their eyes peeled for anything suspicious. If they discovered something that didn't look right, they were to leave it where it lay and let the detectives know. Nothing in the cabinets and drawers was to be touched except any documents there were. As for Andre and Ngau, they would lay out the items on the pier for inspection, and once the boat had been cleared, the two detectives would board to continue their investigation.

Bung's retrieval of the backpack and the plastic folder of documents from a cabinet was slowed by the diesel-slick floor made more treacherous by scattered rice as slippery as ballbearings. With the retrieved items safely in Detective Nakamua's hands, Bung and Tuu opened all of *Atmosphere's* port lights for air circulation before they set to the task of extricating drenched cushions, soaked clothing and bedding, soggy nautical charts, and stored gear in the quarter berth. A bag of syrupy sugar was dropped into the sink.

As the items were handed down from the boat, Andre helped Ngau stage them on the pier, along with the sieve screen, while Sanna photographed each piece, and Nakamua inspected them for any revealing evidence. He detached the Velcro closures of a hefty-size black valise, confirming it was the boat's life raft. The gathering of onlookers formed a wide semicircle around the activity with Chris watching tentatively from the sidelines. When the work on the pier was completed, the only evidence found among the gear were splashes of vomit on the backpack and on a V-berth cushion.

With the boat's belly cleared of rubble, Bung and Tuu vacated the vessel and with Ngau, stood aside to await further orders.

The two detectives slipped on latex gloves and stepped aboard *Atmosphere.* Sanna carefully peeled back the non-absorbent covering Domingo had taped over the smeared blood and photographed the evidence before Nakamua scraped the dried bodily fluid into a plastic collection jar.

With the initial part of the investigation completed, the two detectives lowered themselves, one at a time, down the glistening ladder into the boat's interior. Everything inside, including parts of the ceiling, was coated with a thin layer of diesel. The smell of the fuel was pronounced, but with the port lights open and a purging breeze, not overwhelming. They quickly found that locating any usable evidence within the boat teetered on a fine line between a doubtful maybe and likely impossibility.

The two men switched on their flashlights.

"Check the galley and navigation table," Nakamua told his partner. He himself gripped a ceiling mounted handhold and shuffled, hand over hand, along the slippery floor into the main cabin. After searching through the wet locker, he cautiously moved past the two open in-floor tanks still filled with fuel-tainted water.

Gripping the next ceiling handhold on his passage toward the bow, Nakamua's angle of sight caught the edge of a sealed, Zip-Loc bag lying atop the second in-floor tank, just aft of the tank's open portal. He released the overhead handhold, and gripping the settee table for balance, knelt on the glistening floor. He leaned down and pushed the fingers of his right hand under the flooring and along the tank's oily surface.

"What do you have?" Sanna asked as he raised the navigation table's lid exposing its drowned interior.

Nakamua gingerly withdrew his find. He stood and held out the bag between thumb and forefinger. Within the pint-size bag was a pair of two inch square packets, each filled with a white powder.

CHAPTER SEVENTEEN

Joan sat on her cot perusing a dog-eared copy of TIME magazine with its cover story, "DRUGS, The Enemy Within," when Udui entered Ollei's police station carrying Yao's document folder. He was followed by Detective Nakamua toting a black attaché case and shouldering her backpack. The knees of the detective's pants were blotted with water and carried a subtle bouquet of diesel.

In attendance at his own desk with his bandaged ankle was Deputy Vegas armed with a crutch for mobility, clearly not there as prisoner control. Sitting at home to recuperate while Udui and the two DMLE detectives dealt with the sailboat retrieved from Kayangel Island was too much for the deputy. Offering what assistance he could at the office was far more interesting than daytime television.

"You got my backpack," Joan commented to Nakamua, laying the magazine aside. There was relief in her voice for finally having her possessions. She hoped this signaled a nearness to going home. She stood and stepped to the cell's open door.

Nakamua set the backpack against the office's back wall. Besides a residual aura of diesel, it had escaped the sloshing brew within the sailboat.

"Miss Mackland, please come and have a seat," the detective said.

Joan slipped into her usual chair. Udui and Nakamua took their own seats at the same desk, the constable to one side and the detective opposite Joan. He placed his attaché case on the floor next to his chair.

Domingo hobbled over on crutches, and Ruth pulled up a chair for him so he could listen in more clearly.

"Have you had lunch?" Udui asked Joan.

"Yes, Ruth got it for me."

Ruth saw an opening and said to Udui, "He is on his way over."

Udui smiled his thanks, knowing who she was speaking of, and motioned to the detective it was his show now.

Detective Nakamua opened a notebook and picked up a pen. "The sailboat has been towed to the marina and the diesel and water pumped out," he told Joan. "Detective Sanna and I made a preliminary inspection inside and out, and Detective Sanna has taken a sample of dried blood from the boat for analysis at the community clinic in Mengellang." He looked deep into Joan's eyes. "We found a trace of vomit on your backpack and a V-berth cushion, and a splattering on the toilet which supports your story about being seasick. I'm considering that part of your story as confirmed."

Joan didn't flinch, waiting for the punchline.

"As for the blood sample from the boat," the detective continued, "Doctor Reklai provided us your blood type, A-positive." He looked at his notes and regarded Joan. "There is contact information in Mr. Yao's folder for a Colin Yao. Do you know who that is? I assume he and Wayne Yao are related."

"He's Yao's brother," Joan said.

Nakamua nodded to Udui about what had already been suspected.

"I gave the Koror office Colin's number," the detective told Joan, "and they will contact him about his brother's loss at sea. If Colin does not know his brother's blood type, then hopefully he will know who to contact in Hong Kong to get that information.

"From your description of what happened on the boat and your injury, I am confident the blood type will match your own, but of course, that has to be verified."

Joan gave a nod of understanding. She had no concerns about the dried blood not matching hers, only that she didn't know if A-positive blood was a common type in Hong Kong. Being able to mark this off the list would be a nerve calming relief.

In both Udui's interrogation and now Detective Nakamua's, Joan had cooperated with the full truth, certain the evidence would exonerate her. What she hadn't counted on was an abrupt and unexpected turn from which what she knew to be the truth would no longer hold sway.

"There is one other issue," Nakauma said in a grave voice, giving a grim frown at having to take this next step. "Do you know the reason Mr. Yao was taking his boat to the Philippines and on to Hong Kong?"

Unbeknownst to Joan, the two detectives and Constable Udui had spent the previous hour in Andre's office reviewing the contents of Yao's document folder, including a thorough inspection of Joan's backpack, so they were familiar with all of the evidence, and that familiarity was clear to Joan. It was also clear that they had found something pivotal that directly affected her and the direction their investigation was now heading.

"All I know," she said with hesitation, "is what Yao told me, that he was taking Atmosphere back to Hong Kong to do repairs."

Nakamua gave Joan a measuring look. "When you say he was taking Atmosphere back to Hong Kong, does that mean the boat had originally come from Hong Kong?"

Worry lines furrowed Joan's forehead. Something was seriously amiss.

"I don't think so," she said, guarded. "Yao told me that he bought Atmosphere in Guam about a year ago and had only done local sailing. And the marina manager in Guam confirmed that. I guess Yao meant that he was going back to Hong Kong, not his boat."

The detective nodded that possibility and flipped back two pages in his notepad. "You stated earlier that you had no previous sailing experience before this trip."

Joan's whole body tensed with a feeling of entrapment. "I think I said I had never been sailing on the ocean." She looked from Nakamua to Udui and back again. "I went on a daysail in high school, in Auckland Harbour."

"I see," the detective said thoughtfully, as if this information tied together some critical discovery.

"You found something on the boat." Joan could not stop herself from making this statement, nor could she bring herself to guess what that something was.

Detective Nakamua cut to the chase. He leaned to one side and, opening his attaché case, lifted out a crisp quart-size Zip-lock bag containing the smaller pint-size Zip-lock bag with its two packets he had retrieved from *Atmosphere*. He laid the evidence on the table in front of Joan.

Joan's face flushed. She was afraid to say another word.

A long moment passed before the detective spoke. "Do you recognize this?" He watched every detail of Joan's face as brute reality of her situation dragged a ragged breath from her.

"I don't know anything about drugs," Joan uttered, her eyes welling up.

Nakamua gave Joan a penetrating look. "I didn't say this is drugs."

The detective's statement drove a cold finger into Joan's heart. "I just," she managed. She swallowed. "Is that what it is, drugs?"

"It appears to be cocaine," Nakamua stated. "This will be confirmed at the police lab in Koror."

Joan seemed to run down like a wind-up toy. The secret Yao had stowed on board was a legacy that had now impaled her. Her eyes moved from the packets, to Nakamua and back to the contraband. She slumped in her chair, overwhelmed with emotion. "I swear, I didn't know anything about drugs," she pleaded.

"Miss Mackland," Nakamua asked, looking from one tear-filled eye to the other. "You stated that you didn't know Mr. Yao before departing from Guam."

"I only knew about him through a friend in Auckland," Joan said, feeling as if she had already been tried and convicted and whatever she said now didn't matter. "All I knew was that Yao originally came from Hong Kong and was taking his boat there."

Nakamua sat back and crossed his arms. It was obvious to Joan that he was having a difficult time believing her story.

"So you never sailed with him before this trip," the detective stated, repeating what Joan had already told him.

"No, never. My friend in Auckland, her name is Lois Tomlinson, she organized the trip through her brother, Max. Max sails and is friends with Yao."

Nakamua took Joan's passport from the folder and laid it on the table. "Your passport was issued five months ago and has your arrival and departure from Guam. Have you ever had another passport before this one?"

"Yes, one other, but that passport was lost, so I had to apply for this one." Joan refrained from explaining she suspected her mother had destroyed that first passport after she, Joan, had vacationed in Australia with girlfriends without her mother's blessing.

"And what countries did you visit on your original passport?"

"Just Australia." For Joan, this line of questioning was getting ever more stressful. "I went to Queensland with friends, that's all."

Detective Nakamua placed his hands on the desk top. He looked at Joan flat and steady, getting to the crux of his interrogation.

"Was there a reason why you, with virtually no sailing experience, would make the trip from New Zealand to Guam by yourself to get on a boat that was going to cross an ocean with a man you had never met?"

Joan became very still. She pulled a frown, her breathing rapid for she realized with a rush the reason for this line of questioning. As flimsy as the truth now seemed, truth was all she had.

"I was having problems at home with my mother and an ex-boyfriend," she said, hoping the guilty verdict had not yet been passed. "I agreed to go with Lois on the trip to get away and maybe be able to change my life when I got back. I was worried about going, but Lois has sailed before, and there was a link between her brother and Yao. But then, Lois backed out."

"But you didn't," Nakamua challenged. "You didn't back out."

"I was angry at Lois and too psyched to get away from my mom and ex-boyfriend. If I had changed my plans … If I had not gone, I would have never lived it down with either of them."

The detective looked at Udui and his eyes dropped to the notepad in front of him in a moment of silent assessment. Each part of her explanation seemed plausible with the exception of her reason for going on such a far-flung excursion. Personal problems at home were low on his list of reasons compared to financial gain. He sat up straight and held his gaze on Joan. "Are you aware of any more drugs on Atmosphere?"

Joan looked small and forlorn. "No," she managed. Fear robbed her voice.

"Miss Mackland, I have one more question." There was no banter in Nakamua's voice. "Do you know Christopher Addison?"

Joan's eyes wandered, her mind racing to dredge up a memory, a memory that might exonerate her, a memory that was not there. "No, I don't," she said, looking directly at the detective as she spoke.

What Detective Nakamua saw on Joan's face and in her eyes left no doubt in his mind that to this question; she had told the truth. She indeed did not know Mr. Addison, but this investigation was far from over. He was convinced these two packets contained cocaine, as certain as he was that the trace blood evidence was Joan's, but even those truths could not reconcile her flimsy reason for making this trek. What he needed was clear evidence pointing in another direction, and that evidence could be forthcoming in alternative testimony that would hopefully confirm what he thought was true.

"I'll need contact information for your friend Lois and her brother," Nakamua told Joan.

Joan was numbed by the turn of events. It seemed to her the gods were indeed against her. And why had the detective asked if she knew Christopher Addison, whoever he was?

"Am I being arrested?" Joan ventured in a heavy voice.

"No, you're not," the detective said. "You are being held until details of the blood sample from the boat have been confirmed and the contents of these packets verified. I also have another interview related to your case. Your continued cooperation will be appreciated."

Joan paled, overtaken by an equal measure of relief and anxiety. She wasn't under arrest, but what if Yao had been rescued, and it was he who would be interrogated? The thought of such a bitter-sweet reunion gripped her with agonizing uncertainty. What would she say to him but more importantly, if he was indeed a drug smuggler, what would he say about her? As for Christopher Addison, she figured if this worse case scenario were true, he was likely Yao's accomplice. Pulling courage up by her bootstraps, she asked the detective, "Was Yao rescued?"

CHAPTER EIGHTEEN

Joan's question hung in the air like an innocent prisoner waiting for the jury to acquit or convict. The perdition that had befallen her since being orphaned on the boat deepened her disquiet. Time ground to a halt.

The heavy moment was broken when the office door opened with a slowness that inferred hesitancy. Joan's wide-eyed anticipation of who would step through the door dropped a notch when a thirtyish year old man with sun bleached blonde hair, looking like a California surfer, nodded greeting to Ruth as he stepped inside. "I'm here to see …" Chris said, and noticing the three law officials and woman seated around an adjacent table, he added to the lawmen, "I'm Chris Addison." He looked apprehensive, as if he had troubles of his own.

Detective Nakamua deftly slipped the bagged packets off the table and placed them on his lap, out of sight from the newcomer.

The detective remained seated. "Mr. Addison," he said, "thank you for coming. Please have a seat."

Joan kept her eyes on Chris, feeling as if she was standing on unstable ground at the edge of an abyss, but when the door closed behind him, she sat back in her chair, not knowing how she felt. Detective Nakamua had mentioned a single interview which, with Chris' appearance, signaled Yao had indeed not been rescued.

Constable Udui shifted a chair from the front wall to the opposing end of the desk from where his own chair was located. Chris took his seat. Since receiving a phone call from the marina's manager to come to Ollei's police station for an interview, he had been convinced this request had to do with his two ex-shipmates, and that could spell big trouble for himself.

"Mr. Addison," Nakamua started, "Do you know Joan? Joan Mackland?" He motioned his head toward Joan.

Chris' eyes latched onto those of a tanned, anorexic-looking woman seated behind the desk, to his left. He pegged her as the lady rescued from Kayangel, and though neither one of his ex-voyagers was present, she could be a co-conspirator with instructions from his two ex-friends on what to say.

"No, I don't know her," Chris said with no hint of deception. "Maybe you heard I want to talk to her. That is only to see if she owns the boat, and if she doesn't, who does, and if they want to sell."

"Wayne Yao is the owner," the detective stated.

Chris shrugged his shoulders. "I don't know a Wayne Yao," he replied with no attempt at covering up his own growing suspicions. In his limited view, even if his ex-shipmates had sold the boat, that did not automatically exclude them from continued involvement in drug smuggling. What was crystal clear to Chris was that the detective had a lead that brought him into the mix.

"And exactly what is your interest in buying this particular sailboat?" Nakamua asked Chris.

Chris didn't miss a beat. "My wife and I have been thinking of chartering a sailboat," Chris replied, "and that sailboat is a size and design we like. It's also a fixer-upper." His uneasiness slipped lower on his shoulders, at least until the lawman asked his next question.

"Have you ever owned a sailboat?"

Joan felt uncomfortable watching Mr. Addison almost squirm. The detective's line of questioning had pulled worry lines on the man's face, as if he had just been caught committing a crime. The fact she was privy to a conversation about whether he knew her or Yao before having to explain his interest in buying *Atmosphere* had shifted curiosity to the forefront of her emotions. She saw no bearing on her own case, whether he had previously owned a sailboat or not.

Chris' eyes dilated. His breath caught in his throat. He stared at Nakamua like a spooked rabbit. "I don't know what you've been told," he stated with more than a touch of acrimony. He glanced at Joan with sharp eyes, as if the sole reason for her presence was to incriminate him, and looked away, convinced his intuition was correct, this was a set-up and he was the fall guy. His eyes flashed determination to not allow truth to become lost in the shuffle.

"I was part owner of a sailboat," Chris stated, "but that was years ago." He made a face, looking baffled but his eyes told a different story. "Why do you ask?"

Nakamua posted an elbow on the desk with a hand on his chin, watching Chris' body language. "You were part owner of Atmosphere?" he asked with raised brow. "You do know Damion Lester and Bruce Mills, do you not?"

Chris' worry became canyons on his forehead. His fears had been realized. "Whatever those sons-of-bitches have told you," he said with deep loathing, "or whatever they told her to say …" he indicated Joan, " …or whoever this Yao guy is, it's all a lie. I don't know who she is …" again he indicated Joan, " …I don't know any Yao and I haven't seen or talked to Bruce or Damion for years. I certainly don't know what they have been doing between the last time I saw them and now."

Nakamua removed from Yao's folder a certificate of ownership issued by the State of California. He slid the document to Chris. "Thank you for clarification."

The document showed the stated owner of a boat named *Atmosphere* as Bruce Mills, with two co-owners, Christopher Addison and Damion Lester, verified by their signatures.

Memories flashed in Chris' eyes and Detective Nakamua added to those flashbacks by dropping the double-bagged packets onto the desk in front of Chris.

Chris's jaw dropped. He seemed incapable of speaking, and at that moment, Joan understood what possible involvement this man had in her own story. She leaned in, head tilted to one side to catch every word Mr. Addison had to say. How did any of this relate to Yao, and would whatever Chris revealed lead to her own exoneration, or slip the noose yet again around her neck?

Chris' jaw tightened and his eyes narrowed. "Are they here?" he asked of the two other previous owners.

Without replying, Detective Nakamua asked his own question. "Is this why you want to buy, Atmosphere?" He tapped a finger on the Zip-Loc bag. "I'm betting what's in these packets is cocaine. I'm also betting you are aware there is a larger amount still onboard. Am I right?"

Chris licked suddenly dry lips. Sweat beaded his forehead. A past he thought lost to time had overtaken him and with his undeniable link to the boat, he felt his only recourse was to confess a lie and offer the truth, no matter in which direction it took things, even if up to the top of the gallows.

"Can I get some water?" Chris asked in a humbled voice.

Udui was quick with the request.

Chris drained the glass in three gulps. The room held a stillness as heavy as if a hangman's hand were on the lever that would drop him through a trap door to snap tight and leave the condemned dangling by his neck.

"My wife and I aren't interested in buying Atmosphere," Chris confessed. His face softened with a shadow of relief at having come clean of his deception. "I said that so I could get onboard."

Detective Nakamua motioned to the packets. "For these and whatever else there is?"

Chris couldn't look either officer in the eyes when he said, "No, I wanted a reason to get onboard to retrieve a couple thousand dollars and some grass I hid years ago before I jumped ship, that's all." He looked up at the detective. "I swear. I don't even know if my stuff is still there. I had no idea this coke was still on Atmosphere, and I don't know if there is more."

"So, you are confirming this is cocaine," the detective said in a flat voice.

Chris stared at the packet with a regretful frown. "Yes sir," he stated, immediately adding, "But it's not mine. None of it was mine."

"When was the last time you were in contact with Mr. Lester or Mr. Mills?" the detective asked.

"Like I said, it's been a couple of years."

"How did you know Atmosphere was bound for Palau?"

The detective's question was as curious to Joan as it was disquieting to Chris, especially since Yao had no plans for stopping in Palau, and she had originally thought the island where *Atmosphere* had been grounded was near Yap. Her suspicion Mr. Addison was somehow connected to Yao no longer held water.

"I know what you're trying to do," Chris raised his defense, "but whatever you've been told, it is all a lie. I didn't know Atmosphere was coming here and that's the truth." He looked at both police officers, unflinching.

"I see," Nakamua said in a barely audible voice. He pursed his lips, far from convinced. "Then can you tell me how you knew it was Atmosphere aground on Kayangel and why you were not forthcoming about having been a co-owner?"

Chris blew out regret, looking as if he had bet the farm and lost. Deception was easy when you have an unbeatable hand but in this game, he had dealt himself a pair of deuces and foolishly played them to the end.

"I didn't know it was Atmosphere," Chris explained. "All I knew before I went out there was that the stranded boat was a forty-footer, constructed of aluminum, and Atmosphere is the only sailboat I know that fits that description. I went out just to confirm my suspicions, that's all."

"And with confirmation, you lied to get onboard," the detective said as if fact, "because you knew these two packets and possibly more cocaine was hidden inside."

Chris' reaction was swift and emphatic. "No, I told you that I didn't know," he said, his dander rising at what he saw as an attempt to implicate him in running drugs. "Like I said, I haven't seen or heard from Bruce and Dame for more than two years." He was nearing the end of his fuse. "Bring one or both of them in here and I'll expose their lies."

Nakamua held up a halting hand. "Mr. Addison," he said in a calming voice, "what I am attempting to do is understand what part, if any, you played in Atmosphere being here, in Palau." His bland face showed no emotion. "You've stated that you wanted on Atmosphere to get your money and marijuana, yet you knew there was at least these two packets onboard."

"I guess I figured there could be coke onboard," Chris admitted, "but even if there was, I wouldn't have touched it. My wife and I have a business to run and I don't need to end up in prison."

Joan took in Chris's every word. The spotlight had swung squarely onto his past, seemingly growing brighter with his revelations, and she sensed she was all but out of the limelight.

Nakamua remained silent, watching Chris' body language and letting him build his case or reveal his guilt.

"About four years ago Bruce, Dame and I bought Atmosphere," Chris went on. "We were going to sail around the world. We had weed onboard when we left San Diego for Mexico, but it was just for us. While we were in Mexico, we picked up more grass, but as I found out later, Bruce had bought coke for him and Dame."

"I see," Nakamua said, still suspicious, "so when you departed Mexico, you didn't know about the cocaine."

Chris firmed his jaw. "Dame and I were the ones planning to buy a boat and sail around the world. We had just started looking at used boats when Dame brought Bruce into the picture. I'd met Bruce a couple times through Dame and he seemed an all right dude. At the time, he was looking to buy a boat also, and all of a sudden, the three of us were pooling our money."

"So Bruce bought the coke in Mexico?" the detective asked, still not over his suspicion.

"That's right," Chris stated without hesitation, "but I didn't know anything about it. Dame had used it a few times over the years, but he knew how I felt about hard drugs. Grass was all he and I ever did. I didn't find out about the cocaine until we had set sail for Hawaii. When I found out, I told them to get rid of it overboard, but Bruce promised it would all be gone by the time we reached Hawaii. He also promised that once it was gone, it was gone for good."

Chris paused to ensure the detective and constable understood what he was saying and about his stand on drugs other than marijuana. "Like I said, I have never been into coke, either then or now."

Nakamua gave an encouraging nod. "Go on."

"When we reached Hawaii, we linked up with a guy named, Vince, Dame's cousin. He lives there. Vince went sailing with us a couple times, and the three of them finished off what was left of the coke. After that, I figured that was the end of that. Bruce and Dame bought some weed from Vince, and we headed west to Wake Island and then Guam."

"But that wasn't the end," Constable Udui spoke up.

Chris's face twisted with regret. "No, there was more, a lot more and it had been on board since Mexico."

Joan fully expected both the constable and the detective to give her a high-sign that she had been acquitted by Chris' admissions, but their focus remained on what else the man had to say. Like them, she honed in again on Chris.

"After we left Guam another packet of coke showed up, and that was when Bruce fessed up that he had another ninety-four grams on board, all like this, two grams per pack." He took a deep breath and blew out regret for not having thrown the coke overboard when he had had the chance.

Chris' face darkened again as he said, "Bruce supposedly had had a contact in Manila who was going to buy all the coke he could supply, and when I realized our circumnavigation was a drug run for Bruce, I told him and Dame I was not spending the rest of my life in a Philippine prison or any other prison, and if the coke stayed on board, I was getting off at the next island we passed. That turned out to be Palau.

"Bruce got really angry I was jumping ship but a couple days later, he was all for me leaving. He even put a couple of packets of cocaine in the V-berth where I slept and said they were mine if I wanted them. I didn't and I gave them back."

"Are these the two packets?" Nakamua asked.

"Did you find them in that smaller Zip-Loc bag?" Chris queried.

"Yes," the detective replied.

"That has to be the packets," Chris stated. "I dropped them on the table and told Bruce that I didn't care what he did with the coke, but I didn't want any of it. That's when I realized I had made a big mistake."

"Your fingerprints," Nakamua guessed.

"As soon as I dropped them on the table, Dame stepped between me and the coke. Bruce used a spatula to slide the two packets into the Zip-Loc bag. He warned me that since I had been on the boat from the beginning, and my fingerprints were on the packets, I would be just as guilty as them if they were caught. He was really worried I would rat them out."

Nakamua was not fully convinced Chris was as innocent as he purported, especially since the man thought his two ex-shipmates still owned the boat, and he had been attempting to gain access under false pretences. Retrieving money and marijuana may have been reasons for gaining access, but the coke could easily have been on his list also. Both scenarios were plausible but the man's story, with the evidence in hand, did have some merit. As for Joan, she seemed to be completely out of the picture.

Chris' eyes turned to little rocks. "If either of those bastards told you I had anything to do with what they were smuggling back then or what they're up to now," he stated, "it's a bald-faced lie. They tricked me into handling those packets, and I haven't seen or heard from them since."

"Bruce and Damion were not aboard when Atmosphere left Guam a couple of weeks ago," Nakamua informed Chris. The detective saw no advantage for Chris to continue thinking his two ex-friends were still involved with *Atmosphere.*

The detective turned to Joan. "Ms. Mackland, I would like you to explain what you learned about Atmosphere before your departure from Guam."

Joan appreciated being brought into the conversation, no longer a bystander and no longer a suspect. She herself wanted to believe all of what Chris had said, and if she could relieve some of his stress, he might be able to wrest further details from his memory that could dispel any doubts the lawmen may have had about Yao's part in this.

"Chris, my name is, Joan. I was crewing on Atmosphere when it left Guam about eleven days ago."

"I figured you were the lady who was rescued," Chris commented.

"It should clear things up a little more if I explain what I found out about Atmosphere after your two friends left you here in Palau," Joan said.

"Bruce and Damion went to the Philippines," Chris stated with authority. "That's what happened."

"Maybe they did," Joan admitted, "but when I was in Guam, I spoke with a man who had bought Atmosphere. Actually, when he bought it, the boat's name had been changed to Baccus."

Chris gave a slight shake of his head, not understanding.

"The man I spoke with manages Gregorio Perez Marina in Guam," Joan continued. "He remembered you, Bruce and Damion."

"I remember him," Chris commented, finding a touch of comfort having even the slightest connection with Joan. "He has a really big nose."

"That's him," Joan said. "About six weeks after you three left for the Philippines, Bruce and Damion showed up again at the marina."

Chris' eyes flashed wide. "In Guam? Why would they do that?"

"From what you told Detective Nakamua, about why they tricked you into handling the packets, maybe they had second thoughts about you not being scared enough to alert the authorities about their plans. If you had, I'm sure Palau authorities would have contacted officials in Manila, and your two friends probably figured that too."

Chris shrugged. "I thought about ratting on them," he said, his admission as much for Joan as for the lawmen, "but my girlfriend, my wife now, talked me out of getting anymore involved. I worried about it for a few months, but when the police here didn't serve me with an arrest warrant, I figured Bruce had met up with the buyer in Manila, and it was finally over."

"Well, Norm, the marina manager," Joan said, "told me that after Bruce and Damion arrived back in Guam, they re-registered Atmosphere as Baccus and sold all of the electronics. After that they apparently left Guam because they never came back for the boat."

"And Norm bought Atmosphere, I mean, Baccus?" Chris asked.

"Yes, he bought it from Guam's port authority after they declared Baccus abandoned. He told me that he kept it for a few months, never did anything with it and finally sold it to Wayne Yao, the man I sailed with from Guam."

"I'll be damned," Chris said, intrigued by the story "I would have never guessed they would backtrack to Guam but from what you said, it makes sense."

Like Chris, Nakamua agreed with Joan's assessment that Bruce and Damion had likely been spooked by what Chris could have done, and instead of sailing to the Philippines, they had backtracked to Guam to throw any search off their trail. If that was what actually happened, it indicated they had not jettisoned the coke, for if they had, there would not have been a reason for such a drastic change in their original plan. That also meant most of the coke, if not all of it, had likely been sold in Guam since that island had a population nearly double that of Yap.

For all that Chris and Joan had so far revealed, what was clear to Nakamua was that with Bruce and Damion's coke offloaded in Guam, there was still a plausible link between Yao and the cocaine he himself had recovered after the flooded boat had been pumped out. Though he didn't let on, the light of suspicion once again found Joan.

"Where did Bruce hide the rest of the cocaine?" Nakamua asked Chris, taking back the conversation.

"It was under the cockpit at the stern," Chris answered. "You have to crawl around the engine and worm your way through the cables of the steering quadrant to get to it, which isn't easy. That's why they put it there." He glanced at the packets in front of him. "They must have lost track of these."

Joan let out a long sigh of frustration, for like Detective Nakamua, she too realized the bulk of the cocaine had likely been sold in Guam, and in some strange twist of events, that same stash could have found its way back onto *Atmosphere.* That seemed even more plausible when she factored in her captain's rushed departure from Guam. Mr. Leung, the immigration officer, had clearly stated *Atmosphere* had twenty-four hours to clear port after check-out which meant the boat could have cast off on the following morning's high tide, something, for some reason, Yao had opted against.

Joan's only solace in this convoluted affair was a gut feeling that no matter what else was to be found in another search of the boat, it would coincide with what Mr. Addison had revealed with no direct link to Yao's involvement. She may have only spent a few days with him before his disappearance, but that time in close quarters had given her faith in his intentions, and with that, she admonished herself for doubting her captain in the first place.

Joan drew herself up, fully aware she could be fooling herself, as much as Yao may have fooled her, but he was not there to defend himself, and she would not turn a deaf ear to her gut feeling.

"I am more than certain Yao didn't have cocaine or any other illegal drugs on Atmosphere." Joan stated this with no hint of reservation. "And he didn't know about these packets." She nodded confirmation of what she knew to be the truth. "He certainly had every opportunity while in Guam to stash drugs onboard," she continued, "but the facts are, he forbid me to bring illegal drugs on his boat, and not once did I feel he was trying to hide something from me or keep me from going anywhere in the boat."

Yao's name meant nothing to Chris, but the fact the man owned the boat did. "Shouldn't you be questioning this Yao guy?" Chris said to the detective.

"He's not available," Nakamua replied in passing. He picked up the bagged packets and slipped the evidence into his case. He had heard enough, and with no direct evidence against Joan, he would trust his own intuition that she had been honest in her statements. This was reinforced by Chris' revelations that were as believable as hers, further lifting the veil of suspicion on them both. As for Yao's disappearance, even if the missing captain's blood type was different than Joan's and the blood sample proved to be his, there was insufficient evidence to prove she intentionally killed him. "Thank you, Mr. Addison," he said. "You have been very enlightening, but there is one other matter."

"The marijuana," Chris said with edged voice.

"Yes," Nakamua said. "Are we talking more than a few cigarettes?"

Chris nodded. "Yes, sir, more like three ounces."

Nakamua looked at Chris closely. "Are you aware of the penalties in Palau for possession of more than two ounces of marijuana?"

Chris bobbed his head. "Yes sir, I am."

"Where on Atmosphere do you expect your stash to be?"

"In the anchor chain locker," Chris replied, "with my money. I did all of the electrical work on the boat, and when I installed the foot switches for the windlass, I had to lay on my back and scoot head-first into the chain locker far enough to get my arms in. That's when I noticed a slot between the underside of the deck and the chain locker bulkhead.

"Bruce and Dame went through what grass they could get their hands on like there was no tomorrow. I kept a stash they didn't know about, and any time I was alone on the boat, I would smoke a joint. I didn't get a chance to take it or the money off the boat before they ran out on me. When I realized it was Atmosphere on Kayangel, I figured I might as well see if my stash and money were still there."

Chris drew grim. The proverbial hot water he was in was too deep to touch bottom. "Is there going to be an issue for me if the marijuana is still onboard?" he asked Nakamua.

Chris had been convicted in Palau the year before for possessing an ounce of marijuana, netting him a five hundred dollar fine. If convicted a second time, with more than two ounces, that penalty could jump to a heftier fine and possible prison time, both of which he could ill afford with his business and monthly payments on his sports fisherman, *Chedeng*.

"As long as the marijuana is not in your possession," Nakamua said, "you have nothing to worry about."

"What about my money?"

"If it's there, it will be returned to you."

Chris smiled his thanks.

"Thank you again for coming in," Nakamua told Chris in a concluding voice.

Chris took what success he had had and departed.

To Ruth, the detective said, "Can you contact Ngarchelong Clinic? If Detective Sanna is still there, let him know we no longer need the blood results."

Nakamua turned to Joan. "Thanks for your cooperation," he said. "I have no reason to doubt what you have told me." He packed his notebook and pen into his briefcase. To Constable Udui he said, "You and I need to get back to the marina and make sure there's no more drugs on that boat."

"Detective Sanna is on his way back here," Ruth reported to Nakamua after her phone call to the clinic.

The detective thanked the dispatcher, and he and Udui stood.

"What's going to happen to the boat, to Atmosphere?" Joan asked Nakamua as she got to her feet. She was truly concerned about the boat's future. Through one calamity after another, *Atmosphere* had ultimately saved her life, and though she never wanted to see the boat again, she also didn't want the vessel to suffer any more than it had.

"If Atmosphere is not tied up in some court or neither Colin nor anyone else in Yao's family wants the boat," Nakamua said, "I believe it would revert to you." He said this figuring that in the boat's banged up condition and Palau's distance from New Zealand, Joan would also decline the offer and he was correct.

"If I don't want Atmosphere," Joan said to the detective. "What do you think will happen to it?"

"Atmosphere is probably worth more in parts and scrap metal than the cost of refurbishment," Udui guessed, "but I'm not much on boat salvaging."

A shadow passed over Joan's face. She felt a strong sense of obligation to Yao for his boat and she was thankful *Atmosphere* had indeed been her chariot and not her coffin, but she also understood the reality of the situation. Fate had committed Yao to the sea, and that same hand of providence would either breathe new life into his boat or see it stripped bare and recycled.

"I understand," she told the two lawmen, and through her mixture of remorse for Yao and his boat and thankfulness for her own deliverance emerged what she knew was real. The events of the last eleven days had unfolded as they had, and neither that fact nor *Atmosphere's* likely end would ever change.

Joan followed Detective Nakamua and Constable Udui outside where they stood in a slash of the building's shadow cut from the mid-afternoon sun. The air outside was hot and humid and carried the pungent salty smell of exposed marine vegetation and old fishing nets all wrapped in whiffs of a fresh breeze from atop an adjacent hill.

This was Joan's first time since arriving in Ollei that she had had an awareness of the world around her, and as she scanned her unfamiliar surroundings, she was filled with a deep sense of homesickness. For all that was rolling around in her mind about returning home, she could not ignore a snippet of lingering hope tugging at her soul.

Atmosphere's own fate seemed sealed, but a perchance option just might save the boat and its tangled legacy.

"If no one on Yao's side wants Atmosphere," she queried Detective Nakamua, "can I give it to someone?"

"That would be up to you," the detective said.

"Then, if I do get it, I'd like to give it to Mr. Addison. If he doesn't want it, he can sell it for whatever he can get."

"Minus the marijuana," the detective said with a wispy smile and an approving nod.

The trio's attention was drawn to the rumble of tires on the dirt and gravel road. Detective Sanna arrived from his trip to the community clinic. He parked the DMLE's vehicle in its original slot next to Udui's Land Cruiser.

Sanna joined the others in the widening swatch of shade. He pulled a folded, typed page from his shirt pocket and gave the document to Nakamua.

"Blood type is A-positive," Sanna announced.

Nakamua handed the paper to Joan without looking at it. "Miss Mackland," he said, "I don't expect this next inspection to take more than an hour or so. After that, do you need to get onboard Atmosphere for any reason?"

Joan didn't think twice. With a dark cloud hanging over her memories and the sure to be lingering stench of mouldering cushions and diesel fuel, the thing she wanted most from that boat was distance.

"I really don't want to go back on board," she said, "but I would like a souvenir, the artist's drawing of Atmosphere. It's attached to the bulkhead between the main cabin and head."

"I saw it," the detective confirmed. "Is that all?"

"That's more than enough."

"When Detective Sanna and I are finished here in Ollei," Nakamua said, "we'll transport you to Koror. My office can book you a hotel room."

"That would be great," Joan said, imagining the comfort, privacy and most of all, freedom she would once again have.

"If you need assistance with booking flights to New Zealand, just let me know."

Joan smiled her appreciation. Skyward, a silvery dot pulling a contrail north to south in the cloudless sky underscored her yearning for home. As if to make the moment more meaningful, the subdued knell of a telephone sounded from within the police station.

Ruth brought Joan a box of tissue where she sat alone at what she now felt was her desk. The two detectives, Udui and a hobbling Constable Vegas supported on crutches had reassembled at the marina while *Atmosphere* was treated to one final indignity before the boat was released to its waiting fate.

"Thank you," Joan mimed to Ruth as she accepted the charity, too emotional to speak. She dabbed tears from her cheeks, her face soft with respite.

"I'm so glad he called," the dispatcher told Joan.

As Joan had entered the police station after stepping outside onto the front porch with the two police officers, her eyes had gleamed to Ruth holding out the phone's handset, a call for which no words were needed from the dispatcher for Joan to know who was on the other end of the line. She had burst into tears as she gripped the phone and brought it to her ear.

The ensuing give and take conversation had been a statement of worry and confession of calamity and upon learning of his niece's current situation, Uncle Phil's knee-jerk reaction had been to close his art gallery and travel to the Republic of Palau to personally attend to Joan's repatriation. Joan had been able to dial back his fervor enough to convince him to sit tight, that she would be traveling with two detectives to Koror, Palau's capital city, this very day, where she would check into a hotel and book flights to Auckland. Her explanation had quelled her uncle's urgency and further chastened her own anxieties. The call had ended with reassurance and a promise.

With her world coalescing from broken fragments of hope and despair, Joan's thoughts drifted from her apartment in Auckland to the reasons for making this trip and her first glimpse of Yao on his boat. She recalled how impressed she had been with the boat's comfortable, shaded cockpit, its spacious interior with its wood-scented, homey smell, and of her anxiety-edged relief when Yao agreed to take her on as crew. She had been gratified for the opportunity to prove to her mother and herself that she had the potential of managing her own life, of dealing with the unexpected and coming out a stronger person who could stand on her own, but she had not factored in events that would claim the life of one person and nearly take her own. Of all the anguish she held within, even knowing it no longer mattered, her biggest regret beyond all others was not knowing and never being able to know if she could have changed the outcome that fateful night had she been in the cockpit when Yao was cast into the sea.

CHAPTER NINETEEN

Patches of sunlight skittered across Auckland's downtown district, tantalizing breaks in unseasonable cloudy weather that promised clearing skies from the west.

Joan increased volume on her Volkswagen Beetle's radio as she entered Northern Motorway at Whangarei, on her return trip from Uncle Phil's gallery to her apartment. Half past the hour brought a One ZB radio review of upcoming local events, and she wasn't missing this segment of the broadcast.

"Tomorrow morning," the station's dee-jay announced, "One ZB's morning show will feature an exclusive interview with Joan Mackland, New Zealand's own. Joan will chronicle her fight for survival on the high seas after the captain of the forty-foot sailboat on which she was crewing was lost overboard during a storm. Alone, she spent four desperate days searching for the missing captain before running out of fuel and battery power, enduring dehydration, starvation, collision with a tramp steamer and even shark attack, only to be arrested in the Republic of Palau on suspicion of drug smuggling and murder.

"Don't miss this sure to be fascinating interview with a woman who looked death in the face and refused to surrender. Sponsored by Ponsonby Cruising Club and One ZB Radio. And now, One ZB Sports."

Joan turned down volume as her mind drifted past her upcoming interview to the two weeks since returning home from that cruise from Hell, a fortnight during which she had dealt with re-emerging conflict between thankfulness for reclaiming her life and faltering reconciliation of events plagued with the whys and wherefores of survivor's remorse.

Her struggle with guilt for her mistakes and failures onboard *Atmosphere* had been allayed and finally defeated with the recognition of a restoring point; holding onto a feeling of culpability would not change the outcome. It would not better her life. That would only come with acceptance that the circumstances thrown at her and Yao had been beyond their individual limits, and if anything positive was to come from this, it was that her own survival offered insights to Yao's family of his untimely death, a far better tribute to her captain than his memory existing in the darkness of conjecture by those who had known and loved him.

Joan's epiphany had also revealed that the strength and tenacity she had found to defy her mother and leave New Zealand had been honed to a fine cutting edge of determination over nearly two weeks of peril and suffering, giving her the focus to take full charge of her life and become the woman she aspired to be.

Armed with her new-found self, she had returned to Christchurch three days ago for a long overdue showdown. Like steering *Atmosphere* south in search of reinforcements to find Yao, the time had been nigh to wrest her life, her future, from her mother and chart her own course. Whether her mother would accept this change had been Joan's initial concern, but she hadn't come this far along a new path to backtrack.

Approaching Harbour Bridge on her drive back to her apartment, Joan's thoughts returned to the candid conversation she had had with her mother during that recent visit home.

"Mum, I didn't come here to apologize," Joan had stated, standing her ground after her mother had made a flippant comment about her daughter's selfish behavior in leaving her alone as she had.

"Well, if your father were here …"

"Mum, dad is gone," Joan had cut her mother off. "You and dad divorced, and the only reason he came over here after that was to pick me up. Not to see you."

Joan had been sorry for her bluntness but it had to be said.

Her mother had brought down her eyebrows. "So this is all about you," she had snapped in something short of a hiss.

"Yes, Mum," Joan had stated flatly, "this time it is all about me."

Joan's words had startled herself as much as her mother. As simple as that declaration had been, it had not previously sunk into Joan's psyche until that moment. The responsibility she felt for her mother's emotional needs had been her own failure to erect limits beyond which she would not respond. Over the years, fearful of resentment and rejection, she had catered to her mother's conflation of need and love, unknowingly validating her unacceptable behavior.

"Mum, I'm sorry but …"

Joan's mother had sniffed disapproval, raking her daughter from head to foot in one long stare of measurement and dismissal. "You and your father …" Her words were meant more for her late ex-husband than her daughter, not being one to burn all of her bridges.

"Mum, I learned more about myself during those days on the sailboat than I have in all of my years before. It has been said a million times, but I'll say it again, life is too short and I want to live it, not just exist. Maybe I'll marry and have children. I'll probably stay on the North Island, but no matter what, I want you to be a part of everything I do."

She had caught her mother's perplexed eyes. "I only ask that you start back your sessions with Dr. Kramer." Joan's voice had carried no hope, only expectation.

The long thoughtful moment that followed had been broken when Joan's mother stood and extended her arms for a hug, a welcomed surprise for Joan.

They had embraced, her mom weeping and Joan holding her tight, not certain where this was going. Gripping Joan's shoulders at arm's length and studying her daughter's face as if seeing it for the first time, her mother had said, "Everything I've ever done is because I want you to be happy." She had given her daughter a tight smile. "Maybe I have been a little unfair at times."

"So, you'll see Dr. Kramer again?" Joan was not letting her mother steer this conversation in another direction.

Joan's mother had pulled her daughter close for another hug and stepped back, a distant look in her eyes.

"You go back to Auckland and find yourself a good job. I may need some time to make that appointment, but I won't forget what you've said."

Joan had stood firm. "Mum, I also didn't come to bargain." Her voice had radiated intensity. "Set an appointment this week."

Joan's mother had turned her head ever so slightly. "On one condition," she had said as she fixed Joan with a direct gaze, intent, serious. "Promise me, no more crossing oceans on a sailboat."

"That, I promise," Joan had said with a bitter-sweet smile.

"How about we start dinner?" her mother had suggested.

"Sure," Joan had said but there had been something else on her mind. "I need to make a quick phone call."

"I'll get things started in the kitchen."

As Joan's mother busied herself with preparing dinner, Joan had perched on the edge of the living room recliner and lifted the handset to a phone on a side table. She had been obsessing over this call since listening to her own phone's messages after arriving from Palau, via Manila, Philippines and Singapore, and she had been anxious to bring this part of her life to a conclusion.

There had been three recorded calls received on the evening of her departure to Guam, the first from Lois, checking to see if Joan had actually followed through with her plans, and the second, from Darren, telling her how much he loved her and that he knew she loved him.

The third call had been made the following day. Darren had called again with an anger-filled earful about actually traveling all the way to Guam before droning on about her not asking him to go with her.

Darren's latest call, four days ago, had come while Joan had been meeting with One ZB's station manager and program director to schedule her interview. In this call, Darren had sobbed through a whiny message that mentioned soul mates, true love and repeated apologies, as if reading from some syrupy movie script. He had wanted to meet up to reconcile, promising to do better and devote his life to her happiness. Darren's day of reckoning had now arrived.

Joan had punched out Darren's phone number, unfazed by his previous recorded message, words that she knew were as hollow as her feelings for him. She had earlier considered meeting him in Albert Park, a venue that put her close to her uncle's art gallery, but she had had no desire to stretch this out anymore than necessary, nor drag her uncle into this part of her life. The best Darren would get from her was a phone call.

Darren had answered on the third ring. "Hello." His voice had carried no hint of expectation the caller might be anyone other than one of his beer drinking mates.

"This is Joan, I'm returning your call," Joan had stated in her formal voice.

A palpable sigh on Darren's end, a blend of surprise and relief, had been followed by a desperate, "Joan," and a moment of silence during which Joan had known he was thinking of the right words to say.

"Joan, I've been so worried about you." His emotions had had him barely able to speak. "Are you all right? When can I see you?"

Joan had swallowed, choosing her words and knowing the longer he kept her on the call, the more persistent he would become. "Darren, I'm returning your call to remind you that I broke up with you. There is no reason for you to phone me anymore and no reason for us to meet, now or ever. It's over."

Her abruptness had caught Darren in a stomach punch. "B-b-but, let's at least talk. Please." He had quickly added, "Jake Alister told me you're going to be interviewed on the radio. When is it? I'll be there for moral support. Please, Joan. I love you."

Joan had stared at the ceiling for a few seconds, rocked and stood. "Darren, I told you how things are," she had said drily. "Please don't call me again."

She had hung up her end, knowing there would be other desperate messages on her answering machine when she returned to her apartment, but she would hold firm, and hopefully he would catch on much sooner than later.

As Joan steered her VW across Auckland's Harbour Bridge, she took in the view of Westhaven Marina, wondering if any of the marina's boat owners had ever met Wayne Yao and how many captains and crew would tune in to her interview. She had already decided her story didn't need embellishing. That was for those souls who had never experienced all of what they claimed. She was not looking for fifteen minutes of fame. This interview would be for Yao, a tribute to a man who had been living the dream.

She turned up the radio's volume to Madonna singing, "Live To Tell."

ENDORSEMENTS

Twitty tells a story with a verve that pulls the reader in like a high tide. Full of vivid detail and emotion, *Lady Alone* is a must read for anybody who likes adventure on the high seas or simply wants to understand the challenges of blue water sailing.

Colin Habgood, 24,000 nautical miles under his keel

An intense, yet an enjoyable, captivating story. From the beginning, I felt all the emotions Joan was feeling. From her determination to "show'" her mother and sail when her mother tried to talk her out of it, to the panicked rush to get back to the dock in time to set sail, to the excitement of casting off, and to the sea sickness that led to all going so wrong. I felt her fear when she found herself all alone on this forty-foot sailboat with no sailing experience. Her determination to go on despite all her mistakes and bad luck was admirable. But what choice did she have? She was all alone in the middle of the ocean.

The detail was such that I learned a lot about sailing and the many things that go into it. I liked how information in the beginning tied in with the ending. This whole story was a true adventure. I highly recommend *Lady Alone* if you'd like to take a voyage while in the comfort of your home.

Nan Adel, avid reader

Myriad Pro on LSI 50# archival white
Type and design by Karen Paul Stone

www.ingramcontent.com/pod-product-compliance
Lightning Source LLC
Chambersburg PA
CBHW061234210726
48293CB00003B/767